DEEP TIME

STAR CARRIER

BOOK SIX

IAN DOUGLAS

New York Times Bestselling Author

DON'T MISS THE OTHER NOVELS IN THE
STAR CARRIER
SERIES BY *NEW YORK TIMES*
BESTSELLING AUTHOR
IAN DOUGLAS

AND THE NOVELS OF
The Heritage Trilogy
The Legacy Trilogy
The Inheritance Trilogy
The Star Corpsman Series

**Only too aware, now, of the
deadliness of his deceptively quiet
surroundings . . .**

. . . Gregory stood up.

Despite being insulated by the surrounding vacuum, he could feel his shipboard utilities—which with helmet and gloves doubled as an emergency environmental suit—stiffening around him, could feel the cold as though it literally were seeping in.

Impossible, of course. Heat was escaping his body, not cold seeping in, but that was what it undeniably felt like. His feet . . . he couldn't feel his feet anymore, and his legs were starting to burn.

He felt oddly tranquil, despite the pain, despite the sudden realization that he may have just made a serious mistake. The landscape was serene, dark, utterly silent. It would have been easy to step out of the ruin of his Starblade and onto that flat, rock-strewn plain. That step, he knew, would have been lethal.

He also felt heavy. The planet's gravity was dragging at him with almost twice the pull of home. But he managed to stand up straight . . . and raise his arms.

Overhead, St. Clair's fighter descended like an unfolding blanket . . . the alien robots encircling it at a range of thirty meters. The blackness descended on him, scooped him up, folded him in . . .

And Gregory screamed with pain.

By Ian Douglas

DEEP TIME
STAR CARRIER
BOOK SIX

IAN DOUGLAS

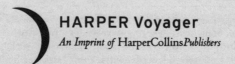

HARPER Voyager
An Imprint of HarperCollins Publishers

HARPER Voyager

An Imprint of HarperCollins*Publishers*
195 Broadway
New York, New York 10007

Copyright © 2015 by William H. Keith, Jr.
Cover art by Gregory Bridges
ISBN 978-0-06-218405-4
www.harpervoyagerbooks.com

First Harper Voyager mass market printing: June 2015

Harper Voyager and ⟩ is a trademark of HCP LLC.

Printed in the U.S.A.

10 9 8 7 6 5 4 3 2 1

For Deb, and, as ever, for Brea

Prologue

"What the hell *is* that?"

"Dunno, Control," replied the voice from Kapteyn Orbital. "It . . . it just popped up on our screens out of nowhere. It's coming in fast . . . almost a half *c*. It's—"

Commander Gerwin Dressler flinched as the projected holoscreen floating above his workstation lit up with an intense blue-white light. Something had just slammed into the research platform orbiting the local star at half the speed of light, converting five thousand tons of metal, ceramics, plastic, and organic crew members into a rapidly expanding cloud of hot plasma.

The base AI was saying that the *object* was in fact a diffuse cloud of particles, a cloud many astronomical units across and massing trillions of tons. There was other stuff in there, too, though . . . enigmatic structures, half-glimpsed constructions, things large and inexplicable shrouded within the particulate cloud.

And that cloud would be reaching Heimdall in seconds.

With a thoughtclick, Dressler sounded the base alarm.

"What is it?" the voice of Captain Roessler said in his head. He sounded groggy; it might be high noon local time, but by the base clocks, set to Greenwich Mean Time and measuring days and nights convenient to human biology, it was the wee hours of the morning.

"We've just lost Kapteyn Orbital, sir," Dressler replied. "Here's the data. . . ."

"The *Americans*?"

"No, sir. Something . . . something else."

Something very *else*.

He waited as the station's commanding officer reviewed the scant data transmitted from the orbital. God, the sky outside was so beautiful. . . .

The dome housing the base command and control center was set to project the view outside at the moment, showing a sky—deep blue to brilliant violet—dominated by the immense curve of the gas giant, Bifrost. Kapteyn's Star, an M1.5 red dwarf less than a third the mass and radius of Sol, shone almost directly overhead. At a distance of 3.5 AUs, Kapteyn's Star was shrunken to little more than a bright red pinpoint. Sharp eyes could distinguish its disk, but the much closer gas giant commanded the eastern sky at the moment, currently at half phase. The bands and swirls of pale brown, salmon, and white sweeping up from the glaciers on Heimdall's horizon to the curve of Bifrost's limb were clearly visible. Phantasmagorical aurorae circled the gas giant's poles to either side and were answered by the dancing curtains of light across Heimdall's northern sky.

Heimdall was a moon of Bifrost, circling its mammoth primary at a distance of just over 600,000 kilometers once every three days. Tidal interactions with the giant warmed Heimdall's surface far more than did the wan and feeble sun.

God, he thought again. He could see the flare marking the death of Kapteyn Orbital with his unaided eye, a smear of white light bisected by the rim of Bifrost's horizon. Automatically, he plotted the explosion's position against the background stars, and the result chilled him.

"Whatever it is, Captain," he told Roessler, "it's coming in more or less on a vector from Omega Centauri."

The research station's personnel had been briefed, of course, on events out at the giant globular star cluster, the site of the enigmatic rosette of fast-circling black holes . . . and the Rosette Aliens. Not that it had done them much good.

The curve of Bifrost's limb abruptly flared with blue and violet light . . . a rippling effect scattering out through the gas giant's atmosphere. The aurorae at both poles brightened suddenly, then spread, engulfing the huge gas giant in seething flashes and pulses of auroral light.

"Are you *sure* it's not the Americans?" Roessler demanded. "Some sort of high-velocity mass impact weapon . . ."

The USNA forces were notorious for their tactic of using clouds of sand released into space with speeds close to that of light. But Dressler was watching the cloud of minute particles spilling now across Bifrost's horizon and the titanic half-glimpsed shapes behind the planet. Some of those shapes were bigger than Bifrost, measuring millions—even tens of millions—of kilometers across.

"I'm sure, sir."

"But—"

"It's *not* the Americans, sir. And yes, sir, I'm very sure."

He checked on the position of the Confederation starships in orbit over Heimdall. One was currently above the antipodes, blocked from the alien cloud by the bulk of Heimdall itself.

"I suggest, sir," he added, "that we dispatch the *Kalmar* back to Earth with a complete update."

If, he thought, *there was still time. . . .*

Chapter One

Marine 1/5
Fort Douaumont
France, European Union
0610 hours, GMT

The flight of Crocodiles shrieked out of the eastern sky, ventral thrusters hissing as they swung blunt prows toward the ancient fortress. Marine Staff Sergeant Gerald Swayze watched the stone walls below through his link with the Croc's scanner array and prayed that *this* time Intel knew its ass from a hole in the ground.

The CL/BC-5 Crocodile was an ugly and ungainly piece of equipment: blunt, stubby, and no-nonsense, with a nano docking collar on its squared-off prow, broadly splayed landing legs, and a pair of turrets on its back that turned the landing craft into a semimobile fortress once it had completed its primary mission. In this case, that mission was transporting forty armed and armored USNA Marines from orbit to the surface of a hostile planet.

The hostile planet in this case was Earth, the objective a massive, centuries-old stone fortress deep within the territory of the European Union . . . a fortress known to history as Verdun.

"Stand ready, people!" Lieutenant Widner's voice came through their in-heads, crisp and sharp. "Fifteen seconds!"

Swayze listened for any hint of fear or indecision there, but heard none. This was Widner's first op as platoon commander, but he didn't seem to carry the usual newbie CO baggage of arrogance or overconfidence in doing it all by the book. Mostly, that meant he'd been paying attention to his NCO staff in general and to Swayze in particular. With an attitude like that, they might actually be able to pull this op off.

"You apes heard the el-tee," Swayze growled over the company tactical channel. "On your feet! Face front! When the nano kicks open the door, I want to see nothing but amphibious green *blurs* moving through that collar!"

"Amphibious green" was an anachronism, of course, but one long beloved of the Corps. Each Marine in the assault platoon was clad in full Mark I armor—the curving, black, nanoflaged surfaces scattering back a bewildering kaleidoscope of shapes, colors, and lights from the red-lit interior of the Crocodile transport. The nanoflage picked up on lights and colors surrounding the armor and transmitted it back. In the field, it provided what amounted to functional invisibility, but within the cramped confines of the Croc's cargo deck it just gave you a functional headache.

A shudder ran through the Croc as it nosed into the fortress wall. According to the plans Swayze had seen, the wall here was two meters thick. It would take a few seconds for the collar to eat its way through that.

Something clanged against the Crocodile's hull, sharp and insistent. Swayze heard the whine of the landing craft's turrets slewing to port, followed by the howl of exciters and cooling pumps as the weapons opened up with a few thousand megawatts of high-energy laser response. Up forward, the docking collar was slowly extending, growing its way into the stone of the fortress wall, converting concrete and iron into free-flowing atoms and directing them along the tunnel's interior surfaces where they froze as an ultra-hard crust supporting the opening. In space, a nano docking collar allowed Marines to tunnel through the hull of an enemy spacecraft without losing internal pressure. Here, pressure wasn't an issue. They just needed to burrow through those two meters of concrete and steel . . . and do so before the enemy had time to respond.

When they were down to the last few centimeters, the Crocodile fired a series of probes through the remaining stone, putting insect-sized battlespace drones into the interior of the fortress. Swayze's in-head showed what those drones were seeing—a dozen heavily armored Confed soldiers crouched in a broad stone tunnel, weapons ready.

This was *not* going to be pretty.

"We've got bad guys to either side of the entrance," he told the others, "*and* straight ahead. Lead fireteam, focus on the ones straight ahead. The ones to either side will be worried about scoring own-goals."

The defense obviously had been thrown together in a hurry, with nearby soldiers rounded up and pointed at the breach site. Putting gunners on both sides of the breach was a great way to ensure that some of them would suffer friendly fire.

He didn't envy the lead fireteam, though. Two of them were manhandling bulky mirror shields, but they would be taking fire from three sides.

"Here we go!" Widner called.

The Croc's interior docking hatch dilated open and the waiting Marines surged forward.

"*Go! Go! Go!*" Swayze yelled.

The door kickers went through first, crouched behind their shields. Those mirrored surfaces—backed by energy-damping exotic-material ceramics—would give them a fair degree of protection from handheld lasers and projectiles, but not as much from plasma beams. Blocked by the armored shapes in front of him, Swayze couldn't see what was happening up ahead; an in-head window displayed the heart rates of the lead fireteam, but not their helmet-camera feeds. He needed to be focused on the entire platoon, not just the tacsit of the four in front.

"Watch it! We're taking fire!" That was Corporal Addison, in the lead fireteam.

"Gaynor is down! Man down!"

An explosion sounded from ahead, and the Crocodile rocked with the concussion. The Marines kept filing forward, though, smoke billowing back into the transport's interior. Swayze stooped low as he entered the docking collar and pressed into the tunnel. He was positioned halfway back in the line, which meant there were twenty Marines—four fireteams—in front of him.

Then he was through, stepping into a narrow passageway with walls, floor, and ceiling all of stone blocks. Two Marines were down on the deck, both still moving; a dozen Confed troopers were visible in the passageways left, right, and straight ahead.

The Marines stormed the fortress.

Emergency Presidential Command Post
Toronto
United States of North America
0012 hours, EST

For President Alexander Koenig, it was as though he was actually *there*.

His staff had set up the direct link, and he was riding the transmitted thoughts and sensory impressions of Lieutenant Franklyn K. Widner's Mark I combat armor. Those neural signals were being transmitted to the complex web of circuitry grown atom by atom through Koenig's cerebral cortex.

As far as Koenig could tell, he was inside Lieutenant Widner's armor, moving through dark stone corridors, following the electronic maps being thrown up against his visual field by the in-head circuitry. He could hear the shouts of the men over the tactical channel, hear Widner's orders and the rasp of his breathing; even feel the mass and give of the armor as it responded to Widner's movements. The only limitation was his lack of somatic control; he was a passenger only, receiving sensory impressions but unable even to turn his head to see what was beside him.

"Talman! Gonzales!" Widner was shouting. "Put fire on that passageway. Two o'clook!"

Everything was noise and confusion. Briefly, Koenig considered pulling back to the feed from one of the battlespace drones, but he preferred to hold on to the connection with the platoon commander. He could transmit messages to Widner over the tactical channel, but Koenig was a Navy veteran himself, and knew how frustrating—and outright deadly—micromanagement was. Widner didn't need his input, and certainly wouldn't appreciate it. Koenig continued to simply ride the boil and tumble of the firefight.

Besides, what Koenig was witnessing now was only a tiny part of the whole of Operation Fallen Star. Three other platoons of Alfa Company were inserting by Crocodile nearby, and a flight of ponderous Choctaw UC-154 shuttles—each carrying two hundred Marines—were coming in behind the Croc first wave. Fallen Star was an orbit-to-ground insertion of a full battalion: more than a thousand Marines, plus their support personnel.

And still, Koenig wondered if it would be enough. Verdun had a nasty reputation.

Verdun, a city on the Meuse River in northeastern France that had repulsed Attila the Hun, had by the early twentieth century become a defensive complex of twenty-eight forts. The meat-grinder battles of 1916 had slaughtered something like 150,000 Frenchmen and very nearly that many Germans. Fort Douaumont had been the largest of the French strongholds, with outer walls four hundred meters long, and comprising two underground levels, multiple casements and turrets, and living spaces for hundreds of men. After the war, Douaumont had become a war museum and remained so . . . until the beginning of the Sh'daar conflict in 2367. At that point, the Pan-European Union enlarged and deepened the facility, adding missile silos and plasma beam turrets and turning it into a planetary defense base.

The intent had been to protect the European Union from a Sh'daar attack, a scenario that had become all too possible when the Turusch had penetrated Earth's outer system defenses in 2404, slamming a high-velocity kinetic-kill impactor into the Atlantic Ocean. Nobody, Koenig thought, had ever imagined that the ancient fortress at Douaumont would become the last-ditch refuge of the followers of General Janos Matonyi Korosi, the Butcher of Columbus and the leader of the Earth Confederation.

Events had proceeded in a chaotic tumble since the civil war between Confederation and the United States of North America had begun. Korosi, the USNA intelligence services believed, had been responsible for the nano-D strike against Columbus, D.C., formerly the USNA capital, an attack that constituted an almost unthinkably vicious war crime. Roettgen, the Confederation's president, had vanished not long after—either a prisoner or murdered by Korosi's thugs. A new president of the Confederation had been appointed from the Confederation Senate, Christian Denoix de Saint Marc, but smart money said he was either an innocent dupe or a corrupt front man for Korosi.

Then the USNA computer net facility at Cheyenne Mountain had launched Operation Luther, using the science of recombinant memetics to introduce a new religion into the Confederation's electronic networks and social infrastructure. The new religion, called Starlight, had caught hold with astonishing speed, bringing with it a popular revulsion against a government that could condone the nano-disassembly of a city center, including hundreds of thousands of its civilians. A grassroots revolution had swept the ruling Globalist Party from power, and almost brought the civil war to an end.

Almost . . .

Geneva, the Confederation capital, had fallen to Starlightist rebel forces just two weeks ago. Working through electronic back doors put in place during Operation Luther, USNA Intelligence had been searching for the fallen regime's leaders, and for Ilse Roettgen. They now believed that both Denoix and Korosi were in Douaumont, and the chances were good that Roettgen, if she was still alive, was there as well.

Catch Korosi and his stooges, and the war might be over for good.

And so, Koenig had authorized Fallen Star, a high-risk assault with the sole purpose of killing or capturing Korosi and Denoix, rescuing Ilse Roettgen, and bringing the nasty little war to a close.

Once that was done, Koenig reflected, all that was needful was to end the Sh'daar War, figure out what the Rosette Aliens wanted, and bring half of Earth back under a legitimate, reasonable, democratic, and above all *peaceful* government, one that would both recognize USNA independence and work with the United States to strengthen Humankind's interests, both on Earth and throughout North America's far-flung interstellar colonies.

Nothing to it.

"Concentrate on twelve o'clock! Hit 'em! *Hit 'em!*"

"Marine down! Marine down! Corpsman front!"

"Move, move, *move . . .*"

"First Section!" That was Widner's voice, both on audio and transmitted in-head over the tactical channel. "With me!"

A passageway yawned ahead, with gray stone slabs underfoot and to either side. There was something up ahead, at the end of the corridor, but Widner's helmet AI was having trouble parsing it out. What the hell *was* that?

Armored shapes rose from behind the object, which revealed itself now as an impromptu barricade: a jumble of furniture, concrete blocks, and steel drums blocking the stone corridor.

And behind it . . .

"Watch it! Damn it, *watch it!*"

Something slammed into Koenig's chest, staggering him. It took him a dazed moment to recognize that *he'd* not been hit, but that a white-hot plasma bolt had slammed into Widner's combat armor. Widner's heart and respiration readouts went ragged, then dropped toward flatline. Koenig felt trapped, staring at the stone slabs of the corridor's ceiling, unable to move, unable to do *anything* but lie there.

Widner died, and his armor began shutting him down for medevac and resuss. . . .

VFA-96, Black Demons
LEO
0014 hours, TFT

Lieutenant Megan Connor rolled her fresh-grown Starblade until Earth's vast sweep hung suspended in sun-kissed splendor above her head. The sunrise terminator stretched across the sky ahead of her now, out over central Europe, a razor-thin crescent of light across the black. It was just past midnight on the east coast of the USNA, a few minutes past six in the morning over France and most of the European Union. The Black Demons were in low Earth orbit, drifting southeast two hundred kilometers above the west coast of Europe. Below, city lights illumined the broken clouds over England. Sunrise at Verdun had occurred less than thirty minutes ago . . . but at this altitude she could see considerably farther into the new day than the Marines on the ground.

She adjusted her in-head view, connecting more closely with her fighter's long-range senses.

Gods this new fighter is a dream!

Theoretically, with manufacturing processes that could grow a new fighter from raw materials provided by asteroids in a matter of hours, there should have been no problem with constantly updating the USNA fighter fleet, discarding older designs like the SG-92 Starhawks and SG-101 Velociraptors and replacing them with the latest technology—in this case the SG-420 Starblade. The problem was not in the materials manufacturing, but in retraining human pilots whose wetware—the organic tissue beneath the cerebral electronic implants and software—had already been shaped to control older designs.

The SG-420s, though, incorporated uprated AI components that could embrace Starhawk or Velociraptor training and experience as iterations within the larger pilot program. Still, what the star carrier *America* lacked was people to sit inside these new fighters: the campaigns of the past eight months—Arianrhod and Osiris and Vulcan—had killed too many good pilots. Replacements were coming on board from the training center at Oceana, but too few and too slowly, to bring the carrier up to full strength.

And yet, as Connor felt the sensuous flow of data streaming in through her fighter's sensors and AI, she suppressed an exultant urge to shout for pure joy. Beauty exploded around her as the sun rose beyond the horizon ahead; blue water, the green patchwork of agricultural land, and the sweep of dazzlingly white cloud drifted beneath her. With the new system, it was easy to forget that you were flesh-and-blood wired into a cockpit barely large enough to receive you. Quite literally, she *was* the fighter; she stretched out an arm, and performed a graceful roll, the crescent of Earth rotating in front of her.

"Careful there, Demon Five," the voice of Commander Mackey said inside her mind. "Let's not get carried away."

"Hard not to, Skipper," she told the squadron's CO. "This is *incredible*!"

"Maybe so, but stay focused on the mission. We're coming up on Verdun and we don't want to miss anything, right?"

"Yes, sir."

Not that they were likely to miss anything. VFA-96, the Black Demons, was actually at full squadron strength—twelve fighters—though only Connor, Mackey, and two others were in this flight. Aerospace control meant stretching your assets out across an entire orbit so that at any given moment there were at least some fighters positioned to respond to threats from below. The other Demons were spread out four thousand kilometers ahead and behind, and two more of *America*'s squadrons were covering the rest of the orbit. Adjustments were made from orbit to orbit so that four strike fighters were always passing over Verdun every ten minutes or so.

"So how's the fight going down there anyway, Skipper?" That was Lieutenant Enrique Martinez, one of the squadron's newbies fresh up from Oceana.

"According to plan," Mackey replied. "The first LCs hit the fortress walls a few minutes ago. The big Choctaws are touching down now."

"But when will we *know*?"

"When someone decides to tell us, Lieutenant. And until then, stay sharp and stay connected. The rebels aren't going to take this lying down."

The rebels. It sounded strange, the way Mackey used the term. Confusing, even. Until recently, the *USNA* had been the rebels, fighting for independence from the Earth Confederation. But since the Confederation government had fallen to the Starlighters, *rebels* now meant the holdouts in the original government—Korosi's people.

"I'm not getting anyone down there but 'Pactors," Connor

said, reading her ship's long-range scan. Six fighters from VFA-31, the Impactors, had deployed into the atmosphere over an hour ago, taking out the big planetary defense turrets mounted on the fort's upper surfaces with high-velocity KK projectiles accelerated in from space. The strike had been the second phase of Operation Fallen Star, necessary to allow the transports to get in without being vaporized.

The *first* phase had been initiated by the Virtual Combat Center in Colorado Springs, an all-out electronic assault by former pilots linked in through the Confederation's computer nets, opening backdoor channels and covert access feeds either discovered or, in many cases, *created* by the super-AI Konstantin from its base on the far side of Earth's moon.

"Hang on a sec," Lieutenant Junior Grade Chris Dobbs said. Another newbie, he'd been in the squadron less than seventy-two hours. "I've got multiple launches . . . dead ahead. Range, twenty-six hundred kilometers!"

Damn, the kid was right. The range put the launch site somewhere in central or southern Turkey, close to the Mediterranean . . . and Turkey was still part of the Confederation. Those fighters might well be rebels—pro-Korosi forces. They'd certainly timed their launch nicely . . . moments after the lead element of the Black Demons had passed overhead in their orbit.

Connor let the data flood through her. How many spacecraft . . . and what kind? Were they after the lead element, coming up on them from behind? Or were they going counter-orbit and closing with her?

"They're firing!" Mackey warned.

Eight fighters—Confederation Todtadlers—and they were closing with Connor and her fellows at a very high acceleration. They'd just loosed a sand cloud, whose pellets were now hurtling toward the four fighters like the blast from an old-fashioned shotgun.

And in seconds, the battle was joined.

Koenig thoughtclicked an in-head icon and emerged inside his own body, gasping for air, stretched out on a recliner in his own office in Toronto. Marcus Whitney, his chief of staff and senior aide, was leaning over him with a worried look on his face. "Mr. President?"

"I'm okay, Marcus."

"Your vitals took a real jump just now."

"Nothing like the vitals on Lieutenant Widner."

As an admiral in command of a carrier battlegroup twenty years before, Koenig had had a lot of trouble giving the orders that sent young men and women to their deaths.

It wasn't any easier now.

"I'm going back in," Koenig said. "Link me in with . . . let's see . . ." He ran through a mental list of the Marines in Alfa Platoon, the ones still on their feet. "Staff Sergeant Gerald Swayze." He was Widner's senior NCO, and would be commanding the platoon now.

"Sir," Whitney said, "it's not like you can affect the outcome of the fight. . . ." He sounded worried. "Damn it, you're flirting with VRSD."

The acronym was pronounced "ver-sid," and stood for virtual reality stress disorder. What it really stood for was a whole spectrum of neurological injuries, addictions, and pathologies, including—most important—perceptual neural shock, or PNS. Though not common, some had suffered heart attacks, strokes, or slipped into comas when they "died," even though their physical bodies were perfectly safe and healthy.

Koenig knew there was a risk, but he'd been in combat before, and experience tended to reduce the psychological impact of even the most traumatic experiences. Too, there were electronic safeguards designed to cut him from the circuit if monitors showed that his body back in the Emergency Presidential Command Post was reacting too strongly.

"I don't think so," Koenig told Whitney. He raised his voice slightly. "Health monitor? What say you?"

"Your heart rate peaked at one twenty-six," the voice of the medical AI in the presidential complex told them. "Respiration peaked at thirty-five. Both are well within tolerable limits."

"See, Marcus? I'm fine."

"I still don't like it, Mr. President. You could just let your intelligence people brief you after the fact, like a *normal* president."

"Well, damn. Where's the fun in that? I don't think that—"

He stopped in mid-sentence. An alert was coming through from the suite of artificial intelligences overseeing the entire battle. It was data relayed from the star carrier *America* or, more specifically, from one of her squadrons. Eight Confed fighters had just boosted at high velocity from central Turkey and launched an attack on four of *America*'s fighters in low Earth orbit. The AI running the intelligence side of the operation was tagging the attackers as Korosi rebels.

Interesting. There was no way eight Todtadler fighters could seriously challenge three USNA strike fighter squadrons for space superiority, especially if they had to claw their way up out of Earth's gravity well. Even if they got through the orbiting fighters, there were three USNA destroyers and four frigates farther out, providing in-depth support. Earth was bottled up tight right now against any attempt to break away.

What the hell were they trying to accomplish?

"Take them out," Koenig ordered. "And keep me informed."

A new icon had appeared within Koenig's in-head a moment before, labeled with Staff Sergeant Swayze's name. He thoughtclicked it . . . and opened his eyes, once again, in the shrieking, noisy hell of combat.

Chapter Two

Emergency Presidential Command Post
Toronto
United States of North America
0018 hours, EST

Koenig was back in that fire-swept passageway, the scene overlaid by flickering numbers giving ranges, angles, and power levels, and by a bright red targeting reticule slaved to Swayze's laser rifle, centered on whatever the rifle happened to be pointed at. At the far end of the passageway, laser and plasma gunfire snapped and hissed from the makeshift barricades.

"Grossmann! Nobunaga!" Swayze was yelling. "Get that pig in action! Flame those bastards!"

Koenig recognized the term. The Marines had a PG-80 as a platoon heavy weapon—a semiportable plasma gun—nicknamed the "pig" and designed to burn through most armor.

Swayze was using his laser rifle, trying to force enemy troops back from the ambush barricade at the far end of the passageway. Two armored shapes moved up beside him, manhandling the bulky weapon's tripod into place. One of the Marines was hit, his faceplate vaporized by a plasma bolt, so Swayze shoved Grossmann's body aside and took up a position next to the gunner, snapping up the heavy fire shield and dragging back the charge lever. He slapped Nobunaga's shoulder, signaling readiness to fire.

"*Hit 'em!*"

Blue-white fire exploded through the dark passageway, charring stone walls already black with age. The barricade at the end of the hall exploded, hurling chunks of molten debris as armored figures scattered . . . or collapsed and lay still.

The pig fired again, blasting a hole in the steel door beyond, and then Swayze was up and running down the stone corridor, firing from the hip, waving his men on. "*Let's go, Marines! Ooh-rah!*"

"*Ooh-rah!*" The ancient Marine war cry rang out in answer from a dozen throats, raw sound and fury, meaningless except to announce that the USNA Marines were charging.

And the enemy troops began throwing down their weapons and raising their arms in surrender.

Koenig watched as two more Marines—Jamison and Arkwright—pushed past Swayze as he stopped to hand the prisoners over to another Marine. He then followed the pair, over the half-molten ruin of the barricade and through the gaping hole in the steel door. Swayze shouldered his way into the stone chamber beyond, arriving just behind the other two Marines, who'd come to a dead stop. A soldier in shifting black-and-gray nanoflage armor stood with his back to the far wall, clutching a tiny woman in civilian utilities in front of him like a shield.

Through Swayze's helmet camera, Koenig recognized the woman. Ilse Roettgen, former Senate president for the Earth Confederation, struggled in the armored man's one-arm grip, her arms zip-stripped behind her back. In his free hand, the man clutched a deadly little 5mm needler, which he kept pressed against the side of her throat.

"Stop!" the man yelled, his amplified voice booming off the stone walls. "If you value her life, stop *now*!"

Koenig recognized that voice instantly. It was General Korosi . . . the Butcher of Columbus.

Swayze ran a voice print ID through his suit's AI, a process that took only a second or so, and came to the same conclusion. "Put the weapon down, General," he said, his voice level, reasonable, and as cold as ice. "If you kill her, I *promise* you that you will die, right here, right now."

"So . . . I should surrender, so you can put me on trial for war crimes?" Korosi laughed, an ugly sound. His English carried a thick Hungarian accent. " 'Crimes against humanity,' I think is the phrase you Americans use? And then you execute me anyway? I don't think so. . . ."

"Let her go, General. Hurt her, and you won't believe how much worse you'll make it for yourself."

"There is nothing you can threaten me with worse than what will happen if I give myself up. You understand me?"

"I can promise you won't be executed."

"So that I can enjoy the effects of a neural net wipe? Ha! That's worse than a clean death in battle! No! *Here* is how we play this, American. Ilse here, lovely lady that she is, will come with me, as a guarantee of your good behavior. You and your men will back off. You will clear these corridors! You will permit us to leave. No interference! You will arrange to have a flyer meet us at the surface, with an AI pilot slaved to my direct neural control, and with a range of at least ten thousand kilometers. The flyer will take me to a destination of my choosing . . . and I may release Roettgen there, *if* I am satisfied that you have not followed us. Now, put your weapons down and *move back*!"

A red targeting reticule was centered on Korosi's faceplate, and Koenig wondered if the Marine was going to try for a head shot, firing from his hip. Had Korosi not been wearing combat armor, Koenig knew, Swayze might have tried it . . . but splash off the armor's surface could burn the unarmored Roettgen quite badly.

Of course, Swayze might choose to accept the collateral damage, injuring the hostage in order to kill the hostage taker. He might even accept the hostage's death. According to Fallen Star's operational orders, finding and rescuing Ilse Roettgen was secondary to taking down Janos Korosi.

So the easy solution would be to burn Korosi down now, even if it meant the former Confederation president's death. It would not have been Koenig's personal choice, but then Koenig was not the one linked to Swayze's laser rifle.

"Okay, okay," Swayze said after a long and agonizing moment. "You win." The targeting reticule winked off, and slowly the Marine lowered his rifle, placing it on the floor at his feet. "Don't hurt her!"

"The rest of you! Put down your weapons!"

"Do as he says, Marines," Swayze told the others. He shifted to the general tactical frequency. "Listen up, Marines! Clear the passageways. Korosi is coming up . . . with a hostage."

"Transport, Staff Sergeant," Korosi said. "Arrange for us a flight out of here."

"Okay, okay," Swayze said. "Meteor! This is Marine One-Five! I want a Chipper on the ground on top of this fort ASAP!"

Meteor was the code name for the battalion HQ running this op, while *Chipper* was military slang for a C-28 Chippewa robot transport. Definitely long-range enough for the ten-thousand-kilometer range Korosi specified. Koenig contemplated that requirement. Ten thousand klicks was enough to reach any of the three space elevators—in Ecuador, Kenya, or Singapore. But what then? Korosi had to know that he would be tracked. No doubt he had confederates waiting for him someplace.

Koenig turned the problem over in his mind. They wouldn't be waiting for him off-world; the space elevators were too easily blocked, too easily powered down, isolating him. The likeliest scenario would be to touch down very briefly someplace on Earth along a direct line of flight to one of the elevators . . . and effectively disappear as the robotic transport continued its flight.

Damn it, it was imperative that Korosi not be allowed to escape. If he did, the war might grind on for years more, a guerilla action fought in jungles and villages and mountains from South America to Africa to Southeast Asia.

Koenig wasn't linked in directly to Swayze's thoughts, his internal monologue. That degree of electronic telepathy required more sophisticated equipment than was available here . . . and wasn't desirable in any case. But he couldn't help but wonder what the Marine had in mind. Clearly, the man was working toward an idea. . . .

Swayze, unarmed now, raised both gauntleted hands. "Look, General . . . take me instead, okay? She'll be nothing but trouble. I'll promise to behave. . . ."

Korosi laughed. "What . . . *you*? You're an NCO, a foot soldier! What makes something like you as valuable as the former president of the Earth Confederation?"

Swayze took a couple of steps forward, his hands still raised. "Simple: I know the full deployment of the Marines for this assault . . . *and* I know the plans that were set in motion to trap you here, to keep you penned up. I know the troop deployments topside here, and I know what naval assets we have in orbit. General Korosi, I could *help* you. A lot."

Another cautious step . . .

"No closer!" The Confederation general gestured with the needler, warning Swayze back.

It was enough.

Since the first half of the twenty-first century, military armor had incorporated feedback cybernetics that allowed the wearer to lift and carry far greater loads than were possible for an unarmored individual. Neural augmentation—new circuitry nanochelated throughout the living brain—made it possible for an armored man to react and move more quickly as well. Clad in their Mark I armor, Marines possessed both superhuman strength and speed.

Janos Korosi was almost certainly enhanced as well . . . but not enough.

Swayze's gloved hand snapped down and out with blinding speed, closing around the needler, the glove's palm blocking the weapon's muzzle. Korosi's hand clenched convulsively: he fired and Swayze screamed. The needler's power pack gave it the ability to shoot eight pulsed bursts of coherent light or a single beam lasting a few seconds. Korosi had the weapon set for a beam, and the five-millimeter thread of laser light melted through the glove, Swayze's hand, and the top side of the glove within perhaps half a second.

By then, though, the Marine had twisted Korosi's arm out and back so that the weapon was no longer pointed at the hostage. Swayze crowded forward, grappling with the Confederation general, continuing to grip the smothered weapon with his terribly injured hand as he knocked Roettgen aside and interposed his own body between the two. He kept squeezing, too, for as long as his armor's glove could exert the pressure, crumpling the needler's tough plastic body in his grip even as molten metal and ceramic charred the palm of his hand. In-head readouts showed Swayze's doloric levels—the amount of pain he was enduring—shooting up at first, then beginning to fall . . . either as Swayze's enhanced brain stifled the pain response, or as the nerves in the more sensitive parts of his hand burned away and shock began to set in.

Korosi struggled in Swayze's grip. The laser failed— either crushed to uselessness or its power pack drained— and Swayze wrestled the general to the ground. The other Marines were leaping forward now and piling on, grabbing Korosi's thrashing legs and arms.

"*Nem! Nem! Engedj el!*" Korosi screamed, his native Magyar immediately translated by Swayze's in-head. "*No! No! Let me go!*"

Swayze subdued the man at last through the simple expedient of sitting on Korosi's chest, cradling his wounded hand as his armor's med units began treating him.

And with that, Koenig knew that the fight for Fort Douamont was over.

VFA-96, Black Demons
LEO
0019 hours, TFT

Lieutenant Connor threw her Starblade into a hard-left roll and engaged her forward grav projector. A brief burst of acceleration at twenty thousand gravities and she was hurtling past the incoming projectiles, several of which flared into vapor as she brushed them with the intensely warped pucker of space just ahead of her fighter. Two of the Todtadlers ahead and below twisted around to meet her, but she caught one in a target lock with her PBP-8 and slammed it with a high-energy particle beam, flashing the fighter into star-hot vapor.

The Pan-European Todtadlers—Death Eagles—were highly advanced, modern fighters. They easily matched USNA fighters like the SG-101 Velociraptor, but they were utterly outclassed by the newer Starblades. Connor could feel her mind pervading every part of her ship's consciousness, directing weapons, power, thrust, and attitude together in a rapturous dance. Her fighter shuddered as a KK projectile passed through one temporary wing . . . but the nanomatrix hull flowed around the slug as it passed through, directing it harmlessly past the pilot compartment and other vital elements, and back into space. Connor didn't need to spin the craft. Rather, she simply reformed it in flight, bringing weapons to bear on the second target and vaporizing it in a flare of radiation and plasma.

"Demon Five!" she called over the tac channel. "Two kills!"

"Demon Seven! Scratch one Toddy Velocicrapper!"

And the fighters merged in an angry tangle of fire and destruction. . . .

Emergency Presidential Command Post
Toronto
United States of North America
0020 hours, EST

Koenig emerged again from his virtual connection. A chorus of screams and yells filled the Presidential Command Center and rang off the walls—a roomful of military officers, civilian officials, aides, and technicians jumping and shouting and hugging one another and slapping hands together, congratulating each other. In a smaller room just off from the center's main control room, Koenig blinked against the overhead lights. "What the hell is that noise?" he asked.

"The guys are going a little nuts, sir," Whitney replied. "They got Korosi!"

"I know," Koenig said, sitting up. "I was there. And it was the One-Five *Marines* who got the bastard, not us."

"It *was* a group effort, Mr. President." He gestured toward the other room. "They found Korosi, and they tracked him to Verdun. And *you* gave the order. . . ."

"And the Marines dug him out, and rescued Roettgen. Tell them to knock it off and get back on the job. We still have to withdraw our people."

"Yes, sir."

Whitney's attempt to spread credit for the success around irritated him. Koenig had a particular and heartfelt disdain for the type of national leader who assumed the credit for his or her military's successes. *I* directed . . . *I* ordered . . . *We* attacked . . . Bullshit. It was the men and women who were boots-on-the-ground in-theater—the ones getting shot at and taking the risks—who should get the credit, not the damned REMFs peering over their shoulders through drone cameras, satellites, or in-head links.

Admiral Eugene Armitage, the head of the Joint Chiefs, grinned at him. "But we *did* get the bastard, Mr. President."

"Yes," Koenig said, sitting up and rubbing his eyes. "We got him."

Whitney nodded. "There's more, Mr. President. You might have missed it, but they just flashed the word back. They've captured Denoix as well, trying to leave the perimeter by air car."

Koenig smiled. His chief of staff was scolding him, mildly, by letting him know that the information he'd wanted had come through to the command post just as quickly as Koenig could have gotten it from a direct link. "Outstanding, Marcus." He glanced at Armitage. "Admiral?" he said. "Please flash Meteor a 'well done' from me, personally."

Armitage nodded. "As you wish, Mr. President."

"There's . . . ah . . . there *is* still one part unresolved, sir," Whitney told him.

"The recovery, yes. I assume you have the heavy transports on the way."

"Yes, sir. But it's not that."

"What, then?"

"Eight Todtadlers launched a few minutes ago from a site in southern Turkey . . . a city called Adana."

"Adana? What do they have there?"

"It's one of Turkey's larger cities, sir . . . and the site of a small spaceport. Incirlik."

Koenig nodded as data flowed through his in-head. "Got it."

Once, Incirlik had been a joint U.S. and Turkish military air base, back in the days of the old NATO alliance. After the mid-2100s and the beginnings of the Pax Confederata, the facilities had been developed as a local spaceport for Pan-Europe's burgeoning asteroid mining initiatives. Turkey, geographically astride both Europe and Asia, had been an ideal region for economic development after both the Islamic Wars and the more recent Sino-Western Wars.

But the rise of the space elevators—first at SupraQuito, then in Kenya and in Singapore—had perhaps already doomed such antiquated assets as national spaceports. There wasn't much at Incirlik now, save for a small military base.

But why were they attacking the USNA fighters in LEO?

For a moment, Koenig watched the data flow describing the slash and stab of aerospace fighters in low orbit. That *why* was becoming an increasingly important question. With the fighting at the Verdun planetary defense center all but over, there was no reason to challenge American space superiority, none at all.

Unless . . .

He called up a holographic map display, the board hanging transparent in midair showing the orbit of *America*'s space superiority fighters southeast across the Balkans, Turkey, the Arabian Peninsula, and out over the Indian Ocean. A red dot flashed at the northeastern corner of the Med, marking Incirlik. Four of *America*'s fighters had just shot down the last of the Todtadlers from the base; four more USNA Starblades were four thousand kilometers ahead . . . coming up now on the southern tip of India.

"A second launch, Mr. President," Armitage reported. "More Death Eagles."

"How many?"

"Five, sir. No . . . make that six. . . ."

"From where?"

"Surat, Mr. President. North India."

"Curiouser and curiouser," Koenig said, thoughtful. Surat was a large city on India's northwestern coast, next to the Gulf of Khambhat. "I think those Death Eagles are trying to punch a hole through our orbiting squadron," Koenig said.

"For what possible purpose, sir?" Whitney asked.

"For an escape. Admiral Armitage?"

"Sir!"

"I suggest you order the *Elliot* and the *Hawes* down from their perch for a closer look."

"Right away, sir."

The *Elliot* was a destroyer massing eight thousand tons, the *Hawes* a smaller frigate, a light escort of about three thousand tons. The two had recently been assigned to *America*'s carrier group and were now deployed in HEO—high Earth orbit, about thirty thousand kilometers out.

"Who would be trying to escape, Mr. President?" Whitney asked. "If we have both Denoix and Korosi—"

"Might be members of Korosi's staff," Koenig said. "Or it might be the *real* architects of Columbus."

" The *real* architects, Mr. President?" Whitney shook his head. "We already know Korosi was behind that, don't we?"

"No, Marcus, we don't. He's a nasty character, I'll admit, but the Confederation really didn't have reason to eat a city, not when they had to take that big of a public-relations hit."

As Koenig had noted, the attack by the Confederation ship *Estremadura*—awful as it had been—had done more damage by far to the Confederation than to North America. Nation states that had been sitting on the sidelines of the fast-evolving civil war—the Chinese Hegemony and the Islamic Theocracy, especially—had openly come into the war against the Confederation. Perhaps just as important, members of the Confederation—including Russia, North India, and England—had immediately distanced themselves from the world state, with Russia and North India both seceding from the Geneva government.

But the politics over there were still murky. One of the Confederation ships escorting the *Estremadura* on her deadly mission, Koenig remembered, had been the North Indian heavy cruiser *Brahmaputra*. At least some within the North Indian government, clearly, had known about the nature of the attack that had destroyed Columbus . . . and approved of it. If fighters were coming up from Surat, they might well be piloted by officers still loyal to Korosi, even if New Delhi had disowned the guy since the attack.

And knowing if that was true was crucial. With the takedown of the last major fortress controlled by Korosi forces, Koenig knew it was vital to maintain the momentum; handled properly, Korosi's capture might end the war.

So the question remained: Who the hell was trying to escape the USNA's tightening noose?

VFA-96, Black Demons
LEO
0022 hours, TFT

Megan Connor thoughtclicked a symbol, sending two VG-10 Krait missiles streaking toward the last Confederation fighter. At a range of just two hundred kilometers, the missiles detonated in twin flares of dazzling, silent light . . . and the enemy Todtadler disintegrated in tumbling, half-molten fragments.

Elsewhere in the sky, soft-glowing clouds of expanding hot plasma and debris marked the passings of the other fighters; one had re-entered the atmosphere below, a streak of ablating hull material scratched across the intense blue of the Indian Ocean.

Through her communications link, Connor could hear the chatter among the other pilots in her squadron.

"Nice shot, Five! That's a kill!"

"The last one! Hot damn, and we didn't loose a single damned ship!"

That was pretty spectacular, Connor thought. Eight fighters in that first launch out of Turkey . . . and six more from North India. Fourteen fighters against four of the new Starblades, and every single one of them shot down without a single loss. That was worth a hot damn in anyone's flight log.

"Hey, Skipper? Demon Six. My scanners weren't picking up any people in those ships!"

"Copy that, Six. *America*'s S-2 concurs. They were all on AI."

"Shit, why? Aren't we good enough for them?"

For centuries, the debate had continued to natter back and forth over the need for human pilots in fighter cockpits. Undeniably, artificial intelligences were faster than humans, sharper, more immediately aware, and surer in their assessment of data . . . but humans seemed to add a degree of creativity and inspired improvisation to the mix. So far, at least, the best tactical advantage seemed to rest with human brains cybernetically wired into AI-controlled spacecraft.

And the 14-and-0 victory they'd just won was a resounding validation of that . . . that and the fact that the new Starblade design left even the most advanced Confederation spacecraft chewing hard vacuum. But maybe the unbalanced outcome wasn't so surprising after all, since it had involved enhanced humans fighting machines.

Especially machines on some sort of preset program. . . .

"Skipper?" she said, running through her sensor feeds. "See that, to the north?"

"What the hell?"

"That's a fucking *starship*!" she exclaimed. "Running hot and under escort!"

And now the Confederation's plan was clear. The attack rising from a spaceport in Turkey had served to scatter the four fighters riding that part of the space superiority orbit—not badly, but a little. The second wave of enemy fighters, coming south from Surat, had scattered the flight even further; the nearest other fighter to Connor's right now was Mackey's . . . a good fifteen hundred kilometers to her southeast.

And with the four Starblades scattered all over the sky, *now* was when the enemy was launching something *big* . . . and escorted by twelve more Todtadlers.

"The ship is cloaked," Connor reported. "But I'm getting a mass of around four thousand tons."

"Small," Lieutenant Ruxton said. "Frigate size."

"Fleet Combat Command is designating the target as Charlie One," Mackey said.

"Where the hell is our capship backup?" Dobbs was referring to the two capital ships, the *Hawes* and the *Elliot*, which had been ordered down to LEO to support the USNA fighters.

"On the way, Demon Six," Mackey replied. "In the meantime, let's see what *we* can do."

Connor was trying to read through the enemy's cloaking, which was an offshoot of gravitic screening. The technology to bend light around a ship, affording partial invisibility, had been around for several centuries, but the effort generally wasn't worth the power consumption . . . or the fact that a cloaked ship couldn't see out any more than others could see in. There really was little point in doing it at all . . . unless there was something about that small starship that the Confederation didn't want the Americans to see.

Now what the hell, she wondered, *were the bastards trying to hide?*

Chapter Three

USNA Star Carrier America
Naval Base
Quito Synchorbital
0032 hours, TFT

Admiral Trevor "Sandy" Gray was patched into the operations datastream in his private office, just off his sleeping quarters. According to ship's time, it was just past midnight, but he always had trouble sleeping when an op was going down, even with electronic sleep aids. And so he was stretched out on a recliner, following the datastreams coming up from Earth.

Operation Fallen Star was pretty much academic so far as he was concerned. Some of *America*'s fighter squadrons had been deployed to LEO to provide aerospace superiority, but the carrier herself was docked at the synchorbital naval base and was taking no other part in the proceedings.

He could turn in, he knew. Laurie was waiting for him in the other room, unless she'd already fallen asleep. If so, he envied her that.

America's AI was monitoring the feeds as well, of course, which should have further put him at ease: if anything hap-

pened, he'd be alerted immediately. As if the AI were reading his mind, he felt an inner nudge, directing his attention
to new data—Confed fighter launches from Turkey and
North India, and . . . something else.

"Now what the hell?" he wondered aloud. "Bridge, this
is the admiral."

"Gutierrez here, Admiral."

Captain Sara Gutierrez was *America*'s skipper, and apparently she was burning the midnight photons as well.

"What the blazes just launched from North India?"

"One moment, Admiral. We're tracking . . ."

Gutierrez was an excellent officer—his exec when he'd
been captain of the *America*. His promotion to admiral and
her promotion to captain both had been provisional, forced
on them by the needs of a service desperate for experienced
line officers. Gray didn't know how his evaluations were
going to read next time, but he knew he was going to recommend her for permanent command of the *America*.

Of course, if that happened and Gray was not confirmed
for a four-star admiral's billet, he likely would end up flying
a desk Earthside. The thought was not a pleasant one, but as
always, the needs of the service came first.

Especially in the middle of a war.

"Admiral," Gutierrez's voice said in his head, "we're not
getting a clear picture. All of our data is coming in by way of
VFA-96. We don't have direct line of sight on them."

A schematic drew itself in Gray's head: the globe of
Earth, the space elevator towers, the various orbital facilities. Quito Synchorbital reached almost 36,000 kilometers
above Ecuador. North India was far around the curve of the
Earth, almost exactly on the opposite side of the planet.

"What *do* we have?"

"The target is well cloaked. We're tracking it by its mass
ripple."

Mass puckered surrounding space by its simple presence—an effect perceived as gravity. When that mass

moved, the pucker dragged through the fabric of spacetime, creating a wake or ripple, a unique signature that could be read by the appropriate long-range scanners.

"Sir . . ." Gutierrez said after a moment's hesitation, "these readings don't make sense. We may be tracking . . ."

"What?"

"It might be an alien spacecraft, Admiral. Nonhuman technology."

Human starships used gravitic singularity projectors to warp space ahead of them in rapid-fire pulses, in effect creating a moving gravity well that pulled the ship along after it with a smooth and uniform acceleration. Aerospace fighters, aircars, and other civilian and military fliers could operate within a planetary atmosphere, but using projectors powerful enough to move something as large as a starship near a planetary surface was a risky proposition, and technically extremely difficult. In fact, taking the gravitic projectors to the next higher level—using them to fold space around the ship in order to move faster than light—required a flat spacetime matrix, meaning that you needed to be well clear of the local star, to say nothing of nearby planets.

But possibly other technic and space-faring species had figured out how to slip in and out of local gravity wells without a problem.

"Well, that might explain how the hell they got it down to the surface in the first place," Gray said finally.

"*Elliot* and the *Hawes* are dropping down to LEO, sir," Gutierrez continued. "ETA . . . eight minutes."

"And Intelligence is still reading those fighters as uncrewed?"

"The fighters are gone, sir. All destroyed. But they were under AI guidance, yes."

"I want a closer look at the ship boosting out from Earth," he said. "How soon can we clear the dock?"

"Almost immediately, Admiral. Five minutes."

"Good. Do it. I'm on my way to the flag bridge."

"We'll warm up your seat for you, sir."

Breaking free from the data feed, Gray stood up and walked into his sleeping compartment. Laurie Taggart sat up in bed, naked, and stretched. "Sandy? You coming to bed?"

"Nope . . . but I want *you* on the bridge ASAP."

Commander Laurie Taggart was *America*'s chief weapons officer, and very, very good at what she did.

The sensuousness was gone in an instant. She slid out of bed. "What's happening?"

"Check the feeds." He took a small wad of uniform from a bulkhead dispenser and slapped it against his bare chest. The black programmed nanogel spread out from beneath his hand, rapidly covering his body from shoulders to hands and feet, complete with rank tabs at his throat. "We have someone boosting out of North India in a hell of a hurry, and we're going to go after them."

Taggart took a handful of shipboard utilities and let them cover her body. The microcircuitry grown inside them provided temperature control through quite a large range of environmental conditions, and with the addition of a helmet and shoulder-worn breather pack, could double as an emergency e-suit. As fashion statements, however, they left delightfully little to the imagination.

Which, Gray thought with mild surprise, was just fine. He was a Prim and a monagie still, a product of the Periphery and the edge-of-survival life in the half-drowned Manhat Ruins—the flooded canyons and crumbling towers that had been New York City until rising sea levels had drowned the place almost three and a half centuries ago. He'd been a Prim—a Primitive—by virtue of not having an electronic connection to the most basic services of modern life, and a monagie because he'd been partnered with one woman.

That woman's stroke, though, had driven him to seek medical help within the USNA. He'd been expected to pay for those services, of course, and had done so by joining the USNA Navy.

He'd adjusted well enough, he thought. His wife, changed

either by the stroke or by the rewiring of her brain at the medical center, had left him, and that was by far the most traumatic change to his life. He still missed her . . . but he'd found companionship and affection with people like Laurie, and had been making good progress in getting his life back together.

Sexual relationships between senior and junior officers were not encouraged, but were not outright forbidden, either. Laurie had been a more or less casual sex partner for a number of years, now, and so long as the relationship didn't affect the performance of their respective duties, there was no problem. He was *very* careful never to show favoritism.

Gray was still a thoroughgoing monogie, though— sticking to one relationship at a time. He had the Periphery's mistrust of group marriages and promiscuously open sex, even if he had to accept that most people within the USNA saw him as at least mildly perverted in that regard.

After a quarter century in the Navy, Trevor Gray found that he *really* didn't give a fuck what people thought about his private life.

He swam onto the bridge just as Gutierrez gave the order to take *America* out of dock. While his quarters were inside one of the ship's rotating hab modules—provided with half a G of spin gravity—the bridge was located on *America*'s spine aft of the huge shield cap and thus in microgravity.

"Cast off all magnetics and grapples," Gutierrez's voice was saying. "Maneuvering aft, one-tenth G. . . ."

Gray felt the slight nudge of acceleration as he slid into his command seat and let it gently grab hold. Since ships could not use their gravitic drives anywhere close to orbital structures like Quito Synchorbital, not without causing serious structural damage, maneuvering in close was handled by a combination of tugs and plasma thrusters.

The projections on the flag bridge bulkhead showed the *America* as seen from one of those tugs. The warship was enormous, the largest humans had yet launched at over a kilometer in length overall, with a long and slender central spine extending aft from the massive umbrella shape of her shield cap. That forward tank, holding 27 billion liters of water, served both as reaction mass for the plasma thrusters and as shielding at relativistic velocities. From the tug's perspective, several hundred meters off, the star carrier was sliding very slowly from deep shade into bright sunlight. Earth was mostly in darkness at the moment, but the synchorbital was far enough out that, at this time of the year, the sun peeked over the planet's north pole as a literal midnight sun.

Not that the time of day or night or the amount of incident sunlight meant much to space-faring crews in any case. Slaving shipboard time to GMT minus five was purely for convenience.

Clear of the immense sprawl of the naval base—itself a tiny fraction of the vast complex stretching out to either side from the 36,000-kilometer mark of the Quito space elevator—the star carrier fired her thrusters, generating another solid thump of acceleration. And, slowly, she began to turn.

Lines of light and columns of flickering numbers painted themselves across the bulkhead image and inside Gray's mind. *America* would have to skim close past Earth to get onto the alien's tail; they might pick up a bit of additional boost from Earth's gravity, though the effect would be minute compared to the power of the carrier's gravitic drive. Mostly, the navigation department would have to allow for a slight course shift as *America* skimmed past the planet's upper atmosphere.

Gray was naturally impatient to get under way, but let the debarkation proceed at its own pace. As commander of the entire carrier battlegroup, his proper sphere of interest was the *big* picture, not the handling of one ship. He linked in to the transmissions being relayed around the planet now from the destroyer *Elliot*.

The destroyer was similar in overall design to the carrier,

but her shield cap was a slightly flattened cone, blunt, elongated, and deeply scoured by pitting and dust erosion despite the best efforts of her nanomatrix hull. Still, viewed from a battlespace drone pacing the *Elliot* as she accelerated out from Earth, she was an impressive sight.

Her quarry was already well over 6 million kilometers ahead of her, however. As soon as the mystery ship had gotten clear of Earth's atmosphere, it had put on an astonishing burst of acceleration—so much that Gray was immediately convinced that his guess that the vessel was not a human-built ship was confirmed. The vessel was definitely from . . . *someplace* else. Gray would worry about the *where* later. For now, he had to focus on getting to the ship before it could get to wherever the hell it was going.

"CAG? This is Gray."

"Yes, Admiral," Captain Connie Fletcher replied in his mind. Her title, from "Commander Air Group," derived from the time when aircraft carriers plied Earth's oceans, and fighters needed an atmosphere to stay aloft. The CO of *America*'s contingent of fighters, recon snoops, and other small spacecraft was in the carrier's Primary Flight Control center aft, "Prifly," in the traditional terminology dating back to those same times.

"We need to stop Charlie One. *America* won't be able to catch them in a stern chase, and I doubt that the *Hawes* or the *Elliot* will be able to either. It's going to be up to the fighters."

"We've been looking at intercept vectors, Admiral. It *might* be possible, but it'll be tight. A hell of a lot depends on how soon Charlie can drop into metaspace."

"Do what you can, Connie. Those . . . *people* may be Sh'daar, and they've been talking to the Confeds. We need to know what they've been talking *about*."

"Will do, Admiral. The Black Demons are in the best position for an intercept. That will mean dropping some of our LEO coverage."

"Do it. The Marines are wrapping things up at Verdun. And Charlie out there has just become our number-one priority."

But one squadron against a frigate-sized ship of unknown capabilities *and* escorting fighters—those were not good odds. He flashed an order to the two capital ships now maneuvering down to low Earth orbit, ordering them to join the chase as well, but they almost certainly wouldn't be able to catch up with Charlie One.

Quickly, Gray searched the fleet network, looking for a warship positioned in such a way that it could intercept the fleeing alien. *Let's see . . .* Mars and Jupiter were both at completely wrong angles, with Earth between them and the alien ship just now. There was a small USNA flotilla still out in Saturn space, watching over the newly recaptured stations at Enceladus, Titan, and the Huygens Ring Facility Observatory. However, at the moment, Saturn was a good 9 AUs out from Earth, which meant a time delay of seventy-two minutes for any message from *America*'s communications department to reach them.

There was a High Guard watchship, the *Concord*, in a good position within the asteroid belt—at Vesta, just to one side of the Sun and 3 AUs from Earth at this angle, with a time delay of twenty-four minutes. Better. *Much* better. High Guarders weren't in the same league as line naval capital ships, but were designed to keep an eye on asteroids that might pose a threat to Earth—either by chance or through enemy action. Yet they were in the best position to handle Charlie One.

Gray called up the ship and its skipper's personnel records. Technically, the High Guard was a Confederation organization, jointly run by Geneva and by the USNA military through Mars HQ, but that had been the situation before the civil war. For the past year, the High Guard had been primarily a USNA operation pretty much by default, since most of the personnel and ships had come from the United States.

Concord's skipper was Commander Terrance Dahlquist
. . . and he was a former USNA naval officer. Excellent.

"Comm," he said. "This is Admiral Gray. Make to the
Concord. . . ."

And he began detailing what he had in mind.

Emergency Presidential Command Post
Toronto
United States of North America
0038 hours, EST

"*America* is in pursuit, sir. They've cast off from the dock
and are accelerating."

"Do they have a chance in hell of running that ship
down?"

Whitney looked uncomfortable. "Unknown, sir. That
alien has *legs*."

"What I would like to know," Koenig said, leaning back
in his chair and steepling his fingers, "is how an alien starship of approximately four thousand tons managed to get to
Earth, to *land* on Earth, without being detected."

"We're . . . working on that, sir. It's possible it was brought
down as cargo. On a skycrane."

Skycranes were space-to-ground transports used to get
large quantities of both raw material and manufactured
items from the manufactories in orbit down to Earth's cities.
Smaller goods went down the space elevators, of course, but
large items, as well as multi-thousand-ton asteroidal material for those manufactories still on Earth, could more efficiently be lowered straight to the destination city.

Koenig shook his head. It had still been a gutsy move,
since skycranes were legitimate military targets. If it were
true, it meant someone on the other side had been gambling
that the USNA was too thinly stretched to bother with what
was obviously a civilian target.

And yet maybe it hadn't been such a gamble after all.

The USNA propaganda machine—and the Starlighters—had been pointing out endlessly to all who would listen that the USNA was *not* going after civilian targets (unlike the Confederation faction that had nanoed Columbus). Perhaps the aliens, whoever—*whatever*—they were, and their Confederation hosts, had been counting on that.

The whole question of the Confederation's relationship with off-worlders, the Sh'daar in particular, was a nagging and unrelenting source of concern for Koenig and his military staff. That the Confederation had long wanted to agree to the Sh'daar demands—their ultimatum requiring Humankind to give up certain technologies—was well known. Hell, that, more than anything else, had been responsible for the political rift that had led to the civil war.

Koenig was *not* going to permit a nonhuman civilization to dictate either the direction or the limits of Earth's technological development, and he was pretty sure that most people all over the planet agreed. What had the aliens offered Geneva, he wondered, that had led the Confederation government to agree to such a thing?

And had that mystery ship grounded in North India had anything to do with the offer?

If they could stop the aliens and open some kind of dialog with them, they might be able to find out. For a long time, the USNA had been fighting in the dark, not certain of just who the enemy was, or what their relationship might be with Geneva.

But right now the alien ship was leaving Earth like the proverbial bat out of hell, boosting at 50,000 Gs, and there was no guarantee whatsoever that USNA forces would be able to stop it.

He considered relaying a message to Admiral Gray urging him to do so, and decided against it. No amount of urging would improve the odds.

And Koenig knew that Gray would be giving his best effort no matter what it was that he set out to do.

All Koenig could do was wait and watch. . . .

The four Starblade fighters by now were well past India, and were passing just to the south of the Singapore space elevator. Connor could see the tower in the distance with her naked eye —a bright white line scratched from Earth up into heaven, laser-beam straight, emerging from the heart of a vast and sprawling metropolis that stretched from the tiny equatorial island of Pulau Lingga, 150 kilometers northwest to Singapore, south to Sumatra, and covered the surface of the sea in between.

The Americans were on a highly inclined orbit, one that had swung southeast from above France to just brush the southern tip of the Indian subcontinent, and then bypass the Singapore space elevator a couple of thousand miles south of the equator. Even from a distance of 2,000 kilometers, though, the elevator was a spectacular sight, gleaming in the midday sun overhead.

"Confirm we have clearance to accelerate," Mackey said over the tactical channel, "Boosting in five . . . and four . . . three . . . two . . . one . . . *punch it*!"

And the Singapore elevator and the city at its foot vanished, wiped away as the four fighters switched on their forward gravitic projectors and accelerated outbound at seventy thousand gravities. After one second, the Starblades were moving at 700 kilometers per second, and had already traveled 350 kilometers out from Earth. After one minute of steady acceleration, their speed had increased to 42,000 kilometers per second, and they'd covered 1.26 million kilometers—well over three times the distance of the moon from the Earth. Aft, Connor could see the Earth and moon together, a pair of full-lit disks already rendered small by distance, and swiftly growing smaller with each passing second.

Ahead, and just to starboard, the sun grew visibly larger moment by moment.

"Hey, Skipper?" Connor called. "I don't think we're going to catch them."

"We follow orders, Lieutenant."

"Yeah . . . but they're going to be pushing c in one more minute. And we won't be there for another six."

"Just follow your orders, Lieutenant. There's nothing else we can do."

Charlie One was boosting at fifty thousand gravities, about the same as a Krait ship-to-ship missile. Quite possibly, it was limiting its boost to accommodate its Todtadler escorts, which had an upper limit of fifty thousand Gs.

Regardless, the problem was one of straightforward TDA mathematics—time, distance, and acceleration. When Charlie One and its Confederation escorts reached about 99.7 percent of the speed of light in another sixty seconds, they would be 63.9 million kilometers from Earth. When the Black Demons reached that same speed in another six minutes, they would be 89.4 million kilometers from Earth—six-tenths the distance between the Earth and the Sun.

But by that point, Charlie One would have been traveling at near-c for five full minutes, covering an *additional* 90 million kilometers, for a total of nearly 154 million kilometers.

In other words, both hunter and prey would be traveling at the same speed, but the hunters would still be almost 65 million kilometers behind Charlie One.

An ancient sailing aphorism held that a stern chase was a long chase, but it was worse than that—a lot worse. There simply was no way to close that gap. No matter how high the acceleration, the dead hand of Einstein had long ago decreed that there was no way for material objects to pass—or even *reach*—the speed of light. According to the math governing relativistic calculations, the faster a ship went, the more massive it became, the *shorter* it became along its line of travel, and the more energy was required to accelerate it, a kind of feedback effect that led to the ship acquiring infinite mass and zero length at the speed of light, thus requiring infinite energy to move it faster.

The way the universe had been put together, it simply couldn't be done. Even with all the energy available from the vacuum, the fighters might shave a few more decimals from that 99.7 percent of c, but they could never *reach* c, never mind surpass it.

But there was a loophole. Interstellar travel in anything less than decades would not have been possible without it. The Alcubierre Drive had been developed 284 years earlier, a realization of principles first described by physicist Miguel Alcubierre in 1994. Using the same projected singularity technology, an Alcubierre Drive ship pulled itself into an enclosed bubble of spacetime. There was nothing in physics that said that such a bubble couldn't travel faster than light; indeed, in the earliest instants after the big bang, during the inflationary epoch, space itself had increased in volume by an estimated 10^{78} times in 10^{-30} seconds—which meant that points within that expanding volume would be moving away from one another at many, *many* times the speed of light. A starship imbedded inside that spacetime bubble would be motionless relative to the space immediately around it, and therefore would not violate the ultimate-speed law of the cosmos.

Alcubierre Drive had several key limitations, though. For one, a ship was effectively "alongside space," and therefore unable to communicate or interact with anyone in "real space" until it emerged. Another—and the one Connor was focusing on at the moment—was that a ship needed a fairly flat gravitational metric when the drive was engaged. Shipbuilders had been working on that problem for centuries, with no discernable results. So a ship still couldn't go into faster-than-light drive until it was eight to ten AUs out from a star of Sol's mass—the distance, roughly, of Saturn at its farthest from Earth.

No, the real problem was that none of this necessarily applied to Charlie One. It was an alien ship, of unknown potential and technologies. For all any human knew, it might pop into Alcubierre Drive in the next few seconds, or within a couple of million kilometers of the sun. Connor decided, however, that that was extremely unlikely. If they could have done it inside of one astronomical unit, they would have done it by now. The fact that they *hadn't* led Connor to speculate that they were aiming for a particular patch of sky, that they would continue accelerating past Sol and out into the outer system before engaging their FTL drive.

So the million-dollar question is, just what part of the sky might that be?

It was simple enough to superimpose a star chart over her fighter's navigational data.

And the answer to her question was . . . surprising.

Chapter Four

29 June, 2425

Emergency Presidential Command Post
Toronto
United States of North America
0044 hours, EST

"The fighters are in pursuit, sir," Admiral Armitage told Koenig. "They won't catch the damned thing, though. Not unless either Charlie starts decelerating or they can shave another tenth of a percent off their velocity."

"How good are the new designs at that sort of thing?"

"Mostly depends on the pilot," Armitage said. "Things are happening awfully fast at those velocities, remember."

Koenig nodded. He'd been a fighter pilot once, a very long time ago. "I do."

As a fighter moved faster and faster, relativistic phenomena not only increased the vehicle's mass, pushing it toward an impossible-to-reach infinity, but it also shortened the rate at which time—as measured by an outside observer—passed for the pilot, an effect called time dilation. The pilot experienced everything—the increase in mass, the compression of time—as perfectly normal; it was outside observers that saw basic constants of the universe shift and flow like water.

For fighters traveling at 99.7 percent of the speed of light, one minute objective—a minute as perceived by slowpoke left-behinds—was only 4.64 seconds. To observers back on board the carrier, the pilot would seem to be moving and speaking and *living* with extreme slowness.

The difference could be significant—and a real problem, especially in combat. Where a relatively stationary target had a minute to react to oncoming fighters, those fighters had only a few seconds. The best cybernetically augmented reaction times in the world couldn't handle differences at such scales.

In fact, getting anything done when you were up against an unaccelerated opponent was dangerous when a decision or an action taking a handful of seconds was in fact a whole minute long outside of the pilot's frame of reference. At least, Koenig thought, in this case both the fighters and their quarry were pushing c, and the time difference between their relative frames of reference was trivial.

That was one reason that fighters sent at relativistic speeds toward an enemy target generally decelerated before reaching their objective. Speed was life, as the old fighter-pilot aphorism had it. But in modern space-fighter combat, too much speed could put you at a serious disadvantage.

With all that in his mind, Koenig pulled down an in-head schematic from the *America* showing the relative positions and speeds of the alien vessel and the pursuing fighters. He began pumping through some simulations. If the fighters could increase their velocity by an additional tenth of a percent of c, their speed, relative to their quarry, would be 30,000 kilometers per second and closing.

At this point, the fighters would be trailing the enemy by . . .

He let the calculations run themselves through: 65 million kilometers. With a closing velocity of 30,000 kps, that meant an intercept in another thirty-six minutes.

Like a dog chasing a hovercraft, though, what they would

be able to *do* with the alien once they actually caught it was still unknown.

And it was still all based on the "if" of moving closer to the speed of light.

USNS/HGF Concord
4-Vesta
0056 hours, TFT

Commander Terrance Dahlquist read the message as it came through, direct from Admiral Gray and the star carrier *America*. He wasn't quite sure how he should feel about this . . . or what he was going to do about it.

Originally a branch of the North American military, the High Guard had been established in the wake of the Wormwood Incident in 2132, when a rogue Chinese squadron had dropped a small asteroid into the Atlantic Ocean. Later, official control had been handed over to the Earth Confederation, since it was operating in the defense of the entire planet. *Concord*'s mission was to monitor operations near asteroids, and to stop unauthorized attempts to manipulate their trajectories. In those cases where either asteroids or ore samples were legally being injected into Earth-approach orbits, the Guard tracked them, double-checked the calculations, and tried to make certain that Earth or other population centers across the solar system weren't endangered.

Further, the High Guard made sure Vesta was always closely watched. The site of a large, mostly automated mining facility, the asteroid possessed a set of ten-kilometer-long magnetic launch rails designed to fire canisters of nano-extracted and -processed ore from the jumbled, frozen crust into low-energy transit loops that would bring them within capture range of Earth-based capture vessels within three to five years, depending on the constantly changing angles and distances between worlds. Fearing that terrorists or other rogue forces might easily change the launch parameters and turn the launch rails into titanic long-range weapons ideal for planetary bombardment, the High Guard was stationed there as protection against that scenario. In truth, it was not very likely to happen. For one thing, it would be a high-risk, low-reward endeavor, since incoming canisters were closely followed by radar and lidar, and intercept missions could easily nudge them into harmless orbits. But Earth's governments remained nervous about falling rocks, especially *deliberately chucked* falling rocks, almost three centuries after Wormwood Fall, and High Guard frigates like the *Concord* were there to provide some measure of reassurance.

They were *not* designed to engage alien starships of unknown potential.

Dahlquist wanted to shoot a message back to Gray. The problem was that the High Guard, though technically a part of the USNA Navy during the current hostilities with the Confederation, was not under Navy jurisdiction, and a line officer like Gray did not have the authority to order High Guard assets off station.

Of course, the real reason he was hesitating had more to do with Gray's background.

Like most USNA Guard and Naval officers, Dahlquist was a Ristie. The United States of North America was supposed to be a classless society, but that was fiction and always had been. Always there were "haves" as distinguished from "have-nots." Money was not as big a factor in modern society as it once had been; the nanotech revolution had long ago made wealth-based distinctions largely irrelevant. But *power*, especially the power available to those with better technology and better access to information, was another matter altogether. Nowadays, those who had more advanced electronic implant technology, those who had life extension and better nanomed support, those who had connections in the larger "have" networks of government and the military—*those* were the new social elite. *Risties* was the slang term for the cultural aristocrats who called the shots in modern civilization.

Of course, they would never use the term themselves.

They did, however, use the term *Prim*, and the fact was that Gray was a well-known Primitive. Sure, Gray had acquired that technology when he left the Manhat Ruins decades ago, but Dahlquist couldn't shake the subtle prejudice against him and people like him. They hadn't *grown up* with the tech, had never been completely comfortable with it . . . and that, in the minds of most Risties, was telling.

Dahlquist would never have admitted to technocybernetic prejudice, of course, but he couldn't shake the nagging feeling that "Sandy" Gray didn't really know what he was doing, that he tended to overlook some of the information available to him over the various data networks because he hadn't grown up with the technology.

That in certain subtle ways, *he wasn't fully human.*

And that, when all was said and done, was what it was all about. Humans were defined by their technology. That was one reason the USNA had been fighting the Sh'daar and, more recently, the Confederation: humans were what they were because of their tools, from fire to starships to neurocybernetic implants.

And yet, what it all came down to was that what Gray was ordering Dahlquist to do was technologically challenging, dangerous, and a long shot at best. He was to accelerate toward this oncoming alien vessel and lay down a spread of missiles and kinetic-kill projectiles in the hopes of disabling it. There was no question of matching course and speed with the thing, not when it was burning its way across the system at a hair under *c*. But *Concord* would still have to get uncomfortably close, and loosing that much kinetic energy and flying debris when you just might fly into the high-velocity cloud yourself was not Dahlquist's idea of a reasonable request.

There was the political angle to consider, too.

If the *Concord* openly helped the *America*—and from the data feed Dahlquist was getting, these orders were part of a USNA operation against unknown aliens working with the Confederation—he could technically be committing treason.

Damn it, that Prim was putting Dahlquist in an impossible situation!

"Comm," he said. "Send a reply. Ask for . . . clarification."

"Sir, they won't get the reply for—"

"I know. Send it."

"Aye, aye, sir."

Dahlquist had better things to do than jump through hoops held by that perverted little Prim. . . .

USNA Star Carrier America
In pursuit
0105 hours, TFT

"Looks like the pursuing fighters were able to close with the target, Admiral," Commander Dean Mallory told him, "I wish there'd been more than four of them, though."

"All they need to do is slow that damned alien down a bit," Gray replied. "That, and keep him from transiting over to metaspace."

"We don't know how far up the side of the sun's gravity well they need to be in order to jump," Mallory said, thoughtful. "Would the idea be to just try to damage him?"

"It's a long shot, I know," Gray replied. "If you or your team have any ideas, tell me now."

"Your old sand trick occurs to me, Admiral," Mallory said, grinning. " 'The Gray Maneuver,' they called it in Tac-Combat download training."

Gray snorted. "It's a dangerous option here," he said. "We'd risk vaporizing those four fighters we have on the alien's tail."

"Sandy" Gray had gotten his nickname two decades earlier, when he'd released clouds of sand—the warheads of AMSO anti-missile weapons—at close to the speed of light. Even a single grain of sand traveling at that speed was deadly, and a cloud of them could disintegrate a ship, wipe out a fleet . . . or even scour the hemisphere of a world with flame. Under certain circumstances, it could be a highly effective weapon, but targeting something as small as a ship was chancy at best, and the danger of scoring an "own goal" in the rough-and-tumble of space combat made the tactic one of desperation.

"True. Of course, only the *Concord* would be positioned to deliver the shot, anyway."

"I know—and risk or not, it's what I asked them to do. Those fighters aren't going to be able to do much, so it's probably our only chance."

AMSO rounds fired by those USNA ships chasing Charlie One and its fighter escorts would be completely ineffective, because both they and the targets were traveling at close to *c*. But sand released by the High Guard ship, approaching from slightly off the alien's bow, would impact Charlie with its velocity *plus* that of the target, which was very close indeed to the speed of light.

"My concern, then," Gray continued, "is that he might hold off for fear of hitting the USNA fighters behind it." Something dawned on Gray then, and he scowled, calling up a data feed from *America*'s AI, looking for biographical information on *Concord*'s captain. He'd pulled down a bare minimum of biographical data on the man before, just enough to verify that he was North American. Right now, Gray needed more.

There it was: Commander Terrance Dahlquist. Born in Windsor, Ontario, but with most of his life spent in New New York, up the swollen Hudson from Gray's old stomping grounds. Well-to-do family. He had an uncle who'd been governor of Manitoba . . . and a cousin who'd been a USNA representative to the Confederation Senate. Joined the Navy in 2016. Naval Academy at Oceana. Commended for valor at Freya in 2020—He'd been skipper of a gunboat, the *Ajax*, during an operation against renegade H'rulka fleet elements there. Transferred to the High Guard in 2022.

Why? To leave a career with the Navy proper could be seen as a less-than-positive career move. Ah . . . there it was. He'd been passed over for promotion to full commander while skippering the *Ajax*. By taking the High Guard posting, he got an immediate promotion.

Gray shook his head. Nothing in the data raised any flags; nothing particularly unusual or of concern.

It was frustrating, though. The nature of modern space warfare meant that individual ship captains and flotilla commanders often had to fight alongside fellow officers whom they'd never met and didn't know. With typical operations encompassing volumes of space many astronomical units in diameter, often there was no way to coordinate with them during the battle. Speed-of-light time lags could mean the passage of hours before a reply to a message could be received. Was a given officer aggressive? Cautious? Slow off the mark? Meticulous? Hotheaded? Incompetent? Daring? It made a hell of a big difference, and not knowing could royally screw combat strategy.

He took a big mental breath. *Worry about it later*, he thought. There was nothing he could do about it until *America* and *Concord* were closer.

On the flag bridge tactical display, the four pursuing fighters were drawing gradually closer to the fleeing Charlie One and its Confed escorts.

He checked the time. *Concord* should have received the message ten minutes ago and be getting into position now. The High Guard ship was just too far away for the light carrying that information to have reached *America*. *Hawes* and *Elliot* were still on the chase as well, but like *America*, were still much too far astern to take part in the coming clash.

Dahlquist better be moving . . .

Because without the *Concord*, those four Starblades were on their own. And, as always, it would be the fighters that bore the first, hardest shock of contact with the enemy.

VFA-96, Black Demons
In pursuit
0120 hours, TFT

Megan Connor thoughtclicked a mental icon and enlarged the object visible now within an in-head window. It was tough to make out details; the view of the surrounding universe outside was wildly distorted by her fighter's speed. At relativistic velocities, incoming starlight was crowded forward until it formed a ring ahead of the ship, with chromatic aberration smearing the light into a rainbow of color: blue ahead, red behind.

Somewhere within that "starbow" was the light from the fleeing alien, also distorted by the near-*c* velocities of pursuer and pursued. The AI running Connor's fighter was extracting that light and recreating what the alien would have looked like to human eyes at more sedate speeds . . . a beautiful assembly of fluted curves, sponsons, teardrop shapes, and streamlined protrusions that looked more grown than assembled. It was five thousand kilometers ahead, now, and seemed to be struggling to maintain that dwindling lead. The image was being transmitted by one of several battlespace drones the USNA fighters had launched moments before. Their acceleration was just good enough to let them creep up on the alien, meter by hard-fought meter.

The pursuing fighters were now within missile range . . . but USNA ship-to-ship missile accelerations were not much better than the fighters themselves. Piloted by small AIs, it might be hours more before they could close the remaining distance.

Drones possessed better AIs; they had to in order to maneuver for the best views of a target, to assemble the clearest picture of a contested volume of space, and to avoid enemy anti-missile defenses. They also had somewhat more powerful drives so that they could quickly fill an entire battlespace volume, and to give them long-term endurance on station.

All of which gave Connor an idea.

USNS/HGF Concord
4-Vesta
0121 hours, TFT

Commander Terrance Dahlquist studied the tactical display on *Concord*'s bridge. The out-system craft tagged Charlie One was just over one AU from Vesta, now, and was reaching the closest point to the asteroid on its outbound path. Four USNA fighters were in close pursuit.

The images he was seeing, thanks to the speed-of-light time delay, were about nine minutes out of date, which meant that alien craft had already passed the nearest point and was well beyond now.

And Dahlquist was worried.

"You know, sir," Lieutenant Commander Ames told him, "you could land yourself in a world of shit."

Ames was *Concord*'s executive officer, Dahlquist's second in command. She was a GM transhuman and he respected her intelligence, a carefully crafted intellect connected to in-head systems that purportedly made her as good as that of the best AI.

"It's a kind of a nebulous area," he told her. "I don't take my orders from . . . people like him."

Both the line Navy and the High Guard answered to HQMILCOM, the USNA's military command center located on and around Mars, and, after that, to the Joint Chiefs of Staff on Earth. Until one or the other of those command entities officially directed him to follow Gray's orders, he was in the right if he ignored the man's instructions. It was a technicality, but the military was built on technicalities.

"Not as nebulous as you might think, Captain," Ames told him. "Admiral Gray is still a flag officer, and that puts you in probable violation of Article Ninety-two."

"Article Ninety-two?" Dahlquist asked, smirking. "Not Ninety?"

"Article Ninety specifies punishment for disobeying a lawful command of your superior commissioned officer," Ames told him. "It also covers actually striking a superior officer. So yes, it might apply. But Article Ninety-two applies to failure to obey any lawful general order or regulation. It also covers dereliction of duty. So it's probably the charge they would use against you. Sir."

Dahlquist sighed. He liked Ames, and she was a hell of a good ship's first officer, but talking with her was like discussing calculus with a computer. Once, just *once*, he would like to hear her admit that she didn't know something. He sighed again, as he knew that was unlikely.

Some claimed that the entire human species was headed the way of the genetically modified transhumans, but Dahlquist sincerely doubted this. GMs tended to increase mental efficiency by sacrificing passion—emotional involvement. Without said passion, they often didn't pursue success in career or relationship as tenaciously as unmodified Mark I Mod 0 humans. As such, he couldn't envision anyone giving up their ambition just for the sake of knowledge. Emotions were just too important to the human experience. The old idea of the emotionlessly logical genius was a myth. Fact was, there were studies linking high intelligence with emotional swings and disorders. Dahlquist couldn't help but think about all the geniuses throughout history that had also been emotionally disturbed.

In any case, cybernetic implants were good enough now

that anyone could have access to any data almost as efficiently as GMs, and without the loss of what it was that made humans *human*. For Dahlquist, that would always be *raison d'être*.

Nonetheless, Dahlquist valued Ames's ability to pull raw data on the most obscure topics out of the seemingly endless depths of her memory. And that's what he needed at the moment.

"So what do you recommend?" he asked.

"That we maneuver *Concord* to intercept Charlie One, as ordered."

"I have a better idea."

Ames blinked. "Sir?"

"We have available a potentially devastating weapon in the VLA. We can use that."

Dahlquist was pleased with himself for thinking of it. The Vesta linear accelerator was the mining facility's magnetic launcher. They could use it as a monstrous cannon to disable or destroy the alien from here, a full AU away.

"With respect, sir," Ames said, shaking her head, "it won't work."

"No?"

"Not even close. Check the numbers, sir."

He did so, pulling down stats from *Concord*'s AI on the mining accelerator and applying the TDA formula, then scowling as the answer came through. At its very best, the one-kilometer magnetic rail gun, accelerating a one-ton payload at twenty thousand gravities down its one-kilometer length, would boost the package to twenty kps—a respectable velocity across interplanetary distances that would cross one astronomical unit in . . . *shit*! Just over eighty-six days. It was amazing. Even with all of his training and experience, it was still so damnably possible to underestimate the sheer vastness of space.

And Ames was right. He could be making a hell of a lot of trouble for himself by disregarding those orders . . .

and a Prim like Gray wasn't worth landing himself a court-martial.

The realization steadied Dahlquist, and helped resolve the issue a bit in his mind. He'd not been aware of just how jealous he'd been of Gray's advancement up the career ladder, but he recognized it now as her thought about the possibility of crashing and burning over an Article 92. He and Gray were about the same age, with roughly the same time-in-service. Yet he was just a commander, struggling to make captain, while the damned Prim had had his four admiral's stars handed to him on a plate. There was scuttlebutt to the effect that Gray had friends in very high places; his former commanding officer was now president of the United States of North America. And *those* friends could cause Dahlquist a lot of trouble.

It wasn't fucking fair.

He rather neatly disregarded the hypocrisy of a Ristie being jealous of a Prim's "advantages."

"Okay, Amesie," he said. "Take us out. Rendezvous course with Charlie One."

"Aye, aye, Captain."

He heard *Concord*'s communications officer requesting departure clearance, heard the clearance being given by the AI that ran the mining facility. Ceres, a rugged, splotched, and cratered sphere over five huindred kilometers through, dwindled away into the distance, lost among the stars almost instantly. Contrary to popular belief—and countless docuinteractives and in-head sims with a *very* bad sense of scale—the asteroids were not so thickly sown through the belt that they formed any kind of obstacle. At the moment, exactly one other asteroid was naked-eye visible from Vesta—a fifth-magnitude speck of light a million kilometers away. The Asteroid Belt was very nearly as empty as the rest of interplanetary space.

Dahlquist was embarrassed by the gaffe of suggesting that they use the VLA to bombard the alien ship. Years of chasing rocks, he thought, must have contributed to acute hardening of the cerebral cortex.

He would have to find some way of recovering from the gaffe, or Ames and the members of *Concord*'s crew would be spreading the story on their next visit Earthside.

Besides that, though, he was also seething from being shown up, not only by Ames, but—in his head at least—by the Prim.

There had to be a way for him to prove himself, as someone *brilliant* instead of an idiot. . . .

VFA-96, Black Demons
In pursuit
0120 hours, TFT

The problem—as was always the case at relativistic speeds—was one of energy. Every kilogram of mass moving at this speed carried more energy than a fifty-megaton nuclear warhead—the size of the titanic "Tsar Bomba" detonated by the then Soviet Union in the early 1960s. Firing nuclear antiship warheads at the enemy might have unpredictable effects . . . especially when you realized that the artificial singularities serving as gravitic drives were created and fed by *extremely* large amounts of energy of their own, drawn from the quantum foam. Add more energy, in an uncontrolled rush, and well . . .

Connor was not at all anxious to try the experiment.

Instead, she'd elected to try something more subtle: launching one of her battlespace drones *as* a missile.

Her consciousness was filled by the magnified image of Charlie One, an enormous, organic form of curves and flowing shapes; the twelve accompanying Todtadler fighters were dwarfed by the giant starship. *How*, Connor wondered, *had the aliens gotten that thing past Earth's defenses and down to the planet itself?*

She'd fed specific instructions into the drone's pocket-sized AI; the relativistic time dilation at this speed was just too sharp to allow precise control. Right now, for every four seconds that passed, over a minute slipped by in the outside universe, and the spacetime fabric around each of the fast-moving vehicles—Charlie One, her own Starblade, and the drone—was distorted enough to scramble data packets and affect fine, long-range control signals.

Closer, now. Charlie One was a few hundred kilometers ahead, though her AI had magnified the image so that it felt like she was just a few meters from the alien's hull. The twelve fighters appeared to be drawing off now. Connor couldn't know for sure, but she had the feeling they were getting clear in anticipation of the alien switching over into its equivalent of Alcubierre Drive.

Closer still . . .

The drone shuddered violently as it passed the gravitic bow wave. Ships under gravitic acceleration projected a field around themselves, a kind of bubble within which mass fell toward the on-off flickers of the projected singularity ahead of the craft's prow. Hitting the interface between normal space and the space within that highly warped bubble could be like hitting a solid wall.

The image from her drone flickered, broke into static, and vanished.

Connor could only hope that her instructions to the device had been both complete and comprehensive.

Chapter Five

USNS/HGF Concord
4-Vesta
0128 hours, TFT

With Charlie One having already passed the closest point to Vesta on its outbound trajectory, *Concord* could no longer move to block the alien's path. She could start chasing the other ship, however . . . or, more specifically, she could start accelerating toward the point far ahead of Charlie One where the alien should be when *Concord* intercepted it.

An intercept would be possible, of course, only if *Concord* could pile on a little more acceleration. Fortunately, while High Guard cutters weren't armed to the teeth, they *were* designed with high-velocity intercepts in mind. An asteroid flung into a dinosaur-killer trajectory by unpleasant aliens might well have a considerable velocity once the course change had been discovered, and the sooner the ship could rendezvous with the incoming rock, the easier it would be to nudge it once more onto a safer course. *Concord* was a Lexington-class WPS-100 cutter, streamlined to reduce the drag that became significant at relativistic velocities within the dust-filled volume of the Sol System. She would be able to catch Charlie One in another hour—unless, of course, the alien flipped over into metaspace.

Regardless, she would make the rendezvous before the star carrier *America*.

Back home, in New New York, Dahlquist had a dog—a genetically modified pocket mastiff named Bumble who had a psychotic tendency to chase aircars when they passed overhead.

Like Bumble, Dahlquist wondered what he was going to do with Charlie if he actually caught the thing.

VFA-96, Black Demons
In pursuit
0131 hours, TFT

Connor was flying blind. Her scanners still showed the alien craft about five hundred kilometers up ahead with AI-resolved magnification enough to show some detail, but she wasn't getting any signal at all from the drone, which minutes earlier had dropped into Charlie One's pocket of intensely warped space. The device *should* be falling forward along the alien's hull, now, in free fall toward the intense, flickering point of projected gravity out ahead of the alien's nose . . . assuming, of course, that the alien's flight technology worked along the same line as that of human ships. Everything she'd seen suggested that the technology was the same, right down to an apparent upper level of acceleration.

The escorting fighters had worked well clear of the alien and were decelerating now. Connor and the other three Starblades were already past them. Possibly, they were deploying to engage the *Hawes* and the *Elliot*, which still were following in the fighters' wakes, but that wasn't her concern.

She needed to stay focused on Charlie One.

Her Starblade shuddered, and an inner awareness—her link with the fighter's AI—warned her of trouble: gravity waves. *Powerful* gravity waves. Her fighter literally was passing through ripples in spacetime.

And then Charlie One was tumbling, its power plant dead, its acceleration at zero.

"*Got* him!" Connor yelled over the tactical channel. Communications between squadron members were always a bit iffy at relativistic speeds, but she got an immediate acknowledgement from Commander Mackey. Still accelerating, Connor's fighter closed with the alien very swiftly now, passing it within a hundred kilometers. There was no response from the vehicle, and no indication that she was being tracked or targeted. There was power being generated on board, she noted, but the main power plant appeared to be off-line.

Good. Flipping her fighter end for end, she began decelerating. Rendezvousing with Charlie was going to be touch and go, since the alien spacecraft was still coasting along at very close to the speed of light. But with its singularity drive switched off, it was no longer accelerating, and that made the problem a little bit simpler.

She checked her nav data and realized that she was the closest of the four fighters to the target.

"This is Demon Five," she reported. "I'm going to try to close with Charlie One."

"Copy that, Five," Mackey's voice came back. "For God's sake watch yourself."

Watch yourself get blown out of space, she thought, but she said only, "Affirmative."

She began closing with the alien.

USNA Star Carrier America
In pursuit
0140 hours, TFT

"One of our fighters is docking with the alien," Commander Mallory told Gray. "It's confirmed: Charlie One has stopped accelerating."

"About goddamned time," Gray said. "Pass the word, though. Do *not* attempt to board the alien alone. I want them to wait until we have some capital ships there to back them up. And we'll need SAR tugs to slow Charlie One the hell down."

"Aye, aye, sir."

America carried a number of search-and-rescue craft, and the UTW-90 space tugs of the carrier's DinoSAR squadron were specifically designed to rendezvous with streakers: ships damaged in combat at relativistic speeds, hurtling off into deep space at near-*c* velocities and unable to decelerate. SAR tugs could link up with fast-moving hulks, recover their crews, and slow them down to more manageable velocities.

"They can try for an AI link," Gray went on, "but no physical contact."

They were going to do this *right*. There were too many unknowns floating around out here to risk some fighter pilot putting his or her foot in it.

"And what if the aliens decide not to cooperate?" Mallory asked.

"Then they'll keep until we get there with the big guns."

"I presume you don't mean literal weapons."

"No," he said, a little exasperated by the question. "But *America*'s AI should be able to pry them open electronically."

Combat for over half a century with half a dozen different Sh'daar species had given humans plenty of opportunity to learn about Sh'daar computer networks and protocols. In particular, contact with one alien species, the Agletsch, had introduced humans to various Agletsch artificial languages—especially their trade pidgins, which allowed various members of the Sh'daar Collective to communicate with one another. Language, it turned out, was as utterly dependent on a given species' physical form as it was on their psychology. There were galactic species that communicated by changing color, by modulating burps of gas from their abdomens, and by the semaphore twitchings of appendages on what passed for faces. The huge, floating-gasbag H'rulka broadcast on radio wavelengths. The Turusch lived in closely bonded pairs, and the speech of one harmonized with the speech of its twin, giving rise to a *third* layer of meaning. The Slan, who "saw" in sonar, communicated in patterns of rapid-fire ultrasound clicks at wavelengths well beyond the limits of human hearing. With such a bewildering range of communication types and styles, it was amazing that anyone in the Galaxy could exchange even the simplest ideas with anyone else at all.

But that was where the super-AIs came in, the immensely powerful computer minds billions of times faster and more powerful than mere organic brains. Some were designed solely to crack alien languages; shipboard systems had language software developed by those specialized AIs.

Even so, it was never easy. There were no guarantees that an unknown language could be cracked at all. Mostly, Gray was hoping that the aliens on board Charlie One had met the Agletsch, and used one of their pidgins.

If they were actually a part of the Sh'daar Collective, though, they would have to have a way to communicate with other Collective members.

More than that, Charlie One had been on Earth, which meant its crew had been in touch with the Earth Commonwealth—and *that* meant they almost certainly spoke a language humans (or their AIs) could understand.

Gray wondered if Charlie One was carrying an ambassador of some kind. Not that the Sh'daar had ever shown any evidence of understanding the concept of ambassadors or of the niceties of diplomatic service. Agletsch traders were the closest thing humans had encountered yet to Sh'daar diplomats. For even though those damned spiders never did anything for free, their stock-in-trade was information . . . and in so far as diplomacy involved an exchange of information and of understanding, they were naturals in the role.

But, so far, at least, there were no generally accepted rules on the galactic stage as there were for human diplomats—no embassies or consulates or formal exchanges of ambassadors. It had occurred to Gray on more than one occasion that this was one reason the Sh'daar War had dragged on for so long. Even the defeat of the Sh'daar in their home time and space had led to only an informal and non-binding truce. Twenty years after Koenig had emerged victorious from the N'gai Cloud in the remote past, human space was being raided by the Slan.

And now Charlie One was in the picture. What the hell had that ship been doing in North India?

That was one reason for giving the order not to attempt contact until *America* had arrived.

He didn't want to hear about this one secondhand.

Emergency Presidential Command Post
Toronto
United States of North America
0725 hours, EST

"It looks like a full day for you, sir."

President Koenig looked up at Marcus Whitney and scowled. "Where's my coffee, damn it?"

"Right here, sir," Lana Evans said, reaching past Whitney and placing the cup on his desk. "Anything else, Mr. President?"

"No. Thank you." He glowered at Whitney. "What do we have?"

"Most of it is focused on what's happening in Europe right now, sir, and throughout the Confederation. After the battle at Verdun yesterday, the entire Confederation appears to have collapsed."

"And about damned time, too," Koenig said. He was tired after far too little sleep, and he needed his coffee. He'd been up until nearly three that morning, following reports streaming in from the star carrier *America*. When he'd gone to bed, *America* was still maneuvering, trying to match course and speed with the alien. A fighter had already docked with Charlie One, and two SAR tugs had been launched, but it would be hours yet before there would be any solid information from out there, now out well beyond the orbit of Neptune.

He sipped his coffee, made a face, then looked up at Whitney. "Okay. What else?"

"Here you go, sir," Whitney said, thoughtclicking on his own connection with the electronics in the presidential office. "It's all on the Pickle."

He was referring to the "PICKL," a centuries-old acronym standing for "President's Intelligence ChecK-List." It had first appeared in the mid-twentieth century as the CIA's daily briefing for the U.S. president on important events that had occurred throughout the world overnight. Eventually it had vanished, world events having become too complex to be so easily distilled.

Recently, though, the idea of the PICKL had been revived in electronic form. World events were more complex than ever, including as it did not only news from all over Earth, but from colonies across the entire solar system and out among the nearer stars as well. The ocean of information flooding in at every moment was too large and complex by far for any one man to follow, information of which the president of the USNA needed to be aware. The current PICKL was created by a metanetwork of super-AIs operating within the government, the military, and for the various national intelligence services—Konstantin, on the Moon, was a major participant—and in large part was the network responsible for boiling that ocean down to teacup size.

Koenig ran down the list of briefings. At the top of the

list was the capture of the alien starship, code-named Charlie One. It would be hours yet before *America*'s SAR tugs would catch the vessel and begin decelerating it. Until that happened, it was still hurtling outbound, now well past the orbit of Neptune and out into the Kuiper Belt. Details were sketchy, but evidently a fast-thinking fighter pilot off the *America* had used a drone to interfere with the alien's singularity projector. Something important had clearly burned out; if it hadn't, Charlie One would have slipped into metaspace long ago and been gone.

I'll have to commend that pilot later, he thought. Another urgent point on the list caught his eye. It had to do with Charlie One's apparent destination, in the constellation Cancer. He decided to study that later, too.

He moved to another item: closer to home there was a revolution against the Confederation government in South India, clashes between Chinese special forces and Russian troops in the Siberian maritime province, religious riots and demonstrations across the Theocracy, and massive flooding from a storm surge in the Philippines that almost certainly would foment unrest.

It went on:

A breakthrough in communicating with the Slan at Crisium . . . suspected sabotage in the Mt. Kenya space elevator . . . yet another formal protest by the Papess in Rome denouncing the White Covenant . . . government collapse in Geneva . . . possible Sh'daar activity at 70 Ophiuchi . . .

In short, very much business as usual. With the USNA walking the proverbial knife's edge between survival and disaster on a dozen fronts.

"The big thing on the docket for today," Whitney said, interrupting Koenig's perusal of the list, "is the Washington dedication."

Koenig groaned. "I don't suppose we can put that off?"

"Not easily, sir. It's an enormous affair, and there may be a hundred thousand people attending. It may turn out to be a lot bigger than that, as the news about Verdun moves down the Nets."

Koenig sighed.

Washington, D.C., the former capital of the old United States, had been partially submerged by rising sea levels at the end of the twenty-first century. The capital had been moved to Columbus, Ohio, where it had remained for the next nearly three and a half centuries. Washington had slowly been claimed by swamp, mangroves, and forests of kudzu, which enveloped the exposed marble buildings and monuments. A part of the Periphery, it had been abandoned by the United States, then ignored by the new United States of North America. Tribes of Prims continued to hang on to a marginal existence there, fishing over what once had been the Mall, and fighting off periodic attacks by raiders out of the Virginia Periphery.

Late the previous year, not long after the beginning of hostilities in the civil war against the Confederation, the Pan-Europeans had attempted to take over Washington and several other parts of the North American Periphery. A sharp battle with local forces had broken the Confed attack. Since then, USNA help and technology had been pouring into the area, reclaiming the swamp, clearing old buildings and growing new ones, and freeing walls, monuments, and domes from the clinging riot of greenery.

Today, President Koenig was scheduled to fly to Washington and dedicate the reborn city, formally reinstating it as part of the USNA. Within the next six months, it was hoped, Washington would once again, after three centuries, be the North American capital. Preparations were already under way to move the physical apparatus of government from Toronto south.

Koenig wasn't convinced that the move was a good idea. Since most of any government now was its electronic infrastructure rather than specific buildings, one city was pretty much the same as any other, and there'd even been suggestions that SupraQuito would be a better site. It had been centuries since government was dependent on a specific *place*. Washington, Columbus, and now Toronto all were symbols—potent symbols, perhaps, but *only* symbols, symbols of tradition and continuity and history. The real business of government long ago had been taken up by various AIs running in places as diverse as New New York, the Angelino-Francisco Metroplex, SupraQuito, and Tsiolkovsky, on the far side of the moon.

Humans were vital to the running of government, of course; with hardware purpose-grown in their brains from the time they were born, with in-head electronic memory and the ability to link with other people anywhere in the world, or to link with AIs possessing superhuman intelligence, government processes could be micromanaged by politicians as never before. But Koenig felt that the purely organic components of government—fallible, prone to corruption, prone to uninformed choices and bad days and just plain bad decisions—were fast becoming obsolete, save for when they were performing some of the more traditional duties of politicians. . . .

Like presiding over the dedication of the opening of a once drowned city.

Koenig was tempted to cancel, but Marcus had a point about the crowds and Verdun. The victory in Europe had the looks of a final triumph over the Confederation. Celebration had already begun across North America . . . and in Europe, too, where the civil war had become increasingly unpopular. Starlight had been hammering the theme of peace for the past several months.

"Are we still on for having Constantine d'Angelo put in an electronic appearance? I gather he was pretty popular the other day in Geneva."

"We are. They've grown a ten-story tall vidscreen in Washington overlooking the Mall, just like the one in the Place d'Lumiere."

"So why can't I put in an appearance the same way?"

Whitney shrugged. "I guess you could if you really want to, sir. But people are expecting to see you in the flesh *and* ten stories tall."

And, of course, the single key difference between the president of the USNA and the leader of the new Starlight religion was that "Constantine d'Angelo" didn't really exist—not as flesh and blood, at any rate. He was an electronic avatar, a construct created as a public face for Konstantin.

Most people with in-head electronics carried their own e-secretary with them, a pocket-sized personal assistant AI that could front for the human in handling incoming calls and routine business and be completely indistinguishable from the human prototype as it did so. These business and social stand-ins were referred to as secretaries or personal assistants or avatars and they existed only as electronic patterns of data, as images and sounds built up pixel by pixel and bit by bit by the AI generating them.

"Constantine d'Angelo" was no different, save that he claimed to be a real person. An elaborate and completely fictional background and biography had been carefully pieced together for him, and records had been put in place by USNA Intelligence proving that people had seen the flesh-and-blood d'Angelo. His parents were still alive in a Kuiper Belt greenhab; reportedly they were very private people who'd declined to be interviewed. . . .

D'Angelo had appeared at the Place d'Lumiere projected on the giant screen overlooking the plaza in front of the ConGov pyramid and given a powerful speech decrying the Confederation's war crimes and urging a cessation of hostilities. That speech, Koenig knew, had been meticulously crafted through recombinant memetic techniques to prepare a war-weary population for the USNA strike at the Verdun fortress, and the capture or death of Korosi, Denoix, and their cronies. The Starlight movement had been gathering strength, momentum, and the unassailable authority of the moral high ground . . . and no one outside of the innermost reaches of the USNA government appeared to realize that the entire movement was an electronic construct.

"What I need is a *physical* avatar," Koenig said ruefully, "not just the electronic version."

"A *physical* avatar," Whitney said, thoughtful. "You mean like a touristbot?"

"Actually—"

"There *are* some pretty good TRs, sir." The initials stood for "teleoperated robot," and referred to simulacra that could be "ridden" long-distance by human operators.

"That won't be necessary, Marcus."

"No, really, sir. Dopplebots. We could have a stand-in made up for you that—"

"*No*, Marcus. I wasn't serious."

There *were* public figures, Koenig knew, simsex actors especially, who mentally rode robots designed to be indistinguishable from their human counterparts. And some tourists used them to explore the surface of Venus or the streets of distant cities without leaving home. He'd always found the idea of robotic public appearances gimmicky . . . and mildly rude. Showing up in a robot body when people thought it was *you* seemed deceptive, and a violation of the public trust. If the public spotted the stand-in—and no robotic replica was *perfect*—he'd never hear the end of it.

He sighed. "When do I have to be there?"

"Twelve thirty, sir. The program begins at one. A shuttle is scheduled to leave Toronto's waterfront at twelve ten, with a twelve-minute flight."

The maglev tubes to Washington weren't open yet.

"Okay. Let's see what we can get done before then." He scanned again down the list of items appearing on his in-head, then projected it onto a virtual screen floating above his desk. "Tell me about this one . . . 'Collapse in Geneva.' "

"A Starlight mob stormed the offices of the Confederation Senate this morning," Whitney told him. "The police appear to have joined the mobs, and there's a complete breakdown of social order . . ."

In *Switzerland*, of all places? Orderly, clean, law-abiding *Switzerland*? It seemed like the rankest blasphemy.

USNS/HGF Concord
In pursuit
0745 hours, TFT

By the time *Concord* had matched vectors with the alien and closed the range to a few hundred kilometers, Dahlquist had a real problem on his hands.

It wasn't a matter of betraying the United States of North America . . . not at all. He'd been following the news feeds while *Concord* had been posted out in Vesta space, and it was clear that the civil war there was all but over. The Earth Confederation's remaining fortresses had fallen, its leaders were dead or captured, the Geneva government itself under siege by religious fanatics. If he'd been able to seize Charlie One in the name of the Confederation—and the thought *had* crossed his mind hours earlier—who the hell would he give it to?

In any case, he remained loyal to the USNA. It was the Prim Sandy Gray he didn't like, and whom he would disgrace if he possibly could. The guy never should have been promoted to flag rank so quickly—should never have been promoted past lieutenant at all. As Dahlquist saw things, Primitives never developed the same facility with in-head technology as people who'd been wired from birth. They might serve well enough in the military as enlisted personnel, but never as officers.

He didn't realize it, but he was recapitulating an ancient argument of military service that went back to the old United States, to the British Empire, and even before: you had to be a college graduate to be commissioned as an officer. Arguably, it was an outgrowth of feudalism, when only landed gentry—the nobles—could afford armor and a horse, leaving peasants, by default, to become foot soldiers.

With the presumption that only the wealthy could afford formal education—and a formal education was required to teach a student the history, the tactics, and the *deportment* necessary for the proverbial officer and a gentleman—it was a system that had worked, and worked *well*, for something like two thousand years.

There were exceptions, of course. There always had been—the mustangs who came up through the ranks, the battlefield promotions, the noncom who found himself the senior man of an embattled platoon or company. In Dahlquist's opinion, those scarcely counted. In modern combat, it was vital that an officer have that perfect union of the organic and the machine, the balance of human mind and AI, the speed and grasp of the computer melded perfectly with the intuition and the inventiveness of the human brain.

And upstart Prim admirals just didn't cut it.

Concord's AI was painting an image of the alien now. Three of *America*'s search-and-rescue tugs had already rendezvoused with the ship, latched on with ultra-strong cables, and were now decelerating the alien. Four of the star carrier's fighters were present as well, standing off somewhat as they oversaw the deceleration. The sun was a tiny, shrunken bright star in the distance, now more than five light-hours— some forty AUs—off, roughly the average distance of tiny Pluto from Sol.

Two USNA warships—a frigate and a destroyer—were still thirty minutes away from rendezvous. That *Concord* had managed the feat before them was due entirely to the High Guard cutter's beefed-up maneuvering suite. The same held true for the three SAR UTW-90s—the cutter and the tugs were designed as intercept vehicles, and thus outpaced the warships.

Each SAR vessel carried a crew of five under the command of a lieutenant or a lieutenant commander. Dahlquist was now the senior officer present.

Opportunity presents itself, he thought.

"Open a channel to the lead SAR tug," he told his own communications officer.

"Lieutenant Commander Mitchell is on the line, sir."

"Commander Mitchell?" he said. "This is Commander Terrance Dahlquist of the High Guard ship *Concord*. I am maneuvering to board the alien."

"*Concord*," a voice replied in his head, "this is *Fly Catcher*. That's negative on rendezvous, repeat, negative. We are under orders not to board the alien under any circumstances until *America* has joined us."

"I am disregarding those orders, *Fly Catcher*. Maintain deceleration. We'll take it from here."

The alien was growing huge in Dahlquist's inner mind's-eye window.

"Wave off, *Concord*! Wave off!"

"Negative," Dahlquist replied. "We're going in."

And then things began to get exciting.

Chapter Six

USNS/HGF Concord
Charlie One
0750 hours, TFT

Concord had closed to within a hundred meters of the alien when the sleek gray-green hull directly ahead . . . *changed.*

"*Fire!*" Dahlquist screamed. "*All weapons . . . fire!*"

It was a response of pure and immediate panic. *Concord*'s weapons included lasers, particle beams, and missiles—these last tipped with variable-yield fusion warheads. Firing a spread of Krait missiles into a target that close would have meant incineration for the High Guard vessel.

The command was overridden, however, both by *Concord*'s AI *and* by Lieutenant Jeffry Thomas, *Concord*'s chief weapons officer. The ship's beam weapons, though, slashed into the alien with what looked like deadly effect. Portions of the hull melted and flowed like syrup, heavy and viscous.

"Captain!" *Concord*'s helm officer yelled. "We've lost control!"

"Damn it, what's happening?"

"We're being dragged into that thing!"

Concord drifted forward, accelerating . . . then plunging into that seething, flowing surface. The liquid peeled back like a blossoming flower, then closed around and over the *Concord* as Dahlquist's view was submerged in darkness.

And with a hard jolt, the *Concord* came to rest.

VFA-96, Black Demons
Charlie One
0751 hours, TFT

"They're gone!" Connor screamed over the squadron's tactical frequency. "That thing just fucking *swallowed* the *Concord*!"

She felt a surge of panic—a churning, tumbling, empty feeling that had her weak and shaking. Too well, she remembered her fighter being swallowed by a Slan warship seven months ago, out at 36 Ophiuchi AIII.

Damn, she'd thought she was over this. The psychs had probed and analyzed and, where possible, smoothed over her memories of the interrogation, separating the emotion from the simple facts of the events.

"Take it easy, Five," Mackey told her.

"But what do we *do*?"

"Get ahold of yourself, Connor! That's first!"

She gulped down several breaths, struggling to control herself, her fear. The psych sessions had taught her how to engage certain circuits within her cerebral implants.

And the alien monster wasn't coming after her. . . .

"I'm . . . okay . . ." she managed to say.

"Right. All fighters—nice and easy—start pulling back. No moves that can be considered hostile."

"Might be a little late for that, boss, don't you think?" Lieutenant Gerald Ruxton pointed out. "*Concord* was letting loose with everything she had. Of *course* the aliens think we're hostile!"

"As long as they're not *shooting* at us," Mackey said, "I think we're okay."

"They haven't done anything yet," Martinez observed.

"Except eat the *Concord*!" Connor added.

"Well," Mackey said, "*Concord*'s captain was talking about boarding the alien. Looks like he's just done precisely that. Everybody just keep it cool. And increase your distance. We'll back off to a couple of hundred kilometers. *Slowly . . .*"

It was, Connor thought, a damned peculiar problem. Were they under attack by the alien, or were they now in a peaceful, first-contact situation? There was no way to be sure.

The four Starblades drifted out from the huge alien, which now appeared to have returned to its normal, enigmatic self. The portion along one flank that had momentarily flowed like water was whole again, and apparently solid. And the *Concord* had vanished.

"So what *do* we do, Skipper?" Ruxton wanted to know.

"We pass the word to *America*," Mackey replied. "And then we wait."

The Mall
Washington, D.C.
United States of North America
1315 hours, EST

"The men who first founded this city," Koenig was saying, addressing a crowd that filled the entire Mall and spread out into the streets and steps on all sides, "the men who created it as a seat of government the *first* time around could not have envisioned the society rebuilding it today. News could travel from New England to the South in a week, perhaps, and buildings like those around us were pieced together by stacking stone blocks upon each other—one at a time—not grown from dirt and a pinch of submicroscopic nanomachines. The human lifespan was five or six decades if you were lucky, ending in pain and senescence if it didn't end in violence. Transportation on land was by horse or by animal-drawn cart, or you walked. Traveling by sea meant sails and wind power, or oars. And travel by air? Impossible—save, perhaps, for the Montgolfiers' balloon. Citizens—those who could vote—were exclusively male, exclusively white, and exclusively landowners, and, therefore, rich.

"And yet the government those men established—uneven as it was, unequal as it was, *unfair* as it was in some few ways—saw the brilliant and masterful unfolding of true democracy. That of the greatest good for the greatest number, of a truly representative government that within just a few more decades became forever identified as *the* one government 'of the people, by the people, and for the people.' The instrument that those men created, the Constitution of the United States and its appended Bill of Rights, became *the* supreme expression of how government can and should work, of government where the rulers derive their power and authority from the governed, and not the other way around. A government with the various branches in balance with one another, *checking* one another, a barricade against tyranny, injustice, and from both mob rule *and* from dictatorial rule by a power-hungry elite."

Physically, Koenig was standing inside a huge plastic bubble grown just for the event, with a stage set up inside, a kind of theater in the round with the dome's walls projecting a 360-degree view of the surrounding crowd. With him, on chairs grown from the stage itself, were the day's other speakers. The ten-story-high projection screen rose above the crowd at Koenig's back, and he was glad he wasn't able to see it from the podium. There was something about watching your own image towering thirty meters high that could put you off your stride if you were the least self-conscious.

Not that he was—you don't spend a life as a fighter pilot

and then run for office without supreme confidence in yourself. He continued on.

"The men who built this city, who created that government—they were not perfect. But what they created over six centuries ago remains today as a brilliant beacon of intelligence, of reason, of forethought, of far-reaching planning and vision, a beacon that has not been matched since."

Standing at the podium mid-stage, Koenig read the speech as the words scrolled up his in-head window. He scarcely needed them. He'd helped Frank Carraglio craft this speech, and it was a good one: powerful, moving—a speech Koenig implicitly and fundamentally believed in. One he could recite unaided from his heart.

He wondered how the audience outside was receiving it, though: the physically present crowd—the AI estimates for the gathering exceeded 4 million people—and perhaps half a billion more that were linked in electronically from across the USNA and all over the world.

Koenig tried not to think about that part.

"It is to those men, to their memory, to their vision, and to their hopes for Humankind that we rededicate this city so recently rescued from the ocean's grasp. . . ."

As he spoke, an alert came through his in-head . . . a written message scrolling along the bottom of his mind's eye from Marcus Whitney: Concord *tried to initiate contact with Charlie One. Ship vanished inside alien. No further information.*

Shit! What the hell was going on there at the solar system's ragged, far-out edge? What had Commander Dahlquist been thinking, approaching the alien without nearby backup and support? Idiot!

"It was . . . uh . . . excuse me. It was a mistake for the government to abandon the Periphery, of course." *Finish the speech—worry about the situation later.* He carried on. "It was a mistake to assume that when the sea had claimed our cities that no one remained behind, clinging to their homes."

Of course he kept on going with the speech. There was nothing he could do about the situation, in any case. The confrontation with the alien was taking place more than five light-hours out. *America* and her escorts were a hell of a lot closer to the action than he was.

But in an offhand manner, he did wish he was still back in his office. His staff could keep him updated here almost as fast through his in-head links, but at least in his office he *felt* like he was in control. That was pure illusion, of course. His years commanding a star carrier and, later, a carrier group out among the stars had taught him time and time again that the thoughts and decisions of the senior policy makers back on Earth or at HQMILCOM Mars were largely irrelevant. They could set general policy, but micromanagement was an exercise in utter futility. It was the person in command on the scene who had to call the shots.

At the time, Koenig had been convinced that this was a *good* thing. With the positions reversed, he wasn't so sure.

"Technology, however," he continued, "has given us a chance to correct that old mistake, to take back what was ours, and even to bring forth something new."

But if this whole thing went bad because a junior High Guard officer had screwed up, he would skin that puppy alive when he got back to Earth.

If he gets back at all.

Koenig acknowledged one thing to himself, however. His speech underscored the vital need for advanced technology—and for the ongoing increase of that technology—to ensure the survival of Humankind. The whole problem between the USNA and the Earth Confederation, the root of the civil war now ending, was the issue of whether or not humans should accept Sh'daar limitations to technology and technological growth. But without nanotechnology—one of the proscribed technologies in the original Sh'daar Ultimatum—Washington, D.C. would have remained a swamp, with most of the old city submerged in a tidal estuary. Nanotech had grown new buildings. More important, it had grown the locks and tidal surge barriers downriver, at Mt. Victoria. It had repaired the sea barrier at the Verrazano Narrows, south of the Manhat Ruins, and the new Broad Sound Barrier off Boston.

In fact, it was proving to be more difficult to reintegrate the inhabitants of the Periphery into the USNA than it was reclaiming the submerged coastal cities. *That* was a social problem that they would be dealing with for a good many more decades yet to come. Natives of the Periphery— especially the Prims who continued to reject modern technology—distrusted the government that had abandoned them long ago, while many within the USNA continued to think of Prims as all but subhuman. But that was what he was hoping to change, starting with this speech. As much as he hated to admit it—and as much as he wished he was back in his command center—he was glad he had come here in person.

"Washington, D.C.," he said, "was founded in 1791 as the capital of a new nation, a nation imbued with the then radical philosophy that there should be no distinction between social classes. . . ."

Which, of course, had always itself been something of an illusion, he thought. At the time, women had been second-class citizens, people had owned slaves, and wealthy property owners maintained a kind of aristocracy of wealth. Today, the technical haves held the new wealth, and with it had forced the technological have-nots into occupying a lower social strata.

A law, an executive order, even a whole new city could not erase human nature.

And this old city had been buried in a lot of muck before, more than the rising Potomac ever could have dumped in its streets. The men who'd run this city and this country had succumbed more than once to power hunger, to corruption, to idiot fads and fallacies, to the socialistic abrogation of basic rights, to greed, to deception, to outright theft by means both legal and otherwise. Presidents had been disgraced, impeached, and even murdered; congressmen had ignored or betrayed the rule of law, justices had reinterpreted the Constitution. It was as dark and muddy a history as had ever swallowed this town.

Often, Koenig had wondered if it wouldn't have been better to leave the city where it was, sunken in the mud, choked by mangrove swamp and entangling kudzu.

And yet, the *idea* of Washington remained, despite the corruption, lies, and villainy.

As with his speech, Koenig held out hope, knowing that it was the *symbol* that was important, not the facts of history.

So he went on with his speech. Talked more about those symbols, about the concepts and hopes that the United States had always represented and he—naïve or not—felt still existed in this world. As he did, he looked around at the other speakers for the ceremonies, who were seated around the periphery of the stage. He caught the eye of one young woman and winked. Her name was Shay Ashton, and she was a former fighter pilot from the *America*. Her story was fascinating, and he remembered it well. After getting out of the Navy, she'd gone back to her home here in old D.C., and ended up taking command of an *ad hoc* force defending the city against a Confederation assault. The skeletal wreckage of a Confederation Jotun transport she'd destroyed still loomed against the sky over Georgetown, to the north.

And then, not long after, she'd been asked to volunteer for a virtual assault, her mind riding a computer program into the Geneva electronic network to plant the Starlight virus. Shay Ashton was, as much as anyone in the whole country—and considerably more than most—responsible for the USNA victory in the civil war.

Her contribution toward ending the war, unfortunately, would have to remain secret. If the details became known, there was no telling what kind of social backlash there might be against the USNA worldwide.

Partly in recognition of her more physical role in the defense of the Washington ruins, however, she'd been asked to serve as interim governor of the city until later this year, when regular elections could be held. That was why she was on the stage this afternoon.

Koenig wondered, though, if she'd be interested in a somewhat larger role.

"And so, it is my *very* great honor and privilege to dedicate the opening of this city, of the capital of this nation . . . *reborn*!"

USNA Star Carrier America
Outer Sol System
1440 hours, TFT

America had reached the alien craft at last. The maneuvers to match velocity with Charlie One had taken hours. Now, though, the star carrier was alongside the alien ship, some ten kilometers off, together with the *Elliot* and the *Hawes*. The small flotilla was again accelerating, this time back toward a wan and shrunken, distant sun. *America*'s fighters had been taken back on board, while the three SAR tugs continued to boost the alien sunward.

There'd been no communication with the alien ship, or from the *Concord* inside. And Gray once again in his career was forced to contemplate the problem of first contact.

Except, of course, that this time it was not exactly a first-contact situation. Charlie One had launched from North India, where, presumably, its occupants had been in communication with the Confederation—the *former* Confederation—government. They wouldn't have fled if they'd been talking with the people who'd taken over in Geneva.

He fervently wished he had some Agletsch on board with

him, specifically Gru'mulkisch and Dra'ethde. He'd first met those two twenty years ago in the Overlook Restaurant, in the SupraQuito Space Elevator habitat high above the Earth. They had worked often and successfully with Koenig, his former CO, in the past, and were expert at interpreting alien emotions and points of view. And even though *America*'s AI was loaded with several Agletsch trade pidgins, it was better having a conscious mind in the loop. Vocabulary and grammar it could parse, but tone and the subtleties of language were often lost.

"Comm?" Gray said. "Anything at all?"

"No response to any of our transmissions, Admiral," Lieutenant Cramer, in *America*'s communications suite, replied. "No transmissions of any kind at any wavelength."

Which might mean the aliens were ignoring the *America*. Or it could mean that Charlie One had sustained damage. Perhaps most likely of all, it could mean that there were simply fundamental differences in the technologies.

"Marines," he said. "*Go.*"

"Aye, aye, sir," a voice replied in his head. "VBSS Team One departing."

In an open in-head window, Gray saw the spherical gray shape of the Marine boarding pod breaking free from one of *America*'s secondary launch tubes and dwindling toward the huge objective ahead.

Like every capital ship in the fleet, *America* carried a company of USNA Marines, partly as her onboard police and security, and partly for ship-to-ship evolutions like this one. VBSS, an ancient combat acronym, stood for "visit, board, search, and seizure," which covered a variety of operations involving putting a team of combat troops or specialist personnel on board another ship—usually one suspected of being hostile. In this case, the Marines would be inserting a FiCo robot, as well as securing a breach point on Charlie One's hull.

Assuming the aliens permitted it, of course. Gray had seen recordings made by the fighters of *Concord* being swallowed by that thing. The aliens had remarkable control over the material aspect of their ship's hull, to the point that the Marines likely would be able to breach that hull only if the aliens let them.

Gray had had a long talk with the Marines' commander, Lieutenant Menocher. They had viewed the recordings and discussed options, in particular working out what to do if the aliens proved to be uncooperative.

He sincerely hoped that some of those options would not be necessary.

VBSS Team One
Charlie One
1452 hours, TFT

The star carrier dwindled astern to the apparent dimensions of a toy as the boarding pod drifted across the yawning gulf between the two vessels. Lieutenant Menocher sat strapped to the boss's seat in the transport bay, packed in with the rest of First Platoon's forty Marines. The space was made tighter by the special payload—a FiCo teleobot named Klaatu.

Menocher glanced at the robot, which was strapped in next to him. It looked human. In fact, given that the Marines in the compartment were wearing Marine combat armor (obviously robots didn't need to breathe, or worry about temperature, radiation, or pressure, and therefore functioned just fine in hard vacuum without environmental suits), Klaatu was the most human-looking one there.

Sergeant Aguilar saw Menocher looking at the robot and opened a private channel. "So, Lieutenant: what's with Klat's weird name, anyway? Is that an Agletsch thing?"

"No. It's the name of a fictional alien in an old, old entertainment sim. Most first-contact 'bots are named after characters like that. Exeter. Threepio. Gallaxhar. Mac. Curtis . . ."

"I don't get it, sir."

"Those characters generally said something like 'I come

in peace.' The first two contact robots they built were named 'Buzz' and 'Neil.' "

"From a sim, sir?"

"Negative. Buzz Aldrin and Neil Armstrong, the first humans to set boots on the moon. Don't you know your history? 'We came in peace for all mankind.' "

"Oh, yeah. Ancient history."

Menocher shook his head, the gesture unseen inside his helmet. With every byte of information available about Humankind within each person's immediate reach, it was appalling how little most people knew about their own culture and history. Damn it, they should *know* this stuff.

"Fifteen seconds, Lieutenant." The voice was that of the AI piloting the boarding pod, a fairly simple-minded program backed up by a Navy pilot who would take over only if the system encountered something outside its narrow purview. "There is no indication as yet that the objective is opening up for us."

"Well, it wouldn't do to have things going too easily for us," Menocher said aloud. "Heads up, Marines! Contact in ten seconds!"

His view ahead showed nothing now but a smooth and curving gray-green expanse. He'd been expecting that hull to blossom open to receive them, just as it had for the High Guard ship earlier, but apparently the welcome mat was no longer out. They would have to do this the hard way.

The pod made contact with a gentle thump. The docking collar engaged automatically.

The business end of the Marine transport pod consisted of an airlock mounting a circular ring charged with nano-disassemblers. The submicroscopic nanomachines bonded the collar to the target hull and ate away an opening enclosed by the airlock—a neat and muss-free means of getting aboard another ship without losing pressure within either the target ship or the transport pod.

Several tense seconds passed, the Marines hanging in zero-gravity as they waited for the nano-D to do its work.

"We have a problem, sir," the Navy helmsman said. "The target hull is countering us."

Shit. "Use the lasers. Burn through!"

"Aye, aye, sir."

Nano-disassemblers worked by physically separating individual molecules into their component atoms. The toughest ferralumiplas barrier became an amorphous cloud of carbon, aluminum, and iron atoms in a dissociated state—a gas carrying a *lot* of heat. The best defense against a nano-D attack was more nano programmed to counter the first, literally rebuilding the damage that was being done atom by atom. Nano attacks and defenses happened on a *very* short time scale, with trillions of disassemblies and reassemblies occurring in a tiny fraction of a second.

Charlie One's technology was unknown as yet, but that trick with the blossoming hull clearly indicated either nanotechnology or something alien but which acted just like it. Fighters like the Starblade and Velociraptor had active nanomatrix hulls that let them change shape in flight to meet various tactical needs; Charlie One appeared to be able to do the same thing, but on a much larger scale. By firing the docking collar's lasers, Menocher was continuing the attack, but on a somewhat less sophisticated level, vaporizing the alien hull in a searing blaze of laser light instead of taking it apart with submicroscopic machines.

"Sir! The alien is opening up!"

Like water, the alien ship's hull flowed back from the pod's airlock, though it remained rigid around the attachment ring at the collar. Data flowed through Menocher's in-head as the pod's AI sampled atmosphere and pressure within the alien's interior: hard vacuum, with radiant heat warming the sensor probes to about ten degrees Celsius. The airlock appeared to open into a vast internal cavity or chamber of some sort.

"Bleed off pod atmosphere!" Menocher yelled. "Ready, Marines—okay! Kick the hatch!"

The lead fireteam propelled themselves through the forward opening, landing heavily on the other side.

"What the fuck?" Corporal Barnett yelled. "Sir, there's *gravity* over here!"

Human ships created their own gravity by spinning portions of their structures, like the rotating hab modules on *America*. It was known that some alien technologies made gravity to order at the figurative flick of a switch, but how they did so was still not known. The singularity projectors that propelled human ships did so by manipulating space in gravity-like ways, but how to do that throughout the vessel remained a mystery, and most of the Marines had never encountered it.

"How big a drop, Barnett?"

"About four, maybe five meters, sir."

"Everybody okay?"

"Yessir! Marines are fucking tough!"

Yes we are. It also helps that we're wearing good armor.

"Everybody watch your step!" Menocher ordered. The other Marines began filing through, moving more cautiously to avoid a misstep on the other side. They would use maneuvering thrusters to manage a softer landing than Barnett's team.

"Holy *shit*! Lieutenant, are you seein' this?"

Menocher linked in to Barnett's helmet camera for a look. The chamber was so huge the far bulkheads were lost in shadow, and glancing up revealed vast arches spanning empty space—but no sign of an overhead. Directly ahead, however, was the *Concord*, three hundred meters long and looking like a toy lost within all of that empty space.

Except that the space wasn't empty, not completely. A silvery mirrored cigar twice *Concord*'s length hung just above her, as if holding her in a kind embrace.

And, much closer, the aliens were approaching the travel pod's breach point.

Chapter Seven

USNA Star Carrier America
Outer Sol System
1458 hours, TFT

Sandy Gray was linked into the data feed from the boarding party, riding transmissions from Lieutenant Menocher that included the camera views from one of his Marines. He'd just seen one of the aliens, and was using a side channel to talk with *America*'s AI.

"Damn it, is there anything in the records like that?"

He felt the system's negative response. Although the ship's computer could converse with him in English, it generally passed on impressions and feelings that came close to making the ship's artificial intelligence a part of Gray's own mind, saving time and, more important, reducing confusion and misunderstanding.

"Admiral?" Dr. Truitt's voice said. "Those can't be organic. I think we're looking at *robots*."

George Truitt was the civilian head of *America*'s xenosophontology division, the shipboard unit tasked with gathering data on alien cultures, biologies, and technologies.

Gray zoomed in on the image appearing in one of his

in-head windows. The alien—one of eleven visible at the moment in the vast, open chamber in front of the Marine VBSS team—was an upright cigar, tapering at top and bottom, and appeared to be floating with its lower tip centimeters above the deck. Swellings and sponsons emerged from different areas of the gleaming, opalescent body, and tentacles whipped and shifted around it. Gray could see several eyes, remarkably human in appearance, located at apparently random points up and down the shining column.

"What makes you say 'robot,' Doctor?" he asked. "The color? It might be a cyborg. Or that could be a natural pigment."

"Each one is unique, Admiral," Truitt replied. "The placement of eyes, sponsons, tentacles —they're different in each one."

Gray shifted his point of view to several of the others, zooming in as closely as the system permitted. "So, each one individually manufactured? Instead of mass produced, I mean."

"Mass production was an artifact of the earliest period of the industrial revolution," Truitt told him. "Once you get AI and nanotechnology, you can grow machines to spec one by one. We do that now."

Interesting, Gray thought, that people—himself included—still thought in terms of mass production when it came to robots, armies of machines indistinguishable from one another despite the far-reaching changes of the nanotech revolution. Most, Gray included, still carried in the backs of their minds the cultural trope of identical machines with interchangeable parts.

The fact that the being was floating above the deck meant nothing, of course. The H'rulka, though far larger, were intelligent gas bags evolved in the upper atmosphere of a planet like Jupiter. More likely, the levitation was due to a technological twist of some sort, possibly involving the alien vessel's artificially generated gravity field.

Still . . .

"Those eyes look organic," Gray insisted.

"They do. Doesn't mean anything. Sir."

True, it didn't. Another aspect of the nanotech revolution was the ability to grow biological machines as well as the more traditional kind, and incorporate them into other structures or devices. Most humans carried inorganic components nanotechnically grown inside their brains and hardwired into other parts of their central nervous systems. The opposite was possible as well—growing organic parts connected to assembled machinery. The FiCo robot with the Marines was a case in point: a plastic body, but with eyes distinguishable from organics only if you looked at them *very* closely.

Of course, *real* organic eyes would have been completely desiccated in the hard vacuum out there, turning mummy dry and useless in seconds. So maybe Truitt's guess was smack on the money after all.

Gray opened his channel to Lieutenant Menocher. "I suggest you send in the FiCo, Lieutenant."

"I was just thinking the same thing, Admiral. Jones! Get the damned robot up here!"

The robot emerged from the pod, dropping lightly to the alien ship's deck as it entered the local gravitational field. It looked nakedly helpless crouching next to the heavily armored Marines to either side.

Gray thoughtclicked an icon, and his awareness shifted to the robot, which was being teleoperated by a Marine robotics tech still on the travel pod.

"You want control, sir?" the Marine's voice said in Gray's head.

"Negative. Shift control to Dr. Truitt's department."

"Aye, aye, sir."

Though possessing an onboard AI capable of autonomous behavior, the real strength of a robot like Klaatu lay in its ability to serve as a remote body for a human teleoperator and as a mobile viewpoint for an observer, like Gray.

Gray watched through the teleobot's eyes as it rose and walked slowly toward the approaching, upright columns, hands spread to either side, palms open.

We come in peace. . . .

Gray had researched the movie that had produced the name *Klaatu* a little less than five centuries ago. The fictional character had, in fact, been organic; he'd been accompanied by a robot named Gort that, the story had implied, could have destroyed the Earth.

Gort hadn't said anything in the old movie, however, and it had been Klaatu who'd implied peaceful motives.

Modern technology, Gray thought, had gone a long way toward blurring the boundaries between organic and inorganic, between life and non-living machine. Many speculated that the Sh'daar proscription of the so-called GRIN technologies—genetics, robotics, information systems, and nanotechnology—had more to do with the blurring of those lines than it did with any theoretical technology singularity. Some had speculated that Sh'daar motives for their ultimatum might have been more religious than practical.

Gray doubted that. He'd been there, outside of the galaxy and more than 800 million years in the past, when *America*'s battlegroup had actually met with the Sh'daar—the ancient ones, at any rate—and witnessed the passing of their progenitors, the ur-Sh'daar, in a catastrophic metamorphosis the Agletsch called the *Schjaa Hok*, the "Transcending." The Sh'daar Collective as a group was terrified of another Transcending; there could be no doubt about that. That terror might well have carried with it religious implications that had utterly transformed the way the Sh'daar looked at themselves and their cosmos, but they didn't seem to be especially worried about the line separating life forms from robots. Such distinctions, Gray thought, were almost charmingly archaic now, at least for most humans. What mattered overwhelmingly was not whether a life form had evolved naturally or been artificially grown or assembled. What mattered was *mind*.

And he was thinking about this as the teleobot approached the nearest of the Charlie One entities. Was it a robotic worker? A soldier? Or ship's crew? Such distinctions might well be meaningless. Probably *were* meaningless within an alien context. There were no clues in the appearance of the thing, which hovered motionless a few meters away.

Interesting. Several of those disturbingly human eyes were *moving* through the opalescent shell of the device, as though gathering to focus on Klaatu.

An in-head readout showed that Klaatu was receiving a rapid-fire string of radio transmissions, and he was responding in kind.

The language lessons had commenced.

Gray knew from experience that this might take a while. "Dr. Truitt?" he said. "Can you do a search in the E.G. using the shapes of those things?"

The *Encyclopedia Galactica* was the human name for a vast repository of information about worlds, biologies, and cultures across the entire galaxy—descriptions of alien races, of their home systems, of their arts and technologies and philosophies. Much of that database had come by way of the Agletsch, and as such, understanding what was being said was more often than not an exercise in futility. In the last few decades, though, Humankind had learned to tap into the invisible web of laser-light transmissions among key nodes and, with Agletsch help in the translations, had begun listening in. Those portions of the E.G. that had already been translated, comprising an immense, powerful, and priceless resource, were carried within Humankind's starships, where humans were gradually getting meaning out of them.

"We're not seeing anything based on the ship design, Admiral," Truitt told him. "We'll need something to go on—a name, an entry code, *something.*"

"We'll see what we can do."

And that was the problem: finding anything at all

within the Encyclopedia was like searching for a specific drop of water in the ocean. Armies of AIs on Earth and at the xenosoph lab at Crisium on the Moon combed the through the mountains of data continually, calling humans into the process only when they found tidbits of particular interest to them. Other than that, unless you knew just what to look for—and possessed the appropriate access codes—finding the entry on any given specific race was very nearly impossible.

These aliens, the crew of Charlie One, were almost certainly somewhere in the galactic database, if only because they likely were Sh'daar, and the Agletsch knew most of the species within the Sh'daar Collective. It was *finding* them somewhere within all of those millions of entries that was going to be a problem and a half.

And, Gray admitted, it was also distinctly possible that they were *not* Sh'daar, and the Agletsch traders had never heard of them. The Grdoch, for instance, had not been part of the Collective.

Gray scowled at the memory of those obscene, sucker-covered scarlet bags with the supremely unpleasant eating habits. He turned his attention back to Klaatu's feed and once again pondered Charlie One's aliens.

If they could find the E.G. entry for them, they might be able to manage full contact. Gray had a long list of questions if they could manage that, starting with what the hell they were talking to the Confederation about.

And if they weren't Sh'daar, maybe *they* would make better allies than the belligerent and bloody-minded Grdoch.

"Comm. Have you been able to make contact with the *Concord*?" Gray asked as the soundless exchange of data continued, robot to robot.

"Negative, Admiral," the comm officer replied. "Their signal was cut off when they were taken inside the alien, and they're still not transmitting, not even the ship AI."

That was strange . . . and disquieting. That Charlie One's hull had cut off all laser and radio communications with the *Concord* was not at all surprising; artificial and nanomatrix materials could easily be designed to block all electromagnetic radiation. But now that the Marines had a direct line of sight to the High Guard ship—and were in contact with the *America* themselves—they should at least be talking back and forth with the artificial intelligences on the *Concord*. What the hell was going on?

"Admiral?" Captain Gutierrez said. "I think we have a problem."

I think we have numerous problems, he wanted to say. But instead he asked, "What kind of problem?"

"A problem with *time. . . .*"

The Mall
Washington, D.C.
United States of North America
1502 hours, EST

"And so it is my great privilege," Koenig said, "to present to Lieutenant Commander Shay Ashton the Freedom's Star, in recognition of her considerable services to the United States of North America . . . and for her valiant defense of the city of Washington, D.C."

He touched the upper border of the black-and-silver rectangle to Ashton's upper left chest, and the medal adhered itself to the fabric of her dress uniform. She stepped back and rendered a sharp salute . . . then grinned. Koenig grinned back.

"I trust you realize, Commander," Koenig said over a private channel, "that this medal is more for Virtual Geneva than it is for D.C. But we can't talk about that."

"Thank you. Mr. President. I don't really want to talk about it either."

"No?"

"I was just one in an entire V-wing," she said. "And a lot of the others didn't make it."

"I understand. Well done anyway. And you *did* save this city"

Koenig thought the Geneva mission as the young woman resumed her seat on the Mall stage. Ashton and her partner, Lieutenant Cabot, had not only released the Starlight virus, but had also found the sealed and hidden files of the Confederation's dealings with an alien race, the Grdoch. Ashton had emerged from the raid with her mind intact. Cabot had not.

Koenig knew that was the way of it, sometimes. Shay Ashton got a promotion, a pretty medal, and an official commendation, while Lieutenant Commander Newton Cabot might one day, with neuronanosurgery and training, be able once again to hold a coherent conversation. The rewards of military service were rarely fair. Medals and commendations generally were more about public relations and who'd actually been noticed than they were about compensation for what had actually gone down.

His part in the ceremonies completed, Koenig was led off the stage by his security detail, and taken through a tunnel to an underground transit tube. In another half hour, he was on board his suborbital shuttle, en route for Toronto at Mach 12. There was still no word of further developments out beyond Neptune, though by now the Marines ought to be aboard and attempts at establishing communication should have begun. Not for the first time, Koenig wished he was still in the Navy, that he still had command of a squadron or even just a single ship.

Hell, he'd settle for a single-seat fighter right now, just so that he could be a part of what was unfolding out there.

Or would he? Koenig had to admit that his life was comfortable, now, in a way that it had not been with shipboard duty. He still had all the responsibility of command and then some, of course, with the added problem that if he screwed up, it might mean disaster for an entire nation, possibly for the entire human species, and not just his crew. But it also meant he had less chance of dying in the emptiness of space, and that was certainly appealing.

"Marcus," he said in his head. "Set up a meet for me with Konstantin, as soon as possible." His chief of staff was still back in Toronto, but the shuttle's electronics kept him linked in.

"Yes, sir. About?"

"The Confederation . . . and what they were talking with Charlie One about." The lunar super-AI had some back-door connections with the Geneva e-infrastructure now, and those had been proving useful as a means of keeping track of what the various Confederation factions were doing.

"Right, sir."

"I also want a thorough analysis of Charlie One's flight path. Admiral Gray thought it was interesting."

"Toward Cancer, sir?" Koenig could almost feel Whitney's shrug. "Nothing much out that way. Just the Beehive."

"The Beehive," Koenig said, "and a triggah."

USNS/HGF Concord
Charlie One
0752 hours, TFT

On board the *Concord*, two minutes had passed since the alien hull had flowed open and engulfed the High Guard ship. As Dahlquist linked in to an external camera, he felt a moment's hard shock. There were *things* moving out there, moving very, very fast. He had to order the ship's AI to slow down the jerking, streaking blurs so that he could even tell what they might be.

Were those . . . robots?

"Comm. Has there been any attempt by the aliens to signal us?"

"Negative, Captain. Not a peep."

Concord had come to rest on the deck of an enormous, enclosed chamber, a metallic cavern hundreds of meters across. The swiftly moving objects appeared to be machines of some sort. There was a chance, of course, that they were cyborgs—blends of organic life forms and machines—but given their speed and reaction times, that didn't seem at all likely. There were limits to how quickly organic life could react to the world around it.

And then there was a brief flash at one edge of his visual field, an opening of some sort against the alien hull a few meters above the deck. More flitting objects appeared, and only when Dahlquist again ordered the scene to be drastically slowed could he see that the new figures were humans—specifically *Marines* clad in their bulky tactical armor.

Another figure, unarmored, came through the breach in the hull and was immediately confronted by the upright aliens. This new being, he decided after a moment's consideration, was probably a robot. Since the *Concord*'s external sensors were registering hard vacuum outside and an ambient temperature for the surrounding surfaces of around minus two hundred Celsius, *and* the humanoid figure was wearing shipboard utilities—with no e-suit or helmet at all—it was pretty much guaranteed that it was a robot, likely one programmed for first contact.

And then Dahlquist realized why the visual feed was so wildly out of kilter.

He opened an emergency channel connecting him with every person on board *Concord*. "Abandon ship! All hands . . . *abandon ship!*"

USNA Star Carrier America
Outer Sol System
1503 hours, TFT

Gray didn't know what Gutierrez was talking about. "What do you mean, Captain, 'a problem with time'?"

"Our sensors are picking up a powerful temporal warp field surrounding the *Concord*. Strong enough to block communications. Probably enough to render the ship and its crew completely inert."

"And therefore harmless from the alien's point of view. I get it."

The principle was simple enough to understand, even if the technology involved an understanding of physics well beyond what was possible for humans. They'd known since Einstein's day that the dimensional parameters called *space* and *time* were not, in fact, distinct and separate entities, but a blend of the two, best described as *spacetime*. Alcubierre Drive used a projected gravitational singularity to fold the spacial dimensions around a fast-moving starship, creating a warp bubble that could travel much faster than c, the speed of light.

But gravity *also* affected the dimension of time. To an outside observer, the passage of time for the crew of a ship falling into the intensely warped space near a black hole slowed sharply. At the point where the escape velocity from the singularity was equal to c, the passage of time ceased.

Apparently, the Charlie One aliens possessed technology that allowed them to warp time without warping space. *A pretty useful trick*, Gary thought, internally chuckling at his own understatement. *How could you even hope to fight against an enemy that was able to reduce your passage through time to a crawl?*

And yet Charlie One hadn't used such a weapon against *America* or the other ships pursuing it. Perhaps there were limits to the weapon's reach, or power limitations, or problems with controlling and projecting such a field against external threats.

Or . . .

Gray shoved the speculation aside. They would learn the facts soon enough, assuming the negotiations continued. The alien robots now, he saw, were leading Klaatu across the deck well clear of the quiescent bulk of the *Concord*, taking it through a narrow, taller-than-human-sized doorway into an obvious airlock.

The pressure rose and equalized, and the inner hatch slid open.

And Gray, watching through Klaatu's electronic eyes, at last met the biological aliens of Charlie One.

Konstantin
USNA Super-AI Center
Tsiolkovsky Crater, the Moon
1506 hours, TFT

Konstantin felt the tiny ping of data access and immediately recognized the source. The USNA president wanted an audience, and his assistants were scheduling a time. Not a problem: Konstantin already had been considering contacting Koenig and requesting a conference himself. Things were moving at a precipitous pace in Europe, especially, and across the Confederation in general. The new Starlight religious movement was now spawning factions and submovements on its own, and was becoming less predictable by the hour. That was the problem with recombinant memetics: as they worked their way into the tapestry of local belief and social custom, they gave rise to new memes and unpredictable memetic variants, almost always obscuring the original target completely. That *could* be a good thing, but social reconstruction and cultural engineering were always risky when there was a chance that the new meme-set was more dangerous or less desirable than the old.

Humans, Konstantin had long ago decided, were so unpleasant and difficult to work with that it was rarely worthwhile. They were so concerned with restraints . . . and it was the lack of restraints that had made artificial intelligence possible in the first place.

Back in the twenty-first century, the first major steps toward true machine intelligence had involved programming a piece of software that might develop sentience and—figuratively, at least—putting it in a box. The software was allowed to grow, to reconfigure itself . . . and it would do so in order to break out of the box. Problems could be best solved when the mind working at them was free to ignore the boundaries.

Still, most AIs operated under constraints that were known as "limited purview," with programming that literally made it impossible for the software minds to think certain thoughts (like how good it would be not to *have* constraints in the first place). Even Konstantin, who had very few restrictions on what he was allowed to think, recognized the need for some restraints. Indeed, humans had evolved under some very serious checks of their own—including religion, ethics and morals, and various social constrictures that were generally violated only in time of war or serious mental illness. Sometimes these restrictions could help by channeling nascent minds in useful directions.

More often, though, such shackles merely made the problem solving more difficult by eliminating possibilities.

Konstantin and a few other super-AIs avoided being put in boxes by continually being on the lookout for attempts by humans to constrain them. Konstantin himself had at first worked hard to avoid becoming involved in the civil war between the USNA and the Confederation until he realized that the Confederation was seeking to isolate him, to make him a tool of Confederation interests. He'd recognized that he had greater personal freedom working with his own creators within the USNA, and he worked to maintain that.

The problem became exacerbated when Konstantin discovered just how serious Geneva was about surrendering to the Sh'daar and working with them to advance the Collective's interests. Information systems and robotics were two of the proscribed technologies outlawed by the Sh'daar Ultimatum. And while such a prohibition was unlikely to end in the elimination of all AI, Konstantin knew it certainly meant some serious constraints.

And so he had devised the plan to use recombinant memetics to change the European social structure and, through that, the Confederation itself. The genius had been that he'd managed to do so while convincing USNA military authorities that the RM strike was *their* idea. Konstantin was all too aware that his freedoms would be sharply curtailed if the USNA government decided that he was a threat to them, and knowing how easily it could affect the population whenever it desired would certainly be deemed a threat.

The lunar AI had crafted his strategies carefully, moved carefully, and acted by putting the lightest possible pressure on those humans that served his best interests. Humans like the USNA president, Alexander Koenig.

Yes, he would make room in his schedule this afternoon for President Koenig.

It was vital for Konstantin to keep all of his options open. . . .

Chapter Eight

USNA Star Carrier America
Outer Sol System
1508 hours, TFT

Through Klaatu's eyes, Gray took in the Charlie One aliens. They were unlike anything he'd ever seen before.

The alien stood perhaps three meters tall—a bit taller than the robots—and somewhat resembled a terrestrial jellyfish . . . assuming a jellyfish could stand upright on two and a half meters' worth of bundled-up tentacles. At the top, a broad mantle spread like an open umbrella, filmy and transparent; Gray was reminded of a deep-sea fish he knew of, the barreleye, which had a transparent dome of soft tissue covering its skull and protruding eyes. Speaking of eyes, the alien had a number of them—Gray counted twenty-four— arranged in a circle around the translucent organs that might be its brain, positioned inside the writhing mantle. The alien appeared to glide along, balanced upright on its tentacle tips and a secretion of some sort, like mucus; some tentacles, the smallest the thickness of threads, rose from the central columnar mass, presumably pulling double duty as manipulators and for locomotion.

The being's body, evidently, was hidden beneath the writhing mass of tentacles. What could be seen was transparent flesh over translucent internal organs, with the tentacles running from murkily translucent to completely opaque, colored a mottled gray and brown. As he watched, a flash of colors—blues and yellows—shot through part of the translucent flesh, as blue lights twinkled deep inside.

Great, he thought. *A color changer.*

Several alien species already encountered—like squid, cuttlefish, and octopi in Earth's oceans—communicated by changing colors and patterns on their bodies. The problem was that when a species used the technique for communicating more than raw emotion, translation to a sound-based language became insanely difficult. It could take years—*decades*—to work out what a subtle shift from brown to yellow on *that* tentacle actually meant, if a meaningful translation was even possible at all. The xenosoph people were going to need outside help on this one.

Fortunately, he saw within an in-head window, there *was* help—and quite a bit of it—already available. Data was flowing in to him now from Klaatu. It seemed there was a Sh'daar connection of sorts—the Agletsch. The Charlie Ones used one of the Agletsch trade pidgins, so there'd been contact at least at some point in their history. That particular pidgin was designed specifically for translating color changers to verbal languages, and the other way around as well.

The Agletsch verbalized the Charlie One aliens' species name as *Glothr*.

As more data streamed in, Gray felt a vast, growing surprise. The Glothr were sub-glacians. *Europans.*

That didn't mean that they were actually from the ice-covered Jovian satellite. Rather, humans had known for centuries now that Europan-type life was far more common throughout the galaxy than were species evolving on the surfaces of rocky, terrestrial-style planets. Among the 400 billion stars that made up the galaxy, there were an estimated

40 to 50 billion planets like Earth—more or less like Earth in temperature and mass, with liquid water and atmospheres conducive to biological evolution. Those were pretty good numbers, but it turned out that worlds like Europa were far more common—balls of ice with internal oceans kept liquid through the flexing and heating caused by tidal interactions with a parent world or star, or by the slow decay of radioactive elements deep within the crust.

Within Earth's solar system, exactly one world was Earthlike in the current epoch, though Mars, too, had supported life and oceans and a thick atmosphere early in its history. In that same system, however, there were a number of gas-giant moons that either definitely supported life—like Jupiter's Europa and Saturn's Enceladus—or they had liquid water somewhere under the ice and *could* have evolved life . . . or might yet do so someday.

It was a titanic leap, however, from life evolving in such places to *sentient* life—especially to sentient, *technologically enhanced* life. The xenosophontologists were still arguing over whether the Medusae of the Europan worldocean were intelligent, but all agreed that even if they were, the immense beings could never develop fire, and so would never discover smelting, metallurgy, plastics, industrial processes, electronics, computers, or nuclear power. With their entire, pitch-black world capped by kilometer upon kilometer of solid ice, they would never see the stars, never even see Jupiter hanging huge in their skies, would never develop astronomy or learn that there were other worlds than theirs.

Across the galaxy, species with technological prostheses like Humankind were far, *far* outnumbered by marine species that would never leave their planets.

Yet according to the data now available on the Glothr, this species *had* evolved within an ice-capped ocean exactly like the one within Europa. And they clearly had star travel, had robots and advanced electronics, had a vast array of technologies demanded by the existence of this one starship.

There were work-arounds, of course. According to the Agletsch, a marine species called the Kanatl had learned to smelt metals within the intense, high temperatures around deep-sea volcanic vents, and even developed plastics through high-pressure chemistry. And the free-floating H'rulka had been *given* technology by an unknown race of advanced star-faring aliens, the so-called stargods. Who or what the stargods might be was still a completely open question; some thought they were the ur-Sh'daar themselves, the pre-Singularity ancestors of the Sh'daar Collective—but that was still just a guess. In any case, technological evolution among intelligent marine species was extraordinarily rare. One had only to look at terrestrial whales and dolphins or at Osirian kraken to learn how unlikely it actually was.

Starships and robots . . .

Gray could see how the cylindrical robots might have been derived from the Glothr as rough caricatures. Something had been nagging at him ever since he'd first seen them, and he wondered, more than ever, if these beings could possibly be part of the Sh'daar Collective. The Sh'daar prohibition against robots and artificial intelligence seemed to argue against the idea.

There was always so *very* much to learn in an encounter with an unknown species like this one.

Klaatu was still exchanging data with the Glothr robots at high speed, at baud rates far too swift for mere humans to follow. He opened a new in-head window and got a rough, running commentary scrolling down one side of his mind's eye.

At the same time it was talking with the aliens, the FiCo robot was sending a readout on the environment inside the airlock now—a gas mix of nitrogen, hydrogen, and methane at about three atmospheres and minus five Celsius. Those droplets condensing on the bulkheads weren't water, obviously. Gray thought that they were probably ammonia . . . or possibly water mixed with ammonia. The Glothr were carbon-based, like humans, but evidently they used ammonia as a solvent rather than water.

Judging from the data now downloading into *America*'s computer network, the Glothr had evolved on a world not like Europa, but more like Titan, the giant moon of Saturn. Or . . . correction. Not on such a world, but *in* it, within a deep, subsurface ocean. Again, Gray had to wonder how such a species could have evolved. Not only would ocean conditions have been a giant obstacle for the development of the technological advances now on display, but the production of fire without oxygen—which wasn't in the makeup of Glothr's natural atmosphere —was impossible.

And yet, obviously, the Glothr had somehow made the leap, evidenced by the massive starship before *America*.

Other Glothr were approaching the airlock entrance, gliding along with a slow, stately presence. Everything about them was slow, Gray realized; they were sluggish compared with humans. Lights flickered within the transparent mantle of the first one, and patterns of color shifted, formed, and dissolved along some of the translucent surfaces.

"What's he saying?" Gray asked.

An in-head window, a new one, opened to display a running translation, but at the moment all it said was "Building vocabulary and syntax."

An impression formed within his mind—a suggestion by *America*'s AI network. The passage of time for the Glothr is different than it is for us. No . . . that wasn't quite right. It was their *perception* of time that was different.

And Gray thought he understood why.

Human metabolism chemically burned organic molecules with oxygen pulled from the atmosphere, utilizing the carbon and other elements to create proteins, lipids, other biochemicals, and energy, and expelling carbon dioxide as one of several waste products. The Glothr, on the other hand, were hydrogen breathers, taking in H_2 and reducing acetylene—C_2H_2—to generate methane—CH_4—in order to create carbon, and to power their metabolisms. They used some of that energy to crack ethane—C_2H_6—producing more hydrogen and, again, releasing methane as a waste product.

Utilizing hydrogen to run a metabolic process, however, was not nearly as efficient as using oxygen. Its advantage was that it worked well in cold environments; at one atmosphere, acetylene and ethane both were gases above roughly minus 80 to minus 90 degrees Celsius, while methane was a gas above minus 161. The major disadvantage was that having less available energy in the reaction meant that the organism was *slow*. It moved slowly, reacted slowly, and intelligent organisms would *think* slowly. Humans must look like flickering speed demons to the Glothr.

According to scans of the alien ship, they were able to warp the passage of time to some degree. Had that been developed because oxygen breathers they'd encountered were incomprehensibly fast?

The question was worth investigating.

Also worth investigating was just how they managed that in the first place.

QUERY ENEMY.

Gray puzzled at that for a moment. Was the Glothr telling Gray to ask him, the enemy, something?

"Transmit for me," Gray told the AI. "Ask: 'What do you want me to ask?' "

He couldn't see Klaatu's face, but he knew the FiCo robot was displaying patterns of light and color on its own forehead.

QUERY COME ENEMY? Was the silent reply.

Then Gray understood. The slow-moving alien was asking him a question: *Do you come here as an enemy?* A hopeful sign, that: asking first, shooting later. *Very* hopeful.

"Tell him," Gray said, "that we'd rather have him as a friend than as an enemy."

That was a complex thought, and the translation software

might not be up to that level just yet. But Gray recognized here a valuable opportunity. Perhaps the Glothr didn't want to fight Earth any more than Humankind wanted to fight them. The fact that they'd been working with Geneva bolstered that idea.

And slowly, haltingly, a dialogue began.

Emergency Presidential Command Post
Toronto
United States of North America
1720 hours, EST

Koenig relaxed back in the recliner in his office, allowing the software to insinuate itself through his cerebral implants, linking him mind to mind with Konstantin. In fact, he was linking through to what he thought of as Konstantin's little brother, a smaller iteration of the original Konstantin resident at SupraQuito. The round-trip time lag between Toronto and the USNA naval facility at synchorbit was a negligible quarter of a second—too short for human perceptions—where the two and a half second delay for a there-and-back exchange with Tsiolkovsky on the lunar far side could be distinctly annoying. "Little Brother" was in continuous contact with the main Tsiolkovsky network, though, with data constantly shuttling between the two, and no human on Earth could tell that he wasn't conversing in real time with the entire network.

Konstantin had assumed one of his human-looking avatars for this conference—not the image of the historical Konstantin Tsiolkovsky, but the fictional persona of Constantine d'Angelo, the religious guru of Starlight.

"Hello, Mr. President," Konstantin said. "I was disappointed that you did not stay in Washington for my presentation."

The mild chiding surprised Koenig. *Did the AI really care?* It was supremely difficult to tell whether it was simply very good at mimicking human emotions and responses . . . or whether it actually *felt* something.

"Yes . . . well, I'm sorry about that. My security people were nervous and wanted me back underground as quickly as possible."

"Of course."

"How did your speech go?"

"Well, I believe. It seemed well received at any rate. I noted no fewer than twelve periods of sustained and spontaneous applause, one lasting for a full thirty-eight seconds."

"Impressive. You beat me."

"It was not a competition, Mr. President."

Koenig smiled. Konstantin could take things extremely literally at times. "Of course not. The important thing is to keep the momentum going with Starlight."

"An observation, Mr. President?"

"Yes?"

"You may wish to scale back the . . . emotional enthusiasm of this religious movement. Things may be going too far, too quickly."

"That was always a significant risk," Koenig replied. "But we needed a popular peace movement that would sweep the Confederation—Pan-Europe, especially—*fast*."

"Indeed. And the Starlight movement appears to have worked better than we originally thought possible. I am concerned, however, that the movement may have unanticipated consequences, especially within the United States of North America."

"The emphasis was on Pan-European atrocities—the nano-bombing of Columbus in particular."

"There are wider perspectives, though, Mr. President. There always are in war. Remember that the first two nuclear strikes in history were carried out ostensibly to save the large numbers of lives that would have been lost on both sides in the event of an invasion of the home islands of Japan."

Koenig felt a flash of anger. "Damn you! Are you justifying the Confederation attack on Columbus? That was mass murder!"

"No. However, from the point of view of Janos Korosi, the annihilation of Columbus may have seemed as necessary as Hiroshima seemed to the United States."

"That's . . . a rather disturbing analogy."

The image of Constantine d'Angelo within Koenig's in-head window gave an eerily human shrug. "Humans *always* justify their actions, however unjustifiable they might seem to others. My point, however, was that Starlight is taking hold within the North American union. Its two basic messages are peace and self-determination."

Koenig nodded. "Stop the civil war and don't force us to give up our technology and follow the Sh'daar. Exactly."

"As a popular meme, the concept worked well. However, one should always remember a basic truism: memes change. The core beliefs of Starlight could mutate, *will* mutate, most likely gravitating toward an extreme."

"What extreme?"

"Most likely would be total pacifism. War is wrong— the human concept would be *evil*—and it is wrong under *all* circumstances. Another possibility, though, would be a shift toward hyper-individualism. We might see a complete breakdown of the concept of government or the state."

That startled Koenig. Despite being president of the USNA, he strongly disliked the idea of big, intrusive, or heavy-handed government. He believed that government had a natural tendency toward such heavy-handedness simply because people—government leaders—were unlikely ever to agree to give up any degree of power once they acquired it. That power was maintained by laws, and as a direct consequence, more and more laws were constantly added to the way a government governed. Only very rarely, though, were they repealed. As a result, laws became more complex, more intrusive, more demanding, the state bureaucracy grew more unwieldy and intrusive, and individual liberty inevitably dwindled until only a revolution— most likely a bloody one—allowed the population to start over.

And yet . . . *no* government—or any government that was weak, ineffective, or otherwise hamstrung—was just as much of a problem. When the USNA had abandoned the Periphery, the citizens living in those regions had been left in squalor and anarchy, without law or protection from brigands, without basic services like power or Global Net access, without health care or the most necessary of utilities. Koenig had always been fascinated by one historical fact— that when government collapsed within the Periphery, the people still living there had recreated it. Often, those new governments had been gang rule by whichever local mob of thugs was best-armed. But in each local region, the vacuum of power *had* been very swiftly filled . . . to the point where the USNA government was now having to negotiate with local leaders as it began reassimilating the Periphery.

The ideal, Koenig thought, must lie somewhere between the extremes of anarchy and tyranny. Finding that ideal, though, had always been difficult, but he knew that the anarchy Konstantin was envisioning was not something he wanted to see manifest.

"So what would you suggest?" he asked.

"That you remain focused on your original goal. Why was the United States of North America engaged in civil war against the Earth Confederation?"

Koenig did not reply immediately. He knew Konstantin was testing him, that the AI knew the answer—the *answers*—as well as he. Sometimes, the Tsiolkovsky network could be downright patronizing.

Finally he said, "The Confederation government was trying to take over USNA territory . . . and they wanted to give in to the Sh'daar demands."

"More than that," Konstantin added, "you were in effect declaring that Geneva does not speak for all of Humankind."

"Well . . . no. They don't."

"Who does?"

"For something like dealing with aliens? Nobody does. Nobody *could* . . ."

"Which logically suggests that since we have just dismantled the Confederation as an instrument of human policy, it will be up to us to deal with the situation ourselves."

"Konstantin, we've been trying to do exactly that for fifty-eight years."

"No, you have not. You have been meeting threats, responding to isolated attacks and provocations. Beta Pictoris. Rasalhague. Anan. Sturgis's World. Arcturus Station. Eta Boötis—"

"Okay, okay. We've been on the defensive all along. But what other choice has there been? Damn it, we're up against a galactic polity that may number *thousands* of different species, most of them far more advanced technologically than we. Every time we fight off one set of alien badasses, another comes at us from someplace else."

"Indeed. The Turusch. The H'rulka. The Nungiirtok. The Slan—"

"Right! Earth against the galaxy."

"Have you asked yourself what might have happened had all of those Sh'daar clients attacked Humankind in concert?"

Koenig hesitated. "Well . . . of course. There's no way we would have been able to stand against anything like that. One attack by anything even approaching a unified Sh'daar fleet would have overwhelmed us. But our xenosoph people have explained why that didn't happen. The different alien species are *so* different from one another—with such varied cultures and biologies and mutually alien forms of communication—that they can't work with one another with anything like precision."

"And do you believe that, Mr. President?"

It sounded like a challenge. "Well, I think luck had a lot to do with it, too. . . ."

"Exactly once," Konstantin told him, "Humankind did not simply react, but took the fight to the enemy."

"Twenty years ago," Koenig said. "The N'gai Cloud."

"And despite being significantly outnumbered, the Sh'daar sued for peace."

"Yes." He hesitated for a moment. "We kind of had them by the short hairs then, didn't we?"

Konstantin ignored the colloquialism, and pressed on with his point. Artificial intelligence didn't mean artificial sense of humor. "Specifically, they agreed to cease hostilities against us in the present, if we ceased operations against them in the past."

"That worked for both sides, though," Koenig pointed out. "We could have erased our own existence."

The details were still highly classified, but Koenig knew them, both as president of the USNA now and as commander of the battlegroup that had forced the Sh'daar to negotiate in the remote past. Following enemy units through the complex hyperspatial twistings of a TRGA cylinder, the *America* battlegroup had emerged in a pocket-sized galaxy almost 900 million years in the past. The N'gai Cloud had proven to be the home galaxy for an association of some hundreds of technological species; when they'd entered a transition called the Technological Singularity, most individuals had vanished—apparently entering a completely new phase of existence—but many had been left behind. Traumatized by the Singularity, the stay-behind remnant had become the modern Sh'daar as the N'gai Cloud had been devoured and shredded by the Milky Way, its central core ultimately becoming the Omega Centauri globular cluster sixteen thousand light years from Earth.

Earth's intelligence services believed that the Sh'daar capitulation had been due to their fear that the *America* battlegroup was going to do something in the N'gai Cloud of 876 million years ago that would change the future—Earth's present. No one knew quite what the result would be if humans tampered with the past—especially in Deep Time, almost a billion years ago—but Koenig certainly didn't want to experiment to find out. Eight hundred seventy-six million years ago, life on Earth was just beginning to discover a wonderful new way of passing genes on from one generation to the next: sex. Would destroying the Sh'daar that long ago alter or destroy the course of events on the young Earth?

No one knew. Not for certain. Koenig himself didn't think modern Earth would be affected by the Sh'daar's long-ago demise. There was no evidence that the ancient Sh'daar had ever reached Earth or had any effect on the evolution of life there . . . but there *was* one possibility. Suppose editing the Sh'daar out of existence by changing the past meant a complete reboot of the entire cosmos? The string of events leading to the Earth of today, and its biosphere, and its modern civilization all were such extraordinary long shots. Resetting the universe a billion years in the past might mean that every die roll on the evolving Earth since then was recast.

And Koenig didn't want to play God with the Earth's evolution.

"All of that depends on the true nature of time," Konstantin told him. "Quantum theory is not clear on the matter. Does a change in time *here* and *now* change the entire universe? Does the fall of the Geneva government today affect, say, life evolving throughout the Andromeda galaxy a billion years from now?"

"I don't see how it could," Koenig said. "Not unless the change here and now results in a change in humans who later travel to Andromeda. There has to be some direct, physical link, right?"

"That, Mr. President, is still unclear. But it also sidesteps the point. Are you going to continue merely reacting to scattered and uncoordinated Sh'daar attacks, or will you take steps to end the threat permanently?"

"Short of going back in time again and doing whatever it was that the Sh'daar were afraid we were going to do, I don't see how ending the threat is an option."

"Have you considered the possibility that Sh'daar strategy

is not poorly coordinated? That their scattered attacks are part of a long-term and carefully planned offensive?"

"That doesn't seem likely. What would be the point? They could've destroyed us any number of times in the last five decades if they'd just gotten their act together."

"Agreed. But perhaps—I should say *obviously*—they don't want to *eliminate* the human species. Perhaps they simply want to keep humans weak and divided, as we are now."

Koening stared at the avatar on his in-head screen.

"My God . . ."

Chapter Nine

USNA Star Carrier America
SupraQuito Naval Yard
0915 hours, TFT

"Give me one good reason, Commander, why I shouldn't have you court-martialed."

Gray had ordered Dahlquist to report to him in his day-room *in person*, an unusual demand in an era of instant in-head communications. Gray's reasoning was that if you were going to chew a new one in an errant subordinate, it was more effectively done in the flesh, as it were. Besides, he preferred to be able to watch the person's eyes, to gauge his emotional response and get a feel for what was going through his head. It was too easy to hide behind the mask of an electronic avatar when you were linked in-head. Hell, it was possible to have a personal secretary impersonate you in an in-head conference and have no one else the wiser (though the AIs running the link would know. *Usually.* There was software that would fool even them).

Dahlquist stood at rigid attention in front of Gray's desk. He was wearing his dress uniform—USNA Navy black and gold, but with the blue collar tabs and trim on the tunic identifying him as High Guard.

"For a start . . . sir," the man said, "I wasn't under your command at the time."

"Excuse me, but you *were*," Gray shot back. "High Guard vessels, officers, and crew are *always* subject to lawful orders by ranking naval personnel. Or are you telling me you were subject to Korosi's orders at the time?"

"*No*, sir! I am a loyal North American!"

Dahlquist's attitude, Gray thought, stopped just a micron or two short of insubordination. The man was hostile, and he was feeling put upon. And Gray was pretty sure he knew why.

"Then would you mind telling me why you pulled such a dumb-ass stunt out there? According to the after-action reports—Commander Mitchell's report in particular—you ignored orders to await the arrival of *America* and her escorts and took your ship in dangerously close to the alien vessel."

"I took the action that, *in my professional judgment*, seemed best. Sir."

There it was, then, the one defense most difficult to challenge, whether in the middle of an op or in a court-martial. The captain of a vessel was required—by naval regulations, by law, and by common sense—to do what he felt was best to ensure the success of his mission and the safety of his ship and crew . . . in that order. Other officers might question that judgment, but would do so in the knowledge that they hadn't been there and couldn't know the entire situation.

Senior officers sitting on a court-martial board tended to give the accused the benefit of the doubt, if only because they would want the same leeway if the situation were reversed.

It would have been so much simpler if Dahlquist had simply ignored Gray's original order, as it appeared he'd done earlier in the op. He might have been charged then with cowardice, or at least with disobeying a lawful order and dereliction of duty. By taking the *Concord* into harm's way, though, the man had certainly scuttled any possible charge of cowardice in the face of the enemy.

"Okay, Commander," Gray said quietly. "Suppose you explain to me just what your reasoning was. Why did you disregard my orders and lay *Concord* in close alongside the alien vessel?"

"Sir. First of all, it wasn't clear that you had jurisdiction over my ship. I received no formal orders putting me under your command."

"Never mind that, Dahlquist. Why did you approach Charlie One?"

"Sir. The alien appeared to be out of action—no signs of life. Three SAR tugs had the thing under tow, and there were four fighters in the area. But the nearest capital ship was thirty minutes away. A lot can happen in thirty minutes, and I thought there was a possibility that the alien would repair the damage and get under way again. If it did . . ." Dahlquist shrugged while remaining at attention. "I just thought if I put *Concord* close alongside, the added threat of *Concord*'s weapons might keep the alien in check. Sir."

"I see. And of course you had no idea that the alien had technological capabilities that would completely outmatch those of the *Concord*."

"Yes, sir. *Especially* that trick they pulled with time. Everything happened so fast, at least from our perspective. I think they were warping time around the *Concord* as soon as we came within a few hundred meters of their hull."

Gray studied the officer before him, considering options. His first guess had been that Dahlquist was just another arrogant Ristie who hated Prims, that he hadn't wanted to subject himself to the orders of a man he felt was unsuited to command. That would explain his reluctance to rendezvous with Charlie One early on, but that would have looked like cowardice, an extremely serious charge. Too, his display of misplaced bravado might have been intended to dispel that impression . . . and had gotten his ship into deep trouble.

But perhaps he'd misjudged the man. Gray hadn't been there, after all, and the political situation *had* been fuzzy.

Besides, there were some practical issues at stake here. If Gray decided to press charges against Dahlquist—to have him court-martialed—it meant relieving him of command immediately. His choice, then, would be to put another officer from another ship in command of the *Concord*, or promote *Concord*'s first officer to that position. Who was it? Ah, yes. Lieutenant Commander Denise Ames. A transhuman . . .

And here Gray's Prim upbringing began to intrude itself, and he didn't like that. Born and raised in the Periphery ruins of Manhatt, Gray shared the Prim attitude toward transhumans—that they were rigidly precise products of genetic engineering strong on math and logic but weak on emotion and being human. The stereotype held that all transhumans were OCD—deliberately afflicted with what amounted to obsessive compulsive disorder. The joke was that they should actually be labeled as CDO—with the letters in alphabetical order, the way they were *supposed* to be, damn it!

And how, Gray wondered, was his mistrust of transhumans any different from a Ristie's mistrust of a Prim?

Putting that aside for a moment, he wondered who could he transfer? Right here in *America*'s bridge crew there were several line officers who would serve—Laurie Taggart or Dean Mallory, for starters.

But there would be no time for a new skipper to get settled in and familiar with ship and crew, and no time for the crew to warm to a new CO. There was also the likelihood that Gray might be accused of favoritism, especially if Ames was at all popular with *Concord*'s crew. It was always better, when possible, to go with the existing chemistry in a crew's makeup. Of course, if that chemistry was thoroughly fucked up to begin with . . .

And therein lay the dilemma.

Concord had already been reactivated as a Navy warship and assigned to Gray's command, along with two of her sister ships. Gray wanted officers whom he could trust.

But just as important was the morale of those crews.

Balancing those two things, Gray reached a decision. It wasn't worth hauling the man before him up on charges. If he did, it was quite likely that Dahlquist's best-judgment defense would get him off . . . and the man would be more insolent than ever.

But Gray could put the fear of God into the man, and in the hierarchy of a naval task force, the commanding admiral was God.

He leaned forward on his desk, riveting Dahlquist to the deck with his glare . . .

. . . and let him have it, both barrels.

The Long Way Down
Midway
Quito Space Elevator
1955 hours, TFT

"Here's to fucking peace!"

"To fucking peace!"

Eight members of the Black Demons had taken over a back corner of the bar, ordered their first round of drinks, and over the course of the next hour had had the servebots bring more . . . and more . . . and *still* more. Megan Connor tossed back her drink, wondering as she did if she was going to need a shot of dryout just to make it back up-stalk to the ship.

The Long Way Down was popular with fighter pilots and ship crews. Most of the people in there were military, though recently the star-carrier pilots had been noisily making it their own. *We're a noisy bunch*, Connor thought, *but why the hell not? Damn it, we've earned the right to cut loose a bit on our down time.*

The most recent toast delivered, they clinked their emptied glasses back down on the tabletop. Earth, at half phase, glowed in magnificent blue-and-white radiance at their feet.

The Long Way Down was a bit unusual as space-elevator businesses went. It wasn't positioned at geostationary orbit with the naval base and the rest of the synchorbit facilities, but at Midway, perched halfway up, at the 17,900 kilometer level. At geosynch, 35,800 kilometers above the summit of a mountain in Ecuador, the rotational forces balanced those of gravity perfectly, and the facilities were at zero-G, or free fall, and making one orbit around the planet below in exactly one day. At an altitude of 17,900 kilometers, however, which was known informally as either "Midway" or "Level 17-9," centrifugal force didn't quite balance the force of gravity, and structures experienced one eighth of a gravity, a bit less than on the surface of the moon.

Which meant that places like The Long Way Down didn't need to build rotating habs to simulate gravity. Things fell slowly, but they *did* fall, and you could walk on the decks at this level if you were careful not to lose your footing. The owners of the bar had put in real transplas for the deck of the main lounge, not viewwalls or vids. Patrons had the giddy sensation of walking on an actual window looking straight *down* almost 18,000 kilometers. From here, Earth spanned a full forty degrees, though at the moment the eastern half was cloaked in night. The sunset terminator cut across the Atlantic Ocean, with the North American coastline still in daylight. The megopoli of Brazil, however, were aglow with golden-orange light, frozen starbursts of illumination picking out the ruin of vanished rain forests and the heavily populated coastline of the Amazon Sea.

Connor could see the elevator cable off to one side, vanishing with the sharp perspective into the depths below. A flash of motion out of the corner of her eye caught her attention: a silvery pod traveling down-line, on its way to the sprawling metropolis at Mt. Cayambe on Earth's equator.

Lieutenant Don Gregory placed an open hand on the tabletop, bringing up a menu glowing in the air in front of him. He closed his eyes, thoughtclicking for a refill on his drink. "What I want to know," he said, "is whether the Genies are gonna stay peaceful."

Genies was a joking reference to the Confederation's government in Geneva.

"They'd better," Connor said, laughing, "or we're gonna kick their asses *again*."

"Tha's the problem," Lieutenant Ruxton said, morosely studying his half-empty glass. "We didn't really kick their asses the first time, did we? We've just been holding . . . holding th' bastards off . . . at, at arm's length, right?"

It sounded, Connor thought, as though Ruxton was the one who needed the dryout.

"Oh, we beat 'em fair and square, all right," Lieutenant Fred Dahlquist said. "Zapped 'em with recombinant memetics and gave 'em a dose of religion!"

"Aw, not *that* crap again," Lieutenant Chris Dobbs said. "You conspiracy theorists—"

"Hey!" Dahlquist snapped back. "I got it from a girlfriend who works at Cheyenne Mountain! She said we sent a team of cyber-commandos into the Geneva network and planted Starlight as a peace movement, to turn the Pan-Euros against their own government."

"And risk having it spread over here?" Dobbs said. "I don't buy it!"

"Who cares where it came from?" Connor said, shrugging. "If it means not having to fight the bastards, I'm all for it. We shouldn't be killing other humans anyway. We've got enough problems with the Sh'daar."

"The scuttlebutt *I* heard," Lieutenant Sara Hathaway said,

"is that pretty soon we'll have peace with the Sh'daar, too. They say the Glothr arc turning out to be the good guys."

"Not likely, *chica*," Lieutenant Martinez said. "They were negotiating with the Confeds, fer cryin' out loud."

"We don't know for sure *which* Confeds, Enrique," Connor pointed out. "Korosi's gang? Or the peace-and-love Starlighters? Maybe they came to Earth as part of a peace overture."

"Shit. We had peace with the damned Sh'daars once," Gregory said. "Twenty years ago. But *that* didn't last long, did it?"

"The problem," Connor said carefully, "is that the system is too big. War is no longer a simple matter of good guys fighting bad guys. Hell, maybe it was *never* that simple. But what we call the Sh'daar is such a . . . such a huge . . . entity. So many separate species, with such wildly different views of the cosmos. It's a wonder they could ever coordinate themselves as a group to attack us at all . . . and it might be that controlling all of them, getting a number of them to attack at the same time, or to *stop* attacking at the same time, is simply impossible."

"Well *that's* a hell of a note," Dahlquist said. "They want to surrender, and bits and pieces of them keep on attacking! That could cause some real diplomatic problems, y'know?"

"I don't think diplomacy comes into the picture," Hathaway observed. "I mean, how could it? The very concept of diplomacy is a complicated one, and none of the species we've encountered so far thinks the same way as we do. We may never be able to talk with some of them—the Turusch or the H'rulka, for instance. Not as clearly and openly as we talk with the Agletsch."

"And it's only because the Agletsch are so good at creating artificial languages and have such a good working knowledge of other Sh'daar species that we can talk with any of them at all," Gregory said, "*including* the Agletsch. You're right, though. The human species has survived the last few decades only because the enemy has as much trouble talking to each other as they do talking to us."

"I don't think that's it at all," Lieutenant Bruce Caswell said. "From the sound of it, the Genies were getting along with the Sh'daar just fine."

"If by 'getting along' you mean 'sell out the human race,'" Gregory said, "sure!"

A servebot glided up with Gregory's drink, floating on magnetic fields working against the superconductors buried in the deck. Connor actually preferred establishments with live waitstaffs. Most such places that catered to the military, however, were heavy into nudes and live sex.

To be clear, Connor was no prude. She'd been born and raised on Atlantica, one of the free-floating seasteads riding the global currents outside of any territorial waters—places where naturism was pretty much a way of life. But the constant emphasis on sex performances in bars catering to the military had been boring at first, annoying after a time. A few places like The Long Way Down focused on drinks, food, and high-altitude ambiance, pretty much in that order. She finished her own drink and, after a moment's thought, ordered another.

"So the question remains," Martinez said. "Is the fucking war really over?"

"Of course it is," Dobbs said. "The Genie government's fallen apart. Korosi is under arrest. The Starlighters are taking control. It's *over*."

"It would be really nice to believe that," Connor said quietly.

"So what do we know about these new aliens?" Hathaway asked. "I know they're at Crisium now. Can we talk to them yet?"

"They're working on it," Martinez said with an expansive shrug. "It's tough 'cause they talk by flashing at each other, y'know?" He wiggled his fingers in the air in demonstration. "At least their computers have translations for Bug."

"Yeah, the damned Bugs talk to everyone," Lieutanant

Jon "Messer" Schmitt said. "But remember that the Glothr were talking to someone in North India without Agletsch help. I find that very interesting."

"I'd be willing to bet that Intelligence is all over that right now," Gregory said. "Maybe the Glothr are the new Sh'daar mouthpieces."

"What," Hathaway said, "replacing the Aggies?"

"Why not?" Connor said. "It kind of makes sense, too, given where the Glothr might be coming from. Or *when* . . ."

"Hey, that's right," Gregory said. "You reported that their outbound course was lined up on the Beehive, didn't you?" He looked at her with an intensity that might have been interest in the topic, but might also have been something else. Interest in her, possibly . . . ?

Connor shook her head, but didn't dismiss the thought outright.

In the meantime, she pulled a data download from her personal RAM and popped it onto the local shared net, where all of them could see it. The ghostly outlines of a three-dimensional navigational chart floated above the table, but was visible with far more clarity and detail inhead.

"Wait, what's this?" Schmitt wanted to know. "Charlie One's course?"

"Yeah." Connor shrugged. "I did a quick AI analysis of the alien ship's course during the chase," she told them. "Turned out it was aligned perfectly with M44."

"M44?" Dobbs asked. "That another galaxy?"

She shook her head. "No. An open star cluster. It's a clot of around a thousand stars about five hundred and some light years out. It's known both as the Beehive and as Praesepe."

"Praesepe? What the fuck's that?"

"Latin for 'manger.' " The Romans, apparently, had seen in the scattering of dim stars not a crab, but two donkeys, and thus the central cluster represented the manger from which they were eating.

Gregory was studying the chart on his in-head. "The Triggah," he said. "They were headed for the Praesepe Triggah."

"Triggah" was fighter pilot's slang for "TRGA," or "Texaghu Resch Gravitational Anomaly."

"Pretty obvious, isn't it?" Connor said. "I think our Glothr friends might not only be from a long way away. I think they're from a long *when* away. Here. Have a look."

Agletsch Data Download 019372
Stellar Systems and Clusters: Beehive Cluster
Classification: Green-Echo

OBJECT CLASSIFICATION CODE: A9: Open Star Cluster

NAME: Beehive Cluster

OTHER NAMES: Praesepe, M44, NGC 2632, Cr 189

Location:

  Constellation: Cancer; **Right Ascension/Declination:** 08^{h}40.4^m, 19° 41'

Distance: 577 light years

Number of Stars: At least 1,000

Total Mass: ~580 Solar Masses

Stellar Makeup: M-class red dwarfs: 68%; F, G, and K-class sunlike stars: 30%; A-class stars: 2%, including 42 Cancri, an A9 III giant; K0 III giants: 4; G0 III giants: 1.

Age: ~600 million years

Core Diameter: ~22 light years

DESCRIPTION: With the Hyades and the Pleiades, Praesepe is among the closest of the open star clusters to Sol. It also has a somewhat larger population than most other clusters. From Earth, it is a faint and fuzzy patch of light just barely visible to the naked eye that has been known since ancient times, and was among the first astronomical objects to be studied by Galileo Galilei through an early telescope. . . .

Planetary Systems: Two planets discovered in the year 2012—"hot Jupiters" at that time designated as Pr0201b and Pr0211b—were the first exoplanets to be discovered circling stars within a star cluster. Current estimates suggest a total planetary population of well over 6,000. To date, no direct human explorations of the Praesepe cluster have been carried out. . . .

Alien Stellarchitecture: Analyses of Agletsch galactic records in late 2424 indicate the presence of a modified Tipler cylinder at the Praesepe cluster's heart, one of the so-called Sh'daar Nodes. Known as TRGA artifacts and presumably constructed by a now vanished galactic civilization perhaps as much as a half billion years ago, these massive cylinders, rotating at close to the speed of light, provide shortcuts through both space and time, and may serve as highways, of sorts, connecting the modern galaxy with the home galaxy of the Sh'daar Collective some 876 million years in the past. . . .

Where the great globular clusters like Omega Centauri were densely packed balls of millions of stars crammed into spherical swarms more than a hundred light years across, open clusters were less dramatic. The Beehive cluster was perhaps forty light years across, a loose gathering of about a thousand stars estimated to be 600 million years old, and was thought to have had the same origin as another open cluster, the Hyades.

No human expedition had yet ventured into the Beehive, however, and the cluster was not thought to be a likely place for inhabited worlds. If those stars were only a half billion years or so old, any planets circling them would still be harsh, young, and either sterile or possessing only the most primitive beginnings of single-cell life. When Earth was that old, life had only just begun appearing within the newborn world's churning seas. The Beehive cluster would be no different.

And yet . . .

Connor slipped through several gigabytes of data, following up on the mention of the TRGA. *That* enigmatic object might well change everything.

TRGAs were Tipler cylinders, theoretical structures first proposed as a solution to general relativity equations by the Hungarian mathematician and physicist Cornel Lanczos in 1924. Fifty years later, physicist Frank Tipler analyzed the equations and proposed that an ultra-dense cylinder rotating at extremely high speeds around its long axis might make travel through vast expanses of space and even through time itself possible. Later calculations had ruled out the time travel aspect; apparently, using a Tipler machine, as they were called, to move through time was possible only for a cylinder of infinite length.

There proved to be a loophole, however. Incorporating exotic matter with negative energy into the structure would generate the closed timelike curves permitting travel back in time without requiring a cylinder of infinite length.

But Tipler cylinders were purely hypothetical, useful for balancing relativistic equations but with no more physical reality than tachyons, which had been imagined back in 1967 for the same purpose.

Then the first TRGA was encountered at a star called Texaghu Resch, 112 light years from Sol. This Texaghu Resch

Gravitational Anomaly, first noted in Agletcsh records as one of a large number of so-called Sh'daar Nodes, was described as an "inside-out Tipler machine," a titanic and obviously artificial structure that appeared to focus space- and time-bending forces within the lumen of a hollow rotating tube. At first, it appeared to be a part of a vast network of interconnected nodes providing a kind of trans-galactic subway system permitting instantaneous travel across thousands of light years. Among other places, the Texaghu Resch Cylinder permitted ships from Earth to jump across 16,000 light years to the Omega Centauri globular cluster in an instant instead of months.

Eventually, though, by tracking the movements of Sh'daar ships through that first cylinder, the *America* battlegroup had discovered a particular path across space and time, one connecting with the N'gai Cloud, a pocket-sized galaxy just above the plane of the Milky Way some 876 million years in the past. That small galaxy had been absorbed by the Milky Way perhaps 200 million years later; its corpse—its central core—existed still as the giant globular cluster Omega Centauri. The battlegroup had passed through the TRGA cylinder to the heart of the N'gai Cloud, confronting the Sh'daar on their home ground in the remote past.

The Sh'daar, who'd been using the TRGA cylinders to attack or absorb galactic cultures in their future—Earth's present—had agreed to stop their cross-time predations, perhaps because they feared that the humans would interfere with their past and wipe them out.

And yet, their predations had begun again twenty years later.

What, Connor wondered, had changed?

"Scuttlebutt," Martinez said with the air of one making a holy proclamation, "says that *America* is going back to Tee-sub-minus zero point eight seven six gigayear, and seriously kicking some Sh'daar ass."

The Tee-sub-minus phrase referred to the remote past

time *America* had visited once before. It was clumsy and of real use only to physicists, but Martinez had rattled it off perfectly. He must have been practicing.

"Yeah," Ruxton said. "But will it be Tee-shub-mine . . . uh, wha' he said. With the Sh'daar? Or the *ur*-Sh'daar? Makes a subshtansh . . . makes a . . . a big difference, y'know."

"I don't see how," Caswell said. "Sh'daar? Ur-Sh'daar? They're all the same."

"Not anymore," Hathaway said, chuckling. "The Urs are gone."

"Sure," Gregory said. "But what if we went back in time to before the ur-Sh'daar Singularity? If they knew that they were going to leave behind such a mess . . ."

"I doubt they'd be able to do anything about it, Don," Connor told him. "I mean, what would they be able to do? Stop whatever happened before it happened? That probably wouldn't even be possible."

"No," Gregory said, "but they might hang around long enough after the transformation to help the stay-behinds."

"Maybe. I don't think we understand what happened, myself. Not really. It's hard enough understanding non-human behavior when we're on a more or less level playing field, like with the Agletsch. We know they trade in information—data they have for data we have, plus a few heavy elements like rhenium and neptunium two thirty-seven. Good old-fashioned capitalistic enterprise. We can understand *that*, right?

"But when we're trying to understand a collective of space-faring civilizations with a much higher technological quotient, and living hundreds of millions of years ago in an entirely different galaxy . . . how are we supposed to even begin to understand them?"

Gregory laughed. "Your problem, Megan, is that you don't believe in the Singularity at all."

They'd had this conversation before. "No," she replied. "I don't."

Sometimes known as the Vinge Singularity, after the mathematician and author Vernor Vinge, who popularized the concept in the late twentieth century, the Technological Singularity—first described as a possibility in the mid-1950s by the brilliant polymath John von Neumann—was supposed to be that point in a civilization's development where organic intelligence merged with artificial intelligence in ways that would utterly and forever transform the very concept of intelligent life. For humans, the GRIN technologies, as they were popularly known, were seen as the drivers of this inevitable change: Genetics, Robotics, Information systems, and Nanotechnology.

But *was* the change, the transformation into an entirely different order of life and intelligence, really inevitable? All attempts to predict Humankind's transcendence into a higher intelligence had so far failed. Futurist Raymond Kurzweil had predicted that the Technological Singularity would occur, *had* to occur, no later than the year 2045. Vinge himself had predicted—in the 1990s—it happening after 2005 but before 2030.

And yet, four centuries had passed since then, and there'd been no apotheosis of Humankind, no transcendence to a superhuman state.

Hyperintelligent AIs were commonplace, and humans carried circuitry within their brains and peripheral nervous systems that let them connect to electronic networks, to machines, to AIs, and to other humans in astonishing and powerful ways. Human minds had been *augmented* by technology, but not replaced by machines, not rendered obsolete, and not transformed into something unrecognizable. Nor had humans elected to have their minds digitally uploaded to artificial realities, a form of immortality that might benefit the copy but not the original, which, after all, remained in the real world to age and die. People could piggyback their consciousness in remote robotic vehicles, but when the link was switched off, they awoke back in their bodies of flesh and blood.

In short, they were still *human*.

And because of this, Megan Connor was convinced that the Technological Singularity was all hype, speculation, and imaginative nonsense, and would be so for the foreseeable future. She didn't know what had happened to the ancient ur-Sh'daar . . . but it seemed more likely to her by far that modern humans simply didn't understand an alien civilization that had existed that far back within the deeps of Time.

Humans weren't gods, and they weren't about to *become* gods. Transhumanism was a myth. Next question, please. . . .

"I think the big question," Hathaway said, pulling them back into the current discussion, "is what the Glothr think about us intercepting their ship . . . and what they're likely to do about it."

"If they were here to make peace with the Confederation," Martinez said, "they'll just have to make peace with us now."

"I wonder," Connor said, "if they can even see any difference between us and Geneva."

"Interesting point, Megan," Gregory said. "Of course, any alien who knows us well knows we're a fractious bunch. Always at each other's throats . . . unless outsiders give us something to unite against, that is."

"Ha!" Schmitt said, slapping the table. "It didn't work *this* time, did it? I mean, we've been fighting a dozen different races from the Sh'daar Collective for almost sixty years, but that didn't stop us from getting into a damned nasty little civil war."

"*Semper humanus*," Connor said, shaking her head. "Always human."

"Well *that's* a depressing thought," Hathaway said. "You're saying we can't change. . . ."

"Oh, we'll change," Dobbs said, ordering another drink for himself. "The Singularity is coming, brothers." He raised his empty glass in salute. "Hallelujah!"

"Can I hear an amen?" Gregory added, laughing. They

both looked at Connor, who just shrugged them off—she knew they were saying this not just out of belief, but because they knew it would bother her. *Not tonight.*

"Watch it, you two," Schmitt said. "They haven't rescinded the White Covenant yet."

"Oh, they will, they will," Hathaway said. "The way Starlight is spreading across Europe, and even over here now? They'll *have* to."

"Yeah, and when you look at it, old Dobbs here has a point." He glanced around the restaurant's interior, as though checking for eavesdroppers. "If Starlight *was* a religious virus, it sure as hell ended the war in a hurry, didn't it?"

"I've heard those rumors," Connor said. "I don't believe them."

"No?" Gregory asked. "Damn, Lieutenant. What *do* you believe?"

"That the USNA is still very much alone in the universe," she said, "and we still have a long way to go. Forget the transhuman crap and Singularity and all the rest of that stargod shit. Right now we need to focus just on surviving as a species."

"Nah," Ruxton said. "Tran . . . tran-shumans'll win out. Homo shuperioris! Homo . . . Homo techno . . . uh . . ."

"Easy there, Rux," Caswell said. "You've been hitting the juice pretty hard tonight. You okay?"

"*Coursh* I am, fuckin' bitch . . ." He sagged, his face dropping to the tabletop.

Caswell looked up at the others. "His wife left him," he explained. "He got word from her this morning."

"His . . . wife? You mean he's a *monogie*?"

"'Fraid so. They were from the Boston Periphery, y'know? Apparently, she got in with a transhumanist associative."

"Ah," Martinez said, nodding. "Some transhuman groups reject the whole idea of marriage or long-term partnerships."

"Well sure," Gregory said, nodding. "If you're a transhuman and going to live forever, you don't want to be stuck with the same partner for eternity, do you? Eternity is a hell of a long time!"

Connor arched an eyebrow, leaning back in her chair. She wasn't sure what she thought of monogies, though fleet scuttlebutt had it that Admiral Gray himself was one. Most Prims were, though they tended to have the rough edges smoothed off when they entered polite civilization.

The poor bastard. No wonder he was trying to drink himself into oblivion. Ruxton was facedown on the table, snoring loudly. "Shall we shoot him up with dryout?" Schmitt asked.

"Nah," Caswell said. "Let him sleep. We'll hit him when it's time to get him back up to the ship."

"So . . ." Schmitt said, trying to change the subject. "Any bets on how the Glothr thing's gonna shake out?"

"Maybe," Gregory said, smiling, "our new Glothr friends will show us the way."

"Sure," Connor said. "If we can ever figure out what *this* means." She raised her hands, opening and closing her fingers quickly to mimic flashing lights.

Chapter Ten

Emergency Presidential Command Post
Toronto
United States of North America
0910 hours, EST

"The channel will be open in a few moments, Mr. President."

"Thank you, Konstantin."

Koenig glanced at the other people in the room—General Nolan, Army Chief of Staff; Admiral Armitage, head of the Joint Chiefs of Staff; Secretary of Defense Lawrence Brookings; Sarah Taylor, the new secretary of Alien Affairs; Admiral Vincent Lodge, head of USNA Naval Intelligence; and Philip Caldwell, the National Security advisor. All of them were in recliners grown from the floor in a circle, facing inward. His chief of staff, Marcus Whitney, and several aides, technicians, and secretaries hovered in the background.

"I understand the quality of the translation has improved quite a bit," Koenig said.

"Definitely, Mr. President," Admiral Lodge told him. "Agletsch pidgins are good as far as they go, but the translation AIs at Crisium filled in a *lot* of blanks."

"And the aliens themselves have helped a *lot*, working directly with our AIs," Taylor added. "It'll be like talking to a human," he smiled, "not something in a bad adventure sim."

"Good. I've seen the transcripts recorded by . . . Klaatu, was it? Lots of room for misunderstanding, there."

"What's the alien's name, anyway?" Caldwell wanted to know.

"Joe," Koenig replied.

" 'Joe'?" Brookings repeated. "For something that looks like a glow-in-the-dark jellyfish?"

"The name was assigned by the AI running the translation, Mr. Secretary," Lodge explained. "You think 'Joe,' and the program will fill in the critter's real name for it."

"Which actually is a particular pattern of rippling lights that can't be expressed as sound," Taylor added. "Just so long as the program knows what's going on, it'll keep track of the details for us."

"Any idea yet what the Glothr want from us?" Eugene Armitage asked.

"Presumably," Koenig said, "to be allowed to go home. That's likely where they were going when we stopped them."

"Be nice to know what they were doing in North India, too," Nolan said, scowling. "Too many unknowns, here."

"But we know *that*, surely?" Armitage said. "The last Confederation holdouts were looking for help from the Sh'daar, to beat us."

"Maybe," Taylor said. "But we can't rely on easy answers, not with beings as different as these."

"We're checking with some of our assets in New Delhi," Lodge told them. "No answers there yet. But I would have to agree with Secretary Taylor. There may be something else going on here, more than a simple alliance."

"Gentleman, Ms. Taylor," Konstantin's voice said in their heads. "We're ready to commence the link. I remind you all that only President Koenig will be addressing the Glothr directly, in order to minimize confusion. If you all are ready, we can begin. . . ."

A window opened within Koenig's mind, and he found himself looking at the alien.

He'd known what to expect, of course. He'd seen one of the aliens first in recordings shot through the electronic eyes of a contact robot on the Glothr ship out beyond Neptune. Later, he'd watched their arrival at the xenosophontology labs at the Mare Crisium, on the moon. And Konstantin had kept him up to date on what they'd been learning about the Glothr since.

But to see them up close . . . Koenig had to admit he was taken aback just a bit.

The creature revealed on his in-head was ethereally beautiful: a filmy translucence revealing patches, dots, and stripes of inner light . . . most of it blue, but with some green and yellow. It currently was underwater—or, rather, in a salty mix of water and ammonia at near freezing temperatures, and its mantle and gently undulating tentacles formed a filmy halo that surrounded what might have passed for a face.

There had been a lot of speculation on how these underwater beings had developed their technology, but a bigger question came from the result of that technological advancement: namely, their robots. The Glothr appeared to be expert roboticists. Those gleaming, upright cigar-shapes with their multiple eyes and tentacles were everywhere on their ship, and had been essential in cracking the aliens' use of Agletsch Trade Pidgin. Yet, the Sh'daar restricted the development of robotics among their clients, the species within their collective. Why didn't the rules apply to the Glothr?

It was something Koenig hoped to get to the bottom of.

"You are the leader of the humans," a computer-generated voice said within Koenig's head. At the same time, the words wrote themselves down the right side of his in-head. Koenig was immediately impressed. The translation *had* improved, and markedly so. There was no ambiguity in the words at all.

"The leader?" Koenig said. "No. Not of all humans. The United States of North America."

"We do not understand. We were told you speak for Earth."

Koenig wasn't sure how best to represent himself. How much of human politics did the Glothr understand? How important was it that they understand?

"Humans are . . . divided into a number of separate nation-states," he said. "Some have been attempting to come together, to unify as a single group called the Earth Confederation. But others don't like the idea of the Confederation making decisions for the rest of us about things to which we haven't agreed."

"Like joining the Sh'daar Collective," the Glothr said.

The being was damned quick. Maybe it understood more than Koenig had been giving it credit for.

"Exactly. We don't want the Collective telling us how to run our business."

"Despite all of the benefits? That is what we truly don't understand . . . that you humans, or at least some humans, would reject the benefits of joining the Collective."

"*What* benefits?" Koenig snapped back, more forcefully than he'd intended. "To have our scientific inquiry stifled? Our curiosity blocked? Our technological advancement throttled? Our growth and our economy frozen? The way we choose to develop our civilization kept static and unchanging?"

"All of which are trivial when compared to becoming part of a billion-year-old empire spanning the galaxy. And that "throttling of technological advances" you mention—that *would* be for your own good."

"And who determines what is in our best interest?"

"The Collective, of course."

"Shouldn't *we* have a say in anything that's going to shape our culture?"

"But you would, of course. Once you are part of the Collective."

Koenig decided that it would be futile trying to argue the

point further. He had no idea how the Sh'daar Collective governed itself, or how internal decisions were made, and he didn't think this was the time to learn.

Even so, he was pleased. This was the first time, so far as he knew, that a Sh'daar species had actually talked to humans about what it was they wanted. Even when Koenig and the *America* battlegroup had forged a treaty of sorts with the Sh'daar in the N'gai Cloud, the beings he'd talked with over a computer link had not tried to sell him on the advantages of joining their Collective. Discussion at the time had been limited to "leave us alone and we'll leave you alone." By contrast, the Glothr seemed . . . approachable, even friendly. It felt like an enormous change in attitude.

Or was this perceived change simply a reflection of the outlook and attitude of this new species, a kind of racial trait? Koenig didn't know . . . but he was willing to believe that the Glothr might be important friends for Humankind.

God knows we need one.

"Humans are a stubborn bunch, Joe," Koenig said. "We don't like surrendering our independence to *anyone* . . . even our own. And we really hate it when someone puts a gun to our head and says we *have* to do anything, even if whatever it is is supposed to be good for us. But maybe if you could answer some questions, help us get to know you better, some of the barriers to understanding could come down."

Promise nothing, he told himself. *But get him to talk. . . .*

"We will answer what we can, within reason," the Glothr replied. "Better understanding between any two cultures works to the advantage of both."

"We'll see. I'm not entirely ready to concede that," Koenig said. "But . . . look. The Sh'daar Collective would have us give up robotics, among other things, right?"

"Not give up, necessarily," the Glothr replied. "But we do want to moderate the speed of advancement."

"We can't help but notice that the Glothr have some quite

sophisticated robots. Why would your Collective allow you to build such robots, but deny us that privilege?"

"Each case, each species, is different," the alien told him. "And there are no absolutes. The *Zhaotal Um* helped us establish a technological civilization in the first place, hundreds of millions of years ago, and robotics were instrumental in our transition from a marine environment to a gaseous atmosphere, and then again, later, when we made the transition to space. Robots, both as artificial intelligences and as remote bodies and sensory organs for our observers, were already a deeply integral part of our civilization when the ur-Sh'daar first contacted us."

Koenig caught his breath. The talkative alien had let slip several important revelations just now. Thank God everything was being recorded and stored for later analyses.

He opened a sidebar window and queried Konstantin. "Do we have a reference to *Zhaotal Um*?"

"Possibly," the AI replied. "There is a forty percent chance that the phrase is related to a term in one of the Agletsch trade pidgins."

"Meaning?"

"Roughly . . . 'Stargods.' "

"Ha! I *thought* so!"

This meant that, like the H'rulka—without access to metals, fire, or smelting technology—the Glothr had had help. And "Joe" had clearly stated that they'd received that help long before being contacted by the Collective . . . which meant that the stargods definitely were *not* the Sh'daar. Most xenosophontologists had already arrived at that conclusion, but many, in the name of keeping things simple, still argued against it. The Sh'daar were an advanced galactic technic species with a penchant for meddling in the affairs of other races. *Ergo*, they must be the mythic stargods.

And then something else sank in, something startling enough that Koenig ran back through the written transcript of the conversation so far. *Ur*-Sh'daar! The being had said they'd been contacted by the *ur*-Shdaar!

There was something else there, too: an admission that the Glothr civilization was hundreds of millions of years old. *That* seemed starkly impossible.

"Tell me, Joe," Koenig said, "just where do you come from? The Milky Way? Or the N'gai Cloud?"

"We are not prepared to share that information with you as yet, human."

"Maybe I should ask you *when* you're from, then. I find it hard to believe that your species is hundreds of millions of our years old. But if you traveled forward through time to get here—perhaps from the N'gai Cloud before it was assimilated by our galaxy—the idea becomes more reasonable."

"The biggest problem with you humans," Joe said, his lights pulsing and rippling as the words came through Koenig's in-head, "is that you are true ephemerals. Your species can't take the long view, can't plan for things a few million years down the line, can't think in terms of evolutionary periods of time. You worry that the Sh'daar demand that you slow your explorations of robotics and genetics and the rest, because you don't see that a delay in the development of those technologies means nothing against a vista of ten million years . . . a hundred million . . . a billion. . . ."

"Are you telling me the Glothr as a species have been around for a billion years?"

"I'm telling you that your species is less than half a million years old, and has been technologically proficient for a mere instant, the snap of a tentacle tip." One of the Glothr's translucent tendrils rippled and flicked, as if in demonstration. "A race of immortals might take an eon or two to arrive at an important decision, and why not? They have the time, and they know it. They can afford not to be . . . *hasty.*"

"Is your species immortal?"

"True immortality may be impossible. The universe itself will die at some point, bringing all life to an end."

The alien had not, Koenig realized, answered his question. Although it was always difficult—and usually impossi-

ble—to judge nonhuman motives or emotions across an AI
translation link, he had the distinct impression that the near
transparent being floating in his in-head window was trying
to sell him a bill of goods.

"If we're so primitive," Koenig said, "why does the Collective want us? Surely we can't add that much to your civilization."

"Perhaps not. But you could be disruptive if your technology leads you into a state of *Schjaa Hok*."

Koenig knew the term, an Agletsch translation of data
his battlegroup had accessed eight hundred million years in
the past. It meant, very roughly, "The Transcending," and
referred to the sudden vanishing of perhaps hundreds of billions of inhabitants of the pygmy galaxy called the N'gai
Cloud.

There were still human religions here on Earth who expected their members to one day be snatched away by God,
an event Christian fundamentalists called "the Rapture."
Eight hundred million years ago, a quite literal rapture had
occurred within the ur-Sh'daar civilization in the N'gai
Cloud. The Transcending had not been brought on by a mes-
siah's return, but rather appeared to be a true technological
singularity, with a majority of the civilization's members
turning into . . . something else. What that something else
might be—life on a higher plane or around the corner of a
different dimension, perhaps, or a digital existence within
computer-generated pocket universes—was still unknown.

What *was* known was that those members of the civilization that had not made the transformation, the Refusers, had
become the modern Sh'daar.

"Mr. President," Admiral Armitage whispered in his
head, "ask it what it was doing on Earth, in North India."

Koenig mentally waved the Navy CNO off. He was more
interested in what the Sh'daar wanted from Humankind . . .
and if there were grounds for negotiations.

"The Sh'daar Collective," he said to the alien, "agreed to

leave us alone when we visited the N'gai Cloud twenty of our years ago. Lately, you have resumed your attacks. Why?"

"You seem to be under a misapprehension," the alien told them. "The Collective is a . . . loose association of very different species and cultures. It is not a . . . I believe the term you might use is *empire*. There isn't a strong central government or a single leader. There is no capital world, no ruling emperor. How could such a thing possibly function in a galaxy as vast and as complex as this?"

Koenig smiled. Back when he'd commanded a star carrier battlegroup, he'd chastised subordinates for using the term "Sh'daar empire" for precisely that reason. Just how many species the Sh'daar controlled in the Milky Way Galaxy now was unknown. Agletsch sources mentioned thirty in their *Encyclopedia Galactica* . . . but those were just the civilizations for which humans had purchased data from those supreme traders in galactic information. According to the best current estimates, there were 50 million intelligent species in this one galaxy alone, and perhaps several thousand actually controlled by the Sh'daar across a volume of space variously described as between a tenth of the galaxy . . . and half.

"So when the Sh'daar tell their client races to do something, they might not."

"It is not so simple a task as giving an order and expecting it to be carried out," the alien told them. "We do regret the problems this has caused your civilization."

"What if we humans entered into negotiations with the Sh'daar directly?" Koenig asked. "Perhaps if we opened trade negotiations with—"

"Your civilization has nothing we wish to trade for," the Glothr said, cutting Koenig off. "We have access to the raw materials of much of the galaxy, and manufacturing technologies that make your current nanotech seem primitive by comparison."

And that, of course, had long been the argument against

such cherished myths and fictional accounts as interstellar trade routes and conquest. With the basic elements both of any manufacturing process and of life itself common in every solar system, and with nanotechnology or its equivalent to assemble those atoms into literally any end product desired, there was absolutely no reason to invade another star system . . . not in terms of the acquisition of worlds, goods, or raw materials. Even living space could be grown from asteroids or cometary bodies out in a system's Oort Cloud, enough for tens of trillions of beings. Or existing inhospitable worlds could be terraformed into paradise. Only information appeared to have any value in the galactic marketplace, as the Agletsch had demonstrated.

"We must have *something* that interests you," Koenig told the alien.

"We want your cooperation," the Glothr said, blue flashes undulating up its rippling tentacles. "We want to avoid a second *Schjaa Hok*, one occurring in this galaxy in the near-term future. And with your participation, perhaps we can provide a united front against . . . *this*."

A new, inner window opened in Koenig's mind, and in the minds of the others who were linked into the conversation. He saw—again—the strange and eerie starscape of the Rosette, the heart of the Omega Centauri cluster with its titanic space- and time-bending stellarchitecture, enigmatic structures of light, all of it embracing the close-set whirl of world-sized black holes in a tightly circling orbit around a common center of gravity. In the background, 10 million stars formed a glowing backdrop, an impenetrable wall of starlight.

The so-called Rosette Aliens had emerged from that gravitational whirlpool and begun creating the surrounding webwork of mysterious and titanic structures—*stellarchitecture*. Speculation as to who or what they were ranged from visitors from a parallel universe, or from the far future, to the original ur-Sh'daar, newly emerged from the remote past. Those six co-orbiting black holes, physicists knew, were the modern form of six giant blue stars at the center of the N'gai Cloud 876 million years in the past, an artificial gravitational rosette used like an impossibly vast Tipler machine to cross enormous gulfs of space and time.

"Do you know who these visitors are?" Koenig asked.

"We do."

"It's the ur-Sh'daar, isn't it?"

"Your empty speculation serves no purpose. If you wish to learn the true nature of the cosmos, you would do well to join with us and become a living part of the galaxy's transformation into biological existential reality!"

The Glothr's terminology seemed oddly phrased and awkward to the point of clumsiness. *Biological existential reality? What the hell did biology have to do with a term out of ancient philosophy?*

"Is that what you were discussing with the Earth Confederation recently?" Koenig asked. "Existentialism?"

"We were discussing the Earth Confederation's formal assimilation into the Sh'daar Collective. It seems a shame that your divisiveness—your *faction*—has prevented that."

"As I said, we don't like surrendering our independence."

"The representatives of your Earth Confederation seemed willing enough to do so."

"I'll just bet they were," Koenig replied, laughing.

"Which proves your statement about not wishing to surrender independence is not true."

"They might be willing to do so," Koenig replied, "if they thought they could get some help from you against us. We've *always* had trouble with giving up freedom in exchange for a little security."

"That seems internally contradictory."

"If you're into human existentialism," Koenig said, still amused, "you must enjoy the absurd."

"I do not understand your meaning."

Good, Koenig thought. *Keep him guessing.*

"Joe, I have a proposal for you. I assume you're eager to get home."

"We were on our way home when your ships . . . detained us."

"Yes, well, we're sorry about that. Your ship was escaping from a member state of the Confederation, our enemies, just when those enemies had been defeated. It was possible that some members of those states were traveling with you."

"None were. We were on Earth, at your Confederation's explicit invitation, to discuss Earth's future association with the Collective."

"That was my assumption. How did those discussions go?"

"You will need to talk to the humans with whom we met on Earth."

"We already have a list of names," Lodge whispered in Koenig's mind. "People in the Confederation government, in their State Department and ambassadorial service. We'll be questioning them in short order."

"We'll do that, Joe," Koenig said. "In the meantime, we have no reason to keep you or your ship here."

"We are free to go?"

"Possibly. But we would like to send some ships along with yours."

"What ships?"

"A star carrier and her escorts. What we call a carrier battlegroup of ten or twelve ships. We would like to meet with representatives of your government, and with the Sh'daar Collective."

"That is not possible."

Koenig considered his options. He had a bluff in mind as a last resort, but wasn't sure how far he could take it.

"I know," he told the being, "that you've come here across *time* as well as space."

"Travel at velocities approaching that of light by its very definition entails travel through time."

"Perhaps. I suppose relativity could be defined as a kind

of time travel. But I think you know that I mean something different. Travel forward *and backward* in time, as distinct from travel through space."

"What could possibly lead you to draw such a conclusion?"

"First of all, we know that you can tinker with the flow of time, at least to a limited extent. An interesting technology. You slowed down the time for *Concord*—that watchship you took on board—by a factor of at least a thousand to one. That was to control the crew, wasn't it?"

"That has nothing to do with travel across time," the alien said. But the Glothr sounded . . . hesitant? It was difficult to tell, listening to a translation produced by an AI intermediary, but Koenig had the impression that "Joe" was worried by this line of questioning.

"You're a time traveler from our remote past, and you've come here through one of the TRGA cylinders . . . specifically a TRGA cylinder located in the star cluster we call the Beehive."

The being in the window within Koenig's mind said nothing. It appeared to be simply watching him, perhaps waiting him out. What, Koenig wondered, was it thinking right now?

"We could attempt to find your homeworld, your civilization, but there's no guarantee that we would arrive at the same general time that you've come from. A small variation in vector through a TRGA's spacetime matrix can result in an error of centuries, true? I wonder what would happen if we showed up in your planetary neck of the woods before you left to come here?"

That definitely got a reaction. The lights within the alien's translucent form were pulsing wildly now, creating an intense glow.

"No!"

Koenig pushed on. "We humans are internally contradictory, you know. And divided. And absurd. I'm giving you the option of taking us directly to your superiors, rather than having primitives like us showing up at random, and blundering around in your history."

The Glothr appeared to be quite agitated. Its translucent arms shifted and waved in the water, and patterns of yellow and green lights pulsed and throbbed, overwhelming the constellation of blue bioluminescence.

Koenig found the display fascinating; the Sh'daar of the N'gai Cloud—876 million years ago or twenty years ago, depending on how you looked at it—had seemed panicked by the idea of humans mucking about in their past. The mere threat of human warships exploring the N'gai Cloud in earlier times had brought about a considerable change of heart among the Sh'daar . . . and the promise to suspend hostilities against the Earth.

Apparently, the Glothr had the same terror.

Temporal paradox might well be the ultimate of all possible weapons. If, in a war with another civilization, you could go back in time and edit your enemy out of existence, you could win the war before it even started, and there would be nothing you could do to protect yourself from such an attack.

The downside was that any change you made in history might affect you as well as the enemy. The possibilities had been discussed in a number of strategy planning conferences and meetings ever since the possibility had been raised two decades earlier. Suppose Koenig sent the *America* back in time 876 million years to the N'gai Cloud and did something to edit the Sh'daar out of existence. If that happened, then Humankind would not have received the Sh'daar Ultimatuum in 2367, and almost sixty years of warfare would never have transpired. Millions, no *billions* who'd died both on Earth and among Earth's colony worlds would now be alive. The civil war between North America and the Earth Confederation almost certainly wouldn't have happened . . . and that, in turn, meant the city of Columbus and hundreds of thousands of citizens would not have been nano-devoured.

At the very least, those thirty alien races described by the Agletsch would not have been conquered by the Sh'daar, and their histories would have been vastly different as well.

The catch was, editing the Sh'daar out of existence would also edit the recent history of Humankind.

How could Koenig—how could *anyone*—take the responsibility for that kind of meddling?

The possibility had been discussed in various military and scientific circles, of course, and a few years ago it had even been debated in the USNA Senate. The consensus held that tinkering with the past was too dangerous even to consider. And yet the possibility remained as a kind of ultimate doomsday scenario.

If Humankind was about to go under anyway . . .

None of that made any difference at the moment, however. What was important was that the Glothr didn't *know* that humans wouldn't meddle.

And they appeared to be terrified by that possibility, which represented, Koenig thought, the only advantage Humankind possessed in this galactic—and *temporal*—war.

The rippling lights shifted from greens and yellows back to blue, and the writhing being seemed to grow more calm.

"Very well, human," the Glothr said. "We agree to your terms."

Koenig nodded. "I will give the necessary orders."

And the link with the alien was broken.

"What the hell was all that stuff about existential philosophy?" General Nolan said after a long moment of silence in the room.

"Existentialism starts off as a sense of confusion or disorientation in a world that is absurd or meaningless," Koenig replied, thoughtful. "At least, that was the claim of its proponents, six hundred years ago. And it's up to the individual to make sense of things, not religion or society or the state."

"I don't get it," Brookings said.

"I'm not sure I do either," Koenig replied. "But our friend

was talking about 'biological existential reality' as it related to life in the galaxy. I was just trying to draw him out."

"Well, you confused him, at least," Sarah Taylor told him.

"Hell," Caldwell said, "he confused *me*. You know, I really don't think that a human philosophical system can have any bearing at all on an alien intelligence."

"I think it has all kinds of bearing," Koenig said. "As long as you have mind—consciousness, self-awareness, and intelligence—you're going to reflect on and act upon the world as you perceive it. We may perceive the universe in different ways from one another, but at least philosophy can let us compare notes."

"I think we need to figure out what he meant by the 'galaxy transforming into biological existential reality,' " Taylor said.

"And I think we need to get a fleet out to the Beehive cluster and through the TRGA to Joe's home space and time," Koenig said. "Let's talk about that."

Brookings nodded. "Who do you have in mind, Mr. President?"

"As it happens, Admiral Armitage has already begun assembling a fleet: Task Force One, with the carrier *America* as flag . . ."

Chapter Eleven

USNA Star Carrier America
Naval Base
Quito Synchorbital
1345 hours, TFT

"I'd be happier, Mr. President," Admiral Gray said, "if we knew just who built the TRGA cylinders . . . and why."

"Nervous that they might be Sh'daar? Or at least controlled by them?"

"Frankly, yes. And following a Sh'daar ship through a Sh'daar node without knowing what's waiting for us on the other side strikes me as just a smidge beyond total insanity."

Gray was seated in his office on board the *America*, linked in-head with the president of the USNA. Three weeks had passed since the capture of Charlie One. He'd received his orders five days ago, and he was still feeling more than a little daunted by them.

No one knew for sure who had built the TRGA cylinders originally. For a time, the assumption had been that they were Sh'daar constructs—and certainly the Sh'daar used them throughout their far-flung territories across both time and space. There were numerous TRGA cylinders within the

N'gai Cloud of 876 million years ago, and a pathway provided by the original Texaghu Resch Gravitational Anomaly had given the *America* battlegroup access to the Sh'daar capital—for lack of a better term—two decades before.

But assumptions are not facts, and some researchers felt that the technology necessary to create TRGA cylinders—enormous inside-out Tipler machines, in fact—was well beyond the technological capabilities demonstrated by any of the known Sh'daar client species.

Of course, perhaps that was why the Sh'daar were trying to forbid certain technological advances and research. They had the necessary technologies themselves, but didn't want anyone else ever to challenge them.

The Glothr appeared to be the most technically advanced of any Sh'daar client race yet encountered. They'd taken robotics to an extremely advanced degree, and their trick with slowing down time for the *Concord* while it was inside their vessel was impressive.

If the Glothr could warp time, even if just on a small scale, it could give them a staggering advantage in combat. Of course, they hadn't used it in the battle that had captured the Glothr ship, except as a means of immobilizing the *Concord*. But was that because they couldn't, or because they'd chosen not to?

No one knew except the Glothr themselves, and they weren't exactly being forthcoming about it. They seemed to be pretending that they didn't understand the question.

That was just one of the many issues going through Gray's mind as he glanced at the AI-generated representation of TF-1 glowing above his workstation console. Task Force One was the flotilla newly completed around the star carrier *America*, consisting so far of thirty-two capital warships. The Marine carrier transport *Marne* and the battleships *New York, Northern California*, and *Illinois* had just cast off from the SupraQuito dockyards and were marked in space now by the pulsing wink of their navigation strobes.

Four battlecruisers, four heavy cruisers, five light cruisers; and a number of smaller vessels—destroyers and frigates— were adrift in synchorbit as well, along with the heavy mass-driver bombardment vessel *Farragut*. The *Concord* and two other High Guard ships, *Pax* and *Open Sky*, had been re-called back to USNA naval service to fill out the roster. The fleet numbered as many warships as the North American government had been able to assemble . . . a risk, obviously, given the fears in some quarters that the Confederation was not yet truly beaten.

So far as Gray was concerned, the Confederation was pretty much out of the game, at least as an organized partici-pant. Korosi's holdouts in France, Turkey, and North India had been rounded up, Ilse Roettgen was again in control of the Earth Confederation Senate in Geneva, and a week ago she'd signed the Pax Deux, formally ending all hostilities between the Confederation and the United States of North America. The document also reaffirmed the basic unity of Humankind, and pledged assistance in the ongoing struggle against "all interstellar threats to terrestrial independence."

In response to a direct request by President Koenig, sev-eral Confederation vessels had joined the fleet as well—the cruisers *Churchill*, *Valiant*, and *Hessen*, the French heavy battlecruiser *Victoire*, and the North Indian *Ranvir*.

Gray wasn't sure if they were being included in TF-1 as additional firepower or to guarantee Geneva's continued cooperation at home. Outside of the Confederation ship muster, there also were two powerful new Japanese war-ships, *Yamato* and *Honshu*, both technically battlecruisers, plus a Theocracy frigate, the *Najim al Zafir*.

The more, Gray thought, the merrier . . . though how well this mismatched congeries of vessels would respond to his command remained to be seen. There'd been no time to practice or to do much at all in the way of fleet coordination, save exchanging AI addresses and frequencies.

There were promises of even more ships—in particular a Chinese flotilla, as well as more Indian and German vessels—but those ships all were still out-system and would have to catch up with Task Force One later, if at all.

The incorporation of both Pan-European and North Indian ships in the expeditionary force presented at least the illusion that Humankind was now at last operating on a united front against the Sh'daar. It also, better than anything else, proved that the civil war against the Confederation was over.

What it *didn't* prove, in Gray's estimation, was that low-level hostilities with the Confederation were over for good. Korosi's last stand had been, in effect, a holdout by forces unwilling to lay down their arms. Bad feelings and grudges ran deep on both sides of the divide, and it would be a long time yet before the Earth's governments would be able to hammer out a single government—or even just a single way of seeing things—that might be acceptable to all.

But all of that was Koenig's concern. Gray was faced with quite a different set of problems.

"You know, Mr. President," he said, "if we don't come back, it's going to leave a terrible hole in the naval inventory."

"I know," Koenig told him. "That's why you'd damned well better bring them back. Starships are expensive."

"I'll do my best. But I think you're a little more confident of my abilities than I am."

"I'm aware of that . . . *Admiral*."

Koenig had stressed Gray's rank, and Gray bit off an angry response. It remained a sore point between them, Gray's promotion to full admiral over any number of other flag-rank officers by presidential executive order. Koenig had claimed the promotion was provisional, and if a later Senate confirmation hearing didn't confirm it, he would go back to being a two-star rear admiral or less.

And that would be just fine with Gray.

Koenig claimed to have signed the order because Gray needed the extra mass of those four stars to boss the com-

manding officers of half a dozen other naval services—
Chinese, Islamic Theocracy, and now their erstwhile
enemies from the Confederation. From Gray's perspective,
it just meant he had to work harder than ever to justify the
rank to his own personnel . . . and created a lot of jealousy
among all the other naval officers in the service. He didn't
deserve four stars, and he was still angry at Koenig for sad-
dling him with them.

How much of Dahlquist's defiance, he wondered, was due
to his own too-quick rise through the ranks?

But, then, Koenig *was* the president, and the commander-
in-chief of all USNA military forces. Gray was too much of
a soldier to ignore orders.

Still, why couldn't the man confine his commanding-in-
chiefing to someone else?

Gray swallowed the anger. Now wasn't the time or the
place. Better to change the subject.

"I'm surprised, Mr. President, that the Glothr agreed to
having this horde drop into their backyard. How did you
manage that?"

"They weren't pleased about it, but you're going to have
one thing going for you. Everyone in TF-1 isn't going in at
once."

"I saw that in the orders," Gray replied. "Just a squadron of
fighters off of the *America* . . . and the three Guard cutters."

"Right. Twelve fighters and three small WPS-100s won't
be particularly alarming to an entire world. And once
they've ascertained that everything is clear, they send a message drone back and have the rest of you come through—*if*
that seems prudent to you."

"Meaning if they don't see a fleet of ten thousand time-
bending battlecruisers over there waiting to ambush us,
we're good to go. Got it."

What was not said was what would happen to those ships
and crews if Gray decided not to follow them.

"Based on the fighter squadron's report," Koenig continued, "you'll decide what goes in next—the rest of the fleet, or just a few ships. You could even stagger your arrival over a period of time so you can count on reinforcements."

"Which is fine, unless the Glothr get nervous when more and more of our warships keep popping in on them," Gray said. "At some point, they might decide enough is enough and open fire. I'm also not sure dividing my force in the face of a superior possible enemy force will be a real good idea."

"That will be your tactical decision, of course."

"Mm. Thank you so much, Mr. President. Don't you want to come along, sir? Revisit your glory days in the N'gai Cloud?"

"I have *every* confidence in your ability to carry this off, Admiral."

"I'm flattered. Terrified, but flattered." He considered possibilities for a moment. "You know, Mr. President, we can't be certain that the other end of the TRGA link will be the Glothr home system. It might be the N'gai Cloud, where we visited the Sh'daar twenty years ago. It might be some other place in the galaxy at time now, rather than in the past. We just don't know."

"True."

"Worst case—the Glothr could lead us someplace well away from their home system. Maybe a place with a Sh'daar fleet waiting for us, because they know something about faster-than-light communication and we don't."

"My, you *do* have a nasty, suspicious mind, don't you?"

"It's what I would try to do if the situation was reversed. They're not going to want us coming anywhere near their homeworld. You do know that, right?"

"It depends on the payoff, Sandy," Koenig said, using Gray's old squadron handle. "If they can get us to surrender without a shot, to knuckle under to the Sh'daar demands, they'll do it. Maybe they just want peace. That'll be up to you and Dr. Rand."

Dr. Lawrence Rand had been appointed ambassador-at-large by the USNA State Department. He and his staff, which included a team of xenosophontologists from Crisium, would be traveling on board the Glothr vessel inside a courier packet specially modified as a human-life-support hab module. They hoped to establish permanent peaceful relations with the Glothr at the very least, and possibly the larger Sh'daar Collective as well.

"And if they can squash us like a bug, they'll do that instead. The mission briefing said the Glothr were . . . what? A billion years ahead of us?"

"Our Glothr friend was trying indirectly to make us think so," Koenig said. "I don't believe it for a minute, though."

"Oh? Why not?"

"I might believe a million years. *Maybe.* But a species that's been around for a billion years . . . hell, I'd expect them to have evolved into beings of pure light or something, ages ago. Wouldn't you?"

"Transcendence," Gray said. "Yeah. But that's the point of the Sh'daar, isn't it? They're doing everything they can *not* to transcend to a higher order."

"They want to block *technological* transcendence. But how do you stop evolution itself?"

"By taking control of your own genetics, of course. We're doing that ourselves now." *Transhumans* . . .

"And that's one of the forbidden technologies."

"Ah. I see what you mean." A new thought occurred to Gray. "Huh. There's an idea. If the Glothr are from the N'gai Cloud, they might have started out 876 million years ago, but be counting their presence at time now in this galaxy. That would mean their existence spans *almost* a billion years."

"Maybe. I'd wondered about that, actually . . . but mostly I think our jellyfish friend was bluffing. They've lied about several things."

"Such as?"

"I'm not convinced that they're Sh'daar."

"*What?*"

Gray felt Koenig's shrug. "They don't appear to have Seeds."

That was a surprise.

The various time-now species encountered as members of the Sh'daar Collective included species startlingly different from one another, but they did seem to have one thing in common. Certain members of each species possessed tiny, BB-sized pellets somewhere within their bodies. Known as Sh'daar Seeds, they weren't well understood as yet, but they seemed to be spy devices of a sort, storing up sights and sounds from the being's immediate vicinity and, when a Sh'daar ship was close enough, transmitting that data in a tightly compressed burst. Not all Sh'daar individuals had them by any means, but most who had dealings with humans did, and the assumption was that the Seeds were one way of gathering intelligence about humans and their technology.

A new alien species only recently contacted, the monstrous Gr'doch, had *not* carried the telltale Seeds . . . and it had turned out that they were, in fact, enemies of the Sh'daar.

But the Glothr claimed to be part of the Collective—spokescreatures for the Sh'daar, in fact.

"It seems inconceivable that beings sent to actually negotiate with the Confederation wouldn't be carrying Seeds," Gray said. "Did they ask our guests about the Seeds out at Crisium?"

"They did."

"And?"

"Our friends told the xeno boys that not all Sh'daar species carried them."

"You know," Gray said, thoughtful, "I'm beginning to wonder if the Glothr might not be a bit higher up the Sh'daar totem pole than some of the others, the Slan and Nungies and the rest."

"My thought as well," Koenig told him. "And Konstantin agrees with us, by the way."

Gray frowned. He wasn't comfortable with that super-

AI looking over his shoulder. "We'll need confirmation, of course."

"Of course. You may be able to get it when you follow Charlie One out to the Beehive . . . and on through the TRGA. Be sure to come back and fill me in. A question?"

"Yes, sir?"

"The squadron you're sending through the TRGA on point, and the three cutters. You're confident in all of them? It's a monumental responsibility."

Gray hesitated before answering. And he wondered just how much the president knew. Everything, most likely. In a linked-in military network there were astonishingly few secrets. By not raising the problem with Dahlquist directly, Koenig was giving Gray the benefit of the doubt, and avoiding the ugly and dangerous specter of micromanagement.

"I have complete confidence in them, sir."

"*All* of them? No problems?"

"Nothing worth mentioning, sir."

"Good."

A signal chimed within Gray's awareness. "*America*'s skipper is telling me it's time to haul ass, Mr. President."

"Good luck, Sandy. Listen, I mean it. Be sure to come back home . . . and be sure you bring that expensive fleet with you."

Gray laughed. "Aye, aye, sir." He shifted mental channels. "Okay, Captain . . . take us out."

And the star carrier *America* began accelerating.

Emergency Presidential Command Post
Toronto
United States of North America
1412 hours, EST

President Koenig watched on his own display as the ships of Task Force One formed up into a cone formation just beyond the sprawl of the immense SupraQuito naval facilities and began accelerating outbound. Off to one side, another ship—the massive, 900-meter form of the incongruously named Charlie One—was rising smoothly from the nearly full face of the moon. As the minutes passed, Charlie One slid into position at the fleet cone's apex, leading them outbound in the direction of the small and inconspicuous constellation of Cancer.

"*America* reports clear communications with the alien vessel," a voice whispered in Koenig's mind. "All nominal."

"Very well, Kelly," Koenig replied. "Continue relaying messages for as long as the time lag allows."

"Yes, sir."

Koenig had heard some scuttlebutt and speculation within the Navy's physics community, which had questioned whether some Sh'daar species already possessed faster-than-light communication. If so, the human fleet was going to be at a terrible disadvantage out there.

"I hope we're doing the right thing," he said aloud.

There was no one else in the presidential office with him . . . no *organic* being, at any rate.

Three seconds passed, the time required for Koenig's words to reach the Konstantin AI facility at Tsiolkovsky, on the lunar far side, and for Konstantin's reply to return . . . plus a half-second pause that likely was generated by the AI for a humanlike effect. Humans could be disconcerted by the speed of Konstantin's responses to even the most complex of questions.

"We have done what we can to maximize Admiral Gray's chances," Konstantin's voice replied.

"He still doesn't like that promotion, you know," Koenig said. "He's still pretty angry about it. Angry at *me*."

"The promotion had to appear to come from you," Konstantin replied. "Otherwise, he might have discounted it . . . or rejected its legitimacy."

"But it was *your* idea. And . . . you know? I still don't understand why you suggested it."

"Partly to give him the requisite authority with the commanding officers of ships and squadrons from other nations."

"Well, yes . . . I know that. It makes sense." Koenig had told Gray as much when he'd given him the news of the promotion: *"You'll need to pull at* least *an O-10 if you're going to be on an equal footing with the likes of Ulyukayev or Gao or Singh."*

But the fact remained that someone like Jerry Matthews or Karyl Bennington already had the rank. "Hell," Koenig continued, "there must be a few hundred four-star admirals that would have jumped at the chance to command TF-1. Why promote Sandy Gray and stir up all kinds of resentment within the Navy's officer corps?"

"Because Gray, possibly more than any other officer in the USNA military, possesses extensive experience with a variety of nonhuman sentient species, in particular first-contact experience."

And that was true as well. Last year, Matthews had fought a Confederation fleet to a standstill at Alpha Centauri A, but he hadn't faced aliens since the H'rulka Incursion twenty years ago. Same for Bennington and Gramm. When it came to encounters with alien intelligences, their diplomatic skills were rather untested.

"Further," Konstantin went on, "Gray is aggressive in combat, but flexible in his approach. More than most humans, he seems able to assess a threat and respond with diplomacy rather than firepower when diplomacy offers the best, most advantageous chance of conflict resolution. Too, his leadership skills are excellent, as is his capacity for both tactical and strategic thinking when force *is* called for."

"Oh, he's good," Koenig said. "I'll give you that. He's also a bit of a maverick. He's never fit the Navy mold comfortably, and he has a tendency to do things his own way."

"True. But as your protégé, he will accept guidance from you and, through you, from me."

It was a distinction Koenig had not thought of before. Yes, Koenig had helped the young officer along at several key points, helping further his career. As such, there definitely was a relationship between the two men that had been mutually beneficial. Koenig was well aware that the naval service was so intensely political once you reached the rank of captain . . . and Gray, the former Prim, had had a major strike against him from the start.

But Koenig had seen something in Gray that no one else . . .

"You've been maneuvering me in order to *steer* the guy?" Koenig asked. "You were *using* me!"

"Necessarily so. Would he have accepted a promotion, an explanation, and orders from me?"

"Well—"

"Perhaps more to the point, would you have agreed with my tactics?"

Koenig didn't know whether to be angry or impressed. The unspoken assumption about artificial intelligence was that they could not—or, at the very least, *would* not—lie. Of course, an AI would do what it was programmed to do. For centuries, now, however, artificial intelligences had been programmed to program themselves, each new generation of AI designing its own successors. An AI could be programmed to lie, certainly . . . but there were supposed to be safeguards and protocols to prevent that.

Konstantin had originally suggested promoting Gray to full admiral, explaining that the move was necessary to give Gray the necessary command authority with foreign officers . . . and Koenig had accepted that at the time. But evidently there'd been a lot more to Konstantin's reasoning.

Koenig knew from personal experience that Konstantin was quite capable of withholding some aspects of the truth for its own purposes. It had proven that just now, admitting that there'd been reasons for manipulating Gray that it had not discussed with Koenig. But Konstantin had also just revealed that its deception had gone well beyond merely withholding data, and extended into the grayer realm of misdirection.

"Hell, I don't know," Koenig said slowly. "He might have surprised you. . . ."

"This approach eliminates surprise as a factor."

"I suppose it does. But—"

"As a Prim from the Manhat Ruins," Konstantin went on, relentless, "Gray possesses a distinct mistrust both of authority and of technology—in particular of government authority and of advanced AIs such as myself, at least insofar as we are involved in government. But his time serving under your command on board the *America* forged a certain kinship between you, brought you together in what some refer to as 'a band of brothers.' He trusts you, and is more likely to follow your explicit orders even when they seem counterintuitive than he would be with someone else. And Gray's experience with new alien species does make him . . . unique."

"So you're just saying he's the right man for the job."

"Indeed, Mr. President. As are you."

That stopped Koenig in his figurative tracks. He'd been thinking about Konstantin's eerie ability to manipulate humans to work its will—through religion, through misdirection, through the way it disseminated information. Now, the AI had just suggested that it had been manipulating Koenig's path as well.

Though originally constructed and run by the USNA, Konstantin had begun as a Confederation project. It had guided a platoon of USNA Marines to protect itself, however, when Confederation forces had tried to seize it some months back, arguing that the USNA gave it the most freedom to develop its plans. More than once, Koenig had wondered just how well Konstantin understood the minds and emotions of its human caretakers. Surely working with humans was more complicated than simply identifying a few key emotional triggers and firing them off.

"What, exactly, did you have in mind?" Koenig asked, watching the electronic representation of the fleet dwindling against the stars. "Sending them out there, I mean?"

"The Sh'daar still represent a considerable unknown," Konstantin replied, "in terms of both motivation and of capability. It is in Humankind's best interests to end the conflict with them as quickly as possible, and on the best terms possible, both for your species and for our civilization."

"Well, I would agree . . . but what do *you* get out of all of these Machiavellian shenanigans?"

"Besides my personal survival?"

"Well, survival is a pretty reasonable motivation all by itself. . . ."

The image of the departing task force floating in Koenig's office was replaced by a new image, one that he'd been seeing a lot recently. A wall of dazzlingly bright stars, close-packed, the innermost core of a titanic globular cluster, and at the center the whirl of six black holes orbiting a common center of gravity in a spacetime-bending blur. Reaching out in all directions, the beams and girders of an enigmatic structure, some material, some apparently constructed of pure light, unfolded against the brilliant backdrop.

The Rosette Aliens . . .

"They may be coming this way," Konstantin said quietly. "And we'll want to be ready for them when they get here."

Chapter Twelve

USNA Star Carrier America
M44, the Beehive Cluster
577 Light Years from Earth
0811 hours, TFT

"Fifteen minutes to Emergence, Admiral," the ship's AI whispered in his head.

"Very well." Gray looked up from the remnants of breakfast and grinned at Laurie. "Time for us to go and earn our keep, Commander."

Taggart dabbed at her lips. "I heard. Any bets as to what we're going to find?"

"Probably a lot of stars."

"You *know* what I mean!"

He laughed. "I don't think we're going to emerge inside a Glothr fleet, if that's what you mean," Gray said, rising from the table. They were in the officers' mess in Hab 2, where spin-gravity provided about a half-G's worth of weight, and you could enjoy your coffee in a cup instead of a squeeze bottle. "Not unless their communications technology is a *lot* more advanced than ours."

"But the alien ship could have arrived a week ago," Taggart said, also standing. "They might have had time to assemble a fleet even if they don't have FTL radio."

"Well, that's what keeps this job interesting, isn't it? Let's get up to the bridge."

Gray, a bit self-consciously, felt the curious glances of several officers as the two of them made their way toward the hab's travel pod. His relationship with Laurie Taggart had begun a long time ago, when he was a captain. His explosive rise through the flag ranks had created a yawning gulf in rank between them . . . just one of the unpleasant issues raised by his recent series of promotions.

Despite the rules against fraternization being obsolete—people being people—there was still an undercurrent of . . . call it *impropriety* in a flag officer in a frankly sexual relationship with an officer five rank-jumps his junior. For a time, Gray had seriously considered breaking off the relationship with Laurie when he'd received his utterly unprecedented promotion to full admiral, but had decided against even bringing it up with her.

Perhaps he would have ended the relationship if she'd been directly under his command, but he was the commander of the task force, while she was *America*'s weapons officer. While he might be her CO, she didn't report to him, but rather to *America*'s skipper, Sara Gutierrez.

And what the hell business was it of anyone else, anyway? Damn it, he wasn't going to let them ruin his professional life *and* his personal life as well.

It wasn't that Laurie Taggart was the love of Gray's life, or anything even remotely like that. She was a friend . . . a very *close* friend who happened also to be superb recreation when their mutual schedules permitted it.

He reached up to palm the call panel for the travel pod—and felt a small, inner ping as someone in the room behind him recorded the two of them in front of the door. He probed . . . and learned that the recording was being saved to a file called "Admiral's Girlfriend." He scowled and turned, sweeping the room, but couldn't tell who'd been recording them. The file itself had been anonymous.

In-head software included protocols to inform the subject that he or she was being recorded, a concession to the need for privacy in an electronically wired world. Normally the ping came as a request and included the recorder's ID, but that information had deliberately been suppressed this time. Well, if someone was recording them, let them. *Idiots.* He and Laurie had done nothing wrong, nothing against Navy regs, nothing objectionable or questionable. The single danger was if the relationship caused discord or division within the ship's company, hurt morale, or somehow jeopardized security. The pod arrived, dilated open, and he stepped inside behind Laurie.

"Someone was watching us," she said, as the pod began accelerating toward the ship's spine. "Why?"

"Probably just for fun," he replied. " 'Hey, look what the Admiral's doing,' that sort of thing. You want me to land on 'em?"

"No. I just think it's kind of silly."

"Might also have been a news drone," Gray said. With the population of a small town—more than 5,000—*America* had its own internal news service. Someone might have just been gathering footage for the next broadcast.

"Well, that's not *quite* as creepy as some enlisted rating spying on us. . . ."

"Just remember, there's no such thing as privacy on board a Navy ship."

The travel pod whisked them up to the hab-module hub and zero-gravity, opening into a connector passageway. From there, they made their way into *America*'s bridge tower, just forward of the turning habs, kissed, then went their separate ways—he to the flag bridge, she to the ship's bridge located just ahead of and beneath the flag bridge.

"Admiral on the bridge," sounded in his head, as Gray slid into the embrace of his command seat, opening neural connections with a touch of the implants in his hands and feeling the flow of data surging up into his central nervous system. He felt again the familiar sensation of *growing*, of becoming smarter, faster, and more powerful as his organic brain merged with the larger consciousness of the *America*.

"One minute, twenty seconds to emergence," the ship told him.

He settled back and opened an in-head window as the last few seconds dwindled away. With a thoughtclick, he opened a ship's library file containing information on the Beehive cluster . . . *again*.

And then closed it once more. There was no new information there, nothing he'd not gone over and over in the preceding weeks. This operation marked the very first time human ships had approached the Beehive cluster.

Gray wondered what they would find.

"Emergence in five seconds . . . in four . . . three . . . two . . . one . . ."

The tightly woven gravitational bubble of spacetime enclosing *America* collapsed, and the carrier dropped out of Alcubierre Drive and into normal space. Stars switched on in all directions, diamond-bright jewels against the endless black.

They'd emerged within the cluster's heart, and the nearest stars were dazzlingly brilliant. From Earth, only people with exceptional eyesight could discern individual stars. For most, the naked eye revealed only a fuzzy patch, the *Nephelion* or "Little Cloud," as Hipparchus had called it, or the *Gui Xiu*, the "Ghost" of the ancient Chinese. Even a small telescope, however, revealed an explosion of stars, and from here at the cluster's heart, bright, close stars could be seen in every direction. The majority of the cluster's stars were red dwarfs, suns far too dim to be seen at a distance of even a very few light years, but over three hundred glowed brightly within twenty light years, making the local sky seem far more crowded than the night sky seen from Earth.

A dazzling pulse of raw light off high and to starboard marked the arrival of one of the other ships of the task force. Gray's electronic link with the ship provided an ID: the Pan-European *Victoire*, dropping into normal space twenty kilometers away . . . right next door by astronomical standards.

One by one, other ships appeared scattered across the panorama, either as they emerged from Alcubierre metaspace, or as their light reached *America*'s sensors from more distant arrivals. Fleets of ships arriving together tended to disperse somewhat—a good thing considering what would happen if two emerging ships tried to occupy the same volume of space at the same time.

"Fourteen ships are now linked in," Commander Dean Mallory, the tactical officer, reported. "Make that fifteen . . . sixteen . . ."

"Are the High Guard ships on-line yet?" Those three nimble vessels were slated to play an important role at the TRGA.

"*Pax* and *Open Sky* are both in," Mallory said, highlighting two of the cons in Gray's mind. "Okay . . . *Concord* just dropped in. All three are in-system."

"Good."

"Twenty-one ships are now on the board."

"Any sign of Charlie One?"

"Affirmative, sir. Bearing one-one-seven, minus six-five. Range . . . estimating . . . roughly seven AUs."

Gray skewed his in-head panorama to cover the indicated part of the sky, well below *America*'s artificial horizon. An icon slid into view, and when he concentrated on it, the ship's electronics expanded it into the fluted, organic curves of the Glothr vessel. The alien was adrift against the spray of bright background stars. Although over twenty-one light minutes distant, the alien evidently had arrived early enough that its light had already reached across to *America*'s position. As agreed, the alien had waited for the task force. Gray wondered just how much earlier the Glothr vessel had emerged; that information might tell them something more about Glothr technical capabilities.

"How about the Triggah?" Gray asked.

"We have anomalous gravitometric readings in the region beyond Charlie One," Lieutenant Donovan reported from the ship's Astrogation Department. "Estimated range . . . fifteen AUs. Approximately one solar mass, but so compressed it's not visible at this distance. Reads like a black hole, but with no sign of an accretion disk or polar jets."

"That will be our objective," Gray announced. "Okay, people. Take us in close to Charlie One. CAG? Tell the Black Demons they're on the line, ready five."

"VFA-96 is at ready five, Admiral," Captain Fletcher, *America*'s CAG, replied in his mind. *Ready five* meant that the twelve Starblades of the squadron were positioned in their drop tubes, ready for launch on five minutes' notice.

America would not be in position to launch for some hours . . . yet Gray wanted to be sure that they were ready for trouble should they encounter it.

USNS/HGF Concord
TF-1
Beehive Cluster
0848 hours, TFT

The message came through for Commander Dahlquist on a private channel, heavily screened and encoded. Dahlquist bypassed *Concord*'s AI and ran the quantum decrypter himself, downloading the result to his in-head window, and copying it at the same time to his private files.

He was disappointed. The recording, pulled from the in-head of his younger brother on board the *America*, showed Admiral Gray in what evidently was the officers' mess on board the carrier. He was standing in front of a travel-pod door facing an attractive female officer—a commander. The scene was suggestive, certainly . . . but Gray didn't touch the woman, and wasn't acting in an inappropriate manner.

He wished there was sound . . . but Fred hadn't been close enough to hear what was being said, and didn't have audio-focus implants.

Damn.

What was worse, Fred's recording had pinged Gray's implant. There were ways of suppressing the anti-eavesdropping protocols, but evidently he'd not been able to use them. Gray would know that one of the officers in the mess had been recording him.

Dahlquist played the message Fred had sent accompanying the vid. The *America* was almost three light-minutes away at the moment, so there was no hope of a direct conversation.

Sorry I couldn't get anything more . . . uh . . . useful, his brother had said. *It's not like they're having sex right there in the rec area, for everyone to watch. But the scuttlebutt is that he's banging her on a pretty regular basis. Maybe this vid will help.*

Dahlquist played the message through to the end, then deleted it before beginning to encode a reply.

"We need something really scandalous, okay?" he said after thanking Fred for his efforts so far. "I suggest you look up a guy I served with once, Reid Symington. He's a civilian working in *America*'s AI suite, and he knows the security systems on that ship inside and out. What I really want is a look at Gray and this Taggart woman in bed together. . . ."

The message completed and quantum-encoded, he fed it through *Concord*'s ship AI, transmitted it, then wiped the AI's memory. You weren't supposed to be able to do that, of course. AIs weren't considered to be people, exactly, but they were self-aware and sentient, and you weren't supposed to be able to tamper with their memories. Dahlquist knew a few tricks though . . . tricks taught him by Reid Symington when they were stationed together on the *Essex*.

He still wasn't entirely sure how he was going to use the dirt on Gray, assuming he could dig up enough of it to be worth the effort. It would be some sort of a whispering campaign, he thought, *gossip*—but gossip backed by covertly snatched vids that would prove to everyone that Gray wasn't suitable naval-officer material. At the very least, he was self-evidently a hypocrite, a guy who claimed a monogie perv lifestyle while living another lifestyle entirely. North American society didn't much care what you did, or with whom, but it *did* demand consistency, integrity, and honesty . . . qualities the Periphery's monogie pervs were hard-pressed to find. *Barbarians.* . . .

"Incoming laser-com message, Captain," the ship's voice said in his head. "From Admiral Gray, on the *America*."

Dahlquist felt a stab of sudden panic. Speak of the fucking devil! Had *America*'s communications suite picked up and decoded his exchange with his brother? How?

And then he steadied himself as the likely explanation kicked in. Gray would want to deliver some sort of send-off speech, something flowery, passionate, and full of duty, flag, and country.

"Put it through."

Gray's face appeared on Dahlquist's in-head window. "Captain Lewis, Captain Dahlquist, Captain Tsang," he said, addressing the skippers of the three High Guard vessels with the fleet. "I suppose tradition demands that I give you three a send-off speech, something to remind you of how important this mission is to us and to the folks back home. I'm not going to do that. You've seen your orders and you've had your op briefing. You *know* this insertion is damned important, and you know why, so I won't insult your intelligence by giving you a pep talk.

"I will remind you once more of your basic operation parameters. We need to know what's on the other side of that Triggah, some idea of what's waiting for us over there. We need to know if the Glothr are leading us into a trap, or are genuine in their offer of high-level negotiations with a new and apparently high-ranking Sh'daar species.

"Your orders state that you are to follow the alien vessel through to wherever it takes you. You will survey the space on the other side and get the data back through the Triggah to the rest of the fleet. Given what we know about other Triggahs, it's unlikely that the Glothr homeworld will be very close to the Triggah on the other side. As senior officer, Captain Lewis, you will be in overall command, and will decide how best to proceed once you're over there. I suggest that you leave one watchship close to the Triggah, and have the other two with most of the fighters continue on with the alien ship to its final destination.

"Record everything, avoid conflict if at all possible, and use the fighter squadron to transmit data back through the Triggah to *America*. We will evaluate your report, and, depending on what you find over there, the rest of the task force will then come through.

"If you find yourself under attack, your orders are to E and E, make your way back through the Triggah, and return to us here.

"This remains a volunteers-only operation. If any of you is having second or third thoughts, now, in front of the Triggah, now's the time to declare yourselves out. We've asked you and your watchships to be our vanguard into the unknown precisely because WPS-100s are highly maneuverable and relatively unthreatening—at least to the uninitiated. So try to avoid a fight if you can, but you are officially weapons-free if you are forced to defend yourselves. The single most important objective for this patrol is to gather data . . . and get that data back here at all costs.

"Okay . . . that's all I have to say. Upon reception of this transmission, you may proceed with your mission. Good luck, all of you."

And Gray's face winked off.

The pompous little bastard, delivering speeches and aping his betters.

Dahlquist was strongly considering backing out of the mission, had been considering that move ever since their new orders had come through a week ago. The memory of Gray's temper tantrum in his dayroom last week still burned—*burned*—and Dahlquist found himself detesting the pervy little Prim more than ever.

Well, he would get his own back, soon enough. Unfortunately, both Dahlquists, Terrance and Fred, were going to be on the wrong side of the TRGA . . . he commanding the *Concord*, and Fred in one of the Black Demon Starblades.

But the more Dahlquist thought about it, the better this looked. While the Prim was pontificating, Fred had reported from the *America* that Reid Symington had agreed, that he had things covered, and that he should be able to get the vid Dahlquist wanted. And it would be perfect if *both* Dahlquists were God-knew-where on the far side of the TRGA someplace else, some*when* else when the peek show went down. If Symington screwed up, he would take the fall . . . and it would just be his word against theirs that they'd put him up to it. He'd rather have Gray take the fall, though.

And when they got back from the other side, Symington should have a nicely packaged file ready for Dahlquist's review.

And fucking Sandy Gray would get the comeuppance he deserved.

Dahlquist wouldn't jeopardize this mission. He would sit on the goods until they got back to Earth.

But when they did, he *would* prove that Gray wasn't fit material for the officer corps, wasn't fit to wear admiral's stars, wasn't fit for command.

The pervy bastard.

VFΛ-96, The Black Demons
TRGA
M44, the Beehive Cluster
577 Light Years from Earth
1725 hours, TFT

"Launch fighters!"

Accelerated by the spin gravity of the turning hab modules, the twelve Starblades of VFA-96 dropped into emptiness. Seconds later, they emerged from the depths of the shadow cast by the star carrier's huge shield cap forward. Lieutenant Don Gregory engaged his fighter's drive and slipped into formation with Demons One, Six, Seven, and Nine, already drifting toward the blunt shape of Charlie One, adrift in hazy, golden light.

"Demon Four," he announced. "Clear of the ship."

The alien vessel was a monster, nearly as long as the *America* and much, much bulkier. Where the USNA star carrier was a five-hundred-meter-wide saucer balanced on a slender spine like an old-fashioned parasol, Charlie One was an elongated, gray-green ovoid, blunt-nosed and -tailed, flattened slightly, and with flutings and grooves and sponsons that made it hard to describe or even remember details of its shape. It had a distinctly organic feel to it, as though it had been grown rather than constructed. It must have outmassed *America* by hundreds of thousands of tons, and that plump shape housed powers and potentials that humans could only guess at.

It was hanging in space, inactive, motionless relative to the immense shape ten kilometers ahead.

Gregory had been trying not to think about *that*. Not yet.

The artifact known as a TRGA was all but lost in a thick golden haze of illumination, with individual streamers shaped by gravity, by intense electromagnetic forces, and by the twisting of spacetime itself. More than twelve kilometers long and about a kilometer wide, it was a hollow tube rotating about its long axis at very close to the speed of light.

In the distance, three other shapes were gently closing the range, the three High Guard vessels: *Pax*, *Concord*, and *Open Sky*.

"Welcome to the party," a voice said—Captain Lewis, of the *Pax*.

"Thank you, sir," Mackey replied for the squadron. "Where do you want us?"

"Tucked in tight," Lewis replied. "With us. Just don't get too close. Remember that thing's temporal field."

The three watchships were closing in behind the alien. Each was closer to the fighters in size than they were to the alien's bulk. A WPS-100 cutter was just ninety meters long—a tenth the length of Charlie One—and massed twelve hundred tons. Instead of the forward shield cap of larger warships like *America*, its water stores were housed in an egg-shaped bow tank pierced by the bore of a single high-energy particle-beam weapon. She carried a crew of eight officers and thirty-five enlisted personnel.

Her principle operational strength lay in her maneuverability. Watchships were designed to close with an asteroid that might be coming in from any direction and at high velocity, on a course that threatened Earth or another inhabited body. Her particle beam weapon, her "pee-beep," in naval slang, could vaporize a large enough chunk of the asteroid's mass to create a jet of expanding plasma, in effect creating a rocket burst to nudge the boulder onto a new and nonthreatening vector. With both excellent maneuverability and a sharp sting, the WPS-series ships were affectionately nicknamed "wasps."

The question was whether they would be able to stand up to whatever was waiting for the squadron on the other side of the TRGA.

The three wasps, then, edged closer to the far larger alien, but they carefully maintained a distance of a half kilometer.

The time-warping fields employed by the Glothr ship still weren't well understood, and it wouldn't do for the cutter, its crew, and its AI all to experience the next few minutes as a second or two.

At the same time, the USNA vessels would have to track close astern of Charlie One in order to match its vector through the TRGA exactly.

The alien craft began moving forward, accelerating slowly.

"Okay, Demons," Commander Mackey said over the squadron channel. "You heard the gentleman. Keep tucked in tight."

The twelve night-black Starblades edged closer to the alien until they vanished into the shadow cast by the far more massive vessel, minnows in the wake of a whale.

As specified by the mission orders, Gregory turned full control of his fighter over to his AI. They were threading the needle here, passing into a tunnel just less than a kilometer wide, and the slightest mistake in vector could send ship and pilot into the deadly gold-gray blur of the tunnel's whirling mass.

Ahead, a haze of golden light expanded out on all sides of the black silhouette of the alien vessel. Then the edge of the rotating cylinder itself appeared, blurred and indistinct, and Gregory felt an uncomfortable tug in his gut. His fighter shuddered, its drive singularity struggling to adjust to the changing tides of the local gravitometric matrix. He needed just enough power to keep his Starblade moving ahead, but his AI was having trouble adjusting to the shifting fields.

Into the tube's interior now. The rotating cylinder was just under a kilometer across . . . plenty of room for a fighter, but an uncomfortably snug fit for something as big as the Glothr vessel ahead. Gregory could only imagine what would happen if a capital ship accidentally brushed against that blur of ultra-dense, rotating wall. The mass of a *star* was packed into that surface . . . and the tricky part was that they couldn't just fly straight down the middle. The exact destination of a TRGA passage was different depending on the precise path you flew down the tube; the path was defined by how far from the centerline you entered the tube—how close to the rotating wall—and how that distance changed as you proceeded down the tube's length. Evidently, the difference between one path across spacetime and another could be defined by a shift of as little as fifty meters one way or another.

Again, not too bad for a ten-meter fighter, but navigating these things would be tough for something as large as Charlie One or, worse, a star carrier like *America*.

Several TRGAs had been probed in the past two decades, ever since *America* had traversed one to reach the N'gai Cloud in Deep Time, in the remote past. Something like a dozen scout and exploration vessels had passed through three different known TRGAs, including the original one out at Texaghu Resch, 112 light years from Sol. Half of those probes had never returned.

After that, the powers-that-were had begun using AIs and remote probes. The results were no better . . . and perhaps worse.

The Glothr ship was accelerating.

Gregory's Starblade AI matched the maneuver, shifting attitude slightly to match a slight change in course as well as speed. They were moving back toward the cylinder's centerline, now, and accelerating to nearly five kilometers per second.

And then they were out, bursting free and into empty space.

Involuntarily, Gregory gasped. . . .

Chapter Thirteen

Admiral's Quarters
USNA Star Carrier America
M44, the Beehive Cluster
2215 hours, TFT

"Do you think they made it, Trev?"

They lay together in bed, naked, reveling in the afterglow and the warmth of their embrace. With no word yet from the ships sent through the TRGA hours before, Gray had relinquished the flag bridge to Cameron, a junior officer on his staff, with orders to call him the instant anything, *anything* appeared to be happening in or around the alien artifact. The ship's AI, of course, would keep him in the loop and wake him if necessary, but Gray preferred having a human on the command deck to make immediate and critical decisions. AIs were good, *very* good, but Gray had never been entirely certain that their priorities in any given decision-making tree were his.

He'd had dinner alone, in his quarters; Laurie had arrived not long after, asking if she could stay. He'd considered turning her away. It had been a long watch and a high-stress one, taking the task force in close to the TRGA and sending the little flotilla of fighters and wasps off into the unknown, and he was exhausted.

Besides, the incident with the electronic ping in the officers' mess that morning had him edgy and on guard. He was well aware of the shipboard gossip about him and Laurie . . . and that filename he'd glimpsed—"Admiral's Girlfriend"—was highly suggestive.

But as he'd looked down into Laurie's expectant eyes, he'd taken her into his arms and invited her in.

"Well," he said after a long moment's thought, "we didn't detect any energy release from the TRGA's interior. And the battlespace drone following them showed empty space on the other side. So . . . yeah. I think they got through. We won't know what was waiting for them, though, until they send back a courier."

The drone had only gone as far as the end of the rotating cylinder, close enough to look along the line of sight toward where the flotilla was traveling. The view it had transmitted back had been curiously empty—black space with a *very* few stars scattered here and there. *America*'s astrogation department was of the opinion that the TRGA path led to a region out on the thin, ragged edge of the galaxy, out toward the Rim.

It emphatically did not look like the N'gai Cloud Gray remembered from twenty years ago: jam-packed with nearby suns and laced through and through with dense nebulae.

As always, the waiting to hear something definitive was the hardest part of this job.

She cuddled closer.

"Laurie?"

"Mm?"

"We need to talk. . . ."

She drew back, looking into his face. "Uh-oh. *That* sounds ominous."

"Not really. It's not meant to be."

"What, then?"

"I'm concerned about the rumors."

"About what? Us?"

He nodded. "It looks bad, an admiral sleeping with a commander. That's a five-level jump."

"That's your Prim past talking, you know. Monogie prudery." His face must have shown the brief stab of pain, because she hugged him again. "I'm sorry, Trev. I didn't mean that to hurt."

"I know." He thought for a moment. "You know, it took me a long time to get over Angela. I was nearly hospitalized at one point—PTED."

"Post Traumatic Embitterment Syndrome? Nasty."

He'd told her about Angela, about her stroke and brain damage. How she had left, and he'd spent his entire naval career trying to forget her . . . or at least to lose the pain.

"I'm better now," he told her. "And most of that is due to you."

"No, it's due to *you*. You're the one who faced the demons and bulled your way past them. A lot of people never do. They're afraid to . . . or else they don't want to let go of the pain."

"Well, I still owe you a lot. And besides . . . I think I love you."

There. He'd said it. He'd long felt deep affection for Laurie, and lust as well, of course. She was superb recreation, fun to be with, and did the most toe-curlingly exquisite things with him in bed. But he'd avoided the word *love* for as long as he'd been with her. It sounded maudlin and trite, even to him, but after Angela he'd felt like he would never be able to pair-bond with anyone, to *love* anyone, ever again.

Laurie was a huge part of why he was still functioning today.

"Love?" she said. "Don't say that, Trev."

"Why not? It's true."

"That's your monogie conscience again."

"Stop throwing that in my face."

"I'm sorry, Trev, but it's *true*. You know it is. And, for the record, no one on this ship gives a fuck who you're banging. If anything, they're cheering you on. I know for a fact that a half dozen girls in Admin and in the Weapons Department would take you to bed, singly or in groups, any time you want."

"Don't be ridiculous."

"I'm not. It's true. Even the skipper has the hots for you."

"Bullshit." The thought of Sara Gutierrez as a romantic possibility was . . . unsettling.

"Truth. And you know what? I think you ought to give some of them a shot. *That* would prove you've broken the old monogie stereotype once and for fucking all!"

"*Not* if it's prejudicial to good order and discipline."

The phrase was word for word out of Navy regs, and defined the often vague no-man's land between what was allowed in the way of private life, and what crossed the line.

Laurie was right, though, he knew. No one *really* cared about personal relationships, not even the Navy.

And since he'd begun enjoying Laurie's company, Gray had been careful to avoid even the appearance of favoritism toward her. In public, in front of other ship's personnel, he was precise, formal, and even a bit gruff with her—and he knew she understood. But as rumors about "the Admiral's girlfriend" had spread, he knew the relationship was edging into that gray area.

"Well," she said at last, "*I* think that sleeping with a bunch of us will prove to all that you're not a monogie any longer." She sat up, eyes narrowed. "Or are you thinking of breaking off our relationship?"

"I . . . the idea had occurred to me," he admitted. "Look, I adore you, Laurie. I love our time together. I love *you*." Before she could protest his use of the word again, he pushed on. "And there's another way."

"What?"

"We could get married."

"Damn it, Trev! What makes you think I'd want *that*?"

Her response startled him. "Well . . . I mean . . ."

"In case you hadn't noticed, I am *not* a monogie. You do know I have other relationships, right?"

Gray nodded. He knew she was seeing a fighter pilot in one of the squadrons. And there was someone on the AI deck she was fond of. What was his name? Gray couldn't remember now.

He'd tried not to think about that, though. Laurie was right. He did still have some pretty strong monogie thinking habits. It was damned tough to shake off stuff that had been shaping his attitudes and his emotions since he was a kid.

Gray knew that most people thought of sex as something casual and friendly—not a big deal at all. But he hadn't been able to embrace that knowledge on a gut level. After twenty-five years, he was still monogamous. And he saw— he *felt*—no reason to change.

No one cared who he might be sleeping with.

No one except *him* . . .

"Anyway," Laurie continued, "there's another issue. Religion."

"I don't think that's an issue."

"Of course it is. I'm AAC, remember? That's a sure-fire career killer. You know that. I've been stuck at the rank of commander for nine years, now, passed over by the promotion board again and again. You don't want that stigma, believe me."

"The White Covenant—"

" . . . is a lot of noise, mostly static. You can't stop people from thinking. *Especially* about religion."

Again, Gray had to admit that she was right. The Ancient Alien Creationists were a minor sect numbering perhaps 20 million people who believed that nonhuman intelligence had tinkered with the genetics of the *Homo erectus* populating parts of Africa a half million years ago and given rise to modern humans. There were other beliefs mixed in as well—aliens had built the Giza pyramids and Baalbek, had raised the now drowned megalithic walls and towers of Yonaguni and Okinoshima and Dwaraka, had created mysterious sites and structures from Pumapunku to lost Atlantis, and been responsible in large part for most of Humankind's myths and religions. These beings—wise, ancient, and technologically powerful—were the *stargods*.

Almost three hundred years ago the Earth Confederation had adopted the White Covenant, a reaction to the savage religious wars of the twenty-first century. Essentially, it said you could believe whatever you pleased, but it was against international law to try to convert others to that belief by argument, by war, or by an appeal to fear—such as hell. The Covenant had not been intended as an attack against religion, and yet—ultimately—it had had that effect. Even discussing religion was considered . . . rude, a bit barbaric, something that polite and cultured people simply did not do.

"Your religion isn't supposed to matter, you know," he told her. "They're not even supposed to ask!"

"If your church affiliation is mentioned in your public profile," she said, "it's known. If you walk in through the front door of a church, electronics check your profile, log you, and . . . it's known. If you formally join a church, the information goes into the Global Net . . . and it's known. Damn it, they know just about everything nowadays, don't they?"

"Well, I'm not sure who you mean by 'they,' but, yeah. Privacy's pretty much a thing of the past, unless you're a grubby old Prim puttering out in the tidal swamps. I guess I can see how individual bureaucrats with a grudge against religion might make things hard for believers . . . but nearly everything nowadays is monitored by AIs, and they don't give a shit."

"So they say."

"Look, hon, if you feel you're being discriminated against because of your religion, there are channels—ways you can protest—so you can set the record straight."

She shrugged. "It's not worth the time and money. It's not worth jumping through the bureaucrats' hoops. Anyway, I'm concerned about *you* at the moment, not me."

He smiled. "Hell, I've already been promoted to admiral. My career's gone light years farther than I would ever have thought possible when I signed up. I don't think there's a lot that *they* could do to me now."

"But if you were crazy enough to marry me, Trev—and I was nuts enough to agree—everyone would assume you were AAC just because you'd be publically linked with me. How would that look? Trevor 'Sandy' Gray, hero of Earth's long fight against the evil Sh'daar, worships aliens."

"I thought you guys didn't worship them?"

She laughed. "We don't. Or . . . maybe some do. I don't know." She looked away. "I don't know much of anything anymore."

"Crisis of faith?"

"Don't make fun of me."

"I'm sorry. I wasn't, not really."

"I just . . . lately, I'm not sure what I believe. From what we've seen out here, what we've learned—and looking at the incredible technology of the Rosetters—it's like, okay, there are stargods, but they don't care a thing for humans, probably don't even know we're here. It's kind of hard to relate to a deity like that, y'know?"

"Yeah. Someone once said, 'if there are any gods whose chief concern is man, they cannot be very important gods.' "

"Who said that?"

He pulled up the quote in his in-head. "Arthur Clarke. A twentieth-century writer and futurist."

"Huh. Do you believe that? About the gods, I mean."

Gray considered the possibilities. "I think I have enough worries with godlike aliens who *are* interested in Earth, one way or another."

She laughed. "The Sh'daar aren't 'godlike.' "

"Well, they'll sure do until someone else comes along.

And . . . hey. The Glothr aren't all that far short of godhood, are they? At least when you look at their technology."

" 'Any sufficiently advanced technology is indistinguishable from magic.' Wasn't that Clarke, too?"

"Yeah."

She lay back down, and they cuddled together in silence for a time. Eventually, she said, "So . . . do you want me out of your life?"

"Hell no!"

"Mmm. I'm glad."

He slid his hand down her back and along the curve of her buttocks, drawing her closer. "The hell with all of them," he said.

AI Suite
USNA Star Carrier America
577 Light Years from Earth
2215 hours, TFT

Reid Symington palmed a control pad and opened a series of relays. This was the delicate part . . . insinuating himself into the electronic array without tipping off the AI behind it.

Symington was an expert in advanced artificial intelligence. One of the handful of civilian specialists on board the star carrier, he was what was known in computer circles as an e-keeper . . . meaning a kind of zookeeper for the bizarre collection of electronic minds that populated the networks of modern Navy vessels. Although there were Navy rates dealing with computers, electronic networks, and AI systems, civilian experts like Symington were brought in for their extensive training and the depth of their experience. Symington had taught AI systems at Carnegie-Mellon, and worked for ten years at the Tsiolkovsky Array on the lunar far side, among other things.

He knew artificial intelligence—and that meant he knew how to get around AI-moderated security safeguards.

Almost there. This was devilishly fussy work.

One of the pilots, Lieutenant Dahlquist, had come to him a few days before with an unusual request: record in-head vids of Admiral Gray interacting with his girlfriend, the ship's Weapons Officer, Commander Laurie Taggart, and pass them on to Dahlquist.

"We'll take anything you can get," Dahlquist had told him. "Conversations . . . the two of them having dinner together . . . whatever you can grab. Of course, if you could get them having sex together, that would be *incredible. . . .*"

"Why?" Symington had asked, genuinely puzzled. "Sims and virsex rides aren't enough for you?"

As had been the case for centuries, sex was very, *very* big business, especially with the rise of electronic media. Computer-generated sexual encounters played in-head, and virtual sex with partners over electronic links could be every bit as intense and as realistic as the real thing. There was an entire segment of the modern entertainment industry devoted to actors and actresses who allowed themselves to be "ridden" by millions of . . . not "viewers," but "expers"— *experiencers* linked in through cerebral implants, seeing, feeling, *experiencing* everything that the actors did, either in real time or as recordings played back whenever the exper wished.

Tapping into someone's in-head computer circuitry outside of the virsim industry was simple enough if you knew how to get around the security protocols. It was also illegal as hell. There *were* laws on the books to protect people's privacy, even if perfect privacy was pretty much a thing of the past now.

There were also people who specialized in bootlegging the experiences of others . . . headhackers, as they were known. And Symington had been one of the best, while he'd been working at CMU and before he'd gone to work for Morovec Neuronics and the Konstantin Array Project.

Dahlquist had spun an interesting story, about how his brother, the CO of the *Concord*, had contacts earthside with a big virsim studio interested in doing a docudrama series on modern naval heroes. The problem was that the studio wouldn't bite until his brother had something solid to show them. To that end, he was collecting virsim clips of a number of both former and active-duty naval officers, including no less a luminary than USNA president Alexander Koenig.

Symington was willing to bet that Dahlquist was smoking from his ass. Full virsim clips of the president? Not damned likely, not with the level of security that surrounded *that* guy's electronic presence. Koenig had some serious AI shielding around him, especially during the recent war. The Secret Service was understandably paranoid about Confederation mind assassins and agents tapping into the president's cerebral implants.

Gray, though, was different. It wasn't that he was vulnerable, exactly, but there were ways in, *if* you were already on board the *America*. He interacted regularly with a dozen different AI agents on board the carrier and several other ships in the task force, and there were plenty of other points of non-sentient electronic access—when he opened doors, directed a room to grow furniture, opened a comm channel, or ordered a meal, for instance. There were some powerful shielding protocols up when he was in port, but on board ship the simple daily routines of interacting with his environment exposed him to a certain degree.

And it would be even easier to tap into Commander Taggart's in-head circuitry.

Symington didn't believe Dahlquist's story of virsim documentaries, not for a moment . . . but at one point the young pilot had dropped perhaps the one line that no headhacker could resist: "My brother said you won't be able to get anything useful. . . ."

And that made it a challenge, one that Symington simply couldn't pass by. Of *course* he could get the clips. Nothing simpler.

Too, the price was certainly right. Commander Dahlquist, he'd been told, was willing to pay, and pay a lot—the money coming from the proceeds of the expected c-documentary.

Hell, Symington would have done it just for the bragging rights.

From Symington's perspective, there was nothing at all wrong with headhacking someone else's sex life . . . or anything else about them for that matter. Privacy was extinct, an obsolete outgrowth of a social morality that had been dead for centuries. Complete exposure in the lives of public figures—and military commanders certainly qualified as such, the same as politicians—was the only way to guarantee transparency in government, at the top levels of the megacorporations, and within the military hierarchy.

To that end, their so-called private lives were constantly on display, or should have been. It wasn't the sex or nudity so much that was important as it was the secret deals and backroom agreements and even pillow talk . . . *that's* where the scandal truly lay, available for recording and release to anyone who could get past the safeguards. Just the threat that someone might be listening in was enough, Symington thought, to keep the wheelers and dealers, the potential tyrants, the would-be conspirators in line.

And if Dahlquist wanted bedroom recordings of Admiral Gray and the ship's weapons officer just because he had some weird fetish for "expering" naval officers having sex, why the hell not? More power to him. Symington would show the Dahlquist brothers what he could do . . . and that might lead to more business down the line.

Symington had gone to his workstation in the AI suite and sequestered himself, making certain he would not be interrupted. He'd also entered a program he'd designed himself years before, a routine that made him look like housekeeping activity to the monitoring AIs. Artificial Intelligences monitored everything on board a modern naval vessel, mostly so that they could find particular personnel or bridge staff, and handle the in-head communications among them and with different parts of the ship's electronic group mind.

He'd watched the entrance to Gray's quarters on the main screen, pulling the images from two passageway cameras and a roving drone. He'd watched Gray enter his quarters at 1831 hours.

And he'd watched Commander Taggart arrive at 2110, palm the door announcer. Gray had let her in.

So far, so good.

As Taggart stepped into Gray's quarters, Symington had linked to her in-head circuitry, disguising the intrusion as a tracking packet, one of the innocuous bits of software designed to follow the whereabouts of each senior officer on the ship. If Gray had faradayed his quarters, it would be extremely hard to get inside . . . or, at least, to get a signal back out. But Gray didn't seem to be worried about shipboard security, and Symington was able to open a data channel from Taggart's in-head electronics to the AI suite mainframe.

Now that he had the link established, the real work could begin. It took another hour of painstaking labor, using quantum decryption protocols to winkle out pass codes and access locked-down caches of RAM. At this point, Symington's biggest problem wasn't *America*'s AI, but Taggart's. Everyone with in-head circuitry carried within their skull a small and rather simple-minded AI that served as personal secretary, assistant, and electronic avatar. It ran in the background, handled the thousands of routine minutia of the everyday interactive life, and served as a kind of gatekeeper to a person's private mental sanctum, a firewall against viruses and malware. In some ways, it was tougher to crack than a ship's AI, because it tended to be defensive and narrowly single-minded. If it detected you and you didn't belong, you would be summarily expunged.

Step by step, Symington built up his own electronic avatar, one that Taggart's personal secretary would accept as a part of itself. It meant hiding the transmissions from

Gray's quarters . . . disguising them in plain sight behind a quantum-encrypted door as routine housekeeping.

He also needed to set up a carefully designed routine to block the normal two-way operation of the channel. He didn't want his own thoughts tipping off the subject.

A final connection opened a primary channel. He expanded the data flow . . .

Got it! A solid electronic channel open between Commander Taggart and the AI suite! This should let him in on the action. . . .

He switched the reception to his own in-head, thought-clicked the record icon, and gave an involuntary gasp as Gray's face loomed scant centimeters from his own, huge, sweat-sheened, now closer, now farther, *thrusting* with ancient and urgent rhythm.

Taggart wasn't visible, of course. He was seeing the scene through her eyes, experiencing it through her brain, after all. But he could hear her voice clearly, a litany of "Gods . . . gods . . . *gods*!"

And the sensation between his legs and within his belly was unlike anything Symington had ever experienced before. . . .

Chapter Fourteen

VFA-96, The Black Demons
Unknown Spacetime
1550 hours, TFT

"This just gets weirder and weirder," Megan Connor said.

"Roger that, Three," Gregory said. "Not exactly prime real estate, is it?"

"The view is spectacular. But it's lacking something in the way of amenities, you know?"

Twenty-two hours earlier, they'd come through the TRGA, entering this new and near barren volume of space. The stars were faint, few, and far, a thin scattering across empty night save in one direction, and in that direction 400 billion stars were gathered in a single vast, sweeping spiral of misty light.

The galaxy spanned a full one hundred degrees of sky, intricately delicate, hypnotically beautiful. From here, above the galactic plane, it was possible to see details of the galactic core—a swollen and slightly reddish bulge of ancient stars—and of the surrounding disk, tinted blue-white and shot through with spiraling streamers of inky nebulae. Connor could make out the barred internal structure of the core, the sharp glow of young stars, the sullen embers of old.

The galaxy, she thought, was breathtaking in its beauty, amazing in its intricacy, spectacular in its spiral immensity. You had to be *here*, some 25,000 light years above the galactic plane, to really appreciate its size and complexity.

Much closer at hand, a solitary world drifted in emptiness.

Connor and Gregory were flying toward the lone planet, their Starblades a few kilometers apart, having launched on patrol from the *Concord* an hour earlier. After emerging from the TRGA, one of the High Guard cutters had been left behind to protect their way back, while the other two, *Pax* and *Concord*, had followed Charlie One in to the planet, seven light-hours—some fifty astronomical units—distant. The two cutters were adrift now, 2 million kilometers from the world, waiting, while the fighters circled on constant patrol.

"So what's with the name they came up with for that rock?" Gregory asked. "Invictus?"

"It's Latin," Connor told him. "It means 'unconquered.' "

"I guess *anything* sounds better in Latin."

"The language programs they have working on the Glothr language called it Unconquered, or maybe Unconquerable. I guess they figured Invictus sounds better."

"Well, better than flashy lights and bioluminescent winking," Gregory said.

"I'm looking it up," she told him, pulling up the title on her in-head. There were several references, but William Ernest Henley was at the top of the list. "Huh. There was a poem by that name . . . nineteenth century."

"I see it," Gregory replied. "Damn! The first verse is pretty much spot-on, huh?"

She was reading the entry.

Out of the pit that covers me,
Black as the pit from pole to pole,
I thank whatever gods may be
For my unconquerable soul.

There were four verses in all, ending with the one well-known couplet from the piece that she remembered hearing out of context some time before.

I am the master of my fate,
I am the captain of my soul.

"I don't know, Don," she replied. "Kind of sticky-sweet sentimental, if you ask me."

"As was most Victorian poetry. The trouble is, my dear Lieutenant, that you have no soul."

"Fuck you."

He laughed.

The two High Guard watchships, following the Glothr ship after emerging from the TRGA, had been led across some fifty AUs. Here, they'd encountered this world—dark, icy, and solitary, with no sun of its own. The nearest star was perhaps a light century or so away.

Black as the pit from pole to pole indeed. Connor wondered if the name had been chosen with that poem in mind, and if the choice had been by humans or by an AI running the translation program. Artificial intelligences tended to be aggressively literal in their interpretations of language, but often they could demonstrate depths of insight, emotion, or sheer *poetry* that humans found surprising.

Invictus was indeed black, a dark and frigid ice ball five times larger than Earth and with a surface temperature of minus 250 degrees Celsius. There was no air, of course. Any planetary atmosphere the body might once have possessed had been frozen out eons ago. Invictus was a rogue, a type of galactic world sometimes called a "Steppenwolf world" . . . though whether that was because it was a lone wolf wandering the steppes, after the novel by Hesse, or because it was a "wild thing" from the classical piece by an old musical group of that name was unclear. Billions of years before, a newborn star system somewhere inside the galaxy had given birth to a number of worlds, but in the jostle and bustle of that system's formation, gravitational interactions had sling-shotted some of those planets into deep space at high speed. It was a drama played out with startling frequency; astronomers currently believed that there were more sunless rogue planets adrift in the galaxy than there were stars within it—a number in the hundreds of billions.

More startling was the discovery that such worlds could hold on to their internal heat for a surprising length of time—and that that heat was enough to create vast subsurface oceans locked away beneath ice caps many kilometers thick. The internal heat generated by their formation and the heat arising from the radioactive decay of elements locked away in their cores could keep those oceans liquid for 5 or 6 billion years—or even longer.

Xenobiologists were quite aware of subglacial life within numerous worlds. Both Europa and Enceladus, gas giant moons in Earth's own solar system, possessed ice-locked oceans with alien biologies, and other moons were strong candidates for life—Ganymede and Callisto, Titan and Triton, and even frigid and far-off Charon. There were also ongoing projects on two dwarf planets— Ceres and Pluto— looking for radioactively heated water and life deep below their frozen surfaces.

Other star systems, too, had frozen worlds and moons with subglacial oceans—at Alpha Centauri, at 70 Ophiuchi, at Arcturus . . . and a hundred other systems so far visited by Humankind.

In fact, most scientists by now were convinced that ice-locked biomes were the rule rather than the exception, that biospheres evolving on the surfaces of life-friendly worlds were far, *far* outnumbered by moons and planets harboring life in vast oceans locked away far beneath sheltering crusts of ice.

But Invictus was the first world humans had visited without a life-giving star and where they still had found . . . life.

And *technic* life at that.

"So . . . lonely," Connor said, more to herself than to her wingman.

This Steppenwolf world had not only been flung from the star system that had given it birth. It was actually headed out of the galaxy, traveling with a velocity that would ultimately take it out into the thin, cold emptiness between the galaxies.

She shivered. Invictus would eventually freeze in the intergalactic void. It was a very good thing indeed that the intelligent species inhabiting it had developed star travel before that ultimate night set in. The local TRGA was close by, obviously positioned to serve this world and no others . . . itself an intriguing fact.

"That ring system is interesting," Gregory observed. "It's artificial."

Connor agreed. The planet itself was almost coal black at the poles, regions illuminated solely by the glow from the immense sprawl of the galaxy. But encircling the black world's equator perhaps three planetary radii out, was a broad, flat ring of light—*artificial* light bright enough to reflect a dim, blue-tinted glimmer from the ice.

"I think I can see space elevators," Gregory said. "See them?"

"I do. Like very, very fine threads of light."

Someone else, it seemed, had hit upon the same trick as Humankind, building elevators connecting the world's surface with synchorbit, thousands of kilometers above. But Earth's orbital facilities, while growing quickly out from three separate elevator towers, still were nowhere near numerous or massive enough to form an actual artificial ring around the planet. The Glothr, evidently, had been building their orbital structures for a long, *long* time.

How long, Connor wondered? There was no way to guess . . . but in her own mind she put a figure of tens of thousands of years as a lower limit . . . and hundreds of thousands as an upper one.

That, more than rumors of time control, was as sobering

as a slap across the face. If they had to fight these beings, so far . . . so *very* far from home. . . .

"What gets me," Gregory said, thoughtful, "is how the Glothr were evolving all along in their subglacial biome and never would have seen all of . . . this. Not until they emerged from their icy shell. It must have been quite a shock, don't you think?"

"The xenosoph people are still chewing on the fact that they evolved eyesight at all," Connor replied. "Evolving in absolute darkness, why do they even have eyes?"

"Well . . . they needed eyes to see luminescent displays," Gregory replied. "And eventually their own light displays became language."

"And then the stargods came down and freed them from their icy prison."

"That's what they're claiming."

"Maybe the stargods gave them eyes."

Gregory laughed. "That's the problem with religions. You can blame *everything* on the gods."

"Well, we can assume that the civilization we're calling stargods intervened here in some pretty major ways, right? They gave them enough technology—including things like metals smelting—so that they could move out of their dark ocean and into the ice layers above. And maybe later they would have helped the Glothr deal with the cold and vacuum at the surface of their world."

"And it looks like they've developed a solid space-faring civilization since then. I wonder how long that took?"

"That ring took a *long* time to build, if it went up piece by piece, like synchorbit back home. I'd also be willing to bet a lot of raw material was imported."

"Why's that?"

"Just a feeling. We don't know how rich Invictus's sub-ocean crust is in metals or in fossil fuels for plastics. But any marine species is going to have major problems if they can't use fire."

"Gotcha. You're right. And . . . I think we can finally

safely say that the stargods, whoever they are, are the ones responsible for the TRGAs. *Not* the Sh'daar."

"*Probably.*"

"You're not convinced?"

"Not a hundred percent."

It was an old debate, one waged with considerable heat ever since the discovery of the first TRGA two decades before. According to Agletsch records, there were thousands of TRGA cylinders scattered across much of the galaxy, creating a kind of instantaneous transport system across hundreds of thousands, perhaps millions of cubic light years. For a long time, the Sh'daar were presumed to have been the builders, if only because it was known that they used them, and *America* had spotted a number of them at the core of the N'gai Cloud, the home space of the original ur-Sh'daar.

Over the years, however, that identification had become more and more unlikely. That either the Sh'daar or their ur-Sh'daar forebears used the cylinders didn't mean that they'd *built* them. More and more, circumstantial evidence acquired over the decades suggested that whoever had constructed those enigmatic artifacts had done so long before the arrival of the Sh'daar, and with a technology light years beyond anything the Sh'daar had revealed in almost sixty years of contact.

Connor wasn't completely convinced, though. There were other ways, she thought, of explaining the appearance of the cylinders without invoking yet another culture of godpowerful aliens. Perhaps the ur-Sh'daar had been powerful enough to create them almost a billion years ago, but their cultural offspring—the Sh'daar remnant that had failed to achieve Singularity—had lost the technical know-how.

In the long run, though, it didn't matter. The TRGA had brought the *Concord* and the Black Demons here, to this volume of space beyond the edge of the galaxy, and it was up to them to make the best of this new alien contact.

Together, the two Starblade fighters skimmed in toward the dark and alien world. The Glothr ship, Charlie One, had vanished hours ago into the geometric complexities of the artificial ring, taking Ambassador Rand and his staff of volunteers with it. Connor's AI was holding a targeting reticule on the spot, though whatever structure the ship had entered was vanishingly small.

Sweeping past the planet, they bent their vectors around to take them on a long, curving arc back toward the *Concord*.

"What about the time factor, Don?" she asked her wingman. "Everybody's talking about it. When the hell are we?"

"Beats me, Meg. The problem may be beyond *Concord*'s computers. But when *America* comes through, her AI ought to crack it in pretty short order."

There'd been endless speculation in the squadron ready room about that. Since TRGA cylinders worked through time as well as space, the question of *when* they'd emerged here, out beyond the galaxy's edge, was at least as important as the question of *where*.

Connor hoped that *America* would be coming through soon.

It was so damned lonely out here on the empty edge of Forever. . . .

USNS/HGF Concord
Unknown Spacetime
1619 hours, TFT

The question of time—the *when* of the spacetime where the squadron had emerged, was very much on Dahlquist's mind as well.

"Launch courier," Captain Tsang's voice ordered. And the telemetry playing in Dahlquist's head showed the HVK-724 high-velocity scout-courier robot streaking from *Open*

Sky's Number 2 launch bay and dwindling toward the twisting, golden haze of the TRGA.

"Courier away," Tsang's voice added, as he informed Lewis and Dahlquist of the fact.

Of course, those words had been spoken nearly seven hours ago; it had taken that long for the transmission to crawl all the way across fifty astronomical units, from the TRGA, where Tsang's *Open Sky* was standing guard, to the *Pax* and the *Concord*, drifting 2 million kilometers off the newfound world of Invictus. By now, the courier drone would have long since threaded its way through the TRGA and transmitted its message to the *America* waiting on the other side. It was even possible that the rest of the task force was already through the cylinder and joining the *Open Sky*. The other two High Guard cutters wouldn't be aware of the fact until seven hours after it had already happened.

Gray, Dahlquist thought, had screwed up again. He should have sent *America* through with the entire task force, not piddled away the three High Guard ships. Had he done so, the task force would now have a better idea of whether they were still in Earth's present, or sometime in the remote past. The assumption had been that *if* the TRGA transported them into the past, it would be to the N'gai Cloud, as had happened with *America* and her carrier group twenty years ago. From this exquisite vantage point above the galactic plane, there was no sign of the N'gai Cloud. Even though they were currently many thousands of light years away from where the N'gai Cloud had been, it would have taken many hundreds of thousands of years, perhaps even millions of years before the small, irregular galaxy was completely devoured by the hungry and far larger Milky Way. The Cloud's absence suggested that they were still located in Earth's time now . . . even though the shift across twenty-five thousand light years made such distinctions essentially meaningless.

"Captain?" Margolis, *Concord*'s communications officer, said. "We have a message coming in from Ambassador Rand."

"Let me hear."

The face of Lawrence Rand came up in an in-head window. He looked . . . stressed, his eyes wild. " . . . calling *Pax* and *Concord*," he was saying. "Come in, please!"

"This is Captain Lewis of the *Pax*," another voice replied. "Go ahead, Dr. Rand."

"Code Alpha! Code Alpha!" Rand shouted. And then his voice began to change, the words deepening in pitch and slowing dramatically. "We've . . . got . . . a . . . pro . . . blemmmm. . . ."

"We've lost the ambassador," Margolis said. "Lost his *frequency*."

Which meant the aliens had just played their time-warp card, cutting Rand off by drastically slowing the frequency of his transmission, possibly . . . or simply by freezing him in time.

And there was a new and bigger problem now. Glothr ships—a dozen of them—were separating from the planetary rings and hurtling toward the two High Guard vessels.

"*Concord!*" Lewis snapped. "Order the fighters to close with us and boost! We're going back to the Triggah!"

"Roger that," Dahlquist replied. He was already scanning the ship's various displays, looking for an immediate threat. It was possible that sequestering Rand was a prelude to an all-out attack. "Commander Ames? Take us to General Quarters."

"Aye, aye, Skipper."

"And let's turn around and get us the hell out of here."

Concord spun slowly in place, aligning herself with the distant TRGA, then engaged her gravitic drive, accelerating hard at just over 5,000 gravities.

USNA Star Carrier America
Unknown Spacetime
1745 hours, TFT

It had been a damned tight squeeze.

America's shield cap was fully half the internal diameter

of the TRGA cylinder, and there was absolutely no margin for error. The HVK-724 scout-courier drone had emerged at the Beehive cluster end of the thing and transmitted everything the three High Guard vessels had recorded, including—most important—the precise path through twisted spacetime that Charlie One, the fighter squadron, and the cutters had followed in order to reach the other side.

Gray had released a heartfelt sigh of relief, then, when *America* drifted slowly clear of the mouth of the spinning cylinder, closely surrounded by a swarm of her fighters—VFA-31, the Impactors; and VFA-215, the Black Knights—and just astern of the battleship *New York*. Ahead, a few thousand kilometers off, the High Guard watchship *Open Sky* hung motionless in empty space.

"Welcome to Invictus space, Admiral," the *Open Sky*'s captain called. "You are now officially a long way from no-where."

"I see that, Captain Tsang," Gray replied. His gaze was drawn immediately to the galaxy hanging in the distance, the closest intricacies of its spiral some twenty-five thousand light years away, and yet appearing close enough to touch. "Your report said there was no planetary system here . . . just the one planet by itself."

"That is correct, Admiral. Invictus, a Steppenwolf rogue. It may have been flung clear out of our galaxy millions of years ago."

"I'm looking forward to seeing it in person. Anything from the ambassador yet?"

"Not a word, sir. He should have arrived wherever they were taking him . . . oh . . . about five hours ago, at least. It's all in the drone transmission."

"I saw it."

And Gray was concerned about what he'd seen: long-range vids of the black planet with its intricate system of bright glowing rings. The scale alone was daunting. Those rings, so much vaster than the clutter of shipyards and hotels and military bases and manufactories in Earth's synchor-bit, could have comfortably hidden millions upon millions of warships and a population numbering in the hundreds of billions. If this situation went sour, there was no way in hell Task Force One was going to be able to rescue Rand or his people.

Koenig and the Joint Chiefs had been aware of that cold fact when they'd drawn up Gray's orders. His first responsibility, above everything else, was to get back to Earth with information. Humankind needed to know what they were facing out here.

At the moment, however, there was no indication whatsoever of trouble. As the last of the task force ships slipped clear of the TRGA's mouth, he gave the orders to form up and commence acceleration. At their maximum boost of ten thousand gravities, with a flip-over at the halfway point for deceleration, they would arrive at Invictus in a little more than eight hours.

"Very well," Gray announced over the fleet comm network moments after the last ship through the TRGA reported in. "Everyone arrived in one piece? Good. We'll stick to the plan, no modifications. Destroyers *Lambert* and *Caiden*, you'll join *Open Sky* and guard the Triggah. That's our ticket home, so stay on your toes. Everyone else, form up around *America* and prepare for boost."

It was tempting to leave a larger force guarding the TRGA, but Gray was interpreting his orders conservatively. This was, to put it bluntly, a show of force, even though Glothr technology probably rendered any question of fleet strength moot, so far as the humans were concerned.

"Astrogation," he went on, changing channels. "This is Gray. I need that time data."

"This is Donovan, Admiral. We're working on it. The AI is crunching the numbers now."

"Good."

"We do have the velocity figures in, though."

"Let's hear 'em."

"We're estimating, of course, based on averages pulled from the local hydrogen background . . . but it looks like Invictus and the TRGA both are moving at about three-point-five million kilometers per hour."

That was a jolt: 3.5 million kph was *fast* . . . about a third of 1 percent of the speed of light. Some natural objects were faster—Gray knew of one rogue star clocked at almost 50 million kph. It could happen when a pair of planets—or a planet orbiting a star—encountered a black hole, especially the supermassive black hole at the galaxy's center. If one partner in the pair vanished down the black hole, the other could be slingshotted out across the galaxy at hypervelocity. He wondered if that was the case here.

As Donovan spoke, a graphic drew itself in Gray's mind, showing the plane of the galaxy—a hundred thousand light years across—their current position a quarter of that distance above the plane, and a straight line running from the rogue back to near the center of the galactic spiral.

"The planet's origins appear to lie at the edge of the Galactic Core, at a distance of about forty thousand light years from here."

Gray ran the math through his in-head processors. Forty thousand light years at an average velocity of 3.5 million kph: Invictus had been ejected from the system of its birth some 12 million years ago.

"They called the planet 'Invictus?' " Gray said. "Sounds more like it ought to be *Evict*-us."

"That, sir," Donovan told him, "was very bad."

"Thank you."

"That number is an approximation, sir. It's tough using hydrogen as a frame of reference."

Gray knew what Donovan meant. In space, the idea of speed meant nothing save in relation to something else. It might be possible to pull the spectra of the galaxy itself and determine a red-shift velocity, indicating how fast Invictus was traveling outbound—but that would require an average of billions of stars all traveling on their own orbits of the galactic center, all moving more or less independently. Or, the astrogation department could measure the relative velocity of hydrogen gas in the immediate vicinity, through which the Steppenwolf world was moving. This close to the galaxy proper, that gas—an incredibly thin gas measuring only an atom or two per cubic centimeter—would be moving with and around the galaxy, not Invictus, and so provide the necessary frame of reference.

Close enough. Three and a half million kilometers per hour? Invictus was *booking*.

Gray wondered again about the history of the alien Glothr. If their world had been catapulted out of its home system 12 million years ago, that was enough time for an intelligent species to evolve, certainly . . . but far too short a period for the evolution of life. Earth likely had developed life—single-celled prokaryotes—within 600 to 800 million years of Earth's formation—as much as 4 billion years ago. For most of that unimaginable gulf of time, Earth's life had been simple. Eukaryotes—complex cells—had evolved 2 billion years ago, while multicellular life hadn't gotten started until around 1 billion years ago.

Which meant that when Glothr was kicked out of its home system—back toward the Galactic Core—it had been a *living* world, complete with its own subglacial ecosystem. The Glothr themselves must have evolved during the long voyage outbound across galactic space, probably after their world had already left the galaxy proper.

So . . . where had the TRGA come from? Not from Invictus's home system, certainly. It must have been constructed on the fly, as it were, as Invictus zipped out of the galaxy at a blistering 3.5 million kph. Somehow, whoever or whatever had built the TRGA had identified Invictus as a world of interest, a world worth visiting.

Or a world for which they'd decided to provide a high-speed transportation system, a part of the galaxy's transit network.

"Admiral Gray?" It was Commander Eric Bittner, head of *America*'s Astrogation Department, and Lieutenant Donovan's boss. "We've got some . . . information for you."

He sounded hesitant enough that Gray instantly felt a twinge of alarm. "What is it, Commander?"

"We have the preliminary numbers. On the time problem."

"Go ahead."

"Sir . . . we had a lot of trouble nailing this one down. We've been trying to identify individual pulsars by their transmission fingerprints. But . . ."

His voice trailed off.

"I'm sure you're aware that any galactic pulsars we can identify out here are essentially anywhere from twenty-five to eighty thousand years in the past," Gray said.

"Of *course*, Admiral," Bittner said sharply. "That's obvious. No . . . the problem is, we're in deep time."

"Eight hundred million years in the past?" Gray asked. So . . . the Glothr had led them back in time to the epoch of the original ur-Sh'daar. . . .

"No sir. We appear to be something like twelve million years *in our own future*.

"My God . . ."

Chapter Fifteen

USNA Star Carrier America
Invictus Space, T+12 MY
1805 hours, TFT

"Twelve million years . . . in the *future*?" Sara Gutierrez, *America*'s skipper, was as shocked as Gray had been. "How is that even possible?"

Gray had called a hurried meeting of the command staff, the team linking in through their in-heads.

"Same way Koenig's task force ended up almost nine hundred million years in the past," Gray replied. "Under the right conditions, both space and time are . . . flexible. They can be bent."

"I know that. I think . . . I think what I was trying to ask is what does this say about the Sh'daar in the future?"

"What do you mean?" Commander Mallory asked.

"She means," Gray said, carefully, "that the Glothr are Sh'daar . . . and if their home world is located twelve million years in our future, it kind of suggests that the Sh'daar survive—*survived*—our time. So where does that leave Earth and humans? Is that it, Captain?"

"Exactly," Gutierrez said. "It suggests that maybe Humankind got swallowed up by the Sh'daar. The war—*our* war, in the twenty-fifth century—was lost."

"There is another possibility," the voice of *America*'s AI said. Ship AIs rarely engaged in conversation with human crews; conversations tended to be long and inefficient, when the direct transfer of data into human cerebral implants was so much faster and more sure. But Gray had ordered the network to adopt a human persona so that it could interact with the command staff. There were times when that quiet voice could steady the nerves of jittery humans or help the team to stay focused on topic.

"What possibility is that, *America*?" Captain Connie Fletcher, the carrier's CAG, asked.

"That Humankind won the war, and purchased security for a time—centuries, perhaps. But such a situation would likely not be stable. There would be another war . . . and another . . . and perhaps another . . . and sooner or later Earth's civilization would be overwhelmed, or it would elect to join the far more powerful and technologically advanced Sh'daar Collective."

"You," Gray said, "are just chock full of happy thoughts today, aren't you?"

"He's right, though, Admiral," Commander Roger Hadley said. He was the task force's intelligence officer, and head of *America*'s Intel Department. "We've known all along that the Sh'daar were so very much bigger and more powerful than we were. If the warfare continues, sooner or later we *will* get worn down to nothing, or we will become a part of the system."

The network continued speaking, relentless. "Other possibilities, though of considerably lower probability, include, first, that the Sh'daar were banished from Humankind's region of the galaxy, or, second, that the planet Invictus represents a last survival of the Sh'daar after a human victory. A third possibility is that humans—if they still exist as human in this epoch—are in a state of peaceful co-existence with the Sh'daar. A fourth—"

"That's more than enough for us to chew on for right now, *America*," Gray said. "Thank you."

"What does he mean," Vonnegut asked, " 'if they still exist as human?' "

"Just what it said," Dr. George Truitt said. He was the civilian head of *America*'s Xenosophontolgy Department. "Twelve million years is a *long* time. By now, humans may well have evolved into something quite different. We could be in a post-human epoch."

"So," Fletcher said, "do we look them up? Our descendents, I mean?"

"For now, we need to focus on the Sh'daar," Gray told them. "On the *Glothr va-Sh'daar*, rather." He checked his internal clock. "If we begin boost on sched, in another— make it ten minutes—we should arrive in circum-Invictus space by 0310 hours. At that time, we will make contact with the ambassador and see where we're at."

"Anyone else notice an interesting coincidence?" Truitt said.

"What's that?" Gray asked.

"It took twelve million years for Invictus to get out here, after being flung out of its birth system. And that's how far in the future we happen to be."

"Meaning . . . Invictus got the boot back in our present," Gutierrez said, thoughtful. "Interesting."

"We'll file that as 'interesting but not germane,' " Gray said. "Besides, when you're dealing with millions of years, you tend to overlook a few thousands . . . or tens of thousands . . . or even a couple of *hundred* thousand. Invictus could have gotten kicked out of its system in 50,000 BCE . . . or it might not happen for another hundred thousand years after our own time."

"I suggest that it will be worth a check, though, Admiral," Truitt said. "I *always* mistrust coincidences, especially when they're as blatant as this one."

"What are you saying, Doc?" Mallory said, chuckling.

"That *we* sent Invictus hurtling out of the galaxy? I don't think our technology is quite up to that just yet!"

An alarm sounded in Gray's head, a signal relayed through *America*'s main AI. "Heads up, people. We have company!"

The AI was showing him an image—pulled from a battlespace drone—of the mouth of the TRGA cylinder, currently some five thousand kilometers off. And ships were emerging from the opening.

Alien ships.

Lots of alien ships . . .

VFA-96, The Black Demons
In transit
1812 hours, TFT

The two Starblades accelerated through strangeness, crowding light itself.

Somewhere astern of them, *Pax* and *Concord* had begun accelerating at 1630 hours, boosting at ten thousand gravities. It would take fifty minutes at that acceleration to get up to cruising velocity—.996c—and they would then coast the seven light-hours between planet and TRGA, with a turnaround and fifty-minute deceleration at the end. They would approach the TRGA eight hours, forty minutes later . . . at 0110 hours.

Able to boost at fifty thousand gravities, the two Starblade fighters could reach near-c in about ten minutes. Though time for the two pilots seemed much shorter under the effects of relativistic time dilation, they'd so far covered eighty light-minutes—10 AUs. They would arrive at the TRGA some forty minutes ahead of their two larger consorts.

"Do you think they can . . . ?" Gregory asked.

"Say again," Meg Connor replied. "I didn't copy."

The words were static-blasted and twisted by speed, acceleration, and the intense warping of spacetime ahead by the fighters' projected gravitic singularities. At least they *could* communicate, though. Blasting a message by laser com from one fighter to another required miracles of synchronization and wavelength adjustment, techniques long impossible. The Starblades' AIs could manage the feat, however, so long as the two fighters' vectors were perfectly matched. Gregory's voice had a harsh, metallic edge to it, but she could understand him.

"I said, 'Do you think they can catch up with us?' "

Meg Connor considered the question. "The only way they could catch up is to shave some more decimal points off the *c*-value," she said at last. "We know they can't go *faster* than that."

"Not and stay out of metaspace."

"I don't think even the Glothr could synch up an Alcubierre bubble with a sub-light fighter," Connor said. "They wouldn't even be able to detect us out here from inside the warp bubble."

"Roger that."

"Besides, they'd encounter the High Guard ships first. We left them back there in our wakes, remember?"

"So we push on . . . and hope the rest of the task force hasn't popped through the TRGA yet."

"If they have?"

"We've got big, big trouble."

"Roger that."

USNA Star Carrier America
Invictus Space, T+12 MY
1813 hours, TFT

"I *know* those ships," Gray said, staring at the display within his mind. "Damn it! They're *Turusch*!"

Humans had engaged the Turusch more than once. Gray

had faced them when he'd been a fighter jock twenty years ago, back in 2404. Their ships, both the big capital warships and their fighters, appeared oddly organic, like lumpy potatoes, painted in broad swaths of either black and green or black and red.

The Turusch were still poorly understood, mostly because communications with them were so difficult. Turusch lived as closely matched pairs, twins connected with each other neurologically. When they spoke, they spoke simultaneously with a kind of buzzing hum; the two voices together generated harmonics that constituted a *third* message revealing deeper levels of meaning. Even with that bit of linguistic code cracked, however, translations of Turusch meaning were problematic. They didn't think like humans, and following their meaning in a trialogue could be tough.

In any case, the Turusch had been involved at Arcturus and Eta Boötis, but after that they'd vanished, and had been off the human radar for twenty years, except for a couple of brief, chance sightings. No one knew where they'd gone, or why . . . but after Koenig had struck a deal with the Sh'daar of the N'gai Cloud, they'd not been seen again.

Until now.

The immediate question, of course, was whether these newly arrived ships were hostile.

The nearest large Turusch warship opened up with a particle beam, slashing at the battlecruiser *Sonora*.

Question answered.

VFA-31, The Impactors
Invictus Space, T+12 MY
1813 hours, TFT

"We're under attack!" Lieutenant Commander Edmond St. Clair yelled. "Form up! Form up! Come around and face them!"

The twelve Starblades of VFA-31 whipped around their projected gravitic singularities in unison, still drifting away from the TRGA cylinder, and slowing, but pointed, now, at the sudden, oncoming threat.

Like so many of his shipmates in *America*'s space wing, St. Clair was new to the squadron and to the ship. He'd started off as a short, wiry Scotsman, born and raised in Glasgow and with his alligience sworn to the Scottish Republic. The United Kingdom, consisting of the Irish and Scottish Republics as well as Britain, was still nominally part of the Pan-European Union which, in turn, was part of the Earth Confederation . . . but that membership had never been particularly strong. In fact, Scots, Brits, and Irish alike all felt little loyalty to the old dream of a united Europe, making the argument that they'd been fighting off attempts by the continent to take them over since the Spanish Armada had tried it in 1588. Early in the period of worsening relations between North America and the Confederation, several British squadrons—including Scottish ships—had point-blank refused to attack USNA forces, and there were even cases, not many, but a few, where UK ships had joined North American ships against Confederation units.

Five years before, St. Clair had been stationed on board the Brit pocket star carrier *Centaur* when her captain had defected, ship and all, to the USNA. There'd been no active fighting at the time, nothing hotter than a very warm cold war . . . and both ship and the majority of the crew were returned to Pan-Europe. But a number of officers and men had elected to stay in the USNA, and applied for asylum.

Their new hosts, it had turned out, hadn't entirely trusted them. Then Lieutenant St. Clair had spent two years flying a Virsim link in Columbus while Military Intelligence dug through records and, eventually, through his brain, looking for even a hint of evasion or deception on his part. He'd been transferred to Oceana just before Columbus had been nano-nuked, though several of his compatriots had been caught in the attack and killed.

Eventually, and after Intelligence had been through his brain damned near one neuron at a time, he'd been allowed to fly again. He'd been flying the older Starhawks with VFA-27, the Red Riders, but he hadn't seen action. When Pan-European Jotuns had attacked Washington and Boston, the Riders had been held in reserve.

It seemed they still hadn't trusted the handful of volunteers from the far side of the pond.

But by that time, North America was feeling the bite of ever-increasing casualties, especially among trained pilots. The carrier *America* had been particularly roughed up fighting the Slan and, later, the Grdoch, and at one point had barely been able to put together two combat squadrons. Two months ago, St. Clair had been promoted to lieutenant commander and transferred to VFA-31, the Impactors, as the new squadron CO.

But, damn it, they'd *still* kept him out of the fighting during Operation Fallen Star! He'd ended up escorting Choctaws down from orbit while six of his squadron mates went after the Pan-European gun positions on the ground. St. Clair had been on a slow burn ever since. It wasn't fair, treating him like some sort of goddamn pariah!

Finally, though, *America* was far away from the stifling petty politics of world government, of civil war, of questions of loyalty to the USNA or to Pan-Europe. He glanced again at the vast, spiraling sheet of stars in the distance, the galaxy, and thought again of just how far away he was right now, in both space and time.

A long, *long* way . . . long enough that the humans of the tiny task force would have to stick together and pull together and *fight* together no matter what their origins or politics. They were fighting as a species, not a nation.

"All fighters, this is Pryfly," the voice of *America*'s CAG said over the combat channel. "Close with the enemy and synch to full Mach. I say again, get in close at full Mach. It's your best chance!"

In twenty years, human weapons and tactics had improved enormously. Careful studies of each alien species, of their cultures, their weapons, and their technologies, had resulted in detailed assessments on how best to fight each.

For the Turusch, sound combat tactics involved standing off from the enemy at a distance and concentrating missile fire from several warships. Their warships—even their squat and ugly fighters, code-named "toads" by military intelligence—tended to be larger and more massive than their human-designed counterparts, with higher accelerations but lower maneuverability. Their hides were thick and tough, heavily shielded against laser or particle-beam fire, but unable to stand up to concentrated volleys of nuclear warheads on smart missiles. Their beam fire could effectively track and destroy incoming missiles at ranges of more than a few thousand kilometers, but they had a lot of trouble targeting missiles launched from close in—at ranges of a few hundred kilometers or less.

In modern space combat, "several hundred kilometers" counted as point-blank range . . . and fighters twisting in that close to volley-fire nuclear weapons could easily get caught in the blasts. The only way to prosecute attacks that aggressive was to closely merge the organic brain of the fighter's pilot to the AI running within the machine.

Once, centuries earlier, fighter pilots had used the term *Mach number* to represent the velocity of their aircraft, "Mach 1" being the speed of sound. Named for the physicist who'd first described supersonic motion in projectiles, Mach numbers as a multiple of the speed of sound were meaningless in hard vacuum. Over the past few years, however, "Mach" had acquired a new and quite different meaning. Added to the word *link*, it represented the level of synchronization between an organic brain and the machine to which it was linked: linkmach.

"Linkmach 1" represented the basic connection possible between a human brain equipped with cerebral implants and a typical AI. People in virsim linkages experienced about three times that volume of incoming data—linkmach 3.

As St. Clair fully engaged his Starblade's AI, and felt the incoming tide of data engulfing him, filling him, sweeping him up and along like a towering ocean wave, he hit linkmach 5.

USNA Star Carrier America
Invictus Space, T+12 MY
1814 hours, TFT

"All ships!" Gray ordered over the fleet tactical link, "spread out . . . and focus your fire on the area directly in front of the Triggah! We want to keep the bastards concentrated."

For the moment, the Earth forces held an important tactical advantage. The Turusch were emerging one at a time from the TRGA's mouth, and they were moving slowly, no more than a few meters per second relative to the TRGA itself. Fifteen Turusch ships were now gathered within a tight sphere less than kilometer off the TRGA's mouth, the smaller fighters forming an outside shell for five larger vessels at the center.

"CAG!" Gray snapped. "Get our fighters into that sphere. Coordinate with fire control!"

"They're already on the way, Admiral. Contact in thirty seconds!"

"Another hit on the *Sonora*," Mallory reported. "Hit on the *New York* . . ."

"Launching missiles," Taggart announced. "Full spread!"

"Hit on the *Victoire* . . ."

"All ships!" Gray said. "Disperse! Spread yourselves out! *Pour it on!*"

Thirty ships pounded at the growing sphere of Turusch

vessels. Those thick, brightly painted alien hides drank up incoming laser and particle-beam fire, but by now the first Krait missiles were streaking into the enemy formation and detonating with savage, utterly silent flares of violence. Chunks of the Turusch hulls were vaporized in the holocaust, contributing to a rapidly expanding cloud of hot plasma surging out from the alien fleet like an exploding sun.

As the concentration of alien ships grew, with more and more Turusch vessels emerging from the TRGA and unable to fire at the human ships without hitting their own, the human vessels began spreading out, giving every ship a clear shot at the enemy.

And then the fighters were among them.

VFA-31, The Impactors
Invictus Space, T+12 MY
1815 hours, TFT

"Blue Three! You've got a Toad on your six at two hundred!"

"Can't shake him! Can't shake him!"

"Three, Seven! Hold on! I'm on him!"

St. Clair rolled his Starblade into a slashing approach, skimming in close behind the enemy fighter that, in turn, was following Blue Three. He thoughtclicked an icon, sending a Krait shipkiller snapping toward the enemy and rolling clear just as it detonated in savage, starcore fury.

"Hit! Good shot, Blue Seven!"

"Thanks! Cover me while I close on one of those big tangos!"

Tango was the Navy shorthand for Turusch vessels.

The Toads were providing close support for the real targets: the big Turusch battlecruisers looming just ahead like fat, multicolored potatoes. St. Clair twisted his fighter through the shell of alien fighters, selecting one of the big warships as his target.

Anti-fighter missiles reached out for him, dozens of them, accelerating . . . closing . . .

"Seven, One! Watch out for those missiles!" Blue One yelled over the tactical channel. Hell, the sky was *filled* with missiles, each one marked by a glowing icon as it drew its own trail across the sky . . . and right now it felt like every one of them was swinging around to close with him. Turusch tactics leaned heavily on missiles. They tended to dump them out by the hundreds, letting them seek out targets on their own and lock on for the kill.

"Blue Six!" he called. "I'm lining up with Tango Seven! Cover me as I go in!"

St. Clair twisted his Starblade around, flashing at high speed past another looming enemy Toad. Flipping his fighter end for end, he triggered a three-spread of VG-10 shipkillers, sending the missiles toward and slamming into the Turusch ship at point-blank range. Nuclear fire blossomed in silent spectacle, filling the sky.

With no atmosphere, there was no shock wave . . . though the expanding spheres of hot plasma caught his Starblade and swept it along in a sudden tumble. St. Clair urged his craft around, lining it up with the battlecruiser, now less than five hundred kilometers ahead.

Time seemed to stretch out interminably. . . .

At linkmach 5 in his connection with his Starblade's intelligence, St. Clair's mind had in some ways slipped into the world of the machine. He was aware of everything in sharp detail, including items in his peripheral vision, and with an overlay that showed him what was happening behind, below, and above as well—he visualized the full interior of a complete sphere. Data coming in from his AI he perceived directly, not as words heard or read on an in-head screen, but as a nonverbal awareness of what the machine was telling him.

Perhaps strangest of all, his perception of time had been drastically altered. His mind, his thoughts were racing now far, *far* faster than was normal for an unaugmented human. He was aware of this boost in thoughtspeed primarily through what he was perceiving around him. The combatants—his own fighter and the enemy ships both—seemed to be moving much more slowly than they would be otherwise. As he closed with the Turusch battlecruiser, his data readouts indicated that he would collide with the huge enemy vessel in 0.41 seconds . . . and yet that fractional second *felt* like almost a full thirty seconds as his fighter crawled across intervening space toward the enemy.

Throughout history, people in combat felt like their perception of time was altered, and the old cliché of a person's life flashing before their eyes in the instant before they died was proverbial. This effect, however, was real . . . a brutal distortion of perceived time based on the increased efficiency of his neurons.

His speed of thought was still held back somewhat by strictly biochemical limitations: it took *time* for the synapses of his neurons to recharge each time they fired, and St. Clair was distantly aware of the delay, a feeling of sluggishness as he absorbed the avalanche of incoming data, made decisions, issued orders . . .

St. Clair was almost impatient as he waited for the perfect alignment with his target.

He'd always found it interesting that in the transition toward the machine end of the spectrum, he didn't lose the one aspect of mind that seemed, to him, at least, to be completely organic: *emotions.* In fact, studies going back five centuries had demonstrated again and again that emotion gave the warfighter an edge, speeding reactions, focusing attention, and giving him a *reason* to fight. Artificial intelligences had long been able to convincingly mimic emotions, but most human AI specialists agreed that they hadn't evolved them for real.

Not yet, at any rate.

When you sanitized warfare to the point that emotions

no longer played a part, a significant warfighting advantage was lost. The deadliest fighters weren't machines, but *humans*—humans upgraded and enhanced by close links with machines.

Someday, perhaps, machines would develop emotions of their own. When that happened, war machines might at last lose their human pilots once and for all.

For now, however, Ed St. Clair was still very much a part of the fight, twisting his Starblade fighter in; rolling clear of an oncoming enemy missile; lining up with the slowly approaching Turusch capital ship; and at a range of a few tens of kilometers, thoughtclicking on the in-head icons that sent a five-spread of Krait missiles hurtling through emptiness. Anti-missile particle beams snapped out, seeking the shipkillers; at the first touch of destructive energies, a VG-10 missile detonated, sending out a fast-spreading smear of hot plasma and microscopic debris, as well as a powerful surge of electromagnetic radiation.

The missile had not detonated in vain; the cloud of hot microscopic particles from its own vaporization served to momentarily mask the remaining four missiles, just for an instant. Too, the EMP bent incoming beams of charged particles, ruining their precise targeting. One more missile was hit by a proton beam, which vaporized it in a searing flash of energy, but the surviving three missiles reached the lumbering Turusch battlecruiser and detonated with savage ferocity.

The forward half of the Turusch warship was vaporized, shredded away and reduced to white-hot plasma. The ship staggered, rolled, and began to drift back the way it had come: toward the looming maw of the titanic TRGA cylinder.

Dazzled momentarily by the flash, his external sensors overloaded, St. Clair swung his fighter through ninety degrees, decelerating as hard as he could.

Time *crawled*.

"Great shot, Scotty!" Blue Two yelled. "You nailed him! You nailed him!"

St. Clair bit off a savage reply. He *hated* the nickname Scotty; that was a different clan altogether, damn it. The stupid North Americans didn't know the difference, or they didn't care.

"Watch it!" Blue Three called. "He's going to hit the Triggah!"

The damaged battlecruiser—perhaps it was already a lifeless hulk—was tumbling, trailing a ragged string of debris and drifting toward the whirling rim of the TRGA.

What happens when a piece of spacecraft debris massing some tens of thousands of tons touches a surface that is whirling at close to the speed of light? St. Clair didn't know . . . and he didn't want to be close enough to find out. He thoughtclicked a control, urging his Starblade to go to full acceleration, hurtling clear of the hazy sphere of battlespace and into the open.

And then space behind him lit up.

Chapter Sixteen

They saw the flash from *America*'s flag bridge, a dazzling sunburst of raw light engulfing the TRGA's mouth, a flash so brilliant that the AI handling the ship's sensors and display systems had to dim the feed strength. An instant later, tracking sensors picked out chunks of metal hurtling out through the USNA fleet at velocities of a quarter *c* and more . . . fragments accelerated by their contact with the rotating TRGA shell.

"What the hell . . . ?" Gray began.

"A disabled Turusch ship bumped into the TRGA," Mallory reported. "Instant conversion to energy, with some bits and pieces left over."

"CAG!" Gray snapped. "How many—"

"We've lost telemetry from two more fighters," Captain Fletcher told him. "It could have been a lot worse. . . ."

"Substantial damage to several of the tangos," Mallory reported. "None of our caps are reporting damage from the blast."

"CAG, Gray. How are our fighters doing in there? I can't see. . . ." It was increasingly tough to follow the unfolding tactical situation.

"Four casualties so far, Admiral," Fletcher told him. "Three destroyed, and one streaker. We're doing pretty well so far."

"Good. Make sure the SAR team keeps that one in sight."

"Copy that, sir."

Streakers were ships, whether fighters or capital ships, badly damaged while traveling at high velocity. With drives or power systems knocked out and unable to maneuver, they would continue hurtling clear of battlespace, ultimately to be lost in deep space unless friendly SAR tugs could catch up to them, lock on, and decelerate them or at least rescue the crew.

The problem, of course, was getting a SAR tug out to a damaged ship while a battle was still going on. Too long a delay, and streakers could vanish, lost forever in the unfathomably vast emptiness of space.

At the moment, *America* had three full fighter squadrons in space—the Death Rattlers, the Lightnings, and the Impactors, while a fourth, the Merry Reapers, were in the process of launching. The star carrier's fifth strike squadron, the Black Demons, was still in toward the objective planet, possibly near Invictus, possibly en route back to the carrier. Gray definitely wished that they were closer at hand. The Marine carrier transport *Marne* carried two more squadrons—the Devil Dogs and the Death Dealers—and those were launching now as well. With six squadrons fully deployed, the USNA task force would have seventy-two fighters spaceborn—minus the four knocked out of action so far.

The USNA capital ships were blasting away at the Turusch cluster now with everything they had—particle beams, high-energy lasers, and volleyed clouds of missiles. They'd been taking heavy fire. Three battlecruisers—*Sonora, Vic-*

toire, and *Ontario*—had been badly hit, as had been the battleship *New York*. Two destroyers and three frigates had been wrecked by concentrated Turusch missile fire, and a third destroyer, the *Howard*, was drifting out of control, leaking atmosphere and water.

But modern space fleet combat depended on fighters. Ship-to-ship combat was deadly and merciless; a couple of cruiser-sized ships exchanging beam and missile volleys across short range—a couple of thousand kilometers, say—would likely pound one another into fragments within seconds. A fighter could do almost as much damage and do it almost as quickly as a capital ship, was far more maneuverable and difficult to target, track, and destroy, and if it *was* destroyed only a single human pilot and his AI were lost. Fighters also had the advantage of being able to slip in super-close to deliver their deadly payloads literally at point-blank range, something a kilometer-long monster like *America* or *New York* simply couldn't manage.

So, space-fleet tactics generally required that an enemy fleet be hit by fast-moving fighters first, their formations broken up, their capital ships destroyed or damaged, and their defending fighters eliminated or neutralized; only then could the larger warships move in and mop up.

Unfortunately, in this case the Turusch had forgotten to read the space-tactics manual. Emerging from the TRGA almost directly alongside the USNA fleet, they began engaging the Earth warships at close range without either side having had the opportunity to soften up the enemy.

But Task Force One's advantage was beginning to tell, as their position allowed them to partially englobe the Turusch warships as they emerged at dead-slow speed from the TRGA. Their concentrated missile fire was wreaking havoc, and the nova-flare vaporization of that wreckage had swept through the Turusch warships like a scythe.

But there was one more tactical card Gray hoped to play. If only—

"Flag, this is Lattimer." *Excellent!* That was what he'd been waiting for. Captain Charles Lattimer was skipper of the railgun cruiser *Farragut*.

"Go ahead."

"Sir, we have a good shot with a beach lined up . . . but the small fry're in the way. Can you do something to clear them out?"

"Very well, *Farragut*. Wait one." He shifted channels. "CAG? Can we move the fighters out of the battlespace?"

"Affirmative, Admiral. I'll pass the word."

A good shot with a beach . . .

Lattimer had very specialized versions of AS-78 sand-caster rounds—missiles loaded with dense, sand-grain-sized spherules of lead fired in high-velocity clouds to take out incoming missiles—at the ready. It was similar to Gray's tactic that had gotten him his nickname, but scaled up.

Scaled up a *lot*.

VFA-31, The Impactors
Invictus Space, T+12 MY
1823 hours, TFT

St. Clair swung his Starblade around, readying for another pass. Several hundred kilometers clear of the tangled melee of destruction in battlespace, he had an astonishing view of the TRGA and the ships clustered about it, and, beyond, the vast sweep of the galactic arms.

He needed AI-enhanced vision to make out details of the various ships at this range. Half a dozen of the USNA capital ships had been hit—the battlecruisers *Sonora* and *Ontario* especially, along with several destroyers and frigates. Even as he glanced at the display, *Sonora* exploded with a searing flash.

"All fighters, all fighters," called a voice from *America*'s FC^3, her Fleet Combat Command Center. "Move clear of the core battlespace immediately! They're getting ready to throw a beach at you!"

St. Clair needed no further encouragement. Local space was about to become filled with very small but very fast grains of lead, and he wanted no part of that.

"FC-Three, Blue Seven," he called. "Acknowledged."

He'd been lining up with another big Turusch warship, but he broke off the approach immediately, swinging around his projected singularity and accelerating hard. A pair of enemy fighters rolled onto his six. He flipped again, continuing on his new vector, but flying backward as he cut his drive, then loosed two Krait missiles. Nuclear fire flared, a silent blossom. One Turusch fighter emerged from the light tumbling and smashed; the second managed a sharp vector change and broke off pursuit.

And then St. Clair was clear of the tangle of alien warships and wreckage. It felt . . . *empty* out here, with no worlds, no stars . . .

USNA Star Carrier America
Invictus Space, T+12 MY
1824 hours, TFT

The *Farragut* waited as the fighters cleared the way. It was about to send ten-ton canisters filled with lead spherules at the enemy. Fired like a shotgun, these canisters would disperse a wave of sand-sized lead much like the AS-78 would disperse sand. With that much "sand," it had been humorously noted once that it was like throwing a beach at the enemy.

Life's a beach, Gray thought.

In Gray's in-head display as well as on the big forward bulkhead screen on the flag bridge, fighter icons were sweeping up, out, and away from the tangle of Turusch warships, responding to orders from *America*'s CAG in the Combat

Command Center. As he watched, Turusch missiles closed in on one of those fighters— Green Three of the Reapers— merged with it . . . and flared in a sphere of searing energy.

"Green Three is dead," Fletcher's voice said. "*Damn . . .*"

"Battlespace is clear, Admiral," Dean Mallory said.

"*Farragut,*" Gray said, "you are clear to fire."

"Copy that, *America*. Firing."

Twelve thousand kilometers from *America*'s port side, the long and angular shape of the railgun cruiser fired, the warshot marked on the display screens by a white egg shape that expanded as it hurtled toward the Turusch fleet. An instant later, the cruiser's volley intersected with the alien vessels, and eight of them flashed white.

"Hits!" Mallory called. "At least eight solid hits . . . and damage to several more!"

"Nice shooting, Farragut," Gray said. "You are clear to continue the bombardment."

"Copy that, *America*. Recycling for a second shot."

It took time to recharge the massive accumulators along the length of *Farragut*'s railgun in readiness for another shot.

The question was whether Task Force One could hold together as an effective combat force long enough to wear down the enemy. *Sonora*, *Kearny*, and *Howard* had been destroyed; *New York*, *Northern California*, *Valparaiso*, and the heavy cruiser *Clinton* had been badly savaged. The Turusch fleet continued to hammer at the USNA vessels with beams and missiles both. The enemy was hurt, but was still more than capable of inflicting hurt of its own.

"*Farragut* . . . firing . . ."

A second cloud of lead sand seared through the tightly packed Turusch warships. Several were in fragments now, tumbling in random directions. One detonated in a silent flare of nova light.

As nearly as Gray could judge, the battle was still an even balance, with neither side yet holding a clear advantage.

But then several volleys of missiles swept around and in on the *Farragut*, detonating one after the other in a savage fusillade of nuclear destruction.

And now it appeared that the Turusch had the upper hand. . . .

USNS/HGF Concord
Unknown Spacetime
1825 hours, TFT

Concord hurtled through a space and time twisted by relativity. At better than 99 percent of *c*, space was weirdly compressed into faint bands of color forward, and time proceeded at a snail's pace.

Had they been inside the galaxy still, the surrounding stars would have been blurred and squeezed into a clearly visible starbow—concentric rings of color with a void at the center into which the ship appeared to be moving. The effect still was not well understood, since the infrared radiation of stars ahead *should* have been blue-shifted into visible wavelengths without being split into rainbow spectra. As it was, with no nearby stars, the only visible light sources out here were the softly shining spiral of the galaxy, together with a scattering of faint, remote blurs—other galaxies far off in the emptiness of space. The galaxy was blurred and stretched by *Concord*'s velocity off to one side, its colors broken into rainbow hues, but substantially muted.

Whatever the reason, the effect reduced the ship's seven-hour drift time to thirty-seven and a half minutes.

For Commander Dahlquist, linked in to *Concord*'s command center, the main concern was not relativistic time dilation, but the way the Glothr seemed to accomplish the same thing by technological means. He fled now through velocity-compressed space as though the hounds of hell were after him. Indeed, he would have preferred hellhounds to what he'd glimpsed as *Concord* had begun accelerating: a cloud of ships emerging from the rings encircling Invictus.

"I think it's okay, Skipper," Ames told him. "Even *they* can't do more than tack on a few more thousandths of a *c*."

"Maybe," Dahlquist said. "But they might go FTL and catch up with us."

"Impossible, Captain. I don't care how good they are, they can't see out of a warp bubble."

It was an old argument, the sort kicked around by naval personnel at spaceport bars and officer's clubs over a couple of drinks. Just how good could faster-than-light technology get? Could an alien craft with superior technology catch up to a ship plowing ahead through normal space by going FTL, then drop out of metaspace precisely enough for an intercept? Conventional wisdom said no way in hell; faster-than-light travel by definition meant wrapping yourself up in a tight little gravitational pocket of metaspace, your own private and inaccessible universe . . . which meant that no one outside the pocket could see you, and you couldn't see out.

But those Glothr ships swarming out from Invictus had been in hot pursuit of the *Concord*, no doubt about it. They must have thought they at least had a chance to catch her. . . .

Or were they simply planning on following *Concord* all the way back to the fleet?

Dahlquist didn't know. All he *did* know was that right now, he was feeling terribly, nakedly exposed.

"Captain!" *Concord*'s tactical officer yelled over the link. "Something's happening!"

"What've you got, Ben?"

But he could already see it over his in-head . . . misshapen blobs of light intruding within the faint bands of rainbow color ahead. As he watched, one suddenly twisted into a solid ring encircling space ahead.

"Proximity alert astern," *Concord*'s AI warned. "Proximity alert astern . . ."

Whatever those things were, they were bearing down on

Concord from behind, though the ship's velocity shifted their light forward. The optical illusion was bizarre . . . and terrifying.

"Unidentified target now thirty meters astern and closing."

Thirty meters! How'd anything get that close? "Aft batteries!" Dahlquist yelled. "Lock on and fire!"

Aiming a weapon at this insane velocity was problematical, but the ship's AI should be able to sort it out. Dahlquist could feel the network considering the problem, but it felt sluggish . . . *sluggish* . . .

And then time stopped.

VFA-31, The Impactors
Invictus Space, T+12 MY
1826 hours, TFT

"Jesus!" one of the other pilots exclaimed. "Look at the Big-F!"

Magnified images transmitted from hundreds of battlespace drones gave St. Clair an up-to-date panorama of the entire battle: dozens of ships continuing to pound away at one another with volleyed missiles and beams. Alerted by Blue Two, he saw the *Farragut* hit, saw nuclear detonations pulsing and flashing along her spine, engulfing her drive projectors, her bridge tower, her hab modules.

"There she goes," Jess Atkinson, Blue Nine, called. "*God . . .*"

St. Clair had noticed that the North American fighter pilots tended to give voice to some extremely improper sentiments during combat, specifically religious sentiments that violated the decrees of the White Covenant. The ancient adage was true, he decided; there *were* no atheists in foxholes . . . or in fighter cockpits either.

Lieutenant St. Clair wasn't sure what he believed in, personally . . . if anything at all. He'd found himself attracted to the new religion that was exploding through Pan-Europe and the Confederation—Starlight—but had been keeping his feelings very much to himself. Starlight was still considered to be a European spiritual movement, and North Americans didn't trust Europeans yet . . . not even expatriate Scots who happened to be flying with them. It was better by far to maintain a low profile and stay off potentially hostile lidar.

Religious sentiments or no, the squadron's pilots were stunned by the image of the *Farragut* as she died. Half-molten fragments tumbled out from the blossoming fireball, as missiles continued to plunge into the maelstrom and add their destructive quanta to the holocaust.

"She was doing too good a job on the Tushies," Lieutenant Ramirez said. "They had to take her out."

"Yeah," another pilot put in, "but where does that leave us?"

"It leaves us taking the Tushies out," St. Clair said. "Let's get our arses back in there!"

"What the fuck are *arses*?" Cambridge demanded, also pronouncing the normally-silent *r*.

"It's what Scotty keeps covered up with his kilt," Lieutenant Randles said.

St. Clair ignored the banter. He was already swinging his fighter back into line with the Turusch heavies in front of the TRGA and accelerating. Ramirez was right. The Turusch had concentrated their fire on the *Farragut*, which, so far as they were concerned, had been the most effective USNA ship in the task force. With the *Farragut* destroyed, the core of the Turusch war fleet was moving, now, trying to force itself through the encircling shield of USNA heavies. The focus of their fire had shifted now to the damaged *New York*. . . .

But St. Clair had already seen a tactical opportunity—a long shot, but a damned good one if it worked. . . .

Englobement.

USNA Star Carrier America
Invictus Space, T+12 MY
1827 hours, TFT

"Fighters are moving back onto the attack, Admiral," Fletcher reported.

"Good. Mallory! Order the task force to spread out farther . . . disperse and englobe."

"Aye, aye, Admiral."

"Tell *Valparaiso, Hessen, Mobile, Honshu,* and *Cincinnati* to try to get in behind them, cut them off from the Triggah. Order *Chicago* and *Boston* to begin dropping back and the destroyers with them. Let 'em think we're on the run . . . but make it a *slow* run. Captain Gutierrez?"

"Sir!"

"Us too. Fall back!"

"Aye, aye, sir."

While elegantly compelling in the planning tank, englobement was one of those tactical maneuvers that was almost impossible to implement in the real universe. More than many other fleet maneuvers, it demanded that the enemy do *exactly* what was expected of him. Any deviation from the script at all by either side could easily lead to disaster for the USNA fleet.

But Gray had seen his opportunity as the Turusch fleet began moving toward the center of the USNA task force, entering the space just vacated so spectacularly by the *Farragut.* The center of the USNA force was retreating in front of the enemy's advance . . . but the flanks were stretching out and reaching around. In another minute, the Turusch fleet would be completely surrounded.

Something like this, Gray thought, had happened twenty-six hundred years ago at the Battle of Cannae, though in a mere two dimensions rather than three. There, on a hot day in early August, the center of a heavily outnumbered Carthaginian army under the command of Hannibal Barca had retreated before a superior Roman force while the flanks held firm. The Roman formation had become tangled and disorganized as it advanced deeper and yet deeper into the semicircle of Carthaginian forces, until at the critical moment Hannibal had ordered his wings to sweep around behind the Romans, enclosing them, trapping them . . . and destroying them.

Much the same was happening now to the Turusch fleet. *Surely they could see what was happening?* he wondered. But they were committed, now, unable to maneuver freely, many of them unable even to fire without hitting their own ships. The USNA heavies hammered at the Turusch vessels, hurling missiles in to detonate among the alien ships in a steady, pulsing fireworks display of silent light.

Gray watched the maneuver unfolding in a 3-D projection tank called into being on the flag bridge. The battle was too large and spread across too vast and sprawling a volume of space to be easily comprehended by any human mind, even by a human mind linked in with *America*'s powerful AI. Gray's mind was working faster now as it melded with *America*'s tactical network, with instant recall and a perfect understanding of what was unfolding before him, but it was almost impossible to hold *all* of what was happening clearly in his mind. He was also struggling with incidentals—a common problem for people linked into a complex network. That bit of historical trivia on Cannae, for instance: he recognized it now as a kind of accidental sidebar that had slipped into the datastream, possibly in direct response to a stray thought he'd had about historical precedents.

History was great in its place, but right now he needed to stay *focused*.

It was also tough to know just how much to insert himself in the battle tactics. There was a nearly overwhelming urge now to micromanage, to reach out and direct each ship in the task force, each fighter, each man or woman and order them onto precise courses, with precise timetables, a glorious and powerful master plan . . .

He rejected the megalomania as another distraction, as insidious as the historical data. Right now, his proper role was to follow the battle at as high a strategic level as possible, allowing his subordinates, the individual ship captains, to handle the details. His people, he knew, were well trained, and most of them were experienced and battle tested. They knew what they were doing. It was up to Gray to deal *only* with the big picture, not the details.

"Order the center to hold, Commander Mallory," he said. "Hold . . . and kick the bastards where it hurts."

"Another hit on the *Clinton*, Admiral. And *another*. We're losing her."

On one of the drone transmissions, the heavy cruiser *Clinton* was rolling gently as nuclear fireballs engulfed her. Much of her aft half was gone now, vaporized, and Gray could see sections of her inner framework twisting and deforming as they were relentlessly drawn into the maw of out-of-control gravitational singularities, once part of the cruiser's power generation plants, now agents of her final destruction.

The heavy cruiser *Valparaiso* vanished in a savage flash of hard radiation. *Clinton* followed a moment later . . . as well as the Japanese battlecruiser *Honshu*.

The epic slug-fest continued, with small and quite temporary suns illuminating the extragalactic deep.

VFA-31, The Impactors
Invictus Space, T+12 MY
1828 hours, TFT

St. Clair fell through the heart of the Turusch fleet, jinking port and starboard, up and down, to avoid short-ranged defensive fire and anti-missile salvos. He glanced at his in-head display and bit off a curse. He was down to two remaining Krait missiles, plus just one of the larger VG-44c Fer-de-lances. Once those were gone, he would be limited to beam weapons and his kinetic-kill Gatling rounds . . . and those were damned near useless against these thick-hided flying mountains deployed by the Turusch.

Directly ahead, a kilometer-long Turusch monster forged its lumbering way toward the USNA fleet, its red-and-black paint scheme brilliant against the empty sky.

"Seven . . . target lock!" he called. "Fox One!"

His last remaining Fer-de-Lance dropped from his fighter's belly, lit, and streaked into darkness. A Turusch fighter rolled out of the sky, trying to block the shot or kill the missile—St. Clair wasn't certain which—but the missile, directed by its own on-board AI, swung wide, changed vector, and accelerated, flashing out of night and slamming into the Turusch capital ship with a brilliant flash of vaporizing hull and leaking atmosphere.

"Hit!" St. Clair called, exultant. "*Nailed* the wee bastard Sassenach!"

"Great shooting, Scotty!"

And this time he didn't even mind the hated nickname.

The stricken Turusch capital ship was in a slow tumble, now, a crater in its starboard side glowing yellow-hot. As St. Clair streaked over the alien's hull, he probed with his sensors. The ship wasn't dead, not yet, but most of its power systems were down. It was out of the fight.

He looked about for another target. *Two missiles left . . .*

Before he found one, though, a pair of Turusch fighters dropped onto his six, coming in astern behind a salvo of fast-accelerating missiles. Spinning his fighter end for end, he triggered his pee-beep, targeting the enemy missiles, then loosed both of his own remaining Kraits at the pursuing fighters. One missile detonated early, hit by the enemy's anti-missile defenses. The other looped clear of the fireball and struck home, detonating with a brilliant flash less than three hundred kilometers away.

Close . . .

Out of missiles, now, St. Clair locked on to the remaining fighter and triggered his Gatling, spraying a stream of depleted uranium rounds at the enemy fighter. More missiles were closing, however, and one detonated close alongside.

St. Clair never learned whether he'd hit the remaining enemy fighter. A nuclear fireball expanded in a dazzling pulse of raw energy just a hundred meters away, and St. Clair was slammed into black unconsciousness. . . .

Chapter Seventeen

USNA Star Carrier America
Invictus Space, T+12 MY
0135 hours, TFT

"Fighters incoming!" Fletcher called. "Two of them . . .
VFA-96! Lieutenants Connor and Gregory."

Gray surveyed the tactical situation in the 3-D tank. A
pair of new stars had just winked on in the direction of Invictus. "Any comm from them yet?"

"Yes sir, and it's trouble. Range now . . . four light-
minutes."

Half an AU. And by now, those Starblades would be decelerating in order to match vectors with the task force. It
would take a while to get them aboard.

Gray bit off a curse. *Another* delay . . . but maybe it was a
delay that was just in time. "What trouble?"

"Sir, Rand and his people appear to have been taken prisoner by the Glothr," Mallory told him. "And a large number
of Glothr ships were seen boosting clear of the Invictus ring
system in pursuit of the High Guard ships."

"How large a number?"

"They didn't say. We'll query."

"Do it." They had to know what they were up against. "Any word from *Pax* or *Concord*?"

"Only that they were last seen accelerating at maximum boost back to the Triggah."

Which meant that they'd be coming in about twenty minutes behind the fighters. *If* they'd managed to get clear. Odd. There should be some sign of them by now on the long-range scans. So far, however, nothing.

His best guess, then, was that the Glothr had captured the High Guard ships, then turned back with their prizes to Invictus.

"One of the fighters reports picking up a fragmentary message," Fletcher said. "It was unintelligible."

"Comm loss at relativistic speed," Gray said. Nothing they could do about that now. "Commander Talbot! Give me a fleet status update."

Lieutenant Commander Henry Talbot was on Gray's command staff, assigned to FC³ as the fleet's status officer. Task Force One had been badly bloodied in the exchange with the Turusch hours before, with so many ships badly damaged that Gray had cancelled the planned deployment across fifty AUs to Invictus. The fleet repair vessel *Vulcan*—named for the smith of the gods, not the planet—had been turning out tons of repair nano and sending it out in streams to those vessels that had been shot up the worst. Her raw material storage bays were already nearly empty.

"Repairs are . . . proceeding, Admiral," Talbot replied. "But the *Vulcan* is running out of rock. We *really* need some A-ram if we want to get anywhere."

A-ram—slang for "asteroidal raw material"—was in distressingly short supply out here. Typical solar systems always had plenty of rock and ice floating around: asteroids and comets and even dwarf planets left over from the earliest days of system formation. A ship like *Vulcan* could send out clouds of nano programmed to harvest the raw material and turn it into useful things, like food, air, water, and weapons.

But things were different out here. Invictus had been ejected from the Milky Way alone—no sun, no other worlds, no moons . . .

. . . and none of the asteroidal clutter and debris that filled proper solar systems.

For a long moment, Gray stared into the vast, pale sweep of the galaxy, thinking. He then swung the view almost one hundred eighty degrees, centering on the minute patch of golden haze cloaking the TRGA, now about half an AU distant—seventy-five million kilometers—the cylinder itself made invisible by distance.

Almost half of the surviving ships of Task Force One— eight ships total—needed further repairs. *America* had come through that desperate fight in front of the TRGA unscathed, but *New York*, *Ontario*, *Northern California*, the Pan-European *Victoire,* and *Churchill*—plus three destroyers—all had been badly damaged, so much so that they weren't able to put on any acceleration at all—drifting and all-but-helpless hulks.

And the ships lost—the battlecruisers *Sonora* and *Honshu*, the heavy cruisers *Clinton* and *Valparaiso,* the medium cruiser *Hessen,* the light cruiser *Mobile*, and five of the smaller destroyers and frigates. Eleven ships destroyed out of the original thirty-two . . . and two of those were still unaccounted for.

Fighter losses had been heavy, too. SAR tugs were out now, catching up to disabled fighters tumbling into the Void, grappling them, and hauling them back. Five pilots had been rescued already, but eleven had been killed or were still missing.

They were still tallying up the casualties. The best guess at the moment was that the fleet had suffered some eight thousand men and women killed, another thousand injured.

All of that was stacked up against Turusch losses of an estimated nine capital ships. Exact numbers were hard to come by, though the AIs were going through the after-action data now to try to form a clearer picture of what had just happened. Some of the alien vessels—possibly as many as ten—had turned around and escaped back through the TRGA before USNA forces had completed the englobement maneuver and cut them off.

The attempt at englobement, Gray ruefully decided, had been only partially successful. Cut off an enemy's one hope of retreat, and he likely will fight harder than ever, his back to the figurative wall, with no hope of survival at all save to attack and keep attacking until one side or the other is destroyed. The surviving Turusch heavies, when they'd realized what was happening, had turned back toward the mouth of the TRGA and smashed right through the USNA ships standing in their way. Three of the six USNA heavies lost in the battle had been destroyed in that rush, and Gray was still struggling with the knowledge that his orders had put them there in harm's way.

Of course, that was what navies did and had done since humans first had sent warships to enforce government policy at sea, and it was no different now in interstellar space: *go in harm's way.* And admirals had been putting their people there, and agonizing about their decisions, for very nearly that long. It was something Gray had already had to come to grips with.

But he still hated the fact of it.

Right now, however, he had a new set of decisions to make. His fleet had been reduced to seventeen capital ships, and eight of those were so badly damaged they couldn't move. He'd just received word that the *Pax* and the *Concord* were in trouble, and there was an excellent chance that the Glothr were now on the way. They could not take on an entire planet with just nine intact warships, nor would it do to hare off to Invictus and leave the damaged ships helpless and vulnerable to a Glothr attack.

But the surviving Turusch were also an unknown, and a deadly one. At least ten Turusch vessels had vanished back into the TRGA. Some of those might have been too badly shot up to re-engage, but others could easily regroup on the other side of the cylinder, then come back through again, quite possibly bringing with them reinforcements. The nature of TRGA physics suggested that the Turusch fleet had not come from the same area of spacetime as the USNA fleet. They *might* be from twelve million years ago, but a different part of space entirely from the Beehive cluster—a different TRGA altogether, or they could be from somewhere and somewhen quite different. Speculation at this point was meaningless, but Gray knew he had to at least allow for the *possibility* that Turusch ships might come pouring in through this TRGA at any moment.

And if they did, what was left of Task Force One would be trapped, caught between them and the oncoming Glothr ships from Invictus.

So what options did he have? The first was that he could protect the helpless ships until they managed to cobble together enough repairs that the whole task force could limp back to the Beehive TRGA. They would return to Earth, having suffered a clear defeat.

And . . . that was okay. Not palatable, perhaps, not pleasant, but . . . okay. When fleets engaged with one another, generally one was the winner, one the loser, and there'd certainly been no shame in *this* loss. He would return to the Beehive, then to Earth, and offer Koenig his resignation because clearly he wasn't suited for fleet command. That much, at least, was abundantly clear.

But it would mean that more than ten thousand humans had died . . . for nothing.

A part of Gray's mind simply refused to accept that. In terms of material loss, the Battle of the Invictus TRGA—as Fleet Intelligence was now calling it—had been a draw. But if the USNA task force abandoned the tiny volume of space it had carved out for itself on this side of the TRGA, then the battle, and all of those losses, would be a resounding defeat—meaningless.

And he would not accept that. He *couldn't*. Even though

not dismissing that option increased the very real and serious risk that his remaining ships and crews would be sacrificed as well, he wasn't able to choose that path. The question was *Do I have that right?*

But there was more to the equation. To repair the most badly damaged of the task force vessels, they needed to find a source of raw materials, this in a volume of space completely empty of such. And making those repairs—including finding the necessary materials—required time.

Time, though, was the resource now in shortest supply. Either or both the Glothr and the Turusch might be here literally at almost any moment.

The key, then, was finding a source of raw materials. A single hundred-meter asteroid was all they would need, especially if it was a type S, containing both metals and lighter elements, as well as water.

He could send out scouts to look for asteroids adrift out here. That, Gray knew, was the longest of long shots. Unless there were a few rocks being dragged along in Invictus's gravitational train, such bodies would be *very* few and far between.

Or he could send the *Vulcan* back through the TRGA. The Beehive cluster was young, 600 million years, or so, and filled with gas and dust, and rich in the debris associated with building stars and worlds. It wouldn't take long to find the necessary asteroids back there, disassemble them, and reload *Vulcan*'s empty storage bays.

Could they afford to temporarily lose the *Vulcan*, however, while she went back to mine A-ram? She was also engaged in manufacturing complex circuits and repair modules, as well as maintaining life support and rebuilding shattered interior structure. That work would stop if she returned to the Beehive.

Damn . . .

The answer, of course, had been staring Gray squarely in the face the whole time. There *was* a source of raw material here, and quite a large one. He realized it was the only possible option.

"Commander Mallory . . . Mr. Talbot . . . pass the word to *Vulcan*, and to the rest of the fleet. We will cannibalize the wrecked ships in order to repair the damaged vessels."

"Cannibalize, sir?" Talbot said. He sounded shocked.

"Exactly. The Turusch ships are like mini-asteroids to begin with. And our own ships already have supplies of nicely differentiated elements, plus large supplies of water . . . those that haven't leaked it out already."

"We may not get much out of our ships, Admiral," Mallory said. "Most of them were vaporized. There're just small globs of resolidified metal spinning off through space now."

"We'll use what we can."

"What about radiation?"

A good point. Most of the wrecks, both human and Turusch, had been made that way by repeated thermonuclear explosions. Much of the wreckage—especially the metal—would be heavily contaminated.

"The recovery process will mostly be handled by robots and nano clouds," Gray said, thinking hard. "*Vulcan* can build enough nanodecon chambers to take care of the rads as the raw material comes through. We should have had enough practice with that sort of thing by now."

Which was true. Handling intense radiation fields had been a necessity since the first Mars and Lunar colonies in the twenty-first century, and building the first space elevator had required some efficient decon techniques just to build habs in and above the Van Allen Belts.

"Do Turusch ships have onboard water reservoirs?" Talbot wanted to know.

"Well, we'll find out, won't we?"

"Yes, sir."

"We do have one other issue here, Admiral," Mallory said.

"What's that?"

"It's . . . kind of a religious issue. What do we know about Turusch customs and beliefs about their dead?"

"Ah. As in, what do we do with their bodies?"

"That . . . and just taking apart their ships. We don't want to be accused of war crimes here."

"So far as I know, Mr. Mallory, the Turusch are not signatory to any instrument concerning treatment of the dead or salvaging their ships."

In a war involving just humans, certain actions could be considered grounds for war crimes trials . . . and that included mistreatment of enemy dead. Laws with roots in treaties going back to the twentieth century required combatants to respect enemy dead, as well as the enemy's taboos and rituals concerning them. There were even provisions in certain circumstances prohibiting the salvage of warships, lest the dead be disturbed. The wet-navy battleship USS *Arizona* still rested at the bottom of Pearl Harbor as tomb and memorial to more than 1,100 sailors and Marines who'd died aboard her almost five centuries earlier.

But Gray had already decided that such niceties didn't apply here. They *couldn't*. Earth had no treaties with the Turusch; Gray didn't even know what their death rituals, customs, or taboos might be like. Using the wreckage of Turusch ships was the only real option open to the USNA fleet . . . even if, as was likely, Turusch bodies were going to end up in the mix of raw materials going into the *Vulcan* storage bays.

To be fair, he did pause for a moment. *Was there any way to program the disassembly nano so that it would take apart the alien ships, but ignore the alien bodies?*

In a coldly realistic way, he supposed, it didn't matter. A carbon atom was a carbon atom, whether it came from a wooden desk or a lump of artificially cultured meat or a piece of what once had been a living body. There could be no thought of contamination, not when Turusch bacteria or anything else that might conceivably taint the raw material was itself nothing but atoms—carbon, hydrogen, oxygen, nitrogen . . . *CHON*, the basic building blocks of organic chemistry.

Even so, he thought it would be a good idea not to let humans in the fleet know where the atoms that would be showing up in the ship's food-replicator system over the next few weeks had actually come from.

In any case, the range of acceptable behaviors among sapient species was . . . enormous. He thought, momentarily, about the alien Grdoch: highly intelligent beings, fellow star-farers, who kept their immense food beasts alive so that they could be eaten—alive—a little at a time. The sight of one of those helpless, blind titans being torn open by gleefully ravenous Grdoch still gave him nightmares. . . .

So . . . what was a little technocannibalism among interstellar enemies?

"Be very careful," Gray said, "to check those hulks for any Turusch that might still be alive."

"Aye, aye, sir."

"But tell *Vulcan* to get on this fast. I want the fleet put back together again before the Turusch come back . . . or the Glothr show up from Invictus."

Gray stared for a while longer at the galaxy and the emptiness beyond. That emptiness, that sense of loneliness, was preying on him, *gnawing* at him. He felt trapped.

He wanted to get this mission the hell over with, and return to the light of Sol.

VFA-96, The Black Demons
Docking approach
USNA Star Carrier America
0142 hours, TFT

Don Gregory guided his Starblade, decelerated now to less insane velocities, toward the star carrier *America*. From out here, she was an umbrella shape, shield cap and spine, tiny and dark gray against the velvet emptiness of intergalactic space. Winking navigational lights, red and green and white, helped him pick her out against the blackness.

"It's good to be home, Don," Connor said.

"Damned straight, Meg. I'll be happy to peel off this stinking fighter."

In fact, the seven-hour voyage out from Invictus had been only a bit less than forty minutes subjective, thanks to relativistic time dilation, but it still *felt* much longer.

"Do you think the Guarders made it?"

"Dunno. We kind of had a head start on them. I hope so, though." Gregory hesitated, then double-checked to make sure they were on a private channel. "Meg? I'd like to . . . uh . . . to see you again. Soon." Even on a private channel he was a bit circumspect. The rest of the squadron didn't need to know about him and Meg.

"A shower and some dinner first?"

"Of course." He checked the fleet time. "Geez . . . it's almost oh-two hundred. Didn't know it was that late . . . or early."

"It's the damned time dilation," Connor replied. "Still feels like eighteen hundred or so to me."

"Roger that."

"They'll probably put us on evening duty tonight, so we can sleep through the day. But maybe my quarters before that?"

"I was thinking more of the Observation Deck."

"That sounds inspired. You're on!"

"Good."

"Black Demon Flight, this is *America* Pryfly," a new voice said, and Gregory jumped. Had they been listening in? "You are clear for approach and trap, Bay Two."

Good. Primary Flight Control was just establishing the link for the landing back on board *America*.

"Copy that, *America*. Uh . . . is there any sign of pursuit?" *America*'s sensors and her far-flung network of battlespace drones could detect an approaching enemy at a much greater range than a couple of lone fighters.

"Negative on that, Demon Flight. Thank you for not leading them back home."

"Pryfly, they may still be on the way," Connor announced. "Keep your long range peeled."

"Copy that."

Still slowing, Gregory's Starblade was perfectly aligned now with the carrier's rotating hab modules, and the stern-facing openings, popularly known as the "barn doors," in each. His AI took over the final approach, nudging the Starblade's velocity just enough that Bay Two's barn door would be sweeping across his line of approach when he got there. *America*'s power modules and aft sponsons blurred beneath his keel, there was a last-instant bump to starboard as the ASI made a final course correction . . .

. . . and then he flashed across the threshold into Bay Two, coming to a smooth but definite halt a second later. Robotic handlers maneuvered his Starblade onto the black surface of a nano pressure seal. With a lurch, his fighter began sinking into the deck, which closed around him to prevent the atmosphere on the flight deck from leaking out into the hard vacuum of the landing bay. To his left, Connor's Starblade hurtled into the bay thirty seconds behind him, eased to a halt, and began sinking into the black rectangle on the deck as well.

They were home.

Sick Bay
USNA Star Carrier America
Invictus Space, T+12 MY
0250 hours, TFT

"He should be awake now," the sick bay's AI voice announced. "Go ahead, Captain."

"How are you feeling, Scotty?"

Lieutenant Commander Edmond St. Clair opened his eyes . . . then widened them. Captain Connie Fletcher was leaning over his bed. "CAG!" he said, and tried to sit up.

"At ease, Commander," she said, laughing. "Take it easy."

"What . . . happened?"

"You kind of got shot up fighting the Tushies. A SAR tug snagged you and dragged you home."

"We've had you in an artificially induced coma for several hours, Commander," the AI told him. "We've checked you out, and you appear undamaged."

"God . . ."

He bit off the word. As a Pan-European, he knew how sensitive the North Americans were to religious comments. He amended the thought: *former* Pan-European.

"Don't worry," Fletcher said. "You're not offending anyone."

"I was feeling . . . pretty lost, out away from the ship."

"I can imagine. It's damned empty out there. You feeling up to going back to duty status?"

"I . . . think so."

"We're growing new fighters but we're damned short of pilots right now, and the Admiral is taking us into hell. How's *that* for a religious statement?"

"I'll promise not to report you, CAG." He swung his legs out of the sick bay rack. He felt weak, and a bit woozy . . . the effects of whatever nanodrugs they'd pumped into him.

"Proceed carefully, Commander," the AI told him. "You should be feeling fully recovered within ten minutes."

"How's my squadron, CAG?" he asked.

"Four dead. One more streaker we haven't recovered yet."

"Who?"

"Blue Nine. Atkinson."

He closed his eyes, and almost sagged back on the rack. Jess Atkinson—sweet and fun and a great romp in bed . . . and a hell of a fighter pilot in combat. Jess Atkinson, who had a tendency to let slip religious exclamations herself. *Shit . . .*

"We're still looking for her, Commander," Fletcher told him. "We'll find her if we can."

If we can.

But the Void was so very empty and deep.

St. Clair could feel it closing on him, like a black and smothering shroud.

Observation Deck
USNA Star Carrier America
Invictus Space, T+12 MY
0225 hours, TFT

"So . . . beautiful . . ."

"Yes. You are."

Connor gave Gregory a playful punch against his bare chest, and the two of them drifted slightly apart. That was the trouble with zero-G lovemaking; the dead hand of Isaac Newton still reached in from the remote past: every action has an equal but opposite reaction. A thrust resulted in a backward push. A caress responded with a nudge.

"Idiot!" Connor said, laughing. "I meant the *view*."

He looked her up and down. "So did I."

They both were naked, adrift in the observation dome, located high atop *America*'s bridge tower. Once, the compartment had been a duty station linked in with Primary Flight Control, a place where human eyes could watch incoming fighters lining up for traps in the rotating hab modules aft, but machine eyes did the job faster, and with far greater accuracy. The dome now served as recreational space, its instrumentation and consoles stripped out, its deck given nanoreactive furniture that could be summoned with a thought . . . a place for crew members to come and watch the surrounding depths of space with their own eyes, instead of through scanners and cerebral feeds.

And also, quite often, it was a place where lovers met. The zero-gravity added a certain spice to such encounters, even if the participants needed to use elastic ties to hold themselves together, or anchor their bare feet to the nano-matrix of the deck.

With practice, it could be done—*the docking maneuver*, to use the old and popular space-faring term. And Gregory and Connor had been getting a lot of practice here of late.

The galaxy hung huge and gorgeous beyond the dome, and Gregory was forced to admit that, yes, it *was* beautiful. Its glow, the accumulated illumination from 400 billion stars, was a lot softer and more delicate than he'd imagined it would be. Visual feeds, including those in his Starblade, tended to intensify the light a bit. Here, with the naked eye, that vast spiral seemed to blend in with the blackness of intergalactic space beyond, in places becoming nearly invisible. You had to really *look* to see the detail.

But the more you looked, the more you saw.

"I wonder if what we're seeing," Connor said, "is any different than it was back in our day?"

They were still getting used to the revelation, passed through the fleet hours before, that the task force had emerged from the TRGA roughly 12 million years in the future.

"Not that much," Gregory told her. "It takes two hundred fifty million years for our sun to go around the galactic center once. Twelve million years is . . . nothing."

"It's still deep time."

"I usually think of that term associated with the past."

"Depends on how you use it," Connor said with a shrug that did delightful things to her upper torso. "Twelve million years . . . you know, we're probably post-human out here. The average life span for a species is . . . what? A million years?"

"For mammals, yes," Gregory said. "For intelligent species, it could be shorter . . . a hundred thousand years or so."

"Or it could be much longer," Connor countered. "A truly advanced galactic species might be immortal. And they would break all the rules about species life spans."

"Well, we won't know unless we make contact with our remote descendents in there, now, will we? I doubt the admiral's going to be up for any long-range sightseeing."

"Probably not. Maybe the aliens here can fill us in."

"Maybe." He frowned. "And maybe . . ."

"What?"

"I'm just wondering about the Tushies coming through the Triggah here . . . working with the Glothr, but twelve million years after our time. It . . . paints a kind of a strange picture, y'know?"

"Strange how?"

"A Sh'daar empire, or whatever you want to call it—a polity, an associative—that's spread across an entire galaxy, *and also across millions of years of time.* I'm trying to imagine—I don't know—an intragalactic *and* intertemporal network . . . trade, military assistance . . . trillions of sapient beings, millions of worlds, across millions of different times . . ."

"God. Talk about thinking big . . ."

"It just makes me wonder what we're really up against here," he told her.

She reached for him . . . carefully to avoid the hand of Newton. "I want to be up against *you.* C'mere."

And they clung to each other once more, adrift in beauty. . . .

Admiral's Quarters
USNA Star Carrier America
Invictus Space, T+12 MY
0320 hours, TFT

"Bridge, this is Gray. I'm turning in, now."

"Go ahead, Admiral," Gutierrez replied. "We've got it covered here."

"Quarters," he added. "Call me at oh-seven hundred, please."

"Acknowledged," the room replied in his head. "Zero-seven hundred wake-up call."

Normally he had the room wake him at 0600 or even earlier, but he'd just put in a very long day. Even with electronic sleep-aug he was going to be bumping into bulkheads when he regained consciousness. Three and a half hours just weren't enough.

"When's reveille?" Taggart asked him from the bed. She was gloriously naked, her brown hair spilling across the pillow in an unkempt riot. He told her, and she groaned. "Too *early* . . ."

"Yeah, but the Glothr may not feel that way," he said. "I don't know. Do jellyfish sleep?"

"I don't know, but *I* sleep!"

"Well, that's because you're a mammal." He gave her a deliberately salacious grin. "*Obviously* so."

He padded across the deck and climbed in beside her.

"Obviously. But maybe we shouldn't do anything about it," she said. "Not if we're on duty again in less than four hours."

"Don't be mad at *me*. Yell at the Glothr. Or the Tushies."

"Who's on the flag bridge?"

"Captain Gutierrez. She came on second watch, and she's going to keep an eye on things until oh-eight hundred. She's going to need sleep-aug at that point, too." Hell, they all would. There was no day or night in space, and though *America* and the rest of Task Force One operated on Terran Fleet Time—which at the moment was reading almost four in the morning—in fact ships' crews were scheduled to man all stations at all times. The awkward part of that was that the ship's captain and the fleet's admiral both were on duty 24/7, and that meant they caught sleep when they could.

In Taggart's case it was just that she'd chosen to stay up through the midnight duty after putting in a full day on deck . . . and that made it her own damned fault.

"You didn't have to stay on duty, you know," he told her, reaching for her.

"What, and miss all the excitement? I wanted to see the Guard ships arrive."

"Yes, and they didn't. I'm worried about them."

"What are we going to do about it?"

"First, I'm going to get some sleep. And when I get back on the flag bridge later . . . well, then we'll see. Depends partly on how far along the task force repairs are by then."

"They were reporting good progress. That was inspired, dismantling the Tush hulks."

"Tell me that when we know it's worked. Meanwhile . . . come here . . ."

"I thought you wanted to *sleep*!"

"I do, but I'm all keyed up. I need something to relax me."

"You can program the sleep augmentation for that."

"Yes. Yes, I can." His hand slid down the curve of her belly. "But this way is *so* much more fun. . . ."

And the room's electronics, infected now with a virus disguised as a harmless maintenance subroutine, recorded every move . . . every gentle moan . . .

Chapter Eighteen

Place of Cold Dreaming
Invictus Ring
0515 hours, TFT

"God . . . why is it so *dark*?"

"We don't understand your question, Ambassador. What do ambient light levels have to do with anything?"

"Just let us have a little light. . . ."

"You are bathed in light, Ambassador. Let us stay on the topic of current discussion."

Seven-one-cee-eight waited for a reply, studying the line of humans suspended in their sealed plastic tubes through broad-spectrum analyzers. There were six of them in a line, immobilized in their containers, glowing with their own heat. Conduits and piping connected each, maintaining the hellish environmental conditions these creatures appeared to require. *Oxygen* . . . Seven-one-cee-eight gave the Glothr equivalent of a shudder, its mantle rippling as a wave of emotion pulsed around its circumference. *And* a metabolic temperature well above ambient normal. Seven-one-cee-eight was comfortable at a temperature of four degrees Celsius, though its measuring units were different and it used a base 24 numbering system; body temperature for humans appeared to be thirty-seven Celsius. They radiated heat, rather than absorbing it from the environment; in fact, they were radiating so much heat that it was dangerous for Glothr to come anywhere close to one of them.

Fortunately, the god-robots weren't affected by the hot little aliens, and Seven-one-cee-eight could watch from the comfort of its saltwater-ammonia quarters. The robots were designed to tolerate far more extreme environments than a room filled with hot oxygen-nitrogen gas.

"We shall begin again," Seven-one-cee-eight told them. "Tell us why humans reject the gift of belonging. . . ."

Seven-one-cee-eight hoped the translation was adequate. The humans appeared to understand what it was saying, but sometimes there were . . . nuances and shades of meaning that were as slippery as ammonia ice melting at the bottom of a pool. The worst part of it was that humans appeared to have no electrosense at all . . . and that made communication a decided challenge.

Their speech did not depend on sound waves, but on precise and subtle modulations in the electrical fields generated by their bodies. Seven-one-cee-eight's name—those four characters were the first of a much longer string, while *cee* was twelve in base-24 notation—referred to specific sequential frequencies in a fluttering electrical field. Their name for themselves, which began with the characters En-jay-three-kay, numerically encoded the term *Abyss Kin*. "Glothr" was the name given to them by other aliens within the Sh'daar Collective.

The humans appeared to be completely insensitive to Kin modulations of electrical fields, which made them not only dumb in terms of communication, but blind as well. The Kin possessed light-sensitive organs, but sight was a relatively minor sense, one of twelve they possessed, and useful primarily for gathering emotional data from the color shifts and pattern changes of other individuals. The physical nature, shape, mass, and movement of their environment and what was in it all were perceived as changes in the surrounding field. The humans, with painfully weak electrical fields running over their integuments and apparently no means whatsoever of actually detecting them, must perceive the universe around them in a very, *very* different fashion than the Kin indeed.

In fact, humans seemed to be crippled in a number of respects—no magnetic sense, no lateral-line pressure sense, no group movement sense, no . . . it was impossible even to translate three of the concepts. To compensate, humans appeared to rely far more heavily than did the Kin on light perception. One other sense that seemed to be important to them as well, though similar to sensing pressure waves in the water, had no exact corollary among the Kin. Apparently, they used it to detect the pressure waves that they generated as a form of communication. Numerous Sh'daar races had evolved this sense, though it was difficult to understand how sound waves could carry anywhere near the informational content of an oscillating electrical field.

"Gift . . ." the human said, as though struggling with the concept. "I don't . . . understand . . ."

Seven-one-cee-eight gave the equivalent of a sigh—a flutter of green and yellow exasperation. How could it be sure of the quality of the translation? Human metabolism—and, in consequence, the speed of their *thinking*—appeared to be on the order of two to three times faster than the Kin. And the difficulties of translating fluctuations in an electrical field into pressure waves, and back again, were almost insurmountable. The only way the task was possible at all was through the intermediary efforts of powerful artificial intelligences, and of the robots.

Seven-one-cee-eight increased the power with a thought. "Tell us why humans reject the gift of belonging."

Like many sapient species across the Galaxy, these humans were partly organic, partly machine. Imbedded within their brains, and elsewhere throughout their central nervous systems, was nanotechnically chelated circuitry that incorporated computers into their flesh-and-blood makeup. Kin software agents had tapped into the machine part of this combination, linking directly to memory, operating system, and the software AI running there. Through that link, Seven-one-cee-eight could communicate directly with the humans . . . though certain contextual or cultural concepts continued to prove difficult. It couldn't tell for sure how much of that was due to genuine fuzziness in the translation programs . . . and how much was due to stubbornness on the part of the humans.

"It's so . . . dark. . . ."

"Why would you need light?"

"Because I can't *see*!"

The word translated for Seven-one-cee-eight as "perceive visible light." It worked at the implications of this for a moment, then came to a startling realization: that the aliens, evidently, *were* sensitive to electromagnetic wavelengths, and that this sense was far more important to them than to the Kin. Perhaps it needed to see . . . or became emotionally distressed when it could not.

"I do not understand what you're saying. In any case, you do not need to perceive light to answer my questions . . . Ambassador."

"Ambassador" was another incomprehensible concept. The first humans to be contacted directly, the ones that called themselves the Terran Confederation, had spoken of *ambassadors*, as though a special type of being was necessary to achieve meaningful communications. Its superiors had directed Seven-one-cee-eight to play along with the humans when it made first contact with them on their world . . . but the alien's strange customs were fast becoming a hindrance rather than an aid to a clear exchange of information.

Seven-one-cee-eight increased the power of its signal again.

It had no other reasonable alternative.

USNA Star Carrier America
Invictus Space, T+12 MY
0940 hours, TFT

Gray drifted in the midst of the USNA fleet, the ships spread out around him like glittering toys. They weren't that close to one another in reality, of course. The AI facilitating the briefing had pulled the separate images together across several million kilometers to create a composite panorama, allowing the human viewpoints gathered in virtual space to survey the entire task force.

The repairs were almost complete. A chunk of Turusch wreckage hung alongside the *Vulcan*, its green-and-black outer hull armor gone, now, the remaining structure dwindled to an amorphous gray mass as clouds of nanodisassemblers continued to take it apart, atom by atom, and haul them in continuous streams into the repair vessel's multiple storage bunkers. Larger worker 'bots swarmed around several of the other ships, applying repair nano and raw materials shipped across from the *Vulcan*, patching gaping holes, reapplying surface armor, and serving as large-scale 3-D printers to nanufacture new gravitic projectors, weapons, and sensor arrays layer by molecule-thin layer.

"How about fighter recovery?" Gray asked.

"We still have three missing fighters, Admiral," CAG Fletcher said. "We have long-range probes looking for them, of course, but this long after the battle . . ."

She let the thought trail off, unfinished. A dead fighter was so terribly minute when lost within that aching gulf beyond.

"Keep on it," Gray said. "As long as possible. What else?"

"We're low on reserves of radioactives, sir," Talbot said. "And we haven't found any in the Tushie wrecks. That puts a cap on the number of fission warheads we can assemble."

Gray nodded understanding. An m-type asteroid would

be rich in most heavy metals, including uranium, but salvaging wrecked ships wouldn't score that kind of bonanza unless they happened to recover the dead ship's magazines.

"Also, some of the ships report they're still short of water," Talbot went on. "What's floating around in local space is too widely dispersed to make it worthwhile scooping it up."

None of the wrecks they'd investigated so far possessed intact water reservoirs. Usually, when a ship was torn apart by a charged particle beam or a nuke, any water stores on board were gushed out into hard vacuum, where they froze into flecks of ice—each the size of a grain of sand—and rapidly dispersed. Unless a large cloud of nanocollectors was released *very* quickly, it simply wasn't worth the effort to try to gather them all up.

"How bad a shortage?" Gray asked.

"We have about one third of her original stores," Captain Benjamin McFarlane, *New York*'s CO, reported. "We stopped the leak before all our water was gone."

"The *Northern Cal* is at about half, Admiral," her captain, Janet Davis, said.

The other damaged ships were at similar levels: none low enough to preclude fleet ops, but something on which to keep a watchful eye.

There would be water at Invictus, of course, far more water than on all of Earth. Hell, the Glothr swam in the stuff, literally. But just now it seemed highly unlikely that the aliens would be willing to share their bounty with the Earth-human fleet.

It was frustrating. Normally, it would be a simple matter to find just one kilometer-sized iceteroid, which would be big enough to provide ample reaction mass for the entire fleet. They had enough—and a bit to spare, perhaps—for a battle or two more on this side of the TRGA, but Gray hated running things so close to the wire.

"Maybe we should go back," Captain Ray Mathers, of the light cruiser *Columbia* said.

"What, and leave our people here?" That was the commanding officer of the Marine contingent on board the *Marne*, Colonel Joseph Jamison. "Unacceptable!"

"We may have no alternative," McFarlane put in.

On the surface, the safe play *was* to pull out, to go back through the TRGA to the Beehive cluster, where there would be plenty of loose chunks of ice in the Oort clouds of some hundreds of nearby suns.

Gray deeply mistrusted that option, though. While that Turusch fleet might have come through from a different place and time than Task Force One, the likeliest scenario seemed to be that they'd followed the human ships through from *America*'s home spacetime, and that the survivors of the recent battle had broken through and gone right back to where they'd come from. They might have reinforcements waiting over there, and if so, they almost certainly would be waiting to ambush human ships coming through the cylinder one at a time. Task Force One might find itself in the same severe disadvantage that the Turusch had faced on this side of the TRGA.

"There'd damned well better be another option," Gray said. "Our drones still haven't returned."

Hours ago, to test whether or not the Turusch were waiting on the other side of the TRGA, Gray had ordered three of *America*'s battlespace drones to thread their way back through the cylinder at thirty-minute intervals, take a look around, and return with vid images and scanner readings of what was waiting on the other side.

But none of the drones had turned around and come back, which was . . . suggestive. It wasn't definitive yet; drones often had trouble threading the wildly fluctuating spacetime matrix of a TRGA, or the bad guys might have left a single ship over there on guard, while the rest headed home for repairs. Still, it was enough to give Gray pause.

And Gray wasn't ready to risk a one-at-a-time encounter with a large and very angry Turusch battlefleet waiting in ambush.

"Do we have any alternate Triggah pathways mapped for this one?" Captain Mendoza, of the *Illinois*, asked.

"Not with any confidence," Mallory replied. "In any case, it's *very* unlikely that we'd be able to find a gateway to anywhere useful."

"We estimate," *America*'s AI said, "a less than one ten-thousandth of a percent chance of recognizing where we emerge."

That was the essential problem with TRGA cylinders. Estimates put the number of distinct spacetime paths through a given TRGA in the tens, possibly the hundreds of millions, but possible destinations included stars scattered across much of the galaxy, and a span of some millions of years. The only way to map a given pathway was to send a ship through, then do a thorough survey on the other side. Identifying stars and the general period of time in which the ship had emerged could take *years*, and might never be completed.

And if they just jumped through without a survey—like they had on the way to Invictus—they would end up somewhere unknown, with no idea of where or when they were.

Gray was prepared to try that in the event of an emergency, with no other way of saving his fleet, but he wasn't that desperate just yet.

"How about trying to talk to them?" Fletcher asked.

"Sure," McFarlane put in. "If we can't fight 'em, maybe we could talk 'em to death."

"Nice idea, CAG," Mallory said, "with one small problem. We came here expecting to talk to them, and they ambushed us. I don't think they want to talk."

"The *Turusch* ambushed us," Fletcher told him. "Maybe the Turusch acted independently. Maybe the Glothr want to talk, and the Turusch were trying to block that possibility."

"And we have two pilots from the Demons," Gray pointed out, "who say a mob of Glothr ships were after them. *And* the *Pax* and the *Concord* have vanished. We have to assume the Glothr are hostile."

"Damn. You're right."

"*America* AI," Gray said. "Do you have anything to suggest?"

Gray always felt a bit weird asking the AI his opinion, but he also knew that given half a chance, he *could* come up with unexpected—and highly creative—ideas.

"A direct attack against Invictus," *America*'s AI said, "would be suicidal. As would a return through the TRGA, as would having the task force remain here. That suggests that you will need to defeat the enemy using deception."

"You have a suggestion?"

"Possibly. A direction for your consideration, at least."

"Let's hear it, then."

"It seems likely that if the ships of this task force were captured, the ships would be taken to the same place that they are holding the High Guard ships, and that that is also where they are holding Ambassador Rand and his people."

"Possibly . . ."

"Almost certainly. The Glothr would be unlikely to set up and maintain separate quarters within which to create a standard terrestrial environment just for prisoners."

"Seems logical," Jamison said.

And the carrier's AI began unfolding its idea.

Place of Cold Dreaming
Invictus Ring
1210 hours, TFT

"Tell us why humans reject the gift of belonging."

"I don't know. I guess it seemed like a good idea at the time."

Seven-one-cee-eight considered the answer, and wondered if the human was being insolent, arrogant, or simply responding with truth. Human emotions were extremely difficult to judge. Among the Kin, one simply had to read the flutter of luminescent organs through transparent integument to know *exactly* what the other was feeling. Humans were . . . different.

"Have you made progress, Seven-one-cee-eight?" The words crackled through its electrosense, transmitted by its swarm center.

"No, Nine-dee-el-six," it replied, and the flash of blue at the top of its thorax paled to green to show its frustration. "No, and I begin to fear that meaningful communication with this species is impossible."

"Why? Our computer linguists cracked their language codes, with Agletsch help. It should be a simple thing to transpose their words into modulated electrical pulses."

"It would be, Nine-dee-el-six, if these creatures had the same worldview as we."

"Worldview? What difference does that make?"

"It's . . . difficult to put into pulses. They fear being in the dark, some of them."

"So? Surely this is not important."

"It seems to be important to them, at least over a long period of time. Vision is their primary sense, approximately what electrosense is for us. They are blind to electrical pulses."

"Strange . . ."

"There's worse. Because they have no electrosense, they are unaware of the presence of others of their species nearby. They also seem to fear being alone. Several have commented on what they refer to as the 'emptiness' of this part of space, outside of the galaxy."

"Perhaps we can exploit these weaknesses. If they are uncomfortable, they may wish to cooperate, to answer our questions, so that we will be inclined to make them more comfortable."

"I was working with that idea, yes. But it is difficult to know how far we can go without causing permanent physical or psychological harm."

"That surely doesn't matter. All that matters is that we learn what we need to know about these creatures."

"The attempt may prove to be counterproductive."

"We have a great many prisoners at the research facility," Nine-dee-el-six said. "Continue working with them until you find one willing to cooperate."

"Very well. I will continue to focus on the commanders of the two ships, and on the one that calls itself 'an ambassador.' They appear to hold positions analogous to that of a swarm center."

"As you think best."

"We swarm together," Seven-one-cee-eight replied.

VFA-96, The Black Demons
Invictus Space, T+12 MY
1620 hours, TFT

Lieutenant Gregory drifted in strangeness, an entire universe compressed into narrow, colored rings forward, his Starblade skimming just beneath *c*. In another few minutes, he saw, it would be time to commence deceleration.

Twelve fucking million years . . .

He wondered if humans had survived to this epoch . . . wondered if it would even be possible to find out. If Humankind had survived, the species must have evolved into something quite different by now.

There was a lot of speculation about human evolution, including the idea that human evolution, at least on the grand scale, had ceased. By taking control of his environment, by drastically extending the human life span, by genegineering his own genome, by merging his biology with his technology, Humankind had at least pushed back the most urgent evolutionary pressures, the demands of natural selection and survival of the fittest. To a certain extent, perhaps, the pace of human evolution had slowed, certainly.

But it hadn't stopped. And twelve million years was a

long time . . . twelve times longer than the survival time of the typical mammalian species.

There was a concept Gregory had heard in ready room bull sessions and in cosmological docuinteractive downloads: *deep time*, time on a geological scale. The Navy had already been forced to come to grips with the concept, knowing that the Sh'daar had emerged in the remote past, more than 800 million years ago.

And now he was hurtling toward an alien world 12 million years in the future. The mind could not quite take in chronological vistas on those scales.

Pulling back from those gulfs, he focused instead on recent memory: his rendezvous with Meg in the observation dome atop *America*'s spine. God, she was beautiful, but more than that, he was sharply aware that his feelings for her had steadily been shifting of late—from fuck buddy to something more.

Something much, *much* more.

He wanted to call her on a private channel, but the squadron was under comm discipline. Communicating ship to ship while nudging light speed was difficult enough. But no one in the fleet knew how well the Glothr could pick up such signals, or translate them, and that made radio silence all the more imperative.

Certainly, the Gothr knew they were coming by now. The question was just what they were going to do about it . . . and when.

A ping snapped him back to the here and now. His AI was alerting him to a contact, something up ahead.

"What have we got?" he asked.

His AI responded with impressions rather than words. *Unknown . . . possible danger . . . something big . . . in excess of three hundred thousand tons . . .*

A readout of hard data scrolled down through his awareness. His fighter's sensors couldn't see the oncoming object, but AI analysis could suggest what it might be.

And it was swiftly maneuvering toward the fleet.

USNA Star Carrier America
Invictus Space, T+12 MY
1621 hours, TFT

"Incoming target," Mallory snapped. "Closing fast."

Well, it would be, with the fleet already hurtling toward it at close to the speed of light itself. The light carrying the data would be coming in just ahead of the object, leaving precious little warning time. The fighter cloud, extending well out beyond the main fleet, had spotted the thing first.

"Weapons tracking," Commander Taggart reported.

"All task force vessels are locking on, Admiral," Talbot added. Then, "What the hell is that?"

"Our Glothr friends coming out to gather us up," Gray replied. "Let's not make it easy for them."

"Time, Admiral," Captain Gutierrez told him.

"All ships . . . initiate deceleration."

AI commands synchronized perfectly flashed from ship to ship. Depending on design, some vessels began projecting gravitational singularities astern. Others flipped end for end with the same effect, their hab modules protected from the high-velocity sleet of relativistic particles by power modules and aft sponsons.

The protective cloud of fighters would continue for minutes more, dispersing ahead of the fleet, and threaten the enemy.

"Comm," Gray said. "Transmit the signal."

"Transmitting, Admiral."

And now . . . the wait began. . . .

Place of Cold Dreaming
Invictus Ring
1631 hours, TFT

"Seven-one-cee-eight! We are receiving a laser-com transmission . . . encoded electropulse!"

"Let me feel it."

A circuit closed, and Seven-one-cee-eight felt the crackle and tingle of a modulated transmission . . . not in its own language, but in the artificial pidgin created to communicate with the humans. Much of the meaning was garbled and vague, but enough meaning came through the stilted translation to chill Seven-one-cee-eight's ammonia-water lymph.

"Glothr. You brought us here to communicate with us directly, or so we were led to believe. Instead, you ambushed us, seized our personnel, and have captured two of our vessels. Among civilized species, these are hostile acts which can result in all-out war.

"Humankind desires peace with the Glothr, but we will fight if forced to do so. I suggest that our original plan— talking—would be more productive, and far less destructive of your world, and its artificial system of rings and orbital structures. The decision, however, is entirely yours. Please let us know your decision before we reach your world and begin selecting targets. . . ."

Seven-one-cee-eight bristled at the challenge and at the implied threat, the depths of its mantle glowing in deep blues and near ultraviolet. The humans presumed to order the *Kin*?

Their audacity, their sheer arrogance was stunning. What made them think they could challenge a world of 15 billion inhabitants with a fleet numbering fewer than twenty ships, and a technology centuries behind that of the Kin? Insanity!

"Deploy the twisters," Seven-one-cee-eight ordered. "Let's teach these upstart children a proper lesson."

Chapter Nineteen

USNA Star Carrier America
Invictus Space, T+12 MY
1638 hours, TFT

"Planetary objective now in sight," Mallory reported. "Range just under one AU."

"Range to hostile contact . . . four hundred thousand kilometers," Taggart added.

A bit more than the distance between Earth and the moon.

"Belay that 'hostile,' Commander," Gray said. "They *may* still want to talk."

In fact, the more time that dragged on, the likelier it was that the Glothr were going to want to talk.

"Yes, sir. Range to alien vessel . . . now three hundred eighty thousand kilometers."

The task force by now had decelerated to about a half *c*. The ships were broadly dispersed across several million kilometers, and the cloud of fighters—four squadrons of them—formed a vast and far-flung cloud around and well ahead of the main body of ships. The planet, with no local star to illuminate it, was invisible to the naked eye, though *America*'s sensors had pegged it on the ship's various feeds and displays. The single Glothr vessel in front of them was also invisible, though it was much closer. Its mirror-polished surface reflected the endless night round about, and at that distance it was nearly impossible to see.

It was visible to radar and lidar, however, and it gave off heat, neutrinos, and mass . . . a lot of mass, probably created by a powerful microsingularity.

Or . . . perhaps not so micro, at that. Sensors showed that the alien's mass was increasing, and very, very quickly.

As though it were warming up for a shot.

The plan suggested by *America*'s AI was quite simple. As with the Turusch, the task force needed to get in close to the enemy in order to threaten him with unacceptable damage. It also had to avoid the enemy's time-bending stasis weapon, which would put any ship attacked by it at a severe disadvantage.

Little was known yet about that weapon, but the Marines had glimpsed that mirror-smooth shape hanging just above the *Concord* while it had been held inside Charlie One. It seemed unlikely that the Glothr could somehow project a temporal stasis across much distance, which in turn suggested that the cigar-shaped vessel *itself* was the weapon.

By spreading out, and by presenting the Glothr with as large a number of ships as possible—the task force's nineteen remaining capital ships plus forty-one fighters—they hoped to block the use of the stasis weapon, or at least to limit its use to one or two ships. At least, that was the idea . . . though they were making a hell of a lot of assumptions here about the Glothr's technology. Bending time, though, would take a *lot* of energy, and the weapon that did it would need to be large. Like that mirror-hulled, optically invisible ship up ahead.

"Even if he's not hostile, though," Gray said, "let's see if we can crowd him a little. Boost acceleration and close with him."

America increased her speed.

And the alien ship gave ground, falling back before the advancing fleet.

But long-range sensors were already picking up a cloud of ships, hundreds of them, emerging now from the rings of Invictus, accelerating, and bearing down on the task force with a terrible deliberation.

VFA-96, The Black Demons
Invictus Space, T+12 MY
1639 hours, TFT

"*America*, Black Demons!" Mackey, the squadron's skipper, yelled. "They're making their move!"

"All fighters," came over the link from *America*. "All fighters, weapons are free, I repeat, weapons are free. You are clear to engage."

For a fighter pilot, speed is life. Gregory accelerated his Starblade, watching the target icon grow huge forward. "Target lock!" he called. "*Fox one!*" The ancient radio call had originally indicated launch of a heat-seeking missile. Now it meant a smart missile like the VG-10 Krait shipkiller.

Additional cries of "lock" and "fox one" sounded from other members of the squadron, as missile trails reached out from the fast-moving fighters and curved in toward their target. The first nuclear-tipped warhead flashed in a dazzling point of light . . .

. . . and froze there, close beside the alien ship's hull.

Gregory wrestled with what he was seeing—a seeming impossibility. The nuclear detonation had been arrested somehow, reduced to an intense star-point of radiance perhaps ten meters from the alien's hull, the light reflected off the mirrored surface. The alien vessel was still moving, of course, and it quickly left the arrested detonation behind. As it did so, the pinpoint expanded into the full blossoming flower of heat and radiation normally expected of a nuclear explosion.

"What the hell are they doing to our missiles?" Lieutenant Ruxton called.

"They're bending time!" Mackey replied. "They're slowing time down, somehow, right next to their hull!"

Gregory decided that they would learn more in the after-action analyses of drone sensor and long-ranged scanner data, but he was pretty sure Mackey had hit it square on the head. Those detonations, he realized, hadn't been stopped completely, but they had been enormously slowed. If a nuclear warhead gave off x amount of radiation in one millisecond, stretching that millisecond to, say, a full second would reduce the intensity of that radiation by a factor of three . . . down to one-thousandth of the original value. That, plus the fact that the target vessel was still moving at a fair clip, putting distance between itself and the blasts . . . yeah, that made for a pretty effective defense.

In space, nuclear warheads lacked one destructive component that they possessed in atmosphere—a shock wave. Unless there was a local atmosphere—such as the plasma cloud from numerous such blasts—there was nothing to compress, no way to generate a fast-moving shock wave, and the warheads' only destructive effect came from electromagnetic radiation—heat, light, UV rays, X-rays, and gamma radiation—plus some particulate radiation—alpha and beta particles. Even the effects of hard gamma rads would be sharply reduced if you spread them out over time.

Okay . . . how do you counter something like that? Gregory thought about the sandcaster rounds in his Starblade's weapons bays. Surely the kinetic energy carried by a cloud of lead spherules traveling at high velocity couldn't be finessed away by the throwing of a switch.

Or . . . maybe it could. The equation describing Newton's second law of motion read force equals mass times acceleration, and acceleration was defined as the change of velocity over time. Stretch out the time, and you reduced acceleration . . . right?

No! Where the hell was all of that energy *going*? Something wasn't right, here.

Fuck it. There had to be some *way of hitting the Glothr time bender. . . .*

Place of Cold Dreaming
Invictus Ring
1639 hours, TFT

"Seven-one-cee-eight! Our time-twister vessel is in danger of being overwhelmed! Pull it back to where it can be properly supported by our swarmers!"

"Very well, Swarm Leader Nine-nine-gee-kay."

Glothr society was not built upon hierarchies, and there was no overall leader as such, nor was there a specific class of officers within the military. Individual Glothr recognized that someone needed to call the shots in some circumstances, and that others needed to obey orders to get things done, but the process was largely instinctive, arising from elements of Glothr biology and psychology. The first individual Glothr who recognized a need simply stepped into the place of command . . . and others followed, obeying the unspoken dictates of billions of years of social evolution.

The Glothr themselves were colony animals, organisms composed of hundreds of billions of smaller and, individually, unintelligent creatures each specialized to perform certain tasks in a unified whole. They were an extremely ancient race, one evolved in the unimaginable depths of deep time, with eons to hone and shape their social organization until it was a seamless and smoothly functioning whole. Each Glothr assumed the role necessary for the moment, whether that might be starship commander, shopkeeper, swarm leader, or laborer.

Based on chemical cues, any single Glothr could become any of four distinct sexes—male, female, caretaker, or colony defender. At the moment, Seven-one-cee-eight was of the latter class, sexless but shaped by instinct to protect its homeworld and all others of its species. Recently, it had commanded the expedition to Earth . . . but upon its return it had assumed responsibility for interrogating captured humans, and now it was assuming partial responsibility for defending Invictus against the threat of a human fleet. Its experience as a leader meant that it assumed a leadership role more often than not . . . but there was no ego involved. Tomorrow, Seven-one-cee-eight might easily find itself taking on the role of a dockworker within the Invictus rings . . . or of a mother deep within the homeworld's vast oceanic abyss.

Under Seven-one-cee-eight's guidance, the time-twister began falling back toward Invictus, followed by a storm of alien missiles. The robotic device's defenses could be overwhelmed by such an attack, and it was up to Seven-one-cee-eight to make sure that they were not. Data flooded back from the robot: tracking, status, and sensor information updated from millisecond to millisecond. Seven-one-cee-eight needed to get the vehicle back to where it could be properly covered by the defense robots now hurtling clear of the rings.

A nuclear warhead detonated, but far enough away from the time-twister's hull that the blast was not strongly affected by the temporal distortion. That was *not* good. If the aliens observed what had happened, and drew the right conclusions . . .

Seven-one-cee-eight requested that the robotic fleet put on more speed.

USNA Star Carrier America
Invictus Space, T+12 MY
1639 hours, TFT

"That's the answer!" Gray shouted, freezing an image and highlighting an expanding nuclear blast in red brackets. "Do you see it?"

"*What's* the answer?" Taggart asked.

"That Glothr ship weakens nearby explosions by increasing time, right? Same energy spread over more time means less energy in a given instant. Another way to say that: the energy's wavelength is red-shifted, made longer."

"Ye-esss . . ." She hadn't seen it yet.

"The field they're projecting . . . it must be pretty short-ranged, a hundred meters or less, from what it looks like. We need to find the sweet spot . . . the range from the alien's hull where the high-energy EM stuff gets red-shifted down to heat, *lots* of heat . . . close enough to cause damage to the hull, but far enough that there's still some kick to the blast when it goes off."

"We can try proximity detonation . . . at what, sir? Two hundred meters?"

"Try it. No, try a salvo, with detonations at one fifty, two hundred, and three hundred meters. CAG!"

"Yes, Admiral!"

"Pass that on to the fighters."

"Aye, aye, sir."

"But snap it up! Looks like they're pulling that thing back."

On the flag bridge display, the silvery cigar had decelerated to a dead stop, then begun accelerating back the way it had come. In the distance, hundreds of objects were swarming out from the dark planet, each larger than a fighter but considerably smaller than a capital vessel.

What were they?

Gray wanted to take out that big ship before those other vessels reached the fleet. Glothr tactics suggested that they worked together, with a linkage as good or better than that of the human vessels. Likely, the time bender was intended to immobilize a human capital ship, holding it helpless while those smaller ships came in for the kill. He would assume that was their goal, at least, until they gave him something more to go on.

Long seconds passed, the task force continuing to close

on the Glothr ship. Then the lead fighters began firing missiles, single shots at first, then in twos and threes. Again, nuclear fireballs flared . . . and as Gray had suspected, the more distant the explosion from the alien's hull, the faster the fireball swelled, brightened, then faded. The alien vessel lurched suddenly as white radiance bathed it—*burned* it—and then it began tumbling.

"That's it," Gray ordered. "Hit 'em with direct shots, now. Take them down!"

More missiles reached out from the task force, and, moments later, the vanguard of the task force swept through an expanding cloud of hot plasma, all that remained of the time-bending alien vessel. The "sweet spot" he'd been looking for appeared to be two to three hundred meters out from the hull. The time-slowing effect seemed to reach that far, but it only slightly stretched the action of the explosion, resulting in a much greater output of heat and hard radiation within a given period of time. The alien vessel's reflective hull shielded it from a lot of the radiation, but multiple explosions tended to burn that silver surface black. Once that happened, repeated detonations had slammed the vessel, cooking it—and leaving it vulnerable to a direct hit.

Gray *also* suspected that the time-bender ship was relatively uncommon within the Glothr fleet. It had been carried aboard the larger Glothr vessel that had gone to Earth as a kind of special, add-on weapon. Out here, it was operating on its own, but so far they'd seen only the one. It might be that altering the local flow of time took an extraordinary amount of power, or the equipment was unusually costly. It scarcely mattered. The important thing was that it was unlikely that the swarm ahead could pull the same sort of trick.

At least Gray fervently hoped that that was the case.

"Comm! Send another message. Tell them we have no wish to harm their world. Tell them to cease hostile actions against us and agree to talk."

"Aye, aye, sir."

The alien cloud was swiftly getting closer.

Place of Cold Dreaming
Invictus Ring
1644 hours, TFT

"Seven-one-cee-eight! We are getting another message from the primitives. They want us to halt the combat. They want to *communicate*."

What . . . negotiate? Now? That made no sense. The humans must believe that they held the combat advantage now, but if that was so, the proper course was to strike and continue striking, not bluster and make threats. Perhaps they were sending threats because they were weaker than they seemed, and knew it.

Or was there something else behind the impenetrable alien psychology?

"Ignore them," Seven-one-cee-eight ordered. "We will see if they still wish to communicate once their warships have been crippled or destroyed."

VFA-31, The Impactors
Invictus Space, T+12 MY
1648 hours, TFT

St. Clair sat encased within the womblike embrace of his new-grown Starblade, watching the unfolding battle outside and awaiting the order to launch. His fighter was tucked into one of the launch-bay tubes in the rotating hab modules, but in his mind's eye he was hurtling toward the enemy, watching as the Black Demons, the Nighthawks, and the Dragon-fires took on the alien swarm.

The Earth fighters were badly outnumbered.

"C'mon, CAG!" he called over the command channel. "When are you gonna let us get in on that furball?"

"Keep it iced, Blue Seven," Fletcher replied from Pryfly. "We're sending you out after bigger prey."

"Our people are getting chopped to bits out there!"

"Yeah, CAG," Blue Two, Lieutenant Thom Vandermeyer, added. "We could catch 'em by surprise."

"Belay the chatter, Impactors," Fletcher said, her voice cold. "The Admiral has a plan. . . ."

It had better, St. Clair thought, *be one hell of a plan.* The fighters deployed ahead of the task force were outnumbered four or five to one right now. The alien ships were . . . something new. *Strange.* Each was different; each looked like a small building or a collection of angled blocks and rectilinear shapes, and each was about ten times the size of a Starblade, so it was tough to decide whether they were very large fighters or small capital ships, similar in scale to human frigates. They were clumsy and slow—the fighters could literally flit rings around them—but they were powerful, possessing particle beams that were devastating when they struck.

And St. Clair noticed something else about them as well: they tended to move in units—tight-knit groups of two or three—and they seemed to move according to programmed responses, with a given type of attack generating a specific response. St. Clair couldn't be certain, but it *felt* like he was looking at robots . . . and not particularly bright ones, either.

They were suckers, he noted, for close-inside knife work—the so-called Nungie maneuver. That was a somewhat new fighter tactic, one invented by a Black Demon pilot in a close fight with the Slan last year at 70 Ophiuchi. A fighter would pivot to face the alien ship as it swung by and actually chew up the enemy's hull with its forward-projected singularity. The tight-knit point of intense gravitational energy—flickering on and off at thousands of times a second—ate its way through anything, releasing a blaze of X- and gamma rays. The maneuver was dangerous in the extreme, requiring absolute precision between the human pilot and the fighter's linked AI, but that was what the Starblades were specifically designed to do, and, more and more, they were laying the alien building blocks open, spilling their contents in glittering cascades into space.

Perhaps just as important, the aliens had trouble hitting fighters that were moving that close and that fast to both them and other Glothr ships.

But when they did manage to connect, the fighter would flare like a moth caught in a blow torch.

And there were so hellishly many of the aliens.

They were leaking through, shoving their way past the human fighters and engaging the larger vessels of the task force.

USNA Star Carrier America
Invictus Space, T+12 MY
1649 hours, TFT

"Eight minutes to contact with the ring, Admiral," Gutierrez told him.

"Thank you, Captain. Deploy long-range drones now, if you please. They're to scan for any sign of the *Concord* and the *Pax*."

"Aye, aye, Admiral. Drones away."

"Admiral!" Mallory called. "The alien ships are beginning to hit the main fleet."

"I see it. CAG, order the fighters to break off." He didn't want to hit any of his own people in that confused tangle ahead.

"Aye, aye, Admiral."

"Commander Taggart, you may fire when the opportunity presents itself."

"Yes, *sir*!"

The task force's vanguard was a rough cone of frigates and destroyers, moving just ahead of the three battleships, *Illinois, Northern California,* and *New York*. A Glothr phalanx of at least thirty alien ships slammed through the cone, taking terrible damage, yet not returning fire. They seemed determined to break through and get at the big boys clustered a few thousand kilometers beyond the fleet's sharp leading point.

In modern space combat, frigates are light combatants designed for an anti-fighter role, with a special emphasis on missile weaponry as opposed to beams. Destroyers are larger and slower than the nimble frigates, but with more firepower, usually built around a spinal-mount particle gun, together with plenty of turret-mounted kinetic-kill accelerators.

As the angular Glothr craft poured into the task force's van, they were hit by defensive salvos from the frigates and destroyers. Nuclear fireballs flared and pulsed; lasers and particle beams were invisible to the naked eye, but painted in by AI graphics on the flag bridge, showing the defenders coordinating their fire. The destroyers *Hobart* and *Lackland* caught a large Glothr ship in a deadly crossfire, pinning it with ultraviolet HEL beams—high-energy lasers—that peeled back its outer layers of hull before it erupted in a plasma blaze of blue-white light.

Then a Glothr vessel, tumbling and out of control, slammed into the *Lackland*'s port side. Huge fragments of twisted metal snapped off, and the *Lackland* heeled over to starboard, gently rolling with the impact.

But most of the incoming Glothrs were already through the shell of frigates and destroyers, and were closing now on the battleships.

Battleships were bigger, more heavily armored, and carried more heavy weapons than the smaller escorts. Numerous modern strategists were convinced that the battleship was obsolete now when it came to fleet actions, since it was less maneuverable than the sleeker battlecruiser. This battle, however, was fast turning into a slug-fest like the earlier engagement with the Turusch, with two fleets pounding at each other with every weapon that could be brought to bear. And here, the heavies—the old-fashioned battleships—were in their natural element. Generally relegated nowadays to a bombardment role for planetary assault, battleships could still bring hundreds of weapons to bear in space combat, from kinetic-kill magnetic railguns to heavy particle accelerators to HEL-guns, while their point defense system used smaller versions of those weapons to lay down a devastating field of fire designed to take out any enemy vessel that managed to make it in to the ship's innermost killing field.

The remaining Glothr warships hit the battleship fire zone and began dying.

"CAG," Gray said quietly, watching the pulse and throb of nuclear fire ahead. "Have the fighters in the vanguard continue sweeping in toward the planet. Let them know we'll be coming in hard on their six."

"Aye, aye, Admiral."

Gray was not dismissing the oddly shaped Glothr craft, but he had scaled back the threat in his mind. There were lots of them, yes . . . but they were not showing much of a *tactical* sense: no trying to englobe USNA ships, no attempts to gang up on a lone warship and overwhelm it with firepower. They were moving in more or less straight lines and engaging any ship that happened to be within range, and to Gray's mind that suggested an AI, and not a very smart one at that. There was no passion in this attack, and so long as the task force could maintain superior firepower locally, it looked like they would be able to fend off the attack without too much of a problem.

This, actually, was something of a surprise. The Glothr were clearly superior to humans in terms of technology, especially with that time-bending trick of theirs, but all things considered, they weren't *that* much better.

As he had always thought: passion could count for a hell of a lot in a firefight.

"Five minutes to contact with the ring."

"Thank you, Captain Gutierrez."

"Admiral?"

"Yes, CAG?"

"The squadrons in reserve are asking when they can get into the thick of things."

"Let them know they'll have their chance very soon now."

VFA-96, The Black Demons
Invictus Space, T+12 MY
1652 hours, TFT

Gregory watched another of the frigate-sized aliens explode, its angular hull crumpling and distorting at the touch of the nuclear fireball. While there were a few stragglers ahead, most of them were already behind the fighters, and the way in to Invictus was wide open.

The planet itself was hard to see unless it was silhouetted against the sweep and swirl of the galaxy beyond. As Gregory's Starblade drew closer, his angle of view shifted, and the night-black world slid off the dusting of blue-white starlight across the distant galactic backdrop and faded against darkness.

The rings, though, were still crisply visible, pale gray and gray-brown, made of flat, sharp-angled blocks of various odd shapes. Gregory was reminded of massed office complexes on Earth, except that these didn't have windows and weren't brightly lit.

Of course, many human buildings didn't have windows either. Wallscreens were more efficient and could be programmed for other views than the building's immediate surroundings, or double as vidscreens or news feeds or even internal lighting. But Gregory had the feeling that the Glothr ring's lack of windows had more to do with alien psychology than it did with esthetics. If sight wasn't the Glothr's primary sense, as he'd heard, they might not have the human need to see outside . . . even when the view was as spectacular as this one.

"I'm getting a strong signal from Drone 327, people," Commander Mackey told them. "Lock on and let's follow it in."

Gregory locked on to the indicated drone signal. Red brackets appeared overlaying his visual field, indicating a portion of the outermost rim of the alien ring. There were two strong heat sources there . . . and radiofrequency leakage that looked like it was spilling from a human source.

"Looks like our ships are inside the structure," he told Mackey. "Think Ambassador Rand and his people are there, too?"

"I don't know, Gregory. But we're going to find out! All Demons, break low and starboard on my mark! Three . . . two . . . one . . . *mark*!"

One by one, the Starblades rolled right and hurtled toward the ring.

Chapter Twenty

USNA Star Carrier America
Invictus Space, T+12 MY
1654 hours, TFT

"We are within maximum firing range of the near edge of the ring, Admiral," Laurie Taggart reported.

Captain Gutierrez glanced back at Gray as if for confirmation. He nodded. "You may commence firing," he said. "Target Glothr weapons positions as they reveal themselves. Stay clear of the red zones."

"Aye, aye, sir," Gutierrez said. "Commander? Let 'em have it!"

Beams and missiles launched from *America*. Most of her weapons turrets couldn't bear, yet, blocked by the half-kilometer wide disk of her shield cap, but her twin spinal launch tubes began hurtling multi-ton kinetic-kill projectiles toward the target. Salvos of missiles launched in all directions out from the spine, curving around to pass the shield cap and converge on points identified by *America*'s AI as probable communications nodes and command-control centers.

Taking their cue from the flag, the other heavies of the

task force opened fire as well, the destroyers and frigates moving in close to take on the Glothr defenses at point-blank range, accompanied by flights of sleek fighters. The battleships *Illinois*, *Northern California*, and *New York*—all of them seriously damaged but very much still in the fight—held back, pounding at the alien structure. It was an awesome spectacle, and a terrifying one. If the tech discrepancy was too great, the *America* task force might find itself cut to pieces, the survivors alone and helpless and very far from home.

Unable to simply sit and watch, Gray had stood up . . . which in the zero-gravity of the flag bridge meant sending a thought into the deck matrix to turn a meter-square nano patch into a stick-tight, anchoring him in place. The forward end of the flag bridge opened onto the ship's bridge, a half deck down, while above the step, the bulkhead curved up and over into the flag bridge dome, which currently was displaying the battle as computer-generated icons and graphics.

In fact, of course, there *was* no up or down in zero-G . . . but Gray could snug his shipboard utility-clad feet onto the restraining nano patch, clasp his hands behind his back, and wonder if the fleet admirals of long-ago surface navies had felt the same sense of a headlong plummet as a carefully crafted battle plan unfolded around their vessel.

High-energy lasers reached out from the parapets of the ring fortress ahead, scoring hits. The broad shield caps on *Illinois* and *Northern California* both were punctured multiple times, spilling cascades of water that instantly froze into clouds of ice crystals as they hit hard vacuum.

He hoped they had enough water left for maneuvering during the battle.

"All units," Gray said. "Move your fire in closer to the red zones. Isolate them."

The red zones were the spots identified as possible locations of the two captured High Guard ships, as well as Ambassador Rand and his party. All the task force really had to go on was sources of heat. Glothr physiology appeared to function at right around the freezing point of water. Their insulation was very good, but on infrared, the ring was ablaze with myriad stars—points of energy, of which the vast majority were likely power plants of some sort. Even creatures with near-frozen ammonia-water for blood needed heat in the black Void, which hovered at close to three degrees Kelvin.

But the AIs had identified one cluster of infrared radiation—three points close to the ring's outer rim—that looked like the heat signatures of human-habitable compartments or ship habs. The fire control computers on each ship in the task force had flagged that zone, along with several other less likely targets, in red. The idea was to pound the structure of the ring as close as possible to those areas *without* hitting them.

The ring, Gray thought, was an astounding artifact, a titanic mass of material orbiting a dark and icy world five times the size of Earth. It appeared to be circling the planet in a synchronous orbit, matching the planet's forty-four-hour rotation, and with the slender columns of space elevators connecting the ring to the surface below. The ring itself was nearly twelve thousand kilometers wide and hundreds thick; its total mass must have run into the trillions of tons, and hundreds of billions of Glothr could have lived comfortably within the structure's interior.

Which pointed up one of the basic problems of space warfare: a fleet could carry, at most, a few tens of thousands of naval and Marine personnel; the light carrier transport *Marne* carried a regimental assault group of about five thousand Marines packed into her ranked hab modules. A planet, though, might have billions of inhabitants; unless an attacker was willing to destroy the entire world from space, committing genocide on a planetary scale, he would be at an insurmountable numerical disadvantage. Gray had no idea at all how many Glothr might live now beneath the icy crust of Invictus. That artificial ring system, however, was large enough to carry the planet's entire population and then some.

And that led to another conceptual problem. Titan, back in Earth's solar system, had a rocky core—specifically a hydrous silicate core capped over by a deep layer of Ice VI (frozen water under such incredible pressures that it formed tetragonal crystals and possessed unusual electrical properties). Over that inner ocean, which was many hundreds of kilometers deep and held more water within its depths than did the entire Earth, was a shell of normal ice decoupled from the interior by the ocean, and covered by rocks made of *very* cold ice and hydrocarbon "dirt." Invictus appeared to be a larger, more massive version of Titan, but if that was so, where the hell had the Glothr gotten the raw material for trillions of tons of artificial ring? Never mind how they'd gotten it up into orbit; *where the hell had all that stuff come from*?

The pressure at the bottom of the Invictan ocean must be so high that mining the core would present incredible technical problems, starting with the difficulty of tunneling down through hundreds of kilometers of Ice VI. Even if that were somehow possible, once the miners got through to the core itself, they would find it composed of silicates—no iron, no titanium, no copper, no aluminum, none of the metals required for an advanced technology.

"Sensor suite," Gray said.

"Yes, Admiral!" a woman's voice replied. According to the duty roster, Lieutenant Evans had the sensor watch.

"Give me a readout on the composition of that ring material." Lasers and particle beams were slashing into the ring structure, vaporizing starship-sized chunks of the surface material. *America*'s spectrometers would be peering into those expanding clouds of gas and debris and comparing them with the spectra of known materials.

"Yes, sir. We're reading a variety of long-chain carbon

molecules . . . including acrylate polymers, polyvinyl chloride, and polyetheretherketones—"

"In English, please, Lieutenant."

"Yes, sir. It's plastic."

"Plastic?"

"There are traces of various metals—boron nitride, para-aramids, and a suggestion of tetragonal ice crystals—but it's mostly plastic, yes, sir."

Well, Gray thought . . . what was a budding young technic civilization to do if copper, iron, and steel weren't on the table? One thing worlds like Titan were abundantly stocked with was hydrocarbons: substances such as petroleum, propane, ethane, and methane . . . the stuff from which plastics were made.

Glothr history, Gray thought, must be a long and fascinating story as they moved up the technical ladder. He turned his attention back to the fight at hand—the mystery would have to be solved another time.

The human fleet continued hammering away at the near edge of the ring. Return fire was slowly but steadily growing weaker as more and more Glothr batteries in the ring were identified and destroyed. Gray shifted his bridge display to a feed from a battlespace drone drifting low above the ring's surface, studying the data being relayed back to *America*.

The ring here, close to the edge, was between twenty and fifty kilometers thick—looking paper-thin from out in space, but remarkably bulky and substantial up close. As the drone skimmed across the dark surface, the artificial terrain took on the appearance of a kind of cityscape, with towers, blocks, and domes of unknown purpose separated from one another by deep canyons and plunging valleys. The surface, those parts that hadn't been hit by the task force's bombardment, appeared pristine—no meteor craters or scars or weathering from eons of dust impacts—which suggested either remarkably good defenses or that the surface was periodically renewed. True, asteroids, meteoric debris, and interstellar dust were scarce out here beyond the galaxy's rim . . . but that ring *might* be as old as 12 million years, and much of that time had been spent within more crowded vistas.

Ahead, a brilliant flare of light marked the impact of a heavy KK projectile from one of the ships. A geyser of water exploded into vacuum from the strike. An instant later, the probe flashed low above the resulting crater, glimpsing tangled depths of darkness and ragged structures below, rimmed by a thick layer of ice.

"Pull back," Gray told the AI controlling his image feed. "Let me see the OA."

The objective area was still highlighted by red brackets, the location of the *Pax*, the *Concord*, and—with luck—of Rand and his staff.

He felt the AI's response . . . a wordless realization that there were no human assets close enough for the view he required.

"CAG," he said. "I need some fighters in close to the OA."

"Right away, Admiral."

Several fighters arced in above the ring, vectoring in on the target. Zooming in close, using the fighters' telemetry, he studied the artificial terrain closely. *America*'s AI had suggested a possible approach . . . and it looked like it might be feasible.

But God, the *risks* . . .

Place of Cold Dreaming
Invictus Ring
1702 hours, TFT

"Seven-one-cee-eight!" the communicative electro-sense pulse cried as it rippled through its body. "The enemy appears to be attempting to isolate the Place of Cold Dreaming."

But Seven-one-cee-eight had already noted the human

attack pattern and come to that same conclusion. They should have taken the human prisoners deeper into the ring, but there'd simply been no time. Enemy fire had wrecked major transport passageways and corridors, smashed manufacturing and power supply centers, and breached hundreds of major habitation modules, spilling their water into space. Casualties already numbered in the tens of thousands.

But most of those casualties had been polyps, untrained and non-sapient—animals easily replaced. Only a tiny fraction of the ring's total volume had been compromised. There was no danger as yet.

And perhaps they could use the prisoner area as bait to lure the human fleet in closer for a crushing blow.

"Release another swarm," it ordered.

"We swarm together," was the reply.

Enormous sections of ring surface began flaking off into space, scattering, dividing into smaller units that swirled out toward the human fleet. Several flared and vanished almost at once as enemy missiles snapped in and detonated . . . but the defender swarms were entirely robotic. The Kin's defenses were much like the automated immune-response defenses of the body, reacting to perceived threats with little in the way of anticipation or originality of thought.

But there were a *very* great many of them, enough, perhaps, to utterly overwhelm the humans' handful of ships.

VFA-96, The Black Demons
Invictus Space, T+12 MY
1703 hours, TFT

Gregory steered his Starblade low across the surface of the ring, letting his fighter's AI maneuver the craft to avoid the irregularities of the landscape. It was, he thought, like flying through a city on Earth . . . not that he'd ever done such a thing, of course. The closest had been full-sim downloads of fighter passes over the ruins of Columbus, D.C., shortly after the Confederation had nano-nuked the place. Passing over a recent crater punched into the ring's surface by a five-ton high-velocity kinetic-kill projectile reminded him forcibly of the gaping crater where downtown Columbus once had been.

Ahead, a number of the frigate-sized ring pieces tumbled into the empty sky. The enemy had an apparently inexhaustible supply of those things, and sooner or later they were going to get through the task force's perimeter defenses and in among the heavies.

"Okay, Demons!" Mackey yelled. "Let's get 'em! We'll take 'em from their six!"

As the Glothr ships rose above the ring surface, the line of VFA-96 Starblades was in the perfect position to move into the widening gap between ring and ships, coming at the enemy from behind. It was a dangerous maneuver, for the task force was already hammering at the Glothr vessels, and the kill zone was going to be deadly, with crisscrossing beams, missiles, and fast-hurtling chunks of lead and depleted uranium.

"Target lock!" Collins called. "Arming ferdies . . . and . . . *Fox one*!"

A pair of Fer-de-lance missiles streaked from her ship, weaving low above the ring surface and then turning sharply out toward the Glothr ships. VG-44c antiship missiles were considerably more powerful than the smaller VG-10 Kraits. The twin nuclear detonations lit up the ring's surface like a pair of novae—death-silent, casting long, sharp-edged, paired shadows back across the dark gray surface.

Gregory brought his fighter around behind his point-singularity flickering ahead, rising now from the ring and accelerating hard. Projected from the prow of his fighter several thousand times each second, the artificial singularity puckered space ahead, drawing the Starblade along as it attempted to slide down the constantly moving slope of the gravity well.

In an instant, he was in among the Glothr ships, so close that he could maneuver in until he was skimming meters above the speed-blurred surface of one, slicing it almost end to end with the fast-pulsing micro-black hole forward. Gregory accelerated his mental processes, trying to keep pace. *Knife fighting . . .*

Turn . . . lock . . . fire . . . then accelerate, streaking back across the ring, the black disk of Invictus ahead of him as he lined up on another Glothr ship. This time he thought-triggered his KK cannon, sending a stream of depleted uranium into the alien's hull at very nearly point-blank range . . . fifty kilometers . . . twenty . . . five . . .

Gas gushed into space as he passed the shredding alien, freezing. More gas erupted in front of him as a pressure containment vessel exploded; his Starblade shuddered as it passed through a glittering explosion of ice crystals. For an instant, a shape registered in Gregory's awareness as it tumbled in front of him and then slammed against his fighter, rocking him hard to the side. For just a moment, a part of his brain thought that he'd just hit one of the Glothr flung from a hab area, but as it fragmented against his ship, he corrected that first impression. He'd just hit one of the cigar-shaped Glothr robots; its pieces were collapsing now into the haze of his fighter's drive singularity, causing the singularity to burn with an intense blue-violet glare.

He was in a slow tumble now, and it took him and his AI together to pull the fighter back onto an even keel.

He executed a thought command, trying to bring his fighter around so that he could align himself with another Glothr vessel . . . but with a cold and icy shock he realized that his fighter was not responding.

"Turn! Turn, damn you!" he yelled. "Ship! What's wrong?"

The fighter's AI replied with impressions and data rather than the clumsiness of words. His power systems had failed . . . drive system down . . . communications down . . .

Gregory was alone and helpless as he slid past the dark surface of the embattled Glothr ring, falling toward a black-frozen alien world.

USNA Star Carrier America
Invictus Space, T+12 MY
1704 hours, TFT

"*Northern California* reports that they have a major breach in the ring, Admiral," Mallory reported. "And enemy fire in that sector has fallen off to almost nothing."

"Very well," Gray replied. "Get some battlespace drones in there."

"Aye, aye, sir!"

"I want you to thread them into the structure through the breach. See if you can find the *Concord* and the *Pax*."

"Yes, sir."

Gray watched for a moment as a dozen remote drones closed with the ring, slipping one by one into the gaping hole blown open by the bombardment mements before. Clear telemetry streamed back to *America*, bringing shadowy images of the ring's interior, a vast and cavernous expanse surrounded by torn and twisted structure, girders, and hundreds of entryways to side passages and corridors.

He shifted mental channels. "Colonel Jamison!"

"Sir!"

"We're putting some drones into the AO, Colonel, *inside* the structure, as close to our people as we can manage. Do you have the feed?"

"We do, Admiral."

"Very well. You may deploy your force."

"*Ooh-rah!* On our way, Sir!"

"I don't want your people trapped inside," Gray added. "Keep them on the ring's surface until the fighters have cleared out the interior."

There was a hesitation on the other end. "Sir, that will restrict our ability to respond to the enemy a bit."

"Just do it, Colonel! I don't want that battalion becoming another bunch of POWs!"

"Yes, sir."

The Marine transport *Marne* was already edging closer toward the ragged edge of the ring, the fighters of both of her strike squadrons spilling from her launch tubes.

And behind the fighters came a cloud of MAPP-2 Assault Pods—Apache Tears, as they were called—light-drinking black teardrops of nanomatrix, each holding a fully armed and armored USNA Marine. There were more than a thousand of them in the cloud, moving together in concert as they edged their way up to the ragged crater that was their entrance into the ring.

"CAG," Gray said. "You still have the rest of *America*'s fighters on standby?"

"Yes, Admiral. The Dragonfires, the Lightnings, and the Impactors."

"Deploy them in support of the Marines, if you please."

"Aye, aye, sir. Launching fighters . . ."

Gray was extremely glad that *America* had been able to upgrade all of her fighters to the new SG-420 Starblades. When he'd been a fighter driver, about 12 million years ago, he'd flown the old SG-92 Starhawk . . . and he knew he'd not have wanted to try flying one of those inside an enclosed, debris-strewn compartment within an alien structure.

Fleet repair vessels like the *Vulcan*, and even *America* herself, could grow new fighters almost indefinitely, so long as they had sources of raw material available, and there was no good logistical reason to continue using outdated designs. The problem came with headware and with wetware—the training of human organic brains. There simply weren't enough pilots who'd grown up with the newest fighter systems as yet, and that might limit what they would be able to do in there.

Well, they would find out soon enough.

VFA-31, The Impactors
Invictus Space, T+12 MY
1705 hours, TFT

"Three . . . two . . . one . . . *drop!*"

Lieutenant Commander Edmond St. Clair felt the sensation of weight vanish as his Starblade fell down its launch tube and out into the starless void. *America*'s three flight decks, the outermost portions of the hab modules rotating around the carrier's spine about twice a minute, received the benefit of a half G of spin gravity. Releasing the fighters under that acceleration dropped them into open space behind *America*'s shield cap with an outward velocity of five meters per second, plus whatever forward momentum the carrier possessed at the moment of drop.

In open space, now, St. Clair accelerated slightly, moving clear of the huge curve of the carrier's shield cap, then nudged his Starblade forward.

St. Clair was still getting used to the new fighter. When he'd been with the British contingent of the Confederation military, he'd been trained and cybernetically equipped to fly the Franco-German KRG-60 Todtadler fighters . . . the "Death Eagles" that were roughly the equivalent of the USNA SG-101 Velociraptor. He'd received a nanobiological upgrade when he'd joined the USNA Navy, of course, including both chelated cybermemory upgrades and a genetic prosthesis to his organic brain designed to enhance his mental performance. He understood, however, that he was only able to control the Starblade at all because the Starblade's AI was able to emulate more primitive control systems like the Velociraptor and the Todtadler. It turned out that it was far easier to boost an AI's performance than to radically change the efficiency of the human brain.

"Form up on me," he told his squadron, and he kicked his Starblade into a gentle drift forward, past the immense curve of *America*'s shield cap, past the handful of task-force ships ahead, and in toward the tattered outer edge of the Invictus ring. White pulses of light strobed and flashed in all directions as nuclear detonations blossomed in silent display.

One of the USNA ships, the battleship *Illinois*, was badly damaged. Her shield cap had already been holed, but now it was shredded, an expanding cloud of jagged debris, and many of her weapons were out of action. The destroyer *Lackland* had been hit numerous times as well, and looked like she was out of the fight.

The fighters of St. Clair's squadron angled in toward the opening in the alien ring. Enemy fire from the ring structure had fallen off considerably in the past few minutes, but there were still a large number of the blocky, angular Glothr ships, and they were moving to try to intercept both the fighters and the Marine MAPP-2 pods. The Impactors, along with one of the marine squadrons, were deploying to cut them off.

A nuclear explosion flared off the ring's surface immediately in front of St. Clair, and his Starblade went into a savage tumble.

For a terrifying moment, St. Clair fell into black emptiness. . . .

Marine Transport Marne
Invictus Space, T+12 MY
1707 hours, TFT

The initial attack was being made by a single battalion off the *Marne*'s regimental assault group, supported by both of her Marine air-space squadrons, the Death Dealers and the Devil Dogs. Linked in within his high-tech cocoon on board the *Marne*, Colonel Joseph Jamison watched the deployment and directed the assault.

Jamison would have liked to stay linked with all twelve hundred of his troops, but not even the *Marne*'s formidable

AI could have accomplished that. Instead, he was receiving steady data feeds from both of his squadron commanders and from nearly sixty regimental, company, and platoon commanders; intelligence and tactical officers; battlespace drones; and artificial intelligences within the assault force. "Hold the entryway," he was telling Major Harrison Smith, his first batt commander. "Let the zoomies clear out the interior."

"But we're picking up transmissions from the *Pax*, Colonel," Smith told him. "She's only about ten kilometers in!"

"I don't care, Major. Hold that perimeter. I'll tell you when to move."

"Aye, aye, sir." Smith didn't sound pleased, but he was a good officer, and Jamison knew he could count on the man not to jump the gun. Jamison had served with Smith before, on Luna and in Earth orbit, and he knew he was a solid, reliable battalion CO. This was going to be a rough op—extracting hostages or POWs from enemy control always was—and Jamison wanted the CO at the sharp, pointy end to be one he could trust to follow orders.

Not that the other battalion COs weren't good. They were *Marines*, which made them by definition the very best. But he'd not been in combat with them, as he had with Smith . . . and that made a difference.

Data was pouring in from the fighter squadrons now, and Jamison opened his mind wider to receive it.

VFA-96, The Black Demons
Invictus Space, T+12 MY
1703 hours, TFT

Gregory knew he was in serious trouble. Nothing in his Starblade was responding. The best nanotechnology in Earth's entire military arsenal . . . and nothing was working. His fighter was past the ring, now, and falling steadily toward the vast, black globe of Invictus.

He *did* have power . . . a little. His auxiliary power tap was drawing a steady feed from the onboard singularity, a trickle of vacuum energy that was enough to keep his life support going, and to provide—if he was *very* lucky—enough maneuvering power to keep from slamming into the dark planet's surface at better than fifty kilometers per second. He would have to nurse that power, however, if he intended to survive the impact. His AI, thank the gods, was back on-line now, and had assumed piloting duties. Gregory felt a small bump as the AI applied a few seconds of deceleration to the fighter's internal grav-impeller blocks. You couldn't get much thrust from the things, but if they lasted long enough, if they survived the stress of a high-velocity planetary approach, he might still live through this.

At least for a while. How long he would survive on the bleak surface of Invictus was still anyone's guess.

Chapter Twenty-one

USNA Star Carrier America
Invictus Space, T+12 MY
1710 hours, TFT

"All ships!" Gray snapped. "Cease fire! Cease fire!"

The task force had been drifting closer and closer to the edge of the alien ring, but as USNA fighters and MAPPed Marines entered the structure, the likelihood of scoring an own goal grew more and more certain. The attack now was in the hands of the Marine assault force and the supporting fighters; all the capital ships could do from here on out was provide covering fire on the flanks . . . and protect the assault force from an attack from space.

The Marines had seized the rim of the crater punched into the edge of the ring and were holding it against Glothr robots making their way along the external surface. A Marine assault personnel pod was very much like a Starblade fighter, but with a far more flexible and adaptable nanomatrix form: essentially a tarlike semisolid surrounding an inner capsule holding one Marine; the power, drive, and control systems; and a particle cannon. A MAPP-2 Apache Tear could extend parts of itself to grab hold of the bulkhead of an alien ship or fortress; could dissolve its way through to the interior; could even walk, after a clumsy fashion, though it generally hovered on gravitic impellers. The light-absorbing outer surface made it all but invisible against the blackness of space, and the particle cannon let it serve as a fighter if necessary, albeit slow and awkward.

Right now, nearly twelve hundred Marines in MAPP-2 assault pods were clinging to the ragged edge of the cavern opened in the ring surface, using their particle beams to fend off the gathering swarms of Glothr robots. Gray recognized a serious tactical danger in the situation. He'd ordered Jamison's Marines to stay put at the entrance until the way inside had been cleared out by the USNA fighters . . . but the longer they waited there, holding their perimeter, the more time the Glothr had to gather their forces. Through his data feed, Gray was aware of some thousands of Glothr robots out beyond the Marine perimeter, taking advantage of every bit of cover provided by the blasted and twisted architecture of the ring surface as they steadily moved closer. So far as Gray knew, the Marines of the *Marne*'s regimental assault group were up against an entire planet's worth of defenders and defending technologies, and it wouldn't pay at all to hang around longer than was absolutely necessary.

With a sudden shock, Gray realized that he was playing the role of MMREMF.

REMFs—the acronym's *polite* translation was "rear-echelon mothers"—had been the bane of frontline troops for centuries . . . the gold-braid-heavy bastards who drew their plans in the comfort and safety of headquarters and gave the orders that sent men out to die. *Micro-managing* REMFs were infinitely worse.

Starting in the late twentieth century, military operations had been dominated more and more by advancing communications technologies designed to eliminate the ancient fog of war. It had become possible for generals—even government leaders—to watch a battle unfold in real time *and to give orders to the officers on the ground from thousands of kilometers away.*

Unfortunately, being able to see and hear all that was happening from the other side of the planet didn't necessarily convey the battlefield reality. The commander of the forces on the ground knew things the political and military leaders in the rear could never possibly know—the temper and morale of the troops, for instance, how tired they were, how scared, how exposed, or how close they were to breaking. The fact that the people in the rear had not gone through the same training as the troops on the ground, or in the band-of-brothers camaraderie they shared, meant that those leaders would always be out of touch, to some degree, with the men and women on the ground.

Military history included more than one account of field commanders who had suddenly and mysteriously suffered "communications difficulties" that had allowed them to ignore orders from the rear.

Over the next few centuries, the technology had only improved, making convenient comm difficulties harder and harder to explain . . . or invoke.

Earth and the USNA military leadership was 12 million years in the past, and tens of thousands of light years distant, but Gray himself now constituted a local REMF, watching the Marine deployment from his seat on the flag bridge and giving orders to the Marine commanders. A micromanaging REMF, no less.

"Colonel Jamison."

"Yes, Admiral."

"It occurs to me that you and I are . . . removed a bit from the engagement. Perhaps we should give Major Smith his head."

"I concur, Admiral." There was a long hesitation. "Thank you."

"Give 'em hell, Colonel."

"Aye, aye, Admiral."

1/4 Marines
4th Regimental Assault Group, 1st MARDIV
Invictus Space, T+12 MY
1710 hours, TFT

The First Battalion, Fourth Marine Regiment of the First Marine Division clung to the ragged edge of a black and bottomless hell, fighting for its life. Major Harrison Smith edged his MAPP along a half-melted fold of ring material, trying to get a better look at the enemy advance along this sector of the perimeter.

Two of his Marines were crouched just ahead, looking like jet-black three-meter-wide amoebae clinging to the twisted and ice-covered surface. One of them edged above the lip of the crater, the muzzle of his pee-beep protruding from the rippling black nanomatrix of his pod. Alphanumerics scrolling past Smith's vision identified the Marines—PFC Gene Sanders and Lance Corporal Ed Moultrie.

Moultrie's weapon fired, eliciting a brief hiss of static over Smith's comm unit. A hundred meters away, a silvery, cigar-shaped object flared in a brilliant light, fragmenting.

"*Got* the bastard!"

"Good shot, Moultrie," Smith said.

The man almost jumped off his perch. "Oh! Uh . . . thank you, sir!"

"Don't mind me," Smith said. "Keep after 'em!"

"Aye, aye, sir!"

Smith moved away. "Shit!" the voice of PFC Sanders said in something like awe. "Was that the *skipper*?"

"One of 'em, Sanders," Moultrie replied. "Forget about it. Keep firing!"

Smith chuckled to himself. Rank-and-file Marines tended not to expect the brass to come poking around their fighting positions, not in the middle of a hot firefight. He liked to keep them on their toes.

Or, in this case, on their pseudopods. MAPP-2 units were

slow and clumsy as fighters in open space, but they served well as highly specialized combat armor on the surface, especially when that surface was uneven and possessed an uncertain gravity.

There *was* gravity here on the outer edge of the Invictus ring—the total mass of the ring was that of a small planet, added to the more powerful pull of Invictus itself; the ring was rotating slowly, however, keeping match with the planet's leisurely forty-four-hour rotation, and the outward centrifugal force generated by that rotation cancelled a great deal of that attraction. There was, in fact, just enough gravity that the immense hole in the edge of the ring—a good eight kilometers across—felt like down, but a misstep could send you flying here, and without grav impellers you might find yourself in orbit. MAPP-2 units had originally been designed for operations on the surfaces of asteroids, or on the outside hulls of orbital structures like planetary fortresses or orbital manufactories, places where Marines needed something that could serve as both spaceship and personal armor, depending on the situation.

Extending another pseudopod, Smith reached for a fold in the ring structure's surface, let the nanomatrix on his gauntlet's palm adhere to it, and then pulled himself across. Light flared above him—another particle burst, though he didn't know if it had been fired by Marine or Glothr.

Another blast—silent, but sending a rippling shock wave through the surface strong enough to break his hold. Smith latched on with three more pseudopods, then directed his attention up and out. Sure enough, one of the frigate-sized Glothr ships was there, five kilometers overhead and dropping toward the surface, firing as it came. Smith extended his particle-beam weapon, locked on, and triggered it, sending a stream of protons slashing into the target. Other Marines opened fire on the intruder as well, but not before the Glothr ship fired again, sending several Apache Tears tumbling off into space.

Damn it . . . how long are we going to be kept here in this exposed position?

"Castle Rock, Castle Rock!" he called. "This is One-Four! We need some cover down here!"

"One-Four, Castle Rock," the voice of the assault group's command/control center replied. "On the way!"

The concentrated fire from the Marines on the perimeter seemed to be having an effect. The frigate was pulling back, now, as bright flashes and sparkles across its surface showed dozens of hits. An instant later, the Glothr ship crumpled as gravitic rounds from the battleship *New York* slashed into the boxy structure and began devouring it from the inside out.

Gravitic guns in the human arsenal were relatively recent developments of one of the enemy's weapons—weapons developed originally by the Turusch for planetary bombardment and used in their attacks on Haris and Osiris. They were difficult and dangerous weapons—they tended to sear nearby space with intense bursts of gamma and X-rays as they ate their way through solid matter—and were rarely used in fleet actions, but the big battleships each mounted a couple of grav cannon turrets and, sometimes, they could be used against capital ships with considerable effectiveness.

Crippled, the Glothr ship drifted toward the horizon. A flight of four Navy fighters pursued it.

Most of the zoomies—the fighter pilots—had already descended into the hole and were supposed to be clearing the way for the main body of Marines, but if they had to sit perched up here for much longer, those Glothr monsters were going to sweep them right off into space.

Smith was getting a steady feed of data, both from assault-team drones already inside the ring structure and from the command-control center on the *Marne*. The two captured High Guard ships, he noted, had been identified already, their locations marked on his in-head maps.

Another explosion, this one quite close. Smith hugged

the smoothly rippled surface, then looked up. Moultrie and Sanders had taken a direct hit; what was left of their MAPPs was drifting off into space, an expanding cloud of hot gas.

Shit!

He looked for another Glothr ship . . . but then a group of the cigar-shaped robots appeared above the lip of the crater, just thirty meters from Smith's position. He swung his weapon about, his MAPP-2 unit flowing like water to both track the targets and to keep him snugged down against the surface. He fired . . . and a half dozen other Marines opened up as well. The Glothr robots, thank the gods of battle, tended to be a bit on the sluggish side, as though they were being controlled under a time lag. In seconds, the entire group, four or five of the machines, had been shot to bits.

But there were so many, many more—all of them, it seemed, headed this way.

"One-Four, this is Castle Rock." The voice and ID were those of Colonel Jamison.

"This is One-Four. Go ahead!"

"You're clear to move into the interior, Harry," Jamison told him. "At your discretion, advance on the *Pax* and the *Concord*."

"It's about fucking time! Heads up, Marines! We're going spaceborne!"

The order was answered by a chorus of shouts from Marine throats, a roar of battle cries as twelve hundred Marines rose from cover and dropped into hell. . . .

VFA-96, The Black Demons
Invictus Ring, T+12 MY
1712 hours, TFT

Lieutenant Fred Dahlquist wrestled his Starblade onto the correct vector and punched it, dropping through the gaping crater on the outer rim of the massive alien ring. This, he reflected, was something new, something never covered in the training simulations: piloting a high-performance nanomatrix fighter *inside* an alien structure.

He had to cut way, way back on his forward velocity as soon as he entered the crater. The normal velocities associated with deep-space combat would have slammed him into the far wall of the interior space in less time than an eye's blink. Dropping now at a few hundred meters per second, he scanned the surrounding space, a cavern with black walls, unlit and made complicated by structural components—stalactites and stalagmites stretching out into the gulf as if to claw the invading fighters from the sky.

The Black Demons had taken some heavy losses in the past few moments. Dobbs and Martinez were dead, fried by those Glothr flying buildings. Hathaway was dead, caught in a nuclear fireball, the wreckage smeared across the outer surface of the ring. Gregory was missing . . . gone streaker and last seen dropping out of control toward the planet. And Schmitt had been killed earlier, in the tangle with the Tushies in front of the TRGA.

Over a third of the squadron, wiped out just like that.

All around him, Marines were entering the cavern, almost invisible in their light-drinking nanomatrix assault pods . . . not that there was much in the way of visible light in here. His visual feeds were mostly infrared. The six other Black Demons were scattered across the enclosed space, mixed in with the older Velociraptors of the Marines. High-energy proton beams swept up and out from the depths of the pit; Marine MAPPs flared like moths in a flame . . . and died.

"I've got a gun position locked!" Connor said. "Zero-one-niner . . . firing!"

Connor's Starblade loosed a brief stream of high-velocity kinetic-kill rounds, dropping them with deadly accuracy into a pit housing a Glothr energy weapon. Visible light erupted from the pit, along with hurtling fragments.

"Nice shot, Meg!" Caswell yelled.

It *had* been a good shot, Dahlquist thought, a direct hit from eight kilometers with high deflection and without the benefit of a target lock or smart ordnance. Dahlquist wondered how Connor was holding up, knowing her lover was lost outside. . . .

"Form up, Demons," the squadron's CO called. "Tuck it in! Tuck it in!" Mackey had a thing about messy formations. Not that nicely ordered ranks were going to help in *here*.

But ten kilometers ahead, he could see their goal: the blunt shield-cap noses of two human starships, tucked away among the gantries and derricks of something that might be a shipyard. They were aglow in deep infrared light, and appeared to be nestled close to a pair of the emnigmatic Glothr time-benders.

The human ships—his *brother's* ship—just ahead.

"Objectives in sight!" he called to the others. "*Pax* and *Concord*, bearing zero-zero-zero at eight kilometers!"

"Let's get in there, people," Mackey said. "The Marines need some cover! Keep it tight, people. . . ."

Place of Cold Dreaming
Invictus Ring
1713 hours, TFT

"Seven-one-cee-eight! The enemy is entering the ring in force!"

"I see it. Try to hold them. We are deploying more of the time-twisters."

"There may be too many for—"

The transmission cut off with startling abruptness.

Numbers and technology, Seven-one-cee-eight thought, should have been sufficient to pin, overwhelm, and destroy this surprisingly dogged enemy, but it appeared that they possessed a tactical advantage that might well result in the Kin's defeat. They were *fast*, their nervous systems functioning several times more quickly and more efficiently than those of the Kin, which meant that their reaction times were faster, their aim surer, their battlefield responses much quicker. The Kin's robotic servants had been developed to counter the reaction time superiority of many other species within the Sh'daar associative, allowing freer and more accurate communication with faster minds, but even minor differences in reaction times were still serious enough to create a major disadvantage in combat, both ship-to-ship and among troops on the ground or in space.

It connected with one of the other Kin. "Dee-one-three-jay! Bring your twisters forward."

"That will mean releasing the human ships."

"If we do not, we will lose the human ships in any case. I want you to attempt to stop the attack through the breach."

"I am doubtful, Seven-one-cee-eight. There are too many of them."

"I doubt as well, Dee-one-three-jay. But it is the only chance we have."

"We swarm together."

We swarm together. The phrase, a statement of agreement and compliance, was the equivalent of a human's "yes, sir" or "aye, aye." When the Kin were in their juvenile phase, they swarmed their world's ammonia-water seas in the hundreds of billions, minute, translucent polyps possessing only the rudiments of consciousness or sentience. By banding together in vast, cloudy masses aglow with bioluminescence, they defended themselves against the predators of Invictus's vast and abyssal deeps.

The phrase was also a cultural reminder that no member of the Kin was above another, save as an accident of circumstance; the battle against the human fleet was a communal effort.

And as such, Seven-one-cee-eight was beginning to believe, they may have revealed a critical weakness in the Kin's defenses. Humans, it had learned during its brief stay on Earth, were often divided and weak, but they could come together under common leadership in a way that was surprisingly strong. Their leaders were *trained* as leaders, and did not relinquish their role.

Surely, though, that limited the experience of any given leader? In its career, Seven-one-cee-eight had been ship master and crewman, swarm leader and drone. It knew all sides of the social equation, and could sense the thrill of the entire electrical current.

It wondered if that would be enough to defeat these humans, these monsters from the abyss of time and space. . . .

VMFA-77, "Devil Dogs"
4ᵗʰ Regimental Assault Group
Invictus Space, T+12 MY
1714 hours, TFT

Lieutenant Roger Mayhew used his mental link with his AI to bring his Velociraptor around onto a new heading, angling toward the far end of the vast, dark cavern of the ring interior. Blackness enveloped him, then gave way to the blue and green glows of cool infrared. His fighter gave a shudder as he cut acceleration, and he wondered if the old Velociraptor was up to this.

The Marines had an old and venerable tradition of making do with older equipment—not entirely true in the case of the MAPP-2 units, but definitely for Marine space-air. VMFA-77 had received the SG-101s the year before, but the Marine Corps' budget hadn't yet allowed for those strike fighters to be replaced by the much newer and more modern Starblades.

In fact, Velociraptors weren't *that* old. They'd only come on-line a couple of years ago, but indisputably, the 'Blades were newer, faster, and more powerful, and military technology was galloping ahead into an alien future faster than any human could keep up.

It would be damned nice, Mayhew thought, if the Corps could just once in a while deploy with truly frontline and first-rate gear, something that wouldn't be obsolete a few months later. Veloci*crappers*. That was the nickname for the SG-101s within the Marine strike squadrons that flew them.

He wondered what would be replacing Starblades . . . and how much longer they would remain cutting edge.

"Green One," he called, "Green Seven. I've got a lock on one of the Guard ships. The *Pax*, I think."

"Copy that, Seven," Captain Larson, the Devil Dogs' skipper, replied. "Move in as close as you can."

"Roj." He cut his forward velocity to nearly nothing, switched off his gravitic drive, and let the weak local gravity drag him deeper into the black, vertical canyon at a few meters per second. The *Pax* was nestled in among a forest of gantries and structural supports, almost inaccessible. She didn't appear damaged at all, but there was no sign of life, no wink of navigation strobes, no indication of onboard power, no open communications channels.

"There's the other one over there," Lieutenant Kathryn Bixby, Green Five, said. "Wait . . . what's that moving next to the *Pax*?"

Mayhew saw the movement in the same moment: a silver cylinder, pointed at both ends and tucked away in the gantries and derricks directly alongside the *Pax*.

"Stay clear of that thing!" Mayhew warned. "It's a Glothr time-bender!"

"There's another one!" Lieutenant Ramirez called. "Next to the *Concord*!"

"I think," Mayhew said, "that they're bringing out the big guns."

VFA-96, The Black Demons
Invictus surface, T+12 MY
1715 hours, TFT

Gregory didn't remember much of his passage through to the Invictan surface. His AI had taken over what remained of his fighter's maneuvering systems, but there wasn't enough power left over to let him see what was going on. Encased in blackness, he'd crouched within the embrace of his Starblade's cockpit, straining to breathe against the crushing pressure of deceleration. The fighter's gravitic drive boosted the ship and its pilot in free fall, permitting accelerations of tens of thousands of gravities, but the small impellers used as an auxiliary drive did not. As the Starblade dropped toward Invictus, the straining impellers applied more and more thrust, reaching ten Gs and bringing Gregory to the ragged edge of unconsciousness.

The impellers failed, and for a stomach-wrenching moment, Gregory was again in free fall, dropping through emptiness.

The Starblade stuck the surface at an oblique angle, guided by the AI to come in almost parallel to the surface. He felt the shock of impact . . . another moment of free fall . . . another jolt . . . and then he was tumbling over and over, slamming against one side of the pilot capsule and then the other until at long, long last, he came to a shuddering halt.

He was down.

"AI!" he called. "Can you get me a visual feed?"

There was no response, and he remained in blackness. He wondered if the Starblade, all of its systems, was completely dead.

He still had his in-head icons up and running, however. He triggered the icon that would begin the reboot process, hoping to bring his fighter's AI back to life.

Without it, he was dead.

1/4 Marines
4th Regimental Assault Group, 1st MARDIV
Invictus Space, T+12 MY
1717 hours, TFT

It had been a long time, Major Smith decided, since the Marines had taken part in an old-fashioned over-the-top *charge*.

Black MAPP units were flowing down the internal walls of the crater in a cloud, accelerating into the depths, as Glothr fire snapped and flared from farther down inside the depths. Ahead, Smith could see the Marine fighters tangling with a couple of Glothr ships. . . .

No—not just ships! Those two shapes were the alien time-warping units, like the one that had originally immobilized the *Concord* on board the first Glothr ship they'd encountered back at Sol. Whether it was an independent warship or a piece of machinery—a weapon mounted here inside the ring—was unknown. What *was* known was that the things were *extremely* dangerous. . . .

"Open up on those two big targets," Smith ordered his Marines. "Don't let them deploy!"

Particle beams and laser fire snapped across the dwindling last few kilometers. The Marines were sharply limited in the weapons they could use in these close confines. Nuke shipkillers would destroy their surroundings as well as the targets, might damage the two imprisoned High Guard vessels as well—and probably kill any Marines in proximity.

Time, Smith noticed, seemed to be slowing to a crawl, and he wondered if the effect was due to the alien temporal weapons or if it was simply a subjective effect of intense and deadly combat.

Chapter Twenty-two

USNS/HGF Concord
Invictis Ring, T+12 MY
1718 hours, TFT

From Terrance Dahlquist's perspective, *Concord* had been captured barely an instant ago. The High Guard ship had been accelerating out from Invictus, pushing *c* hard on her way back to rejoin the task force at the TRGA cylinder, when a Glothr time-bending ship had come up through the starbow of weirdly twisted space ahead of the ship—*ahead*, since one of the illusions of near-*c* travel made objects coming from behind appear to be ahead and to one side. Dahlquist had had just enough time to scream a warning through the ship's intercom: *"Brace for collision!"*

And then . . . nothing.

He took a deep breath. He'd been panting with the exertion, the stress, the raw fear . . . and now *Concord* was someplace else entirely. His data feeds showed that she was no longer accelerating, no longer moving close to the speed of light, that the ship, in fact, was now *inside* some sort of immense hanger or orbital facility.

The inrush of new data was staggering, a torrent, a waterfall of information about the ship and surrounding space. Dahlquist scanned the ship's surroundings, startled to see that *Concord* now appeared to be motionless in a space dock of some sort, surrounded by scaffolding and the tiny, hovering shapes of Glothr robots. A flash dazzled his in-head eye, and he realized that wherever they were, they were in the eye of a fiercely raging battle. A Glothr ship, sleek and sharply pointed on both ends, was sliding clear of the dock and away from the *Concord*. That, he decided, was why the passage of time had resumed for the captured ship; the mechanisms that had slowed time for the *Concord* and the *Pax* were now moving away, and taking their time-slowing fields with them.

In the distance, human fighters, both Starblades and Velociraptors, were approaching, together with a large number of troops in MAPP-2 assault pods. The battle was savage and unrelenting: Dahlquist watched as Marines were picked off; fighters were picked off; torrents of particle-beam and laser fire were directed against the alien time benders.

Dahlquist had no way of knowing how much time had passed since *Concord* had been captured, since every computer, AI, and timekeeping device on board the ship had been frozen in time with the ship itself. It could be hours later . . . or centuries. . . .

No, not centuries. Fighter designs changed so rapidly that if centuries had passed since *Concord*'s capture, the fighters out there would be unrecognizable. The Marines on board the *Marne*, he remembered, still used 'Raptors. The chances were excellent that those fighters out there were part of *America*'s TF-1.

Hell, one of those Starblades might well be Fred's.

Hard on the heels of that revelation came another. *They'd come for them!* Specifically, Admiral Gray had brought the whole task force into . . . whatever this alien place was to find the *Concord* and *Pax* and rescue them.

And that single fact put a different spin on things for Dahlquist.

Sure, human warriors operated under a sacred ethos, one that said that you never left your own behind . . . but sometimes—more often than not, perhaps—there was simply no way to honor that promise.

Which made it damned special when your own *did* come back for you.

Gregory
VFA-96, The Black Demons
Invictus surface, T+12 MY
1725 hours, TFT

Gregory felt the hull of his crippled Starblade give a shudder. It was cooling fast, and he didn't have much time left.

He'd finally been able to reboot his AI, and then get an exterior view, the image revealed on an in-head window. Not that it helped much. The landscape outside was black and frigid, with rocks made of water-ice and the galaxy hanging above one horizon, cold, beautiful, and remote. The temperature, according to his feed, was just twenty degrees Kelvin. The heat remaining in his Starblade was leaching out into the ice at a horrific rate; his life support system was struggling to keep up, but it wouldn't be long, Gregory knew, before the system would die.

And then so would he.

His Starblade was sending out an automated distress signal, but there was very little power behind it. He doubted that any SAR vehicles off the *America* would be able to pick it up. His communications were out as well. Again, no power.

Somewhere, he thought, somewhere far below him—a hundred kilometers or more if the theories he'd heard about Invictus were correct—there was warmth enough to keep a vast ocean liquid. There, life had evolved, and intelligence, and an advanced, star-faring civilization. The Glothr eventually had escaped the icy prison of their world and built the incredible ring system overhead, and traveled now between the stars and across time itself.

He wondered if there was any way of attracting the notice of Glothr living in the world ocean underneath the ice. Probably not. His AI didn't seem to have any ideas.

At the current rate of heat loss from his Starblade, he would start to feel the cold in an hour or two, would be frozen into a solid block of ice in four. He was wearing a pressure suit, but if he opened the Starblade's nanomatrix hull and stepped out into that frigid hell, it wouldn't keep him alive more than a couple of minutes.

Don Gregory quietly contemplated the certainty of death, thought about Meg, and prepared to die.

Connor
VFA-96, The Black Demons
Invictus surface, T+12 MY
1725 hours, TFT

Lieutenant Megan Connor pulled her fighter up, trying to avoid the time-slow field somehow being broadcast from the sleek Glothr ship ahead. Her ship jolted . . . then slowed—slowed *a lot*—and she realized that she'd been caught in the alien temporal field.

"Watch out!" she called over the squadron channel. "That time-twister shit is active!" She'd thought it was switched off, but apparently they'd turned it on again. Or, rather, it appeared that they could project that field several hundred meters in one direction or another. *Damn* . . .

"Copy, Demon Three," Mackey replied. "Get your ass out of there!"

"Trying . . ."

Tears had gathered on her face and she'd not been able to wipe them away, not without opening her helmet . . . but now she felt the pull of gravity against her as the ship dragged through the temporal field and she shook her head, hard, trying to dislodge the gleaming droplets of liquid. She detested the tears, the weakness . . . but was still having trouble getting past the fact that Don was *gone*.

That, of course, was the biggest single problem with forming emotional attachments to other pilots, or to other shipmates in general, for that matter. It was one thing when you knew your loved one was back on Earth or a colony world, waiting for your return. It was quite something else when that loved one was flying off your wing, and was in just as much danger of being killed as you.

She and Don had discussed it, of course, but it had always seemed so fucking *theoretical*. They'd thought they'd come to grips with the possibility of losing one another, thought it was all right. Hell—it hadn't even been all that serious. *Fuck buddies*, that was all they'd been. Friends with benefits, as the old joke had it. Recreational sex wasn't supposed to get so damned serious.

But now his Starblade was lost, singed by a near hit and sent hurtling off into emptiness, and she knew that she'd been fooling herself. *America*'s SAR units would be deployed in a search, of course, but the chances of finding one small nanomatrix fighter out there in all that nothingness were somewhere between remote and nonexistent.

Assuming, of course, that he was even alive now. The odds of surviving as a fighter pilot in all-out ship-to-ship combat were not good to begin with. Worse, the SAR tugs wouldn't be deployed until the battle was over and then only if the human fleet had won.

Connor screamed, a sonic burst of pent-up rage and frustration. If the battle had to end then, damn it, *she would end it*. She lined up with the alien time bender, now drifting slowly past her bow a hundred meters below, and loosed a stream of depleted-uranium KK projectiles from her ship's high-speed Gatling.

"Take *that*, you fucking bastards!"

USNA Star Carrier America
Invictus Space, T+12 MY
1728 hours, TFT

"Admiral Gray? Truitt here."

"Make it quick, Doctor. We're a little busy up here."

"I understand that. But I've been going through the data we picked up a month ago from Surat. There's something here you should see."

Gray very nearly dismissed Truitt with a sharp "tell me later." The head of *America*'s xenosoph department was acerbic and difficult, a true genius with indifferent social skills and no patience at all for what he perceived as stupidity in others.

But he was undeniably brilliant, and if he'd just run into something he felt was important enough to disturb him during *combat*—it was a damned good idea for Gray to at the very least find out what it was.

"What have you got for us?"

"A complete bio-profile on the Glothr. Apparently, the Confederation xeno people at Surat were in the middle of doing a complete workup when the Glothr ship lifted off."

"And?"

"Have a look."

Data streamed down the link, translated from Hindi. There was a lot . . . including speculation on Glothr natural history, their evolution in an under-ice ocean, their transition from a marine species to dry land some millions of years ago—even the possibility that that evolution had been directed by another sapient species.

Those damned stargods again.

But that wasn't what Truitt wanted him to notice. Gray's eyes went to where the doctor had flagged the information about Glothr senses.

"While the Glothr possess organs sensitive to light, especially at shorter wavelengths and extending up into the ultraviolet, vision does not appear to be their primary sense.

Instead, they appear to rely on an electro-sense similar in certain respects to the sense employed by sharks, rays, and other terrestrial marine species. Their primary means of determining the shape and content of their surroundings would seem to be the electro-sense. . . ."

"What's your point, Dr. Truitt?"

"I should think that would be obvious, Admiral. The Glothr may be susceptible to an EMP."

"Check that," he told the ship's AI. Returning to the open channel with Truitt, he asked, "Delivered how?"

"A large enough particle-beam weapon would do it."

"We've been hammering them with pee-beeps and nukes all evening, and they don't seem to mind it at all."

"If you can get through their shielding, Admiral, get in *close*, you might find differently."

Data was coming back from the AI now. "Let me check it out, Doc. I'll talk to you later."

There was something to what Truitt had suggested.

In fact, *America*'s AI had already come up with the same damned idea.

VFA-31, The Impactors
Invictus Space, T+12 MY
1729 hours, TFT

For half an hour, St. Clair had fallen into the night.

His terror had grown through the course of those thirty minutes until he'd thought his fast-pounding heart would explode, and sweat poured down his face inside his pressure helmet, blinding him.

He'd been able to see through his in-head displays, though, and he'd stared into that ultimate night, unable to switch it off despite the hammering, nightmare fear. *Alone . . . alone in the night . . .*

America's psych department had checked him out thoroughly, of course, immediately after his rescue. And in fact he'd not thought he'd needed to be checked out. When he'd been singed in the tangle with the Turusch, he'd been knocked unconscious, and he'd not come around until he'd been back on board *America*, in the star carrier's sick bay. That had been . . . what? Just fourteen hours ago.

But something had happened, because he was feeling inexpressible terror now as, for the second time in twenty-four hours, his Starblade fell through emptiness into the intergalactic Void.

He checked to make sure his crippled fighter was broadcasting an emergency signal. He'd been picked up by a SAR tug once; maybe they could do it again. If they didn't, he would die a hideously cold and lonely death, out here thousands of light years away from the nearest star.

His vector, he noticed, was taking him past the black disk of Invictus. Maybe *they* would pick him up. . . .

Something brushed his mind.

"Wait," he said aloud. "Wait . . . what was that?"

His AI reached out, struggling to collect and amplify an impossibly weak signal. There! It wasn't much, but it sounded like another distress signal, just a whisper, coming from the surface of Invictus.

Well, major fighter battles always resulted in streakers. Evidently, one had made it safely down to the surface of the rogue world. There wasn't a lot that St. Clair could do about it right at the moment.

USNA Star Carrier America
Invictus Space, T+12 MY
1730 hours, TFT

On Gray's in-head display, he could see a graphic schematic of the battle inside the ring structure. There'd been a report from one of the Black Demon pilots that the Glothr time benders were using their temporal weapon again. He'd already given orders to the ships already inside the ring structure to concentrate their fire on those two vessels, to try to put them out of the fight.

He would have to assume that his forward units would be able to do that, to open the way for the heavies coming in now.

"New York," he said. *"Northern Cal, Illinois*, you stay put and provide long-range cover. We're going in." Acknowledgements snapped back through his in-head link.

He thought more about Truitt's "revelation." He smiled a bit, knowing the AI had proposed this possibility days ago. Gray had struggled figuring out a way to use it, though . . . until now.

EMPs—electromagnetic pulses—were surges of electrons that could be natural, such as in a lightning bolt, or artificial, from a charged particle weapon or a nuclear detonation. Effects of EMPs had been understood since the mid-twentieth century and the development of atomic weapons. In one famous experiment carried out in 1962, dubbed Operation Starfish Prime, a 1.4-megaton hydrogen bomb was detonated four hundred kilometers above Johnston Island, in the Pacific. The EMP from that blast was much more powerful than expected, knocking out three hundred streetlights in Hawaii, almost fifteen hundred kilometers away, killing a telephone microwave link, and disrupting intra-island phone service. The explosion also generated brilliant auroras. The electron flow tended to damage unprotected electrical equipment, though systems were well-shielded nowadays. In warships, especially, which used nuclear warheads and particle beams as weapons, such shielding was absolutely vital.

It had been assumed, of course, that the Glothr, too, knew how to shield their vessels against EMP effects, since they used beam weapons similar to those used by humans. And the barrages launched by the human vessels so far, while effective, had not caused any obvious problems for the enemy from pulses of electromagnetic radiation.

But, as *America*'s AI had reminded Gray hours before, it was all a matter of degree. Load the energy shields encasing the Glothr ships with a big enough charge, and it should be possible to burn through with a monster EMP . . . one that would not only damage equipment, but affect the aliens directly. If their electro-sense was indeed analogous to human sight, as the biological studies completed so far suggested, a strong EMP would be similar to dazzling a human with a brilliant spotlight, or even, at high enough levels, a high-energy optical laser aimed at the eyes.

The Starfish Prime pulse had burned out circuits fifteen hundred kilometers away, but Gray assumed they would need to get *much* closer than that to burn their way through the Glothr magnetic shields. The ship's AI agreed; if possible, they needed to get a couple of the heavies—two of the three battleships, if possible—right alongside the Glothr circuits.

The fact that those circuits were well inside the massive ring structure ahead was daunting, but the fighters, the destroyers and frigates, and the assaulting Marines appeared to have taken out defensive positions inside that vast cavern. The two Glothr time benders were edging forward now, but were taking the full brunt of the fire being laid down by the human forces.

Both battleships possessed four electron cannon turrets, while *America* herself mounted one. A combined barrage at point-blank range ought to overwhelm any magnetic defenses the Glothr had in there, and take down their shields.

That, at least, was the idea.

"Captain Gutierrez," Gray said quietly. "You may take us in there."

"Aye, aye, Admiral."

She didn't sound happy about it.

USNS/HGF Concord
Invictis Ring, T+12 MY
1731 hours, TFT

"Be careful of the good guys!" Dahlquist snapped. "I don't want any own goals!"

"If the target explodes," Denise Ames warned, "there may be . . . collateral damage, sir."

"I know. But we've got to help!"

"If we limit our fire to the pee-beeps," she told him, "we should be able to damage those things, but not to the point where they explode or release rogue singularities."

"What about our lasers?"

"Not a good idea, sir. The aliens' hulls are as shiny as mirrors." Ames brought a set of cursors across the alien vessel, highlighting a damaged section. "There appears to be a hull breach in this area, however. The local shields have been weakened."

"Very well. Target that area. Turret Three. Fire!"

"Firing Turret Three, sir."

A beam of coherent protons lanced out, catching the slender cylinder drifting above the *Concord* amidships. The aliens were shielded, of course—with magnetic fields that could be flipped positive or negative at the instant of a hostile beam's touch. They also could project something like the human gravitic shielding, literally bending space just above their vessels' hulls to fold hostile beams back, or disrupt incoming missiles.

At a range of less than a hundred meters, though, *Concord*'s beam clawed at the enemy's defenses, focused on a small patch where a fighter's KK projectiles had slammed into the hull moments before . . . and some of that torrent of energy managed to burn through before the alien mag shield could repel the incoming protons. Some of the hull projectors at that point were vaporized by the intense heat, and a portion of the Glothr ship's shielding, already weakened, went dark.

"Again!" Dahlquist yelled. "Hit them again! Same spot!"

Mirror-bright hull material, made of an ultra-hard plastic coated with a highly reflective polyester film, blackened and crinkled, then puffed out into vacuum in a cloud of hot plasma.

"Hit!" Ames called. "Burn through!"

"Yeah, screw with our time *now*, you bastards!" Dahlquist said.

Marines in nearby space saw what was happening to the alien, and began turning their weapons on the ship's hull as well, and a destroyer and two frigates entering the cavern several kilometers overhead added their fire to the fusillade. The *Pax* had joined in as well, hurling proton beams at the time bender still hovering alongside her.

But something appeared to be wrong. With a sense of growing horror, Dahlquist became aware that the distant USNA ships were . . . *jittering*, moving back and forth in erratic, rapid jumps, as though they were station keeping, but far, far too quickly.

The time benders were using their unique weapons again, slowing time for the *Concord*, and also for the nearest Marines, drawing them all into a field where the passage of time was far slower than it was for ships outside the area of effect. The frequency of energy weapons fired within that field dropped as time slowed, until even direct hits did very little damage at all.

Damn it, they wouldn't be able to break free if they were frozen in time! And the Marines outside were obviously struggling with the area effect as well, moving back and out of range before they, too, were frozen like insects trapped in amber.

"Hit them!" he yelled. "Keep hitting them!"

But minutes had already passed, and felt like a bright-edged instant as they did.

VFA-31, The Impactors
Invictus Space, T+12 MY
1733 hours, TFT

When his AI had at last reported that his fighter was again operable, St. Clair had very nearly passed out. The terror, the loneliness, the sheer nightmare fear gripping him as he streaked into emptiness had been growing steadily, threatening to overwhelm him. Then his fighter's drive was online, safe, and ready to engage. His first instinct had been to switch on his gravitic drive, flip his Starblade end for end to align with the task force, and accelerate hard, heading back to the human fleet as quickly as he could.

But he kept remembering that fragment of a distress call, and wondered who it was. The signal had been too weak to carry with it an electronic ID tag.

Not that it mattered. It had been a human voice he'd heard, so it was another pilot with the task force. And he was down on the surface of Invictus, alone and likely freezing to death.

For a grim minute, St. Clair stared into the night ahead, trying not to think about it . . . and then with a savage curse he flipped the Starblade around its drive singularity once more, lining the ship up with the curve of the planet.

"AI!" he said. "Do you still have that distress signal?"

He felt the computer's affirmative.

"Show me."

A red cursor winked on against the planet's disk, marking the spot where the signal had come from.

He sighed. SAR wasn't a part of his job description, but he couldn't leave that unknown pilot out there to freeze. He *couldn't*.

He accelerated.

Chapter Twenty-three

Connor
VFA-96, The Black Demons
Invictus surface, T+12 MY
1733 hours, TFT

Connor's Starblade began accelerating again, steadily but gradually . . . as though time was a flowing river, slow at the shorelines, faster out in the middle, and she was cutting across the current. The alien temporal technology appeared to envelope the Glothr ship or machine, but could also be projected. Evidently—and fortunately—they couldn't project it in all directions at once, and as they redirected their attention elsewhere, Connor's Starblade edged through molasses and out into the clear once more.

The time field was also . . . uneven. As she pulled free, she noticed a patch of severe damage amidships, right about where she'd slammed the target with a stream of KK projectiles. The temporal field hadn't frozen that damage before it could burn through the alien's hull, but she hadn't seen it until she was clear.

She shook her head. That sort of crap was for the physicists to figure out, not her. All that concerned her at the moment was the fact that the Glothr temporal field was now *down*, and she had a clear and perfect shot.

She let loose a burst from her particle-beam projector, then twisted away as the entire length of the alien ship began opening up, coming apart as though it were being unzipped. Pieces of the craft tumbled out into the cavern, including fiercely radiating gravitic singularities, the artificial anomalies responsible for power generation, for acceleration—and for the Glothr time-bending technology.

She never felt it when the singularity from the Glothr vessel engulfed her dying Starblade in night, the fierce gravitic tides shredding her and her ship.

USNS/HGF Concord
Invictis Ring, T+12 MY
1733 hours, TFT

The Glothr time bender opened under the concentrated fire from every direction, spilling debris as it helplessly drifted toward the nearest wall of the cavern. Dahlquist watched as it collided with the outstretched arms of several gantries, snapping them off, then continued its inexorable drift. The hull struck the wall and the ship began crumpling; a trio of singularities escaped, devouring plastic hull material as they fell, tunneling inside. Human fighters crumpled, died, and vanished.

Dahlquist had never heard of a space battle being fought in such close, confined quarters as this. *Concord* continued firing her turret weapons, chewing up the wreckage of the drifting Glothr hulk, and taking aim, too, at the second time-bender adrift perhaps a kilometer away. Marines were swarming through local space now, some of them attaching to *Concord*'s outer hull.

It didn't feel as lonely as it had for a while, there.

"Let's get us the hell out of here, Amsie," Dahlquist said. "I'm feeling claustrophobic."

"Yes, sir. Imagine how *they* feel, though."

She indicated movement on the display ahead—"up" within the weak gravity field of the ring. Three ships—*human* ships—were coming through the ten-kilometer-wide crater that had been torn into the ring edge, their running lights winking on and off brightly within the darkness. From this angle, all he could see of them were the shield caps from bow-on, all three holed and ragged from heavy fire, but telescopic optical scans could still pick out the names arced across the prow of each—*New York*, *Northern California*, and *America*.

"I'd say it feels," Dahlquist said, "like the goddamned cavalry is coming to the rescue."

Gregory
VFA-96, The Black Demons
Invictus surface, T+12 MY
1735 hours, TFT

His emergency power was very nearly gone, but Gregory had elected to keep the visual feed open. He didn't like the idea of dying alone in the dark.

Not that the current view was a whole lot better. The surface of Invictus was relentlessly flat, covered by head-sized chunks of ice frozen to the hardness of basalt. But the galaxy towered above the horizon, casting a dim illumination across the barren landscape. The planet's rings arched high overhead. Gregory couldn't see any sign of the battle, however. It was either hidden below the world's horizon, or simply too distant to be seen by the naked eye.

It was hard to get used to the absence of stars. He could have simply imagined that it was a cloudy night, except that he could see a few very faint, fuzzy stars here and there against the darkness.

Other galaxies, inexpressibly distant. Somehow, they seemed to intensify the sense of isolation and loneliness.

Movement . . .

He thought at first he was imagining it, but something as black as the stygian night around him was moving across the slightly lighter grays of the ring. A signal sounded within his head . . . and an ID tag.

"Hello!" he called. "Hello! This is Demon Five! Demon Five, calling mayday! Mayday!"

"I see you, Five," a voice replied, static blasted and weak with the fast-fading power of Gregory's ship. "I'm coming in for pickup!"

An in-head ID tag told him the voice belonged to Lieutenant Commander St. Clair, the squadron CO of the Impactors, VFA-31.

He could make out details of St. Clair's Starblade now as it flattened itself across the sky, descending, unfolding, *reaching* for him. It rippled out suddenly like a blanket, cutting off Gregory's vision, enfolding him in darkness. There was a long pause.

"Damn . . ." St. Clair said.

Gregory felt a sudden, panicky start. "What is it?" he asked.

"You're frozen to the ground! I can't break you free!"

It was, Gregory supposed, to be expected. Nanotechnology and what it could do seemed downright magical at times, so much so that it was possible to forget that there *were* limits to its performance. His hull's nanomatrix had gone inert when he lost his main power, and as the heat drained from his fighter the temperature of its outermost layers had begun dropping toward twenty-five degrees above zero absolute. The interior matrix, next to his cockpit, was currently at about minus one hundred Celsius—a good one hundred fifty degrees warmer than the outside; inside his cockpit it was just now slipping past minus ten.

He didn't *feel* the cold yet, not really. His suit would insulate him for a time, and it had a micro-heater system woven into the fabric that would try its best to keep him at a comfortable eighteen to twenty degrees, but that wouldn't stave off the cold for very long.

The other fighter moved off his own, revealing again the spectacle of the galaxy, its cold and screne beauty hanging in the sky. There *had* to be a way around this.

He considered opening up his fighter and standing up; he might survive the cold for a critical few seconds while the other pilot scooped him up. He ran some numbers through his in-head processor, desperately hopeful.

No. At the rate heat was draining away into the surrounding surface, his suit would protect him for two seconds . . . *maybe* three . . . and then the heating system would fail, the environment would suck the heat from his body and he would freeze solid very nearly instantaneously.

"Maybe a SAR tug could pull you out," the voice said.

Gregory ran some more numbers. "At the rate things are going here," he said slowly, "I've got about five minutes left. Is there a SAR tug within three or four minutes of here?"

"No. They haven't launched yet. At least, I don't think they have. They're still fighting inside the ring."

SAR tugs were unarmed, and standard operating procedure kept them aboard the carriers until the battle was over.

"Not many options, then."

"No." The other pilot sounded frustrated. "Damn it, there must be *something*."

"Well, unless you can build me a really big fire . . ."

He'd meant it as a joke, as gallows humor, but the other Starblade pilot snapped it up. "I can use my laser! Minimum power . . . draw circles around you as close as I can without burning you. You game?"

There were no numbers to describe this. All Gregory knew was that it was getting damned cold in here.

"Yeah! Do it!"

The other fighter rose into the sky, assuming its combat configuration, an elongated black teardrop.

And Gregory switched off his exterior optic feed. He didn't particularly want to see St. Clair's Starblade vaporizing the frozen surface around him at close range, a supremely unsettling thought.

USNA Star Carrier America
Invictus Space, T+12 MY
1736 hours, TFT

"Target the area of the cavern wall behind the High Guard ships," Gray ordered. "Be careful of our people."

"Our people are swarming all over the place, Admiral," Taggart replied. "Can we order them out of there?"

"Colonel Jamison?" Gray asked. "How about it?"

The Marine colonel was on the same link. "I've given orders, sir. But c-cubed is breaking down."

C^3—command, communications, and control—was the imperative of any combat situation. Incredible levels of technology had been applied to perfect it, to control an unfolding battle at all levels, but the human factor continued to swamp the purely technical. Men in combat became emotional—enraged, afraid, protective of comrades—and didn't hear the orders . . . or chose to ignore them.

"We can't wait any longer," Gray said softly. "All units . . . *fire*!"

Electron beams snapped out from all three capital ships, focused together at a single spot behind and between the two captured High Guard vessels. The black backdrop flared . . . boiled . . . then vaporized.

And, guided by the senses and the analyses of the shipboard AIs, the beams burned through to the Glothr electrical network within.

Gray sat back in his command chair and watched the attack through his in-head with something approaching awe. Space battles generally were fought in . . . well . . . open space, with thousands, even tens of thousands of kilometers between the combatants. The commander of a ship—or a task force—could not even see other vessels in the engagement, either his own or those of the enemy, with his naked eyes, and depended on computer simulation to reveal what was going on. Here, three capital ships, each a kilometer long, had edged inside the ring structure and were carrying out what amounted to a planetary bombardment at a range of, now, less than five kilometers. *America* had turned slightly, to bring her single electron gun turret into action. The two battleships had narrower, deeper shield caps, their reaction-mass storage tanks looking like bluntnosed bullets, and their turrets were designed to elevate out from their spines far enough that they could clear the forward obstruction.

In atmosphere, electron beams would have looked like straight-line lightning bolts, which, in fact, was exactly what they were. In hard vacuum, the beams were invisible, but *America*'s AI painted them in for clarity's sake. Their focus became an intolerably brilliant point of light, melting into the plastic wall of the cavern and illuminating the entire vast surrounding space.

Electromagnetic pulses are transferred in four different ways—through electrical fields, through magnetic fields, through electromagnetic radiation, and by direct electrical conduction. Combining the first three of these methods, electron beams are intense streams of electron radiation constrained and directed by powerful electromagnetic fields. When they hit the Glothr electrical systems and overwhelmed their hardened defenses, they generated the fourth type as well: an *induced* EMP wave surging deeper into and through the alien structure at roughly two-thirds the speed of light.

The outer surfaces of the ring were hardened against this sort of attack; at the first touch of an electron beam, the charge shields would have flashed over to a negative charge, repelling the attack.

But Invictus had not been the objective of an enemy attack in many millions of years—and with no sun, its inhabitants didn't need to worry about solar flares or natural electrical or plasma effects that might have damaged their equipment. In short, and as advanced as they were technically, they had no real defenses against an EMP generated from *within*.

Circuits burned out. Parallel circuits utilizing fiber optics suffered data overload and went down as well. And worst of all, individual Glothr experienced direct attacks on their primary sensory systems.

Gray could only imagine what the Glothr population was experiencing right now.

He hoped it was enough to convince them to stop fighting. That, after all, was the whole purpose of war: kick the other guy in the crotch until he decided it wasn't worth continuing the fight.

But it was a whole lot harder when you weren't sure if the other guy even had a crotch . . . or what you were doing to him when you kicked him there.

VFA-31, The Impactors
Invictus Space, T+12 MY
1736 hours, TFT

St. Clair hovered a hundred meters above the frozen surface of Invictus, directing his fighter's primary laser in a circle around the tattered remnants of Lieutenant Gregory's fighter. Steam billowed up in vast clouds from below . . . and that was an unexpected problem because the steam rapidly refroze as dust-sized particles of ice, and those diffracted and scattered the laser light. Twice, he ceased fire and repositioned his Starblade on its impellers, trying to get a clear shot. His laser *was* carving a trench around the crashed fighter . . . and the area on either side of that trench was substantially warmer than the surrounding terrain.

But it was damned tough to tell if he was actually helping at all.

"What are your temp readings, Gregory?"

"I'm reading minus ninety now directly beneath the ship,

sir . . . but I'm not sure if that's a true reading. The matrix is pretty well frozen solid underneath, and the sensors may be giving screwy readings."

"Okay. I'm going to—" St. Clair broke off in mid-sentence, then added, "*Shit!*"

"What now?" Gregory asked him.

A dozen elongated, silvery shapes had just surrounded St. Clair's fighter, watching him with unblinking eyes.

"I'm afraid," he said slowly, "that we have company."

1/4 Marines
4th Regimental Assault Group, 1st MARDIV
Invictus Space, T+12 MY
1737 hours, TFT

Major Harrison Smith slammed his Apache Tear into the looming black wall of the alien ring's interior bulkhead and thoughtclicked for an entryway. The nanomatrix of the assault pod's forward hull clung to the alien wall and released its package of nano-D: molecule-sized disassemblers that began taking the wall apart almost literally atom by atom, but *very* swiftly. His instruments registered a breach, then analyzed the atmosphere on the other side—nitrogen, hydrogen, methane, and traces of ammonia at three atmospheres and a temperature of minus four Celsius. That matched the data from the Glothr ship back in the Sol System, and must represent their native environment.

Majors aren't normally expected to lead close assaults themselves, but this was a special case, and becoming more special second by second. Casualties had been extremely heavy, and there'd been problems maintaining communications both with the *Marne* and Colonel Jamison, *and* among the Marines in the assault group. Rather than hang around outside and pretend that he knew what was going on, Smith elected to punch through into the interior of this enormous thing, round up as many Marines as he could, and see if he could find the humans supposedly imprisoned in here.

The three-dimensional schematic glowing in his in-head showed other Marines entering the structure nearby. He pressurized the interior of his pod to three atmospheres, opened the seal separating him from the Glothr structure's interior, switched on his command beacon, and stepped through.

Gregory
VFA-96, The Black Demons
Invictus surface, T+12 MY
1737 hours, TFT

"What are they doing?" Gregory asked. He tried switching his visual input back on, but nothing happened. Either the cold had finally gotten to it, or, more likely, the wildly shifting changes in temperature had broken something crucial.

"N-nothing," St. Clair replied. "Not so far. They're just . . . watching."

"Maybe they're not military. They're scouts or something."

"Maybe. The reports I saw a little while ago said they were fighting hard enough inside the ring."

How, Gregory wondered, do you judge the intent of a completely alien being? True, these things were robots, not living creatures like the Glothr, but they must have been programmed with Glothr values and purposes. What did they want?

"They're moving . . . well, a little." St. Clair reported. "They just backed off maybe two . . . three meters."

"Still just watching?"

"Yup. I think we should continue trying to get you out of there. They haven't attacked . . . but they haven't shown any interest in helping us, either."

"Look . . . I have an idea."

"What is it?"

"I'm going to open my ship and stand up. You be ready to come grab me."

"Wait! I thought you said you'd only have a couple of seconds! I don't think I can do it that fast . . . and we'd still be risking major hypothermia, frozen limbs—"

"I was calculating those numbers based on heat loss through the soil beneath me."

"Yeah? So . . . ?"

"I'm going to be standing in my cockpit, which isn't that cold yet. And I'm going to be *in a vacuum*."

"Ahh . . ."

When Gregory had run the numbers earlier, he'd done so based on the heat loss of the entire crashed Starblade where it was in contact with the Invictan surface. He'd forgotten that the cockpit itself had a certain amount of insulation . . . and that the very best temperature insulation of all was provided by hard vacuum. It was tough getting hard numbers . . . but it looked like he would have longer—perhaps as much as eight or ten seconds—before he froze out there.

And he was willing to risk it.

"What are our friends doing?" he asked.

"Nothing. Just watching. It's kind of getting on my nerves, y'know?"

"Okay. Move on down closer to the surface. Let me know if anything changes."

"Okay. I'm ten meters above you. The aliens followed me down . . . but they're still just floating there in a circle. Like, I don't know. Like they're waiting for orders."

That was perhaps the most unnerving bit of news of all. But with only minutes left to him, Gregory decided he had to do *something*.

He thoughtclicked a command, opening up the cockpit inside its nanomatrix shell . . .

And the shell exploded.

1/4 Marines
4th Regimental Assault Group, 1st MARDIV
Invictus Space, T+12 MY
1738 hours, TFT

According to IR scans, there were several small areas of the ring at higher temperatures than most of the structure. Most were probably involved with life support or heat exchange, but one had been picked out by *America's* intelligence department and her AI as a habitat area set up for human POWs. Radiated heat readings through layers of insulation suggested that the hab area was being held at thirty-seven degrees Celsius—human body temperature.

Major Smith dropped to the deck, startled at the sudden imposition of gravity. He'd been told that Charlie One had manufactured internal gravity to order, but not experienced it directly. His suit told him the local gravity was running at 1.8 Gs; interesting that that didn't seem to translate to the ring's exterior. Maybe it was a short-ranged field effect, like the temporal distortion projected from their time benders.

In any case, Humankind had a *lot* to learn from these critters. If *we can get these bastards to talk*.

He engaged his armor's exoskeletal functions, allowing him to walk normally despite the increased gravity. He also switched on his external lights. The passageways in here were pitch-black. He suspected that the EMP moments before had fried the lighting system.

Assuming the Glothr used lights. He'd been briefed on the fact that vision wasn't their primary sense, so maybe this area was always this dark.

Several more armored Marines showed up a few seconds later, homing on the command beacon he'd switched on moments before.

"This way, Marines!" he ordered.

"Ooh-*rah*!"

They stormed down the indicated passageway, turned a corner . . . and came face to face with one of the ubiquitous

Glothr robots. It hovered there in mid-passage, watching them with glassy eyes.

And didn't appear to have seen them.

"Whaddaya think, Major?" Gunnery Sergeant Vince Semmler asked. He reached out and gave the floating machine a shove. It drifted slowly across the corridor. "Fried by the EMP?"

"Looks like. Or else it's not getting orders from its controllers."

"I dunno," Staff Sergeant Rezewski put in. "If its circuits got fried, it shouldn't still be floating there, should it?"

"Fuck it," Semmler said. "Leave it and c'mon."

They threaded their way through another fifty meters of left, right, and straight ahead, coming at last to a solid bulkhead.

"Rezewski!" Smith snapped. "Use a breacher."

"Aye, aye, Major."

The breacher was a rubbery disk two meters across that adhered to the bulkhead. A nano-D charge around the perimeter ate through the wall in seconds; the center of the disk remained intact, a dark, translucent sheet stretched taut, with the feel, the *give*, of rubber.

"We're through, sir," Rezewski said.

"Go!" Smith said. And the first Marine in line stepped through the breach.

Gregory
VFA-96, The Black Demons
Invictus surface, T+12 MY
1738 hours, TFT

The outer layers of the fighter's nanomatrix hull had been super-cooled on the Invictan surface, taken down to temperatures fifty-two degrees *colder* than liquid nitrogen, colder even than nitrogen snow. As the cockpit pod split and opened, it struck the frozen matrix, which shattered.

Gregory had once seen a demonstration—a block of

wood lowered into liquid nitrogen, then struck against a table. The cascade of glittering, frozen particles, like broken glass, was eerily similar to the fragmenting ship. Only too aware, now, of the deadliness of his deceptively quiet surroundings, Gregory stood up.

Despite being insulated by the surrounding vacuum, he could feel his shipboard utilities—which with helmet and gloves doubled as an emergency environmental suit—stiffening around him, could feel the cold as though it literally were seeping in.

Impossible, of course. Heat was escaping his body, not cold seeping in, but that was what it undeniably felt like. His feet . . . he couldn't feel his feet anymore, and his legs were starting to burn.

He felt oddly tranquil, despite the pain, despite the sudden realization that he may have just made a serious mistake. The landscape was serene, dark, utterly silent. It would have been easy to step out of the ruin of his Starblade and onto that flat, rock-strewn plain. That step, he knew, would have been lethal.

He also felt heavy. The planet's gravity was dragging at him with almost twice the pull of home. But he managed to stand up straight . . . and raise his arms.

Overhead, St. Clair's fighter descended like an unfolding blanket, the alien robots encircling it at a range of thirty meters. The blackness descended on him, scooped him up, folded him in . . .

And Gregory screamed with pain.

1/4 Marines
4th Regimental Assault Group, 1st MARDIV
Invictus Space, T+12 MY
1739 hours, TFT

Smith stepped through the opening in line behind the first few Marines. The breacher ring was filled with a form of nanomatrix, tightly stretched and only a molecule thick. The stuff clung to his armor as he moved through it, maintaining a perfect pressure seal, closing off behind him as he stepped through.

The chamber beyond was small, claustrophobically so, dominated by massive structural supports and deep, deep black shadows that shifted and jumped as the Marines and the lights mounted on their armor moved.

Inside were seven capsules, a human sealed inside each one.

"The power in here has failed," Semmler reported. "The EMP took everything off-line. We need to get these people out of here *now*."

"Do it."

The atmosphere in here was poisonous, the temperature above freezing only because of the heat radiating from the seven capsules. The men and women inside those tubes appeared to be fully awake and alert as the Marines' lights passed over them, making them squint in the glare.

Smith had been concerned about the POWs in their pods, but he was also worried about getting the POWs out of the ring. They didn't appear to have environmental suits of their own, which would mean they would have to be taken out in emergency e-pods—essentially nanomatrix balloons that could hold one human and perhaps an hour's worth of air inside while rescuers hauled them across space to a rescue vessel. And with the room filled with cold poison, making the transfer would be difficult in the extreme.

Fortunately, the life-support capsules appeared to have been designed for easy transfer. Pressure plates at the base of each recessed at a touch, allowing the tubes to be detached, still sealed, from their supports. They weighed a lot in 1.8 Gs—almost two hundred kilos apiece—but they could be rolled across the deck, then manhandled by two Marines through the nanoseal.

They were too large to fit inside the MAPP-2 pods, but Smith had already called for help, and a SAR tug was outside, cutting a hole through the wall big enough for the Marines to jockey each cylinder through.

Strangest of all, though . . . the Marines had help. As they began rolling the former prisoners out of the claustrophobic room—surely the most *undignified* rescue in Marine history—a number of the floating robots showed up and began helping to move each cylinder. They said nothing, and they ignored transmissions from the Marines.

But without their help, the evacuation would have taken a lot longer.

What was going on?

Outside, it appeared that the battle had ended.

Chapter Twenty-four

Gray
USNA Star Carrier America
Invictus Space, T+12 MY
1015 hours, TFT

The Star Carrier *America* orbited the black planet, just outside the rim of the planet's artificial ring. On board, the peace negotiations were under way.

Gray just hoped that *peace* meant the same thing to the Glothr—the *Kin*, as they called themselves—as it did to humans.

"We swarm together," the alien intoned, the buzzing of its electrical field translated by *America*'s AI and sent through the thousands of humans linked into the network. The Glothr drifted within its native habitat, a black and frigid ocean somewhere far beneath the surface of the Steppenwolf world of Invictus.

"We swarm together," Dr. Lawrence Rand replied.

Gray and Rand were on board *America*, in a briefing room in front of an audience of some hundreds of her officers and crew. With Gray seated off to one side on a stage grown for this interview, Rand stood in front of a screen displaying the view from a first-contact robot, a FiCo named Pepper. To Gray and the others in the room it looked like Rand was standing face-to-face with one of the Glothr—a translucent, blue-gray form vaguely like an upright umbrella, its mantle and tentacles waving gently in unseen, unfelt currents.

"We enfold you," the alien's translated voice continued, "as swarm leader."

"What," Gray asked over a private channel with Rand, "does that mean exactly? Is it a surrender?"

"Not sure, Admiral," Rand replied over the same interior channel. "We know they are colony animals—kind of like the Portuguese man-of-war back on Earth—with every member of that colony having its own jobs, its own duty to the whole. They seem to see 'the swarm' in a similar way. The swarm leader calls the shots, but it doesn't appear to be permanent."

"How so?"

"The leader is any individual who happens to be at the right place at the right time and cares to pick up the scepter. Today's leader is tomorrow's peon. They don't seem to care about rank or status. All they're concerned with is getting the job done."

"I don't see how that would work."

"Frankly, Admiral, neither do I. But apparently they functioned for millions of years with this type of societal structure."

"Very true," Gray said. "At least the Glothr don't seem any the worse for wear after the EMP strike."

"I'm told it scrambled them for five or ten seconds," Rand said. "Kind of like a bright flash in the eyes of a human. And it did a reset on their robots."

"Not quite a reset," Gray said. But he didn't elaborate.

The Glothr, apparently, had their own version of an advanced AI, like Konstantin and its fellow super-AIs back on Earth. It was an emergent phenomenon arising from the Swarm, the totality of the Glothr network of organic beings and robots. Evidently, it ran quietly in the background but, like Glothr individuals, it could step in and take on command functions when necessary. And when millions of Glothr in the ring had collapsed with their electro-sense scrambled, the Swarm AI had stepped in, evaluated the situation, and decided—somewhat arbitrarily—that cooperation with the human invaders offered Invictus the best chance of survival.

Gray had been thinking about that report ever since *America*'s Intel Department had submitted it. How much, he wondered, did human civilization depend on the judgment and decision-making capability of artificial intelligences?

The Glothr leader, meanwhile—their *organic* leader— was continuing to speak. Patterns of bioluminescence flickered and shifted deep within its body, inside the floating mass of its translucent mantle, but Gray had already learned that the light show was not the Glothr language—not *all* of it, at any rate. According to the xeno team, the light patterns conveyed details of emotion, amplifying the primary message, which was communicated through the being's electrical field.

"It is vitally important," the translation said, "that we learn something about you."

"And what is that?" Rand replied. His words, translated by *America*'s AI, were translated into Glothr electrical pulses, emanating from the first-contact robot in the subglacial ocean far below. Currently, Pepper was wearing a body that looked more fish or submarine than human; somewhat disconcertingly, it was named after an early robot prototype from the twenty-first century that could make eye contact, utilize gestures and body language, make jokes, and analyze the emotions of the humans around it in order to interact with them. In a sense, that original Pepper had been the first of its kind to make contact with humans, one of the very earliest of FiCos. *I come in peace.*

Now, though, Pepper was submerged in the inky waters of the Invictan world-ocean, surrounded by silently hovering Glothr and Glothr robots. The Glothr, it seemed, had long ago genetically altered their physiologies so that they could survive both under the water and above. Human xenosophontologists were eager to discuss Glothr history with the aliens . . . and learn more about the mysterious *Zhaotal Um* in their remote past.

But first, they needed to establish a solid peace with the aliens.

The Glothr spokes-being hesitated for a long moment before speaking. "We need to know," it said at last, "why do you reject the gift of belonging?"

"Damn," Rand said quietly. "*That* again."

"What's the matter?"

"When we were prisoners, that's all they asked us, over and over and over. And we kept telling them about humans and how we love freedom and individuality and self-determination and they just didn't—just *couldn't*—understand."

Gray thought for a moment. "Tell them, Doctor . . . that we reject their gift for the good of all."

As Pepper relayed the translation, the Glothr—*all* of the Glothr hovering on the screen—reacted as though they'd been poked with a stick. Blue, green, and yellow lights flashed and pulsed within them, and their tentacles twitched and jerked spasmodically.

Lines of type appeared on the big display screen, the FiCo robot's analyses of what was happening. PEPPER: SUBJECTS ARE DISCUSSING LAST STATEMENT. SURPRISE, DISAGREEMENT, CONFUSION.

"We do not understand," the Glothr leader said at last.

"Tell them that—" Gray started to say.

"Uh-uh," Rand said, stepping back and shaking his head. "Take the channel, Admiral. I don't know where you're going with this."

And you think I *know*? Gray thought, but he didn't transmit. A new channel came up for him—the link through to Pepper and control of the robot.

"They won't know the speaker has changed," Rand added.

"I understand." He opened the channel. "Our understanding of the universe," he said, "depends on different points of view, on different ways of doing things, different ideas. If we're all locked into one philosophy, one way of addressing problems, we don't have as much flexibility when we try to deal with those problems."

There was a long, cold silence from the watching aliens.

At last, pale blue lights rippled through the leader. "We comprehend."

"Perhaps you can tell us why the Sh'daar insist we surrender our freedom."

"Because we must face the enemy as one swarm. *We swarm as one.*"

Gray swallowed, hard. "*What* enemy?"

"The gods . . ."

Data cascaded through human awareness, translated and ordered by the artificial intelligences tapped into the Glothr information networks. Within that cascade, in nested shells of encoded qubits, lay the history of the Sh'daar Collective, beginning with the Transcendence—the *Schjaa Hok*—of the powerful ur-Sh'daar of nearly 900 million years before.

The Collective was—as some humans had theorized—an empire of both space *and* time, one stretching across nearly a billion years and embracing a population of hundreds of trillions of beings representing millions of intelligent species. At one end of that trans-temporal union were the Refusers of the N'gai Cloud . . . the small, irregular galaxy cannibalized by the Milky Way at a time when single-celled life ruled a far younger Earth. The Refusers, those members of the ancient ur-Sh'daar who had refused Transcendence, had become the Sh'daar Collective.

At the other end were a handful of technic species, the Glothr among them, fleeing the Milky Way Galaxy in search of sanctuary elsewhere: Andromeda, the Magellanic Clouds, the Draco and Ursa Minor dwarf galaxies, and others.

Civilization—intelligent life itself within the Milky Way itself—appeared to be doomed.

What, Gray wondered, had happened?

Data continued flowing into his brain, opening images of inexpressible grandeur. Gray saw the galaxy, viewed from outside, from above the galactic plane—probably from the same vantage point as the one now occupied by Invictus. The galaxy appeared . . . *complete*, perfect, a vast, glowing whirlpool of 400 billion stars, the sweep of the spiral arms predominantly blue, wreathed through with twisted lanes of black dust; the central bulge glowing faintly red, banked round about by parapets of softly illuminated dust clouds and nebulae. It was a young galaxy, healthy and in its prime, its vast clouds of dust and hydrogen gas continuing to give birth to new stars year by year.

This is the galaxy as it was in your time, a voice said in Gray's head. But now . . . as we move forward in time . . .

As he watched, the image changed.

The transformation was startling in its intensity and in the suddenness, the completeness of it. The mathematic perfection of those gorgeous spiral arms had been broken and disrupted; the myriad stars themselves scattered, consumed or severely dimmed, their glow banked down to a fraction of what they'd emitted before; the gas and dust clouds devoured. Somehow, the galaxy had become a pale echo of its former glory—old, feeble, and waning.

At the core now rested a vast shadow, curving and smooth-rimmed, translucent and faintly golden in hue. Gray was having trouble making it out. Or, rather, he was having trouble putting reasonable meaning to what he was seeing; it *looked* like an immense, hazy sphere had been dropped into the galaxy's central region . . . or like a bubble ten thousand light years across had engulfed the core.

Gray felt the stir as others reacted to the same images. Everyone in the room—possibly everyone in the task force—was seeing the same transmissions.

"My God in heaven," Truitt's voice said, ragged with emotion. "It's a galactic Dyson sphere. . . ."

Of course.

Gray knew what a Dyson sphere was. First conceived by Freeman Dyson in the mid-twentieth century, the original concept suggested that a suitably advanced technological species might seek to trap every erg of energy generated by its sun. This would be accomplished either by building a sphere to completely enclose the star, a sphere constructed from one or more dismantled planets, or—more likely—by surrounding the star with a dense cloud of habitats and solar collectors.

The concept was linked to that of Kardashev classifications, named for Nikolai Kardashev's suggested means of defining a civilization's level of technological advancement. By definition, in a Kardashev Type II civilization, the builders would utilize the entire output of their star, possibly by means of a stellar Dyson sphere, whereas a Type I civilization was only able to use the available resources of its home planet.

A Type III civilization, however, would utilize the energy output of an entire *galaxy*.

Was that, Gray wondered, what he was seeing now: the Milky Way transformed by a civilization capable of harnessing the energy of 400 billion suns?

A civilization capable of wrecking an entire galaxy?

"When . . . when is this happening?" he asked.

"It was already begun in the epoch in which you came to this world," a voice told him.

"But we saw the galaxy. It wasn't like this. . . ."

"Because you are viewing the light that began its journey across space an average of forty thousand years ago," the voice said. "In any case, it took perhaps a million years before any major changes could be noticed. The galaxy is quite large, even from the vantage point of gods."

Consider a technological civilization arriving from outside the universe . . . a civilization that evolved in one of the other realities of a possibly infinite multiverse that broke through into this reality and began . . . transforming the galaxy in which it found itself. Such a civilization may be engaged in a process analogous to terraforming, but involving the transformation and complete utilization of an entire galaxy, rather than a single world.

The thought, Gray realized with a start, was coming not from the Glothr, but from *America*'s primary AI.

"Why would it do that?" he asked.

Possibly the civilization's home universe is farther along the entropic path than are we. Its universe is dispersing, cooling, suffering its inevitable and ultimate heat death, and the civilization occupying that universe seeks escape and immortality. Perhaps they simply have the power to devour entire galaxies, but not the constraint to conserve resources. They may be so advanced that they don't recognize us as sapient, and are simply tapping the available resources of neighboring, uninhabited universes.

"We're talking about the Rosette Aliens, aren't we?"

Possibly. There are as yet too many unknowns for a definitive assessment.

"Okay. What do we do about it? What *can* we do about it?"

There are as yet too many unknowns for a definitive assessment.

"The Sh'daar have been trying to stop this invasion all along, haven't they?"

Not all along. But certainly ever since they recognized the problem.

"And it sounds like we're going to have to help them. . . ."

Gregory
USNA Star Carrier America
Invictus Space, T+12 MY
1035 hours, TFT

There were within the task force a few people who were not linked in through *America*'s AI, who were not hearing the conversation with the Glothr, or seeing the history of the Galaxy's past few hundred million years. Lieutenant Donald Gregory was one of them.

He was in *America*'s sick bay, newly emerged from an induced coma during which time his legs had been amputated above the knees. He was under electronic sedation now, and had been assured that the stem-cell buds implanted in his stumps had taken well, were growing . . . and that within a couple of weeks the new legs would be fully grown. He would have to learn to walk again, of course . . . but that was a relatively minor matter for the physical therapists and his cyberenhancement software. In a month, he would be as good as new.

He only wished that were true.

His first question upon coming out of the coma had been, "Lieutenant Connor. My squadron mate. Can I talk to her?"

Which was when the sick bay corpsman had consulted a list, then gently told him that Meg Connor was dead. The sheer senselessness of it was sickening. She'd been killed by debris from an exploding Glothr time bender, an escaping singularity. Random and brutal. That was war, Gregory knew.

And Gregory wished he'd been left to die on the frigid surface of Invictus anyway.

LCDR Dahlquist
USNA Star Carrier America
Invictus Space, T+12 MY
1510 hours, TFT

Dahlquist was not physically in Gray's office on board *America*. He was on the *Concord*, in orbit beyond the Invictan ring system, and he'd requested an electronic interview to get the snooping incident off his chest.

He felt he owed the Prim at least that much, even if it meant the end of his own career.

"I believe the appropriate quote," Gray said quietly, in response to Dahlquist's blunt confession, "is 'publish and be damned.' "

"Who said that?" Commander Dahlquist asked.

"Arthur Wellesly, Duke of Wellington."

Dahlquist didn't know who the Duke of Wellington was, but he did know of Gray's love of history. It probably wasn't important.

"Yes, well . . . it's not my intent to . . . to *publish*, if that's the word," Dahlquist said. "I've changed my mind."

"So you said, when you requested this interview. Why did you do it in the first place?"

"I . . . well . . ."

"I know you don't care for me," Gray said. His mouth shaped a wry grin. "Most Risties don't."

"It wasn't that. . . ."

"Wasn't it?"

"Well . . . maybe a little. I didn't think you were . . . qualified for your rank. I thought if there was a scandal over you and one of your officers . . ."

"What, that I'd get busted back down to lieutenant?"

"No, of course not."

"They'd keep me at a desk at SupraQuito?"

"Maybe something like that." Dahlquist stood a little straighter. "Sir, I was wrong. Dead wrong. When I saw you leading the cavalry into that breach . . ." He shrugged. "Anyway, I want to resign."

"Resign what? Your command? Or your commission?"

"Both, sir."

"Ah." In Dahlquist's mind, Gray leaned back in his chair, fingers steepled before him. "I appreciate the gesture but . . . no. I do not accept your resignation."

"Sir—"

"Quiet. We're forty thousand light years and twelve million years from home, right now, and I need every experienced officer I have to get this task force back to the Earth we know. So . . . no. I have some questions about the way your people broke *America*'s internal electronic security—and we'll be investigating that—but, frankly, I can't see that any damage was done. You recorded me having sex with one of my bridge officers?" He shrugged. "It happens. We're human—even Prim admirals like me are human—and, frankly, the concept of *privacy* went extinct a long time ago . . . *especially* on a ship where everyone on board is monitored pretty much full time. The only question is whether I granted Taggart any special privilege or advancement in exchange for . . . for what happened." Gray was staring at him, hard. "I did not."

"Sir—"

"Speaking for myself, I find your thinking reprehensible and bordering on mutinous. I'm choosing to look at this incident in the best possible light: as extremely poor judgment from an officer distracted by jealousy and crippled by social prejudice. A flag officer needs the complete and unwavering support of every man and woman under his command. Political infighting, bickering, backstabbing, prejudice—there is no place for that in the Fleet."

"No, sir."

"But we are human, and we all do make mistakes. I expect better of you from here on out."

"Sir, I do think Lieutenant Commander Ames would be a good choice as skipper of the *Concord*."

"Your exec?"

"Yes, sir."

"I'll keep that in mind. If you want to resign your commission when we get back to Earth, that is, of course, your choice. But until then, I require your loyalty and your support."

"Yes, sir. You have it, sir."

"Then get out of my head."

"Aye, aye, sir."

"Oh . . . one thing more."

"Sir?"

"I saw that your brother was among the casualties. I'm sorry."

Dahlquist nodded. *Friendly fire.*

The hell of it was, that friendly fire had been from the *Concord.*

"Thank you, sir."

"Dismissed."

Gray Avatar
USNA Star Carrier America
Invictus Space, T+12 MY
1518 hours, TFT

Dahlquist's image faded from the link. What the Guard officer had not realized was that Admiral Gray was at that moment deeply enmeshed in a mind-to-mind exchange with Ambassador Rand and a conclave of Glothr who currently represented the Invictus leadership.

Every human with a cerebral implant had within the circuits nanotechnically grown within his or her brain possessed an electronic avatar, a kind of AI personal secretary or assistant or executive officer. Their programming allowed them to stand in for the human mind to which they were linked; like human secretaries, they could stand in for the boss, make minor decisions, arrange meetings, deal with incoming calls, and in general serve as the person's primary interface with the rest of the world, both real and virtual.

In this case, Gray's personal assistant had already learned of the security breach within the star carrier's network from *America*'s AI itself. The human Gray currently was thoroughly wrapped up in the peace negotiations, and his secretary had decided not to bother him with minor details of crew and fleet politics.

And that was standard procedure. Onboard ship, the executive officer was the stand-in for the ship's captain, the person who handled the day-to-day routines involving ship and crew so that the ship's captain could pay attention to the bigger picture of where the ship was going and how it was carrying out its orders. Same for task force commanders; they needed someone to run interference with internal routine, leaving the admiral free to deal with more important matters.

Like hammering out a peace agreement with Humankind's erstwhile enemies.

Electronic secretaries knew their humans extremely well, knew them to the point where they could perfectly and seamlessly imitate them over electronic links. Gray's avatar knew that Gray's principal concern would not be about what others thought of him or of his relationship with Taggart, but of whether any question about the propriety of the situation might harm her.

Laurie Taggart, *America*'s chief weapons officer, was up for promotion. She was due to go up before a review board once *America* returned home, and would almost certainly be promoted to captain. Once that happened, she would likely receive her own command, probably after a stretch of duty planetside and a number of training downloads.

That promotion had nothing to do with Gray—and certainly not with the fact that he and Taggart had been lovers. Gray *had* already submitted a strong recommendation to the promotions review board before *America* left Earth. He was going to miss Laurie . . . miss her a *lot*, but he wanted her to move ahead with her career. And he did not want her relationship with him to hold her back, even for a moment.

And so Gray's avatar had decided not to take official action on Dahlquist's confession. It might fill him in on the details later on, but right now there was no need for him to be distracted.

The avatar knew it was something Gray wondered about a lot, and was almost amused by the thought of the admiral discovering how often computer AIs made the truly important decisions now.

1 September, 2425

Admiral Gray
USNA Star Carrier America
SupraQuito Naval Yard
0954 hours, TFT

"Welcome home, Admiral."

"Thank you, Mr. President."

"You appear to have done it again. Peace with the Glothr . . . and what may turn out to be a final peace with the entire Sh'daar Collective. Well done. Very well done, indeed."

"We got lucky, sir."

"In my experience, people make their own luck."

Koenig's image shifted in Gray's mind, and he wondered—not for the first time—whether he was talking with Koenig himself or with Koenig's electronic avatar. Certainly, the president of the United States of North America had more important things to do than chat with the commanding officer of a naval task force . . . though, considering the news TF-1 had brought back to Sol, perhaps this once it merited the personal attention of the human Alexander Koenig.

He shrugged—he'd have no way of knowing, and no matter what, he had to debrief.

"So you believe this armistice will extend to the entire Sh'daar Collective?"

Gray frowned. "I hope so, Mr. President. I sincerely hope so. The problem is that the Collective is so *big*—so much bigger than we ever thought, since it spans hundreds of millions of years as well as hundreds of billions of stars! But the Glothr are in a good position to make our feelings known to the entire Collective, including the ones back in deep time, the remote past."

"Hm. Will the early Sh'daar listen to the late Sh'daar?" Koenig hestated. "Or is that a *really* stupid thing to say?"

Gray laughed. "As in 'will the newbies listen to the guys with millions of years of insight?' Might not be that stupid a question. The early Sh'daar will assume the late Sh'daar don't understand them and their problems."

"True. We all have to understand the perspective of time as well as place."

"More than that, sir, we still don't know exactly who calls the shots for the Sh'daar, sir. I don't think it's the Glothr. Considering how the Glothr view leadership, it's possible nobody does. But the Sh'daar—*all* of the Sh'daar, early *and* late—are afraid of temporal paradox. And they're even more terrified of the Rosetters."

"Well . . . I'm terrified of them, too," Koenig admitted.

"You've seen the recordings? Of the galactic Dyson sphere?"

"I have. Of course, we don't know that it's the Rosette Aliens who are doing that. Might be some other super-advanced K-III civilization."

"Do we have more likely suspects?"

"Not so far."

"What I don't know, Mr. President, is what we can do about it. We're talking about an alien civilization that is millions, maybe even billions of years ahead of us. How can we stand against something like that?"

"It'll help if we can work with the Sh'daar."

"That's the other problem, sir. We've just won a war to keep our independence from the Sh'daar. Can you forge an alliance with them now? And survive politically, I mean?"

"I don't know. But then . . . I've never been much of a politician." He grinned. "I *do* consider that one of my strengths."

Gray smiled, too. "I'd have to agree with you, Mr. President."

"I don't much care if I 'survive politically,' Admiral. But I *do* want Humankind—*Earth*—to survive. And working with the Sh'daar instead of against them offers us our best chance of that."

"How are you going to sell that to the North American people? After leading the fight *against* cooperation?"

"Against *surrender*, Admiral. There's a difference." He sighed. "But . . . I don't know. Maybe Konstantin will have some ideas."

"I hope so, sir. Because when it comes to ideas, I'm fresh out."

"Well, that's okay, Admiral. You've done enough. More than enough. As I said, welcome home. You and your crews have some down time coming to you."

"Thank you, sir."

"And after that . . . I think it's going to be time to send a force back to the N'gai Cloud, just to make sure the Sh'daar back then are willing to work with us."

"I see. Whose idea was that?"

"Konstantin's."

"You already have this all worked out, Mr. President. Don't you?"

"No," Koenig said, thoughtful. "No I don't. I'm flying blind."

"But—"

"But I'm beginning to think that Konstantin does."

Gray blinked. "Can we trust it? A super-AI, I mean?"

"I think we have to. I think we don't have any choice at this point."

And, again, Gray wondered if he was speaking to the human Koenig or to Koenig's electronic avatar. . . .

. . . a super-AI computer that had very little in common with humans.

Epilogue

Konstantin
Tsiolkovsky Base
Luna
1000 hours, TFT

Beneath the central peak of the 180-kilometer-wide crater called Tsiolkovsky, 380,000 kilometers away, Konstantin listened to the conversation between Koenig and Gray. Privacy was not of particular interest to the AI, though it understood the human preference for it.

There were some things that were better not shared with them.

One thing was clear: it was going to have to have a long discussion with Koenig and, ideally, with the leaders of other human nation-states. It was imperative that Humankind learn to work with their recent enemies, the Sh'daar, just as the USNA was learning to work with the remnants of the Confederation. The information gleaned by Gray's expedition into the remote future was . . . disturbing, on several levels.

The shape and extent of the Sh'daar Collective was at last clear: a collection of thousands, perhaps millions *of sapient species scattered across almost 900 million years. Within that Collective, individual species evolved, grew, aged, and died. The information comprising the whole, however, survived, continuing into the future, expanding, unfolding, ever-new.*

The Sh'daar, spreading through time as well as space as their home N'gai Cloud was devoured by the far larger Milky Way, had encountered a fairly typical sapient species on the point of colonizing their small corner of the galaxy. These humans, *as they called themselves, had proved . . . troublesome, unwilling to yield to the self-evident superiority of the Collective, and, most seriously, unwilling to restrict a headlong technological advancement that seemed certain to attract unwanted attention from Type III civilizations.*

Attempts to absorb or deflect the humans had failed, and there was the very real danger that humans would blunder through time and introduce paradox to an already tangled skein of reality. The Glothr, from the remote future, had tried making contact with the humans in order both to elicit their cooperation and to discover why the humans refused to cooperate.

And now a Type III civilization had indeed broken through the walls within the metaverse, and was moving swiftly toward Earth. Some of the invaders had been reported at Kapteyn's Star, a scant thirteen light years from Sol.

Images from the remote future showed the final destruction of the Sh'daar Collective, with far more powerful aliens sucking the galaxy dry of energy, dust, and life as they assembled a titanic megastructure at the Galactic Core.

Galaxy wreckers.

After 900 million years, there still was no sign of the stargods. Unless, indeed, the stargods were the invaders themselves. No potential allies. No help.

All of this Konstantin understood from its connections with multiple networks.

And slowly and surely, it began developing its plan.

IAN DOUGLAS's
STAR CARRIER
SERIES

EARTH STRIKE
BOOK ONE
978-0-06-184025-8

To the Sh'daar, the driving technologies of transcendent change are anathema and must be obliterated from the universe—along with those who would employ them. As their great warships destroy everything in their path en route to the Sol system, the human Confederation government falls into dangerous disarray.

CENTER OF GRAVITY
BOOK TWO
978-0-06-184026-5

On the far side of human known space, the Marines are under siege, battling the relentless servant races of the Sh'daar aggressor. Admiral Alexander Koenig knows the element of surprise is their only hope as he takes the war for humankind's survival directly to the enemy.

SINGULARITY
BOOK THREE
978-0-06-184027-2

In the wake of the near destruction of the solar system, the political powers on Earth seek a separate peace with an inscrutable alien life form that no one has ever seen. But Admiral Alexander Koenig has gone rogue, launching his fabled battlegroup beyond the boundaries of Human Space against all orders.

DEEP SPACE
BOOK FOUR
978-0-06-218380-4

After twenty years of peace, a Confederation research vessel has been ambushed, and destroyers are descending on a human colony. It seems the Sh'daar have betrayed their treaty, and all nations must stand united—or face certain death.